Pearl of Arabia

Connor Black

ما طار طيرٌ وارتفع إلا كما طار وقع

She who flies away comes back.

–Omani proverb

Prologue

Twenty-Five Years Ago

In the back seat of the elegant sedan, the two girls locked eyes simultaneously. They'd each sensed the same rising tension as the car rolled down a wet, potholed street in East Oakland.

The older of the pair, only six herself, turned to her father in the driver's seat. Mohammed al Abdali, his posture erect, tightened his grip on the steering wheel and strained to see through the rain-streaked windshield. She watched his glance flash quickly to the navigation system and then back to the slick road.

"What's wrong, Baba?" she asked.

Mohammed's eyes caught hers in the rearview mirror. "Nothing to worry about," he said through a forced smile. "The map is taking us on a little detour."

The younger girl watched the brief exchange and, despite being barely two years old, recognized something was wrong.

She didn't know that Mohammed was entirely unfamiliar with the area. She didn't know that somewhere on the circuit board of the Mercedes APS navigation system, a chip had received a signal and issued a zero instead of a one. She didn't know that ordinarily, a code snippet would have caught and resolved the anomaly. And she didn't know that tonight, the error-checking code had been disabled.

They'd attended a fundraiser in the Oakland Hills and were making their way home to Pacific Heights in San Francisco. A road closure, presumably caused by the weather, had turned what was usually a straightforward route into a mess, forcing them off the freeway and into a less desirable part of Oakland.

The course correction wound them down a bumpy, narrow street. At first, Mohammed wasn't too worried. They were headed in at least the general direction of the Bay Bridge. But at a traffic light next to an empty lot and an abandoned thrift store, the navigation system instructed them to turn off. He trusted the computer and obeyed, steering them deeper into the confines of dark, narrow streets.

Another turn later, a man as wide as he was tall stepped directly in front of the car and pointed a gun at the windshield.

Mohammed twisted the wheel to the left and shouted to his wife and the two girls to get down. A graffiti-covered van quickly blocked his way and thwarted the sole avenue of escape. Before he could put the car in reverse, a second figure appeared on the driver's side, brandishing a pistol. The man was hyped up and agitated, and his feet moved rapidly as he pulled at the door handle and shouted, "Don't even think about it! Outta the car!"

In the back seat, the girls screamed. Mohammed's wife, Maha, hurriedly searched for her seatbelt release, her hands shaking. "It is just the car they want," she cried.

Mohammed only hoped that was true. "Get the girls out and run," he snapped.

The older girl understood and swiftly unbuckled her seatbelt. She unclipped the toddler and pulled her out of the car seat. As she reached for the door, she could hear her mother frantically trying to get the folds of her dress out of the way, still struggling to find the buckle release.

The girl lifted the toddler out and set her on the curb. "Hide! Over there!" she barked, pointing to a row of scraggly bushes. The little girl wobbled a second as she was set down but understood and teetered into the shrubs.

On the other side of the car, Mohammed slowly emerged from the driver's door, hands high, pleading to de-escalate the situation.

The older girl leaned in the passenger door and unclipped her mother. As they extracted themselves, they could hear Mohammed. "The key is inside. Take the car. Plea—"

A gunshot to the center of his chest stopped the next words.

"The girl!" one of the criminals yelled.

Maha pivoted her body between the voice and her daughter. Just as she reached out to wrap the older girl in her arms, two more shots rang out.

Mohammed, blood bubbling from his mouth and chest, dragged his head across the oily pavement, searching. Beneath the car, through the rain and dim reflection of a somber street lamp, the last thing he saw was his wife, her eyes glassy and lifeless, lying atop his daughter.

The toddler was nowhere to be found.

1

Present Day

Adira Eastmont exhaled and tapped her badge against the time clock outside the nurses' locker room. A camera came to life, and the screen beneath it returned an image that surely couldn't be her. A countdown began, and she hurriedly tamed the errant strands of hair that had escaped her scrunchie on the bus ride to work. Before she could finish, the screen flashed and revealed the photo that had been saved—a mass of curly, dark brown hair, two blurry hands, and the hint of one amber eye below a furrowed brow. Frightening. At least the clock at the top of the screen showed she was on time.

Clocking in for a shift at Highland Hospital flipped a switch for Adira, shutting off thoughts of the past-due electric bill for her tiny apartment, the suspect bread on the peanut butter sandwich she might not even find time to eat, and the hole in her right running shoe just above the big toe. Working in the ER required presence, compassion, and efficiency. There was room for little else.

The night nurse made quick work of the handover, running through the charts of the three patients who would carry over into Adira's shift. She had an ETOH—alcohol intoxication—likely close to discharge, an elderly woman with shortness of breath, waiting on labs and chest imaging, and a male with abdominal pain tender to palpation.

Adira checked on the abdomen first, noting the fever, chills, and vomiting on his chart just as the internist arrived. The doctor palpated the man's belly as Adira ran through the chart again with him, confirming her suspicion of appendicitis. She drew blood for pre-procedure labs and hung antibiotics while gently explaining to the patient what to expect next.

She switched to the elderly chest patient for her turn in X-ray, then checked on the ETOH, dropping a breakfast tray off for him and running through a portion of her well-practiced alcohol abuse speech. Her last stop was an empty bed, ensuring it was clean, stocked, and ready. It didn't stay that way for long. There were more cardiopulmonary cases, trauma from violence and accidents, and a few codes called. Toward the end of her shift, a boy was brought in just as things began to settle.

"Well, who do we have here?" Adira asked as she closed the curtain around the bed.

"It is my little brother, Khalid," replied the young woman who'd brought him in, urgency in her voice. "The machine, the heater, fell out of the wall when he tried to turn it on! Will he be okay?"

Eyes red and filled with tears, the boy of no more than ten years old looked to be in quite a bit of pain.

"Let's have a look," Adira said. Turning to Khalid, she continued, "You're going to be fine, Khalid." Her voice was calm, slow, and deliberate as she began her assessment.

While his eyes were red and his breath short from crying, the only injury was a set of deep lacerations on his left leg. His pants were torn and stained, but the bleeding had slowed.

She removed a hand towel wrapped around the wound using a saline wash. Next, she used a set of shears to cut away the pant leg. As she worked, she asked, "*Naametan chist?*"

One of the exciting parts of being a nurse in Highland was the diversity of patients that came through. While there were plenty of Central Americans, the halls and waiting rooms were filled with people from Africa, Asia, and the Middle East. For the most part, English and Spanish were spoken across the complex. Still, Adira was comfortable trying other languages heard in the hallways and always made an effort to learn greetings and calming phrases from patients. Seeing the hazel eyes, strong jaws, and sharp noses of the boy and his sister, she'd guessed they were from Afghanistan and had asked what the girl's name was in Dari.

"Nahal," she said absently, closely watching her brother, her hands wringing.

"*Naameman* Adira, and your brother will be fine, dear." An elderly female professor in nursing school had called her *dear,* and it always felt comforting. Adira often used the word herself with children in the hospital.

Turning to Khalid, she said, "Well, young man, it looks like you'll need a few stitches. But we'll take an X-ray just in case."

"Will it hurt?" he asked.

Adira put his hand on his shoulder. "The X-ray? Not at all. But I'm going to have to clean the wound up a little. That will sting. But you look pretty tough to me."

He gave a clipped nod, and Adira gently cleaned the laceration.

He winced more than once as she proceeded. She asked softly, "I'd guess you were in third grade?"

"Second," he replied.

"Well, you certainly look strong." Turning to Nahal, she asked, "How about you?"

"I am in grade nine," the girl replied, worry still etched across her face.

Treating family members that came in with a patient was part of the job. Understanding cultural dynamics, especially in East Oakland, came hand-in-hand. "Is Khalid your only brother?"

The girl bobbed her head, thankful Adira understood.

"What's your favorite subject in school, Khalid?"

"Soccer," he replied.

"Well, don't worry about your career in the pros. We'll get you fixed up just fine," Adira promised. "How about you, Nahal? What's your favorite class?"

Nahal hesitated and took a breath, the conversation beginning to calm her. "Computer science."

"I bet you're good in math."

The girl managed a smile. "I like maths."

"Math is always straightforward, isn't it? Clean and structured," Adira said. "I always liked math too."

They went on to talk about school as Adira finished with the wound and took the pair down the hall for an X-ray. Soon after they returned, an elderly doctor, who had taken care of Adira years ago and was a large part of the reason she worked in this hospital, arrived.

"It looks like you two have found my very favorite nurse!" he said after passing through the slit in the curtain. Dr. Green's cheerful face showed a broad smile made only brighter by the contrast with his ebony skin.

The children were immediately captivated.

"How did the film look, Adira?" he asked.

"Khalid has two perfect legs, Dr. Green. Looks like he only needs a few stitches."

"Well, that's some good news, Khalid. How about we get you fixed up, then?"

Nahal looked to Adira as if asking if this was okay.

Adira leaned toward the girl. "Dr. Green's fixed me up before, and he did a great job."

Just as Green took a stool, Adira's name was called from outside the curtain. They both recognized the nasal tone of a senior administrator. Green nodded that Adira could leave to speak with him. She told the kids she would return shortly and made her way to the nursing station.

Tom Miller stood at the desk, his face radiating impatience. The despicable man was always trying too hard, frustrated that nurses and staff didn't show him the respect he felt he deserved. After ignoring his flirtations when she first arrived, Adira soon became his favorite to bully. This, she was sure, would be another rebuke.

"Down here," he commanded, turning down a hall that led toward the lab, expecting her to follow like a flea-covered dog.

When they'd reached an alcove away from the patients and foot traffic, he stopped and looked down at her. "Beds three and five weren't restocked. Both turned over, and critical items were missing."

"After the pneumonia in two, I cleaned both beds and restocked nearly everything before the leg wound came in. I didn't get the chance to go to the supply room for one splint and a backup set of EKG leads. Going as fast as I can. Wouldn't exactly call those critical."

"The ER is about pace. Your keeping up is critical."

Adira turned and looked back at the nurse's station.

"They're not going to help you," he sneered.

This wasn't the first time Miller had manufactured a problem to deliver an unnecessary reprimand. Recently, it had become somewhat of a habit, and she'd reluctantly voiced her concern to the head nurse. The woman had said enough to Miller to stop the issue for a couple of weeks, but his obsession soon returned.

Adira turned a foot in the direction of the nurse's station.

"I will get right to it, Mr. Miller," she murmured. "Thank you for your concern."

The words came out reluctantly, but it was time to escape. Challenging him would only make it worse.

He let a moment pass, relishing her irritation.

"I also saw that you let the girl go with the boy to X-ray. You know that's against policy."

She froze, her body tense, and turned back to face him. "Aren't you the one who tells us to treat the family? To respect the needs of different cultures? Well, that girl is scared to death that she'll be in trouble for not taking care of the family's only son."

His response was a disparaging smile.

"But I guess looking after your people isn't something you're very familiar with, is it?" she said, turning her back to him and taking a step away.

His hand shot out, seizing her arm from behind and spinning her around. "Don't get smart—"

His unwanted touch was like a hot iron. She twisted away to break his grip, then immediately spun back and stepped forward, using both hands to push him into the wall. He quickly regained his footing and looked down at his shirt. After smoothing a wrinkle and straightening his tie, he turned his gaze back to her.

"We'll see what that earns you," he sneered.

She made a threatening feint forward, immediately erasing the smug look off his face, before turning abruptly for the nurses' station.

"Stretch givin' you a hard time again, 'Dira?" one of the nurses asked when she returned.

"Guy creeps me out. Grabbed me. From behind."

"Mhmm," she replied. "You gonna need to report that."

"A report that will just go to admin? To him and his buddies? Not worth it."

"Well, you got to tell Marissa, then." Marissa was the head nurse and, for the most part, an ally. "She ain't gonna be back for another hour. We'll keep Lurch away till then."

"Thanks. I'm going to finish restocking and check on Dr. Green and the boy."

" 'Fore I forget, 'nother one of them fancy envelopes came for you."

The nurse pointed behind the counter before heading back to her patients. Adira went and retrieved the letter. Like the one before and the two emails before that, it bore the red-and-green seal of the Sultanate of Oman. Placing it in a back pocket beneath her scrubs, she saved it to read at the end of her shift.

Oman, of all places. When they'd first emailed her about a job, she'd had to look up where Oman was. The country of only five million people was on the east side of the Arabian Peninsula, framed by Yemen and Saudi Arabia, and just across a gulf from Iran. The best she could learn from the few websites that knew something about it described it as a peaceful country. She doubted that was possible in the Middle East.

She'd dismissed the offer quickly. Her practical side understood that she had a good job and leaving it to venture into the unknown was simply out of the question. After their second message, her opinion remained unchanged and indifferent. The third, sent via post to the hospital and printed on fancy stationery, was rather personal. It had arrived on a particularly tough day and had boosted her confidence at the time.

Today's letter was similarly flattering.

Dear Ms. Eastmont,

It is with great pleasure that, on behalf of His Majesty Hamad al Sabir, the Sultan of Oman, the Ministry of Health extend again your nomination to the Nursing Care Leadership Advisory Program. This program is a vital initiative of the Ministry of Health. It will serve as the foundation for our goal of providing the finest care possible to the citizens of the Sultanate of Oman.

You have been nominated due to your exemplary university achievements, outstanding performance at Highland Hospital, and the esteemed care you have been known to bestow upon your patients.

We understand that accepting this position is a significant decision. As such, we again extend our offer of remuneration commensurate with your value to the program, including transportation, lodging, generous stipend, and further compensation as detailed in the attached.

Your skills, and indeed your specific personal experience, will ensure the great success of our program.

It is with pleasure that I await your reply.

Yours sincerely,
Zahra al Abdali
Office of His Majesty the Sultan of Oman

While the compliments were a bit over-the-top and perhaps not entirely accurate, the message did make her stand a little taller. Flipping to the offer's details, she noticed that the numbers were higher than before, with her salary alone nearly three times what she made at Highland.

2

"Sure is a flattering letter," Dr. Green said before passing it to his wife, Imani, later that night. "And since you know how much I support traveling, I say it's something you should consider. Great experience, working in another country. Looks good on your resume too."

The three sat around the small table in the Greens' old house in Rockridge. The couple had invited her over for dinner after their shifts at the hospital. Walking into their home after work and seeing the piles of books and eclectic African crafts still made her happy. It had been a place of transformation for her years ago. A place of refuge, and she loved and trusted the pair implicitly.

"I know it sounds good on paper. But the reality is that if I leave the county hospital system, I leave the union. And if it's terrible there, I might never get my job back."

"There will always be nursing jobs, Adira," Green said. "Don't make a decision based on the union or fear of losing your place."

"The other thing is that, well, it's an Arab country. And I'm not too sure about working as a woman there."

Green regarded her quietly for a moment. "Heard there was an issue today."

Adira glanced at Imani, who had just flipped to the second page. "Yeah. Tom Miller. Guy's like a creepy stalker, always looking for a reason to pull me aside," Adira replied.

"I'll talk to Catherine tomorrow," Green said. Catherine was the head of nursing across the entire hospital network, and since she operated at the leadership level, would carry some weight.

"Thanks, but I can handle it."

"You sure? Happy to go out with a bang." Green was due to retire at the end of the month, a change Adira still wasn't happy about.

She forced a smile and put her hand on his knee. "Promise. You and Imani have done enough."

Imani had been listening to the two of them carefully. She enjoyed the peaceful sincerity and affection in how they spoke with one another. It was something that couldn't have made her happier. "So," she said, holding up the letter. "If I get this straight, you want to stay in a poor, decaying public hospital system when the sultan—a title which means more than king—of a paradise in Arabia wants to shower you with praise and money?"

As she spoke in her deep singsong tone, the lovely old African woman began to laugh. Her braids, a bright blue this month, shook and twirled, their vibrancy bringing a smile to Adira.

Adira opened her arms. "Well, when you put it that way, it does sound pretty good."

"It's more than pretty good. And since he didn't say it, I will." She got up from her chair and leaned down to hug Adira. "I am so proud of you," she said, finishing it with a loud kiss on Adira's cheek.

Green tried to recover. "My congratulations were, ah, implied."

Imani made a mocking face. "Implied, were they?" She caught Adira's eyes, and they both began to laugh. Once they'd caught their breath, Imani continued, "Now, dear girl, you do know that Oman is my part of the world, don't you?"

"You're from Tanzania!" Adira replied.

Imani tipped her head forward. "Yes, but Oman once controlled the coast from Tanzania all the way up and across to Iran. Even though the country is smaller now, it's still full of every type of person. East Africans, Arabs, Persians, Indians. It's a melting pot."

Adira forced a small smile. "Glad you know something about it because there's not much online."

"I think you do know something about it. Everyone does," she asserted, popping her eyebrows. "Sinbad the Sailor? The Queen of Sheba? And I'm sure you've heard the story of Aladdin."

"Those are from Oman?"

"Of course. Sinbad was from Oman. Even sailed an Omani ship. Sheba, whose story is told in the Bible, brought frankincense from Oman to King Solomon. And where do you think Aladdin found the lamp and his princess?"

"But still, it's the Middle East. Not exactly a Disney movie over there."

Imani's hand waved off Adira's concern. "The media gravitate to drama and threats. None of that in Oman. It's known as the Pearl of Arabia."

"Really? But even if it's a great place—and working there would be a good move—I don't think I'm ready for that sort of change."

"Change is always hard," Imani admitted, standing and again wrapping Adira in her arms. "You do what's right for you, okay? Just remember that we will always love you no matter what you decide."

Adira knew they would. They'd been the ones to reach out. The only ones.

***

A family of recently relocated Afghans had heard the gunshots that rainy night in East Oakland so many years ago. They'd hidden under the beds and in a closet. Only after blue police lights strobed across their ceiling did they feel it was safe to look.

They'd watched an ambulance take one victim away. A second removed two bodies that had been covered by police. A few officers worked the scene for about an hour, taking photographs and knocking on doors to take statements. After a tow truck removed the Mercedes, the last police car left, and the street took on an eerie silence. The family's eldest son had been the first to go outside.

The rain had stopped, but even still, there wasn't much to see. He paced the street for a while, wanting his father to see that he could be protective of his younger sisters. After a few minutes, he turned back.

As he walked past the side of their house, he heard a noise. It sounded like someone crying. Someone small.

Hidden in the tall weeds behind their garbage can was a terrified little girl.

They brought her inside, and while the mother and daughters tried to console the toddler, the father and son spoke in hushed tones about what to do. Calling the police to return her would have been the best option, but the ink on their Special Immigrant Visas was still wet, and their trust in local authorities had yet to be established.

The daughters wanted to keep the girl, even if for the night, until she wasn't so upset. The father and son decided that would be okay, and maybe the girl would be able to tell them her name.

But hour after hour, the toddler cried. No amount of water or tea or hugs from the daughters would calm her. It wasn't until the early morning hours that she finally fell asleep.

When dawn broke, the father instructed his daughters to wrap the girl up in the blanket she'd fallen asleep on and walk with him to the Eastmont Medical Center. They'd received care there since their arrival and knew where to go. They also knew when the doors opened and had timed their arrival to be just before then. There was no sense in being questioned.

When the guard stooped down to unlock the main door, he wasn't shocked to see the toddler. It wasn't his first time, so he knew to get on his radio for a nurse and Child Protective Services.

The toddler was given a physical while the CPS officer filled out the paperwork. There'd been a name written on the tag of her sweater: Adira. But there was no last name, so as was customary with abandoned young children, he was free to select one of his choosing. Unfortunately, he was not a very imaginative sort and simply used the name of the medical center: Eastmont.

With those two blanks filled, Adira Eastmont entered "the system." It was an institution that would do her no favors, sending her through a revolving door of wretched foster homes and failed adoptions. Her eyes, a piercingly light shade of gold, were a constant problem. Other children called her a witch, all too often making a scene that only drew more unwanted attention. And attention, at least in the world of preteens, triggered jealousy and abuse that had a tendency to become more than just verbal.

She had things stolen by other kids in nearly every home. Like the Vans a social worker had given her and the soap a bully threw at her after telling her she stank. Fights were a constant, usually bullying between kids in a home but sometimes a foster parent coming unhinged.

Adira wasn't always totally innocent. Ever, really. But there was enough blame to go around. The cycle started early. She'd break a house rule and get punished. She'd push a little further the next time, and the punishment would dial up. It would start easy. A blanket taken away, a week without a shower, or a couple of days sleeping on the floor in a windowless room. After those came the rough ones. Slaps that became punches. Belts and, once, a cigarette burn. She carried the resentment into the next home and the one after that. Each time, the triggers came faster, and the results hurt more.

As Adira had developed into a teenager, her problems expanded. Boys became attracted to her caramel brown skin and long hair but fell into a tortured mixture of fear and lechery upon seeing her bright eyes. Only her fast-moving elbows prevented an assault behind the gym during her first year in high school.

A month later, two of them tried at once. Her elbows hadn't been enough.

After her feral survival skills had failed her that night, Adira became detached. Angry and irritable. Tired. Depressed. So tired every day that it became a struggle. It became too much of a battle to face life any longer.

The couple fostering her at the time found her on the bathroom floor, a dark pool of blood slowly spreading from her wrist. Seeing their monthly check from the county seep across the curled linoleum, they acted quickly, raising and wrapping her wrist and bringing her to the Highland Hospital emergency room.

On duty was a former Navy flight surgeon who quickly read the situation and acted with purpose. Adira was in hemorrhagic shock, unconscious, presenting with extremely low blood pressure and fingernails turning blue. Dr. David Green ensured the bleeding was controlled, then immediately worked to bring her fluid levels back up with saline and a blood transfusion. When she'd finally stabilized, he continued to monitor her progress, ensuring there was no organ damage and the circulation had returned to her limbs.

He then moved to the next problem and, with no small amount of force or effort, arranged for her to be placed under the care of foster parents trained specifically for teens who had been through severe trauma. When she was finally released into their care, that would have been the end. But for some reason, Dr. Green took it upon himself to check on her once she settled in and began therapy.

He found the teenager guarded, her golden eyes always on alert, much as he expected. What he didn't expect was to see her so inquisitive and intelligent. Questions about her wound, homeostatic pressure, and prognosis were clear and detailed.

But then she dug further, asking his motivations for addressing her foster care and why he had visited. After each well-structured question, she'd listened carefully, almost clinically, to his response.

His visits increased, even joining her for therapy sessions after a time. He'd been cautious at first, making sure a dependency didn't form. Over time, her therapist confirmed that their relationship wasn't unhealthy but a shared level of respect.

As a group, Dr. Green, Imani, and the new foster parents worked to give Adira the stability she'd never had. She returned to high school, retaking the previous year and eventually graduating near the top of her class. Having been through the transformation she had, she pursued medicine and received a full scholarship to a respected four-year nursing program.

Adira began her studies with her nose buried in books and medical journals, quietly and with a fair amount of her armor still in place. As she moved into clinical work at the university's hospital, adjusting to the constant presence and pressure of administrators, doctors, and senior nurses was challenging. They pushed her, constantly questioning, teaching, and demonstrating. They forced her to verbalize, assess, act decisively, and lead in stressful, chaotic situations.

Through countless hours in the hospital and community clinics, she discovered that her weariness of people—or more specifically, distrust—was somewhat of an asset. With an ease that startled even herself, she was able to transform her life experiences into an empathy that consistently won patients' confidence. She found that she worked exceptionally well with children and people from neglected communities.

She graduated with honors, and while job offers came from a couple of health networks, she was drawn back to Dr. Green and Highland Hospital at the foot of the Oakland Hills.

Of the more than twenty thousand kids that age out of foster care each year, only half leave the system with a job. A scant 3 percent earn a college degree.

Dr. Green had been the only person in her life to reach out. To connect. Without his support, she would have been on the wrong side of every statistic. He'd made a difference simply by caring.

3

Adira clocked in the following day with a bounce in her step, happy to take on whatever cases the day had to offer. But just as she clipped on her pager, a message came through for her to report to a conference room in the administrative wing. Her spirits immediately fell, sensing this was once again the work of Tom Miller.

She entered the glass room to find three people, one of whom was the head nurse, Marissa. While they got along well, the look on Marissa's face was grim. "Good morning, Adira. This is Mr. Witcolm, from HR," she said, gesturing toward a pasty man in a suit and tie seated to her left at the round table. Turning to her right, she continued, "And this is Martina Lopez, a representative from the union."

Adira gave a single nod but said nothing.

"Have a seat, Adira," Lopez said. Once Adira took her place, she continued, "I first want to let you know that I am here as your advocate. We are going to discuss an incident that transpired yesterday."

Adira stiffened. "I imagine this has to do with me being grabbed? I don't know how you heard about it, but it wasn't a big deal. I'm happy to clear the air, though."

Lopez exchanged a glance with Marissa.

"Adira," Marissa said. "We aren't aware of an incident where you were grabbed. We're here because Tom Miller filed a complaint."

"Two complaints," the pale man interjected.

"He filed a complaint? About what?" Adira asked.

"Ms. Eastmont," began Witcolm, "Mr. Miller has submitted that while the two of you were discussing work matters yesterday, you acted inappropriately."

"*I* acted inappropriately?" Adira asked, baffled.

"Yes. He has indicated that you made advances toward him. After he did not respond, you physically pushed him with considerable force into a door."

"Advances?"

Lopez leaned forward, interrupting. "Adira, please take a moment." She then reached out and put a hand on Adira's arm. Adira looked down at the woman's hand before extracting her arm and placing it out of reach beneath the table.

The gesture didn't go unnoticed. "Why don't you tell us what happened yesterday."

And so Adira did, going to great lengths to hold her emotions in check. She went through the encounter clinically, providing specifics without interpretation.

Lopez responded. "Thank you for clarifying. But I can tell you are holding back. So please share any context that might be helpful."

Adira explained that she felt Miller showed an unhealthy interest in her. And while she didn't have specific dates and times, she conveyed three prior instances where Miller had singled her out for reprimands, followed by unspoken invitations on how to rectify the problem.

"And did you make your manager aware of the issue?" Lopez asked. Without waiting for a response, she turned to Marissa and asked. "Did you know of these events?"

Marissa, who had entered the room thinking she would be looking after one of her nurses, was not pleased to have the tables turned on her. "I was made aware of one or two and dealt with them accordingly."

"Did you file a report? Email HR or journal it in any way?" Lopez asked.

"I did not," replied Marissa, now crossing her arms. "I didn't feel it was significant enough to escalate. But I did speak to Mr. Miller and asked him to dial back his tone."

"Any harassment is significant," Lopez snapped, glaring at Marissa.

Her supervisor flailed, and Adira couldn't help but be disappointed. Yet another figure of authority letting her down.

Witcolm cleared his throat. "These past events, whatever they may be, can be addressed. But today, they're not relevant. What I have, Ms. Eastmont, is an official record of your misconduct. It's something I cannot ignore."

Adira prepared to respond, but Lopez interjected first. "So you're telling me, Mr. Witcolm, that since a white man filled out a form, he's right? And since a dedicated nursing staff member didn't file a report, she's the bad apple here?"

"I can only rely on the documentation I have here," Witcolm replied.

"Oh, is it documentation that you want? Well," Lopez said, thumbing through pages in her folder. "I have some performance reviews here from Marissa herself. Let me give you a few quotes. 'Adira can express empathy for patients while still showing great efficiency with attending physicians.' Or how about, 'The department has come to rely on Adira for her engagement with children, especially new immigrants nervous about visiting a government-run facility'? Sounds like she's just the kind of nurse you need here, Mr. Witcolm."

"Be that as it may, we've yet to address your advances on Mr. Miller."

"*My* advances? Please. The guy is a creep."

"How about the assault?"

"I didn't assault him," Adira said. "He grabbed me, and I reacted. Sure, I pushed him, but to get him off me. Have you ever been taken down a hall and grabbed, Mr. Witcolm?"

"He has indicated that he was fearful of his safety."

"*His* safety. Got it." Adira remembered the first time this had played out in a home. It was the first day, and she'd been excited to find a plastic doll. One of the arms was missing, as were the clothes, but that didn't matter. Adira had picked it up, only to have her arm grabbed by a wicked, big girl with a wide, flat nose. Adira pulled away, breaking the grip, only to be shoved hard by Flat Nose's other hand. Adira fell, and the doll was snatched away. But her fall had made enough noise to draw the foster mom's attention. As soon as she appeared in the doorway, Flat Nose grabbed her stomach and, feigning intense pain, claimed Adira had punched her.

Adira had been sent to bed without dinner that night, and Flat Nose received a double serving.

"Look at me, Mr. Witcolm. I'm five-five." Adira got to her feet, her heart beating faster. "Why don't you stand up?"

"Ms. Eastmont, this is hardly the place."

"You're doing an investigation, right? This is exactly the place. Stand up."

"Adira, let's all take a seat," Lopez said. "I know I got a little dialed up there, but I don't want you to."

Adira turned and looked down at Lopez briefly before turning back to Witcolm. In a calm and steady voice, she said, "Mr. Witcolm, I would like you to stand up so I can demonstrate the scenario Mr. Miller described."

Witcolm frowned at Lopez before reluctantly pushing back his chair and standing.

Adira projected a calmness that wasn't felt. "Tell me, how exactly would I assault you? You have, what, six inches on me? And he's another few inches taller than you. Am I really a 'threat to your safety'?"

"Ms. Eastmont, this is making me very uncomfortable."

"Uncomfortable?" she asked. "How about if I grabbed you like he did?" Her hand shot forward, grabbing his arm. She squeezed tightly. She squeezed like she'd been squeezed, not by Miller, but long ago. She let him sense that she wasn't one to be reckoned with before finally letting go. "Scared, Mr. Witcolm? Now you know what I felt yesterday with that pervert grabbing me."

Witcolm swallowed and then pulled down his jacket sleeve, collecting himself. "Ms. Eastmont, I think your demonstration went too far," he said.

"Now you know what it feels like being a woman," Lopez snapped. "Every goddamn day."

"Yes, well, her account differs significantly from that of Mr. Miller. And as past events are only alleged, there's little that can be done."

Adira glared at Marissa, who looked down at Witcolm's papers, now more concerned with her career than Adira's. It was despicable how this had played out. How one man's ego could force this to happen.

She wasn't going to be a victim. She was a nurse, lending her hands to real victims. Healing defined her. Not this.

Still standing, Adira pulled her shoulders back and took a slow, deep breath before speaking. "Ms. Lopez, thank you for your help. Thought you were a paper pusher for a minute there, but I'm glad the nurses—the female ones at least—have you on their side."

Lopez nodded, wondering where this was going.

"And Marissa, to be honest, I expected more from you."

Marissa, still uncomfortable, looked away.

Adira then turned to Witcolm. "I'd ask what our next step would be. I'd ask what you are going to do about harassment like this in the future. About men filing bogus claims." He began to stammer a reply, to which she held up a hand, stopping him. "But I won't ask. Because it's clear that you are more interested in using those papers to cover your ass."

The look on Witcolm's face showed he was even more desperate than before to have this meeting come to an end. He began to pack up his papers. "Yes, well, it appears I have some decisions to discuss with my colleagues."

"I'll save you some time," Adira announced. "Consider this my exit interview."

She spun on her heels and reached for the door. She stormed through the hallways, her face flushed with anger, and stomped all the way to the street outside. Since restarting school, she'd been very aware of not lashing out, not being impulsive. She'd tried being disciplined. Careful. But now, she'd let anger get the best of her again. Let it torch a bridge to the only thing she really had, her job.

She curled up in the bus shelter, wedging her back into the corner and raising her feet onto the dirty bench. It was Miller who'd caused this. And Marissa. And the whole admin office. And the foster system. When the bus finally pulled up, she was even blaming Dr. Green for retiring and leaving her all alone.

That wasn't fair. He'd been the one to lift her up. None of it was his fault.

By the time she walked up the creaky stairs to her apartment, she'd turned the blame on herself. It was her fault for not being brave enough to file reports on the creep, for not following up. For not reaching out to people and making some friends over the years at the hospital.

It was her fault for feeling so alone.

She curled up on her bed in the tiny studio and wept. She looked around the room, wondering what to do next. It was such a depressing place, with its chipped paint and mismatched secondhand furniture. How could she even afford to keep it without a job? How could she afford to live?

She wanted to call Dr. Green but was embarrassed. Embarrassed by what she'd done and for even considering blaming him. Embarrassed by the feeling she'd failed the one person who had ever cared about her.

She had to do something. She had to do something that would make him proud. That would make her proud of herself. At the very least, something that would pay the bills.

She pulled the crinkled letter out of her pocket.

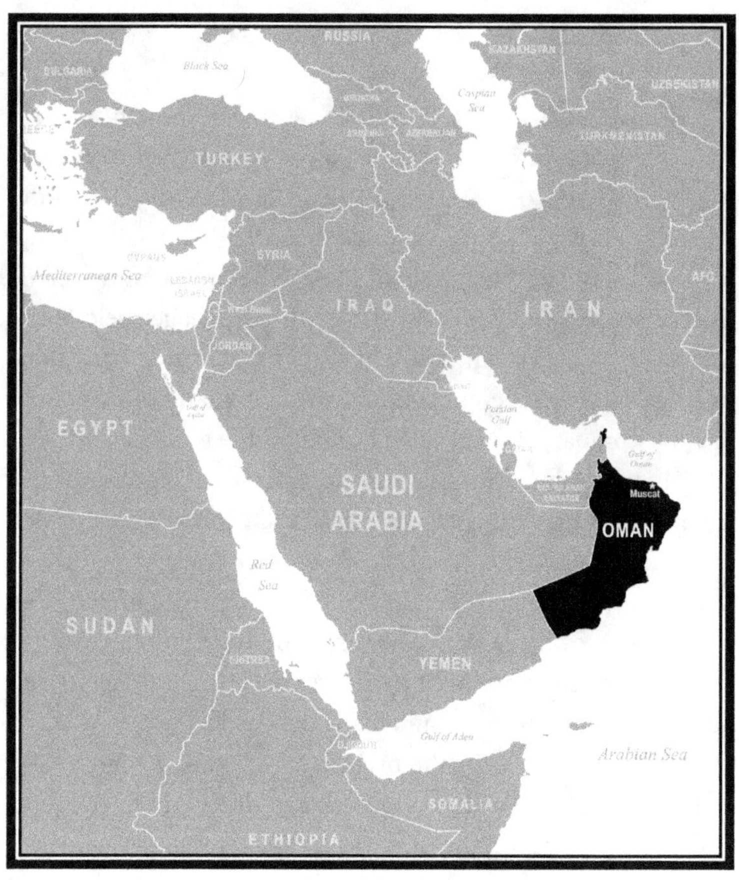
RUSSIA
KAZAKHSTAN
Black Sea
Caspian Sea
UZBEKISTAN
TURKEY
TURKMENISTAN
AZERBAIJAN
CYPRUS
SYRIA
AFG.
Mediterranean Sea
LEBANON
ISRAEL
IRAQ
IRAN
JORDAN
EGYPT
Persian Gulf
Gulf of Oman
SAUDI ARABIA
Muscat
OMAN
Red Sea
SUDAN
ERITREA
YEMEN
Gulf of Aden
Arabian Sea
ETHIOPIA
SOMALIA

4

Adira wasn't new to international travel, though this was only her second excursion. After high school, the Greens had encouraged her to see more of the world than the Oakland to Fremont corridor, going so far as to match her savings for an on-the-cheap backpack tour of Europe before nursing school. That trip had begun as a disaster, with her meager belongings and cash stolen within hours of arriving overseas. Back then, only luck—a chance encounter with a woman who owned a fashion company—had pulled her out of the gutter.

This trip, by contrast, was starting on a highly positive note. The Oman Ministry of Health had booked her in first class, complete with a luxuriously soft seat that reclined into a flat bed. She slept well on the first leg to London, but excitement got the better of her after the connection. Once the flight attendant announced they were on final approach, Adira slid closer to the window and lifted the shade.

The sea sparkled in the bright sun, changing from a deep indigo beneath her to a vibrant turquoise where it met a ribbon of pale sand. The city was a tight mosaic of low-slung white buildings stretching along the shore, none more than four or five stories tall. Behind them, like the back of a vast stage, a jagged mountain range stood sentry.

She pressed her head as close as she could to the window. The city had no prominent center, nor any tall, mirrored skyscrapers, rendering it almost timeless. Just as she began to take in more and more detail, a soft thump came from beneath her feet, and the plane started to slow.

While she'd expected to be pushed down crowded, bland corridors to slow immigration and customs queues, she was instead greeted by name and escorted to a private arrivals lounge where uniformed officials took care of her entry paperwork in minutes. She was processed efficiently and then escorted outside. Once out in the bright sun, she expected it to be searing hot and dry. Instead, it was surprisingly humid, and the heat was not oppressive in the slightest.

A spotless green Range Rover bearing a red crest of two crossed swords beneath a *J*-shaped khanjar knife waited for her along with two men and a woman. The woman stepped forward with the help of a slim cane, unusual for a someone who appeared to be around thirty, fit, and very sophisticated.

Her outfit was a perfect combination of elegant and strong, with a long-sleeve cream dress over matching slacks and expensive shoes. Tiny gold sequins on her black hijab sparkled in the midday sun, complementing her subtle yet immaculate makeup. Adira was immediately conscious of her comfortable clothes and sleep-tangled hair.

"Welcome to Oman, Miss Eastmont," the woman said. An awkward second passed while her dark brown eyes closely considered Adira.

Just as Adira was about to break the silence, the woman continued.

"I am Zahra, and this is Suhail," she said, gesturing to the uniformed man at her side.

"Nice to meet you, Zahra," Adira replied. "And you, Suhail."

The uniformed man bowed his head slightly but made no effort to extend his hand.

Zahra turned to Adira. "Ahmed, our driver, will take your bag."

"Thank you, Ahmed," Adira said, doing her best to make the *h* sound slightly sharp in the back of the throat as Zahra had done.

He smiled at her pronunciation, finding it closer than the attempt of most foreigners. "You are welcome, Miss," he replied, holding his right hand to his chest. "May I?" he asked, gesturing to her tattered suitcase. The ends of his eyelids were darkened with eyeliner.

"Yes, thank you."

As he placed the bag in the back of the vehicle, Suhail held the door for her, his expression stoic if not sour.

"It is my pleasure to thank you for accepting our offer, Miss Eastmont," Zahra said as they drove down the arrow-straight airport access road. "We are very pleased to have you here."

"Please, Zahra, call me Adira. I'm looking forward to the program and meeting everyone involved."

Zahra glanced forward briefly. "Yes, well, before that, we would like to introduce you to Oman. We have arranged for you to have a few days at our finest hotel. Once you are rested, I will give you a tour of Muscat, the mountains, and the desert sands."

"Thank you, Zahra. But you don't have to make this a vacation for me. I know I'm here for a job and am happy to get right to work."

"Please accept our hospitality, Miss Eastmont. There are a few days before your work begins, and it will give you a chance to get oriented to our culture."

Adira took some time to look out the window, taking in the brilliant blue sky above the mountains that gave not even the hint of a cloud. They passed low-slung offices and shopping malls, the men walking in and out dressed in long white tunics with white caps atop their heads. The women she saw wore hijabs, mostly black, and she was relieved that it didn't seem to be common for their faces to be completely covered. But like the men uniformly in white, almost all of the women wore a black dress or robe that covered them from neck to ankles. She was quick to realize she'd landed in a culture that was a complete one-eighty from California's T-shirts and hoodies.

"Okay, Zahra, I'll take you up on your offer. But you really need to call me Adira, okay?"

Zahra's eyes warmed with an exhale. "If you insist, Adira," she said with a genuine smile.

They left the motorway and wound down a cut between two hills into the oldest part of Muscat surrounding the port. Zahra pointed out the souq, the mosques, and the remnants of lookout towers built by the Portuguese late in the sixteenth century. In one of the denser parts of the old city, a collection of perhaps two dozen men had gathered, chanting and holding up signs.

"Is that a protest or a celebration?"

Zahra looked out. "A protest, though I am surprised to see it. They are scarce here."

"Anti-government?" Adira asked.

Zahra waggled her hands back and forth. "Not exactly. There is a defense purchase that some do not like. There is a feeling the money would be better spent on jobs than warplanes."

"I thought oil was an unlimited resource here."

"In some of the other Gulf countries, that's the case. Oman has oil, but not to the volume you find in Saudi or the Emirates."

Before Adira could ask more about the issue, they turned off the main road and soon faced a hotel that was fancier than anything she'd ever seen.

"Al Bustan Palace," Zahra said. "While it was once a home for the sultan, it is now a Ritz-Carlton hotel."

"It's incredible," Adira whispered as they came to a stop.

Zahra led them into the lobby. Polished marble throughout the vast space sparkled in the gentle light of a crystal chandelier at least three stories tall. The interior was beautiful, and Adira was stunned that she would be brought to stay in such a place. Never in her wildest dreams had she thought it possible. "My goodness, Zahra. Are you sure this isn't a mistake?"

Zahra smiled at Adira's genuine reaction. "We enjoy spoiling our guests. So yes, this will be yours for a few days," Leaning closer and lowering her voice, Zahra added, "After this, you'll be staying in the desert. You should take advantage of having a few small luxuries."

Adira looked up to the chandelier again. "Not so small," she mumbled.

"Shall we go to your suite?"

"Don't we need to check in?"

Zahra withdrew a keycard from her bag. "It has been arranged. Please, follow me."

The suite could only be described as majestic. There were sweeping views of the sea from a living room straight out of a magazine and a sparkling bathroom larger than her apartment in Oakland.

"This is incredible!" Adira said.

"I will leave you to have a rest. You must be tired from your journey. But if I may," she said, gesturing Adira to a small dining table where a leather folio had been placed before her arrival. "This is for you. Inside is a local SIM card for your phone, the number for which is on the reverse. There is also a card with my mobile number and Ahmed's. He will be available should you need to go anywhere. Inside the envelope, you will find money and a credit card that you are free to use during your visit."

"Zahra, I don't—"

She waved her hand dismissively. "These are yours. Part of your compensation."

"Thank you," Adira replied. "When will we meet again?"

Zahra looked at her watch. "It's nearly two now. Perhaps I could join you for dinner here?"

"Perfect. Gives me time for a shower and a nap."

"Shall we say half past six?"

"Deal. I'll see you then."

After Zahra left, Adira took an apple from a large dish and went out to the balcony. She leaned over the railing and took a bite, marveling at the lush green grass below, the beach, and the gulf beyond. She sent a text to the Greens, smiling to herself as she added a few pictures to the message. After a long shower, she lay on the bed, wondering if what was happening to her was real.

A loud trill woke her. She rolled across the bed, disoriented, before realizing it was the phone. "Hello?"

"Good evening, Miss Eastmont. This is the front desk. I wanted to let you know that your dinner guest has arrived."

"Oh, shit!"

"Ahh—"

"Sorry! Tell her I'll be right down!"

Adira quickly rose, looking outside to see the sun had already set. The clock showed it was just past seven. "Oh, shit!" she said again.

She'd fallen asleep in a robe, which was quickly cast to the floor as she dug through her suitcase for something to wear. Modest. The Muslims she met at the hospital always stressed modesty. A pair of slacks and a loose-fitting top with shoulders—one of her only two "nice" outfits—would work. After quickly pulling them on, she slipped into a pair of sandals and dashed to the bathroom.

Running her fingers through her hair, she looked in the mirror. No time for makeup, and thankfully no dried drool on her cheek. She grabbed her key card from the table and was in the lobby two minutes later.

"I am so sorry!" she said, slightly out of breath.

Zahra held a hand over her mouth and smiled. "It is okay, Adira. The time difference for you is eleven hours."

"Thanks. Sorry to be such a mess."

"You look very nice. Please," she said, gesturing. "I have a table for us in the Turkish restaurant. I hope that will be okay."

"Never had Turkish food, but it sounds great." Adira followed her across the lobby and through a gorgeous entryway. In the dining room, they were surrounded by tables of women in black abayat, groups of men in crisp white dishdashas, and a few Western guests in sport coats and conservative dresses.

Zahra noticed Adira fidgeting. "Are you all right?"

Adira spoke quietly. "Zahra, I'm a mess compared to these people, even in one of my nicest outfits. I might be out of my league here."

"We can stop in some shops if you'd like. But really, as long as you are respectful and do not show your shoulders or too much of your legs, you will be just fine."

A waiter arrived and asked if they might like a drink.

Zahra asked for sparkling water. After Adira did as well, Zahra said, "This is a hotel, so alcohol is available if you prefer."

"I'm not much of a drinker."

"Neither are we. It is actually forbidden for us. Is there something on the menu that interests you?" Zahra asked.

"It all sounds interesting. But why Turkish food here? What about Omani food?"

"We will have local food soon enough. With our long history of trade—from spices to precious metals and everything in between—you'll find that our cuisine spans from African to Indian and European. Turkish especially is found in most places."

The waiter returned with their drinks and offered to take their order.

"If you would like, I could order for us?"

"That would be perfect."

Zahra spoke with the waiter, and Adira listened carefully to the rapid changes in tone. Arabic could sound harsh but also had a lovely cadence.

"Can we get back to clothes for a minute?" Adira asked. "Most of the women here are wearing black dresses. But it looks like they also have clothes underneath."

"It is not a dress. Perhaps robe is a better word? It is an abaya, worn over clothes when one is outside of the house in the city."

"And your scarf—head covering—is it still called a hijab here?"

"Hijab is the broad term for a head covering. There are other names, like shayla, specific to a region and the way it is worn. You might even hear it called a lihaf when it has something sparkly sewn in."

"So you can show your style?"

Zahra laughed and held her hand up as if posing. "Of course! But the hijab shows modesty before God—or Allah, as we say—and is a reflection of your relationship with Him. It is not much different from other religions that use head coverings."

"Ahmed and the local men also wear caps."

"Yes, the embroidered cap is a kummah. It is worn with a dishdasha, the pressed, long-sleeve tunic, which is usually white. These are part of our heritage. In Muscat especially, you will find almost all men in white dishdashas and women in black abayat."

"Is it a law to dress that way? Everyone the same?"

"Not a law. But it is recommended as a way to celebrate our culture and history, especially in the city. When we leave Muscat, you will notice more differences. Ahmed will wear a turban—though we call it a mussar—wrapped in the Omani style. It will even have small tassels on the edges."

Adira leaned forward and, in a conspiring tone, asked, "Was that eyeliner he was wearing?"

Zahra put her hand to her mouth and gave a light chuckle. "Kohl. Yes, some men wear it. There is indication that the Prophet did as well, so while I know what you're thinking, I wouldn't read that into it."

Just then, the first of several dishes arrived. Zahra had ordered a variety, wanting to make sure her guest would find something she liked. Smelling the beautiful foods, Adira found she was famished and utterly intent on trying everything.

"Tell me about yourself," Adira inquired as they ate.

Zahra wasn't entirely prepared for Adira's question and carefully said, "I lived overseas when I was young but have spent much of my life in Muscat."

"Married? Boyfriend?"

"Alas, no." Zahra lifted her cane up. "This isn't much of a help, really."

"I watched you walk when we came in. Spinal or hip?"

Zahra again hesitated. "A little of both. Accident when I was a little girl."

"So do you let that define who you are?"

"You do get right to the point, don't you?"

"I'm sorry. That was rude of me."

"No, it was honest. But let's not discuss me. I want you to get to know Oman, get to know our people and our nation."

"How about Suhail? Why did we have an army guy with us today? Isn't Oman safe?"

"Oman is very safe, I can assure you. And Suhail is part of the Royal Guard of Oman, the people who protect His Majesty. I work in the Palace Office, and when we borrow a vehicle, they usually come with a driver and guard. It is simply procedure."

"So he's like Secret Service guarding the boss. Got it. Does the sultan have a lot of enemies?"

"Actually, quite the opposite. His Majesty is well known throughout the world as a mediator. It is often here that nations in conflict negotiate peace. Our stance has always been neutrality."

"Must be nice," Adira replied.

Zahra tilted her head agreeably. "We like to say that Oman is friends with everyone and has no enemies."

"But what about Sunni and Shia? They've been fighting forever, right? I'd have thought you'd have an enemy through that alone."

"We are neither Sunni nor Shia. The Omani are Ibadi, and our practice of Islam is not a part of this rift. It is one of the reasons we can work with everyone in the Muslim world."

"Never heard of Ibadi."

"Most people haven't. It's found almost exclusively in Oman and a few parts of Africa."

"I saw a lot of women out today. Does Ibadi treat women differently?"

"That is more due to His Majesty Sultan Hamad than anything. Thanks to him, we vote, have equal pay by law, and own land just as men do."

"So women here are entirely equal? The guard today—Suhail—he looked a little grumpy about protecting us."

Zahra straightened the placemat beneath her plate. "By law, women here are equal. But in practicality, we dress differently and play different roles in society. Suhail may come from a family that looks at life the old way. There will always be progress to be made."

Adira didn't want to press further. "Or he could've just been having a bad day."

Zahra smiled and dipped one side of her head briefly.

Adira brought her back to Oman's leader. "I'm glad to know the sultan's an advocate for women."

"He has accomplished a great deal in fifty years. When he came to power, our country was primitive and isolated, much like North Korea, in fact. We had only a few kilometers of paved road, three schools that were only for boys, and only one small hospital. His Majesty drove a renaissance of modernization, everything from infrastructure to education and healthcare. He brought us to the world stage in a way that was respectful of our history."

"You're painting the picture of a pretty amazing country."

"You will see for yourself tomorrow."

"Have to say I'm excited," Adira admitted, her cheeks drawing upward.

The two shared tea and dessert before saying goodbye. By the time Adira reached her room, the jet lag hit again and she was struggling to keep her eyes open.

Housekeeping had cleaned up the mess she'd left behind. Her clothes were unpacked, neatly pressed, and hanging in the closet. Next to her toiletries bag, her hairbrush rested on a perfectly folded washcloth. She didn't remember using it before rushing down to meet Zahra. It struck her as curious, but she was too tired to worry about it.

5

Adira's tour the following day began in Mutrah, at the apex of a horseshoe-shaped harbor framed on both sides by sharp mountains.

Zahra drew her hand across the expansive view. "The mountains surrounding this inlet protect ships from wind and storms. Since it was such a safe place to drop anchor, the harbor became the center of old Muscat."

"Is that what the ships looked like?" Adira asked, pointing to a pair of old dhows anchored in the center of the calm water.

"Exactly like that," Zahra replied. "We still build them using the original techniques as a way to preserve our heritage."

Adira watched as a pair of seagulls danced around the small ships before landing among a flock bobbing across ripples in the blue-green water.

"Because the ships sheltered and resupplied here, Mutrah became our center of trade. Even though container ships now unload in another town, commerce is still at the heart of Mutrah. Over there is the fish market," Zahra said, gesturing to the left. "It is fun to see in the early morning, but be prepared because the smell is quite strong!"

Adira smiled, and Zahra gestured for them to proceed along the corniche at the water's edge. The wide pedestrian walkway curved around the full perimeter of the harbor. A gentle breeze blended mechanical city sounds with the soft lap of water against the seawall and trills from the birds.

They passed a man wearing a polo with bright stripes standing next to the stone railing, two cats expectantly eyeing his fishing rod. Nearby, a man in a sand-colored dishdasha spoke emphatically into a mobile phone, his free hand gesticulating wildly. Further down, they came across a family, the mother rocking a stroller back and forth, the father wiping a dribble of ice cream from his older daughter's face.

Opposite the road that separated the corniche from the water were shops and apartments, more old than new, but all whitewashed and contrasting beautifully with the rough, dark peaks in the background. After passing a mosque with its single minaret tiled in vibrant blue, they crossed the road and entered the Mutrah Souq.

The market's warren of covered cobblestone passageways was lined with dozens and dozens of tiny shops. Each store was its own miniature theater, with bright lights highlighting the tiers of tables featuring their wares and luring customers inside.

It was clear that anything and everything could be found in the souq. The first shop they passed was clearly a metalworker, his pieces sparkling under bright spotlights. Intricately carved platters sat below tea and coffee pots, all perfectly arranged smallest to largest. Above them, hanging from fishing line, were perforated tin lanterns, each of a different shape and size.

They strolled past a shop selling stuffed toy camels and T-shirts. "These are for tourists," Adira said.

Zahra replied with an upward pop of her shoulders.

"But I haven't *seen* any tourists."

"We have tourists," Zahra replied, tilting her head across the passageway toward an elderly European couple in shorts. "Not many, though. It's a part of the economy we would like to develop."

"So is this market for tourists or locals?"

"Both. Let's go in here." Zahra pointed to an entrance framed on one side with pressed, white dishdashas and colorful dresses and scarves on the other.

Adira followed her up two stone steps, past a tiered display of white caps arranged in circles much like a wedding cake. She paused and took a closer look.

Zahra turned back. "Do you remember what they're called?"

"Kummah. For men," Adira replied. "But the pattern embroidered on them is much more intricate than I thought. And each one is different."

The shopkeeper took this as his cue and stood up from his small stool in a back corner. "They are embroidered by hand, madam, not machines. Each one is very special."

Adira picked one up, feeling the soft bumps in the dense stitching before replacing it just as it was.

"Perhaps you would like a dress? Or this?" He pulled a folded scarf off a shelf and gently shook it open. It was electric blue with vibrant gold embroidery. "This blue is nice with your top and the gold matches your eyes!"

Adira saw the corners of Zahra's lips turn up. "That's a bit too bright for me, thank you," Adira said, letting him down gently.

"Actually, do you have something to cover with?" Zahra asked. "We are going to the Grand Mosque later."

Adira shook her head, then pointed to an off-white scarf with a simple fringed edge. "Could I please see that one?" she asked.

Zahra leaned toward Adira. "Hope you're ready to bargain," she whispered.

Adira gave her a wink in return.

"Yes, of course," the shopkeeper said, unfolding and laying it out for Adira. "This one is very soft. From Kashmir."

Adira felt the shawl, and loved it immediately. The cashmere was soft and light as air, perfect for the climate. "How much?" she asked.

"This will be twenty rials," he said. "It is one of our finest."

Adira took her time before replying. "You have a very nice shop here, but that is too much for me."

"I can make a special price for you. Eighteen rials."

"I think eight would be fair," Adira said, her voice level.

The man shook his head. "I am sorry, but that is far too low. These are some of the most delicate pashmina threads. Very thin. Very difficult to make."

Adira handed the scarf back to the man. "Thank you anyway," she said turning away and gesturing for Zahra to leave.

Before she crossed the threshold, the shopkeeper called out. "Wait! For you, I can make the price fifteen rials."

Adira turned her head back. "Ten is my limit."

"Oh, madam," he said, shaking his head.

"Let's go, Zahra," Adira said, gesturing down the passage.

"Ten!" the man said. "You leave me no choice."

Adira paid the man, and he handed her the scarf nicely folded in a small plastic bag. She thanked him and joined Zahra outside the shop.

"How'd I do?"

Zahra laughed. "Not bad for your first try."

Adira held a hand to her chest. " 'Not bad?' I got him down 50 percent!"

Zahra lifted a shoulder and smiled. "You'll get better with practice."

Adira feigned exasperation before they both began to laugh.

Together, they wandered deeper into the market, passing shops that sold everything from undergarments to sweets. Some shopkeepers had small pots of frankincense burning just outside their doors. The earthy scent of the smoldering resin combined with the worn cobblestones beneath their feet and the carved wood shading the meandering old alleys rendered the market timeless.

At the opposite end of the market, they returned to the bright sunshine. As Adira blinked and her eyes adjusted, their green Range Rover arrived. A guard opened the door for them, and after seeing them safely inside, drove them up winding streets to the base of an ancient wall. There, Zahra led Adira up a series of stone steps, explaining that they were ascending to a sixteenth-century Portuguese tower.

After passing the decayed remains of an old cannon, they arrived at the lookout level. Stretched below them was a postcard-perfect view of the harbor and the Sea of Oman beyond.

"Beautiful," Adira said, leaning her arms on the stone parapet.

A cooling breeze found its way up from the sea.

"Okay, you were right. It is kind of a paradise," Adira said.

"I am glad you see it this way," Zahra replied.

"Can I make a confession?"

Zahra's eyebrows rose. "If you wish."

"I was a little scared to come here. The Middle East has a reputation. Unstable, unsafe…"

"In some places, that is true."

"That's the thing. I guess I thought of the Middle East as a single culture. But it's not. The people we passed on the corniche. They were just people being people."

Zahra smiled and let Adira sort through her thoughts.

"Did you see the family earlier? They were giggling without a care in the world. Swap his dishdasha for a T-shirt and her abaya for a sundress, and they could have been anywhere."

Zahra opened a hand. "They were being a family."

"Exactly. And there were guys being guys, and women chatting like us as they strolled along. Some smiled a hello. I didn't expect all of that, and I just wanted to say I'm a little embarrassed."

"Don't be, Adira. Just enjoy how *normal* it is here."

Adira pointed a finger at Zahra. "I didn't say *normal*! I know better than that!"

"I was only teasing," Zahra laughed. "Let's go and have lunch."

They walked down from the tower and were driven to a restaurant near the fish market for lunch. Afterward, Zahra showed Adira the Royal Opera House where they caught a few minutes of concert preparation.

Their last stop for the day was the Sultan Hamad Grand Mosque. Zahra showed a couple of ways Adira could fold her new scarf to cover her head before taking her through the enormous prayer hall.

The next day, they met at the Al Mouj Marina, where a boat took them to the Daymaniyat Islands. The captain threw an anchor into shallow, crystal-clear water. Fish and sea turtles drifted around colorful mounds of coral, the tropical scene a striking contrast to the dry, stony islands that barely broke the surface. They went below deck to change, Adira donning a simple one piece and Zahra appearing in a much more modest suit that covered her like a thin wetsuit from her ankles to the top of her head.

Seeing Adira look at the burkini, Zahra shrugged—"It's how we do it!"—before rolling off the side of the boat with a laugh. The water temperature was ideal, and they spent the day snorkeling and enjoying a picnic on one of the pebbly beaches under glorious blue skies.

On their last day, Zahra asked Adira to meet in the hotel lobby early in the morning with her luggage. They drove high into the Al Hajar Mountains and stopped for a swim in a wadi nestled deep in a canyon before continuing farther south.

As the roads changed from smooth to gravel and eventually mere markings in the sand, Zahra explained they would have lunch at a Bedouin camp. While the nomadic tribes didn't migrate across the deserts in search of pastures for their herds as they once did, their heart and spirit were still strong in many villages.

In a camp at the edge of the golden dunes of Wahiba Sands, Zahra led Adira into a large tent made of wooden stakes and a patchwork of canvas tarps. They took a seat on thick carpets covering the sand in a corner opposite a young girl weaving bracelets. She said hello in Arabic but, otherwise let them be. Eventually, the girl's father entered, carrying plates of chicken, grilled fish, and rice. Zahra taught Adira to eat as an Omani with the right hand, using three fingers to compact the rice with some meat, and the thumb to act as a pusher.

After three days together, they'd become comfortable with one another and laughed easily as they ate. Adira had never been one to make friends quickly, so she was surprised at the bond she'd formed with Zahra in only a few days.

More than once while they were eating, the little girl coughed. She did so once again when they were finished, this time wiping mucus onto her sleeve.

Adira got up and went to sit with the girl. Using some of her limited Arabic, she said, "*Ismi* Adira. *Mas-muki?*" *My name is Adira. What's your name?*

"Tala," the girl said.

Adira made a show of putting her hand on her own forehead. With raised eyebrows, she asked if she could do the same to the girl. Receiving a modest shrug in reply, Adira felt for the girl's temperature. A little warm, but certainly not hot.

"I'm going to listen to you breathe, okay?" she said, pointing to her ear. She then put her hand on the girl's back and made a show of taking a deep breath.

"*Hasanan,*" the girl said, turning slightly.

Adira pressed her ear to the girl's back and listened, hearing lungs that were mostly clear. Sitting back up, she noticed the father had been watching. He spoke to Zahra, asking if the girl was okay.

"Tell him Tala appears to have a cold," Adira explained. "Plenty of water and rest would be a good idea. If her temperature spikes or the coughing worsens, he should take her to the doctor."

Zahra translated, and the man thanked Adira before briefly stepping out of the tent. He returned a few minutes later with a long-beaked coffee pot and dates. Adira sipped spiced coffee from a small cup while the little girl showed the bracelets she'd been making.

After saying their goodbyes, they drove across a stretch of desert to a small block of concrete villas built right on the edge of the sands. Turning into the courtyard of one, Ahmed brought the vehicle to a stop. Suhail, the guard, went off to a small official-looking building nearby without so much as a goodbye.

As Ahmed unloaded Adira's suitcase, Zahra explained that her work would begin in the morning, and this was the house where two doctors and a nurse lived while on rotation at the village. Adira was to spend a week with the mobile clinic serving the Bedouin while the Ministry made more formal arrangements for her in Muscat.

"Aren't you staying?" Adira asked. While she was excited to dive deeper into the land she'd only had a taste of so far, she was a little nervous about Zahra leaving her.

"I am afraid I must get back to the Palace; it is a long drive."

"I have enjoyed you showing me around, Zahra. Thank you. For the tour and for the job. I can't wait to get started."

"I have greatly enjoyed your company, Adira. It has been a pleasure, and I will see you when you return to Muscat."

The two embraced, and Zahra joined Ahmed in the car and drove off with a wave. Adira picked up her bag and walked inside.

6

"Hello?" Adira called, walking down the hall of the old house. There was no response other than her echo, so she took it upon herself to look around. It was a simple place made of concrete with tall ceilings. The air was stuffy, so she looked around and found a switch for the rusty split-unit air conditioner. Only a few clicks and clacks came in return.

The main living space showed a haphazard array of well-used furniture. What may have once been a second living room was used to store medical supplies. An industrial freezer had been added for medications. A quick look showed it filled with the latest COVID vaccine doses. So she'd be working in vaccination clinics. Not a problem, as she'd done plenty with the Highland staff since the virus had arrived in the US.

Down a short hall were a few bedrooms, each a bit of a mess, one with a bed that looked to have been wheeled in recently.

She returned to the living room and tried the AC again, flipping the switch off then on a few times. If she had to guess by the clicks, the problem was electrical. She checked the plug, then wiggled the wire where it entered the unit. The high-voltage line gave a sharp crackle in return. After unplugging the unit, she grabbed a chair and the one knife in the kitchen that could substitute for a screwdriver. One of the wires had come off a post. After fixing the connection, she put the housing back on and plugged the unit back in. This time, it came on immediately after she flipped the switch.

"You have fixed it!" came a man's voice.

She turned to see a thin man in a white dishdasha. "Wire was loose, that's all. I'm Adira, the new nurse," she said.

He came closer with a broad smile that genuinely projected his expression of happiness. "We have been banging on that thing for the past week without even Allah's good fortune," he said, walking forward to embrace the cold air. "Luxurious!"

He spoke in the same manner as Zahra, slightly formal, with a touch of a British accent.

"I am Amir," he said. "And we have been looking forward to your arrival." He took a moment to look carefully at her, then smiled mischievously.

"What?" Adira asked.

"You will know soon enough," he replied. He then turned to the door and called out, "Chevy, Nabila! Adira has arrived. And she has fixed the air conditioner!"

A small, middle-age Omani woman wearing a red-and-blue tunic and cream hijab walked in. She introduced herself as Nabila, the nurse, before excusing herself to clean up and pray.

"New girl fixed the air con? God bless her bloody soul!" came a loud female voice in a frighteningly sharp Australian accent.

"She did," said Amir. "And I must say you will want to see her straightaway!"

Adira wasn't sure what he meant by that, but the man chuckled and then sat down on one of the couches.

Footsteps echoed in the hallway. Adira turned to find a tall young woman with bottle-bleached, short-cropped hair sticking up in all directions. She stepped forward to look at Adira, and her mouth fell open. She dropped the box she was carrying and ran straight at her. Adira froze, too shocked to move.

"Bloody hell, they're spectacular!" The woman quickly pulled a chair from the kitchen and pushed Adira into it. "I'm Chevy, by the way. Stay right there. Stay!" She then ran into the supply room.

"Chevy? Like the truck?" Adira asked Amir.

"I believe it to be the informal version of *Chevannah*," Amir said.

"Amir! Where the hell is the bloody ophthalmoscope?" Chevy shouted through the doorway.

"How many times must I ask you to watch your language! It is right where you left it yesterday."

"Oh, calm your dress-wearing ass down, Princey." There was a bang, followed by another shout. "Got it!"

This woman was proving to be a life force all her own. Amir looked over and rolled his eyes; Adira tried to hold back a smile.

Chevy sprinted back into the room, grabbing a chair for herself on the way.

Adira recognized what was coming next. She did her best not to laugh at Chevy's excitement, and sat still, her eyes straight ahead.

The light on the ophthalmoscope came on, and Chevy peered through the eyepiece. "Bloody brilliant! Did you know that amber eyes are like this perfect mix of all the stuff that colors eyes? The recipe is super rare, like less than a hundredth of a percent."

Adira felt Chevy's hand move slightly, adjusting the angle of the light.

"Your iris has every color between yellow-white and copper. Usually, you only get a part of the spectrum. Never seen anything so sparkling and gold like this. Gorgeous depth in the pattern too."

" 'The stuff that colors eyes.' Is that a medical term? You doctors are *so* impressive," Adira said in mocking admiration.

"New girl's got some cheek! I like it!" Chevy said, jumping up and moving to Adira's other side. "Now keep still!"

"Yes, ma'am!"

"The stuff that makes them gold is a combination of more than a dozen genes plus a balance of eumelanin and pheomelanin," Chevy said, looking through the scope. "The pigment in brown and blue eyes is mostly eumelanin. People with green eyes really get me hot and bothered. That's pheomelanin. For amber eyes, you need the perfect cocktail of both. You got a top shelf pour, so yours are uniquely vibrant. They really glow in the scope." She paused a moment and changed the magnification. "Wear sunnies a lot?"

"Sunnies?"

"Yeah. Sunglasses."

"Sure. Why?" Adira replied.

"Good. Light eyes need more protection. You get called *Wolf Eyes* or *Cat Eyes* when you were a kid?"

"*Witch,* mostly. You an ophthalmologist?"

"Witch! Love it! We do family medicine here. My focus is endocrinology, not ophthalmology. At med school, I shacked up with an ophthalmologist. God, he was hot. Hooked me into all this eye business. Even drove me to publish about it once.

People here are going to love you. They believe in the mystical, *jinn* they call it. Can't wait to see their faces when they meet a real witch!"

"School was in Australia, I'm guessing?"

"Sydney on a full scholarship for pikers," she said, turning off the scope.

"Wrong-side-of-the-tracks scholarship for me, too. Only BSN, not MD."

"Poor kids rule!" Chevy said, holding her fist out for a bump. "What're you doing here?"

"Government invited me for the Nursing Leadership program."

"Never heard of it. But glad to have you on board."

"That reminds me," said Amir. "We will need to take some blood. Nothing serious; we just keep a record as a baseline for you in case we come across something new." He rose and went into the supply room just as Nabila returned.

"She always like this?" Adira asked Nabila, pointing to Chevy.

Nabila laughed. "How bad was she?" Her English was good, but she wasn't as comfortable speaking as Amir.

"Like someone who had a coffee IV running all day."

"Then she is very calm. Most days, she is like a stick of dynamite."

Chevy rolled her eyes and returned to the box she'd dropped earlier.

"Given the freezer, does this ah, clinic, focus on vaccinations?" Adira asked. She tried not to be rude, but it was hard to think of the house as a medical clinic.

Chevy gave a cackle while carrying the box away.

Nabila smiled and said, "The house itself is not a clinic. We are a mobile clinic, sleeping here and using it for storage. A proper clinic is planned for the village but not built yet."

"What type of medicine do you practice?"

Amir answered. "General—or what you may call family—medicine, primarily. Since we are mobile, the Ministry of Health uses us as a temporary measure to service communities where facilities are planned but not yet built. And you are correct about the freezer. Being mobile also means we provide vaccine doses for certain communities."

"So what is in store for me?"

"Family care for a few days, then we will shift to a farming village for boosters," Amir said. Looking at his phone, he added, "And after that, it looks like we'll be on the coast vaccinating fishermen."

"I'm looking forward to it," Adira said. Turning to Nabila, she asked, "Are you a part of the Nursing Leadership program? I'd like to know what to expect."

Nabila looked at Amir, who replied for her. "The program is small," he said. "But important. Our medical schools are advanced, but it's a way for us to learn from other countries and assemble best practices, if you will. And we've found that it is better to have practitioners in the field than lectures. We can learn from watching you and asking questions. You'll be with the three of us for a while, then put with a hospital team."

He took her left arm and set it on the table. A tourniquet went around her bicep, and a quick wipe with alcohol cleaned the site. Nabila held open a package containing a needle for him, and he very quickly had the vein. She passed over one vial and then another. Once they were filled, she labeled them while Amir withdrew the needle and held a sponge on the site for a few seconds.

"Do I get a lollipop?" Adira asked.

"We could manage a beer. That is if Princey hasn't sculled them all again," Chevy replied from the kitchen.

"I hope you know that not to be true," Amir said to Adira. "Omanis generally do not drink."

"Why's she call you Princey?" Adira asked.

"*Amir* means *prince*," he explained. "I have learned that Australians love to put an *ee* sound at the end of everything. I really do hope that all Australians aren't as offensive as she can be."

"I love you too!" Chevy said, making a show of blowing him a kiss as she sat down on the couch and propped her feet up on the table.

They shared stories for a while before turning in for the night. As Adira made up the extra bed in Nabila's room, she heard the front door open and some footsteps in the courtyard. Scraggly plants in front of the window obscured the view, but it looked like Amir had gone outside to speak with a woman. Adira turned back to the bed, not giving thought to her being anyone other than a patient.

The following day, Adira was up early and took the time to familiarize herself with their available supplies. The collection was small and relatively simple but perfectly adequate for working in the field. Eventually, Nabila arrived and took her outside to show the equipment and supplies stored in their two Land Cruisers. It was important for her to understand what they had and where to find it to efficiently work as a team.

They spent the morning as a foursome, familiarizing Adira with the Bedouin village. It was interestingly split almost in two, with half living on the edge of the sands in tents and half making their home in a growing number of concrete houses and buildings. The traditions, however, carried across both sides, the most interesting of which was an approach to care quite unlike her work in America.

Rather than the rush she was accustomed to in the ER, everything here moved at a slower pace. The medical team would be invited into a tent or home for tea or coffee and often introduced to the extended family. Only after initial pleasantries would a patient's care be discussed, and even then at great length before proceeding. The healthy approach left Adira feeling fresh and fulfilled by the time her day wrapped up—a striking contrast to the exhaustion and sore feet after a shift back home.

7

In Muscat, more than one hundred miles away from the sands, Rashid bin Tamim, the Minister of Defense, sat in a lavish suite on the top floor of the Chedi hotel. Isolated from the public areas of the hotel and known to very few, the penthouse was a discreet meeting place away from prying eyes inside the Palace's state offices.

In this particular case, he met with a Brit named Jonathan St. Marks. One of life's necessary evils, St. Marks was a broker, a role required by any defense company selling across international borders.

"Your terms are beyond what is possible, Mr. St. Marks," Rashid said.

St. Marks wore a smug look. "Perhaps. But it seems your deal with the Americans has unfortunately fallen through."

Rashid knew why the thin man was so full of himself. Over the past few months, St. Marks had used his contacts to sour the sale of $800 million in American fighter jets to the sultanate. He'd done the same to a similar size contract with the French earlier in the year. Clearing these options off the field meant Oman was left with a single offer of $1.3 billion for twelve British fighters and their assorted munitions.

"Indeed it has," Rashid grumbled. The number, which exceeded what he could authorize on his own, was a problem. But doing business with the arrogant Brit did have its benefits. They would come soon enough.

"As I have explained, Mr. St. Marks, I cannot agree to this deal for anything greater than one billion."

"Your Excellency," St. Marks said, finally using the title bestowed upon ministers. "I've felt a little underwater myself a few times. And what I've found is that there's always an alternative. Another dial to turn, maybe even a few."

"One billion US, Mr. St. Marks. That is what the sultanate can do." Rashid stood as if to leave, smoothing his starched dishdasha.

"I've been authorized to go down to one-point-one-five."

Progress, Rashid thought. He remained quiet, knowing St. Marks would fill the silence.

St. Marks needed the deal. With the sultan childless, Rashid, as a distant cousin, was the odds-on favorite to take the throne. And once Rashid ascended, he would need a broker to handle more than just arms. There would be oil, mineral, and infrastructure deals and more to be made. St. Marks wanted them all. He wanted that seat at the table.

Rashid took two steps toward the door.

"Please, Rashid. How about this: one-point-one. And as I know it will be a struggle," he continued, reaching into his left jacket pocket for an envelope, "perhaps this will offset any difficulties."

Rashid took the envelope and withdrew a card upon which was written a single figure. "Your offer is kind. But perhaps not kind enough," he said, handing the paper back.

St. Marks took it back, making a show of looking at the number. "My apologies. I meant to give you this one." An envelope from his right pocket was retrieved and presented.

Rashid read the second card and found it in keeping with what he expected the man to offer. While it would still require some effort with the Palace Office to have the extra cost allocated and the purchase approved, at least his personal side of the deal was taken care of. "Do you have a pen?" he asked.

St. Marks produced a pen from the more generous of his two pockets.

Rashid wrote an account number on the card and returned it. "Please, remain our guest here for a few days, Mr. St. Marks," he offered as he walked to the door. "It would be our pleasure."

Once out of the hotel and in the back of his Bentley Flying Spur, Rashid directed his driver to take him to Al Alam Palace. As he entered the large complex of buildings, his phone rang.

"How did your meeting go, Rashid?" a low, gravelly voice asked.

"I was able to get him to one-point-one," Rashid replied.

"Plus, I imagine, something extra?"

"Of course not."

The line hung in silence. The caller knew Rashid would need his help to get the overage approved but was not going to come out and offer assistance. He wanted to be asked.

"It seems we will have to get this approved together," said Rashid.

"Meaning?" the voice asked.

"Meaning," Rashid said uncomfortably. "Meaning that I would like your help to get this through."

"Of course, my friend. I would be delighted," the voice smugly replied.

Rashid reluctantly shared his thanks before hanging up. *Inshallah*, at least he'd be done with the insufferable man soon enough.

***

Just across the expanse of the Palace grounds, in one of the few residences other than His Majesty's own, Zahra al Abdali spoke with her staff.

"Anything back from Stanford yet?" she asked.

"Not yet. Day after tomorrow," a young man seated at his workstation replied. He read the look on Zahra's face and added, "That is still fast."

"Yes, I know," she replied. Turning to two men dressed in Western clothing, she asked, "Are your flights still on time?"

"*Na'am, sayyideti*," they replied in unison. *Yes, ma'am.*

"And the samples? You each have both?" She knew they did. She knew that every detail had been planned out. But it was important to hear her emissaries confirm if only to reassure her once more. She reviewed a few last details before sending them out to waiting cars. While they were both headed to the airport, it was important they take separate routes from this point forward.

After they left, the young man spoke again. "You really think she is the one, don't you?"

"It does not matter what I think. We need concrete results. But it's her, Abdul. I could tell the moment we met."

8

Over the course of several days, Adira found herself enjoying work in the desert more and more. There were wellness checks and vaccinations, follow-ups to minor aches and pains, and the time to carefully review and diagnose illnesses. Importantly, improving the health of hard-working people in the brutal climate of the desert was fulfilling.

Chevy introduced her to a study she was working on related to changes Bedouin go through during urbanization. For centuries, the Bedouin have lived on diets based on what was immediately available in the golden sands. As villages moved closer and closer to the edge of the desert, they brought easy access to manufactured and high-sugar foods. They also brought machinery that reduced the hard labor traditionally required in an agrarian lifestyle. And then there was stress, the pressure of transition from barter to currency. Chevy explained that these factors had significantly impacted the Bedouins' collective health, and she was researching these changes at a more granular level.

While Adira proved her worth in the field supporting Amir and Chevy, she also spent time between calls and in the evenings reviewing their operational plans and supplementing them with input from her experience in California.

This open exchange of ideas between colleagues had been working well for the week, and they functioned exceptionally well as a team. It was something that proved critical late one Thursday afternoon.

During peak travel time at the end of the work week, when tired sons and daughters drove back to the desert for their mothers' home-cooked meals, there'd been a multi-vehicle accident. Royal Oman Police, the lead coordinator in such emergencies, dispatched ambulances from Isa'af, the National Ambulance Service. But with Isa'af response times at least twenty minutes in rural areas, Amir and Chevy were also contacted.

Thankfully, they weren't out on the sands but quite close by and arrived only a few minutes after the call. The accident had occurred not far off the main road, on a small dirt intersection surrounded by a few small markets, a garage, and a chip shop where they'd grabbed burgers once before. At the site, they found a large eight-wheel truck laying on its side diagonally across the road. The rear of a silver sedan was pinned beneath the truck's cargo box, and a white SUV had collided with the front of the truck just as it had rolled. The air still held the dust and sand that had been stirred, along with the scent of hot metal. Fortunately, there was no evidence of fire.

"Bloody hell," Chevy exclaimed, grabbing the basic life support bag.

Amir took the larger, advanced kit. "Get the spinal and airway kits too," he said to Adira and Nabila.

Adira assessed the scene, where a small group of locals had frantically gathered. The injured would need care, but the uninjured and bystanders would need direction. And as she'd learned long ago, everyone was going to depend on them for calm clarity.

Adira identified a protected expanse of road that could be used safely for staging transport and treatment. "Transport here," she said to Amir, pointing. "I'll have the police clear the area while you and Chevy triage."

Around her, men and women moved every which way through the vehicles. Adira quickly dispatched two policemen to move them a safe distance away and clear the staging area. She was thankful English was the default second language taught in Omani schools, and they understood her perfectly.

That done, she rejoined Nabila, and they approached the closest vehicle. She pointed to Chevy, a few steps ahead, and said, "They're triaging first. Go with Chevy, and I'll take Amir. We'll sort and assess, then treat and transport."

They efficiently classified the casualties with loud, clear voices across the scene. Of seven total, there was one critical—the truck driver—and two urgent. The other four were either fine or with only minimal soft tissue injuries and labeled as "greens."

The greens were sent under their own power to wait with police near the staging area. They did not need immediate treatment, and clearing them allowed the team to focus on the three more severe injuries.

One was a female in the sedan's back seat, contorted agonizingly close to the compacted trunk now stuck beneath the large cargo box. Her head was wrenched back in pain, but thankfully, there was access to her from the door on the opposite side. The second urgent injury was to the woman driving the SUV. While the airbag had saved her head and torso, the momentum had driven her knee into the lower dashboard, resulting in an open fracture.

Most worrisome, and therefore labeled "critical" in the parlance of casualty scenes, was the truck driver. While his appearance wasn't as visually gruesome as the SUV driver, the injury sustained when his head impacted the cab's doorframes—first left, then right—was significant.

"I've got the spinal first, then the fracture," Chevy announced, pointing at the sedan and then the SUV. Chevy and Nabila would strap up the woman in the sedan and, if possible to do safely, extract her for transport.

"I have the truck driver," said Amir. Adira handed the spinal bag and board to Nabila and waved a policeman over to meet her at the cab of the truck with Amir.

"We'll need transportation for three," she said to the officer. Pointing to each of the vehicles, she continued, "When the EMTs arrive, send them here to the truck first. Then the neck injury. Leg fracture after that. Got it?"

The man gave a quick nod and was on his radio quickly. Adira turned back to the truck. With it resting on its side, Amir had needed to climb up to the driver-side window and carefully lower himself down. "He's unconscious now. Pupils fixed and dilated," he said.

Adira understood that meant a possible subdural hematoma, a bleeding on the brain. Minutes counted. "We're going to need a medevac," she said to the officer. Seeing the questioning look on his face and one of his hands twisting, she added, "An air ambulance. Helicopter." She pointed to the sky and twirled her finger.

His forehead rose in understanding. "*Aiwa.* Yes," he replied before getting back on the radio.

"Want to keep him in for the EMTs to move or get him out now?" she asked Amir.

"Time's the issue," he said, looking back up to the door above. "Let's get him out."

Adira visualized moving the driver out through the side window now high in the air, knowing they'd also have to then safely lower him down the outside of the cab. "The windshield," she said. "Kick it out, and we'll have him right here. Safety glass should come out in one big sheet."

Wedging his back against the back of the cab and careful to stay above the driver, Amir used the heel of his boot and kicked firmly around the top edges of the windscreen. After a few swift kicks, a portion separated. The window shattered into tiny fragments, but the thin membrane inside held it together as a single sheet.

Adira grabbed the rubber around the exposed edge and pulled, but it would require some effort. To the side, the policeman with the radio stood with a tall teenager next to an old man. She extended her hand to the policeman and teenager and called them over with a downward wave of her hand as she'd seen Amir do the day before.

"Pull here and here," she said, directing them to the corners. They had the window peeled away in no time, and the young man pulled it clear.

Another policeman had seen what they were doing and smartly grabbed a second backboard from the Land Cruiser. Together with him, Amir and Adira carefully extracted the driver. They placed him on the board, and Amir checked his pulse and breathing.

"Airway's blocked," he said. With the traumatic injury to his brain, the driver's tongue had gone slack, blocking the oxygen he desperately needed.

Adira grabbed the ALS bag and rolled the top layer out. "Combitube," she said, correctly assuming that Amir would prefer the airway device to a field intubation. She withdrew the bulbous form and split the packaging open for him. He took it with his right hand, then used his left to hold down the driver's tongue. Carefully and confidently, he inserted the airway into the driver's mouth.

Adira filled two syringes with air and connected them to small leads. Once Amir was ready, they depressed the syringes, inflating two small bladders in the combitube. One held the tongue back while the other sealed the airway.

Once the syringes were removed, Adira attached a bag and squeezed it to effectively breathe for the driver. As the sound of a helicopter reached them, she also checked his pulse, finding it weak.

As she squeezed the respirator, she took a moment to look up. In any emergency, staying calm and situationally aware were vital. Adira's strength in the ER had always been her clarity in that regard.

She'd caught a glimpse earlier of an ambulance and knew that Chevy and Nabila had already sent their possible spinal injury off. They now tended to the driver of the SUV. The woman was alert but in significant pain. On the other side of the scene, the patients they'd labeled green had been given chairs and water from the chip shop. Some policemen were talking to them, one with a first aid kit tending to a superficial wound.

After the helicopter had landed, two EMTs arrived with a stretcher. Amir described the patient in clear, clipped terms, and Adira briefly stopped respirating to allow them to get the man onto the stretcher. One took the respirator, and they efficiently wheeled the driver back to the helicopter.

Adira quickly rolled up the gear bag and went to Chevy and Nabila. A third pair of EMTs had arrived, placing the young female driver on their scoop stretcher. The open fracture had been tended to skillfully, and while the woman's eyes were puffy from tears, she thanked Chevy and Nabila profusely.

Once the ambulance departed for a secondary hospital a few towns away, the scene became decidedly calmer. Chevy and Amir moved to the staging area while Nabila and Adira repacked the bags and disposed of used material.

"I suppose you're used to this in the emergency department in America," Nabila said, her relief that the ordeal was over clear.

"Goes fast, doesn't it?" Adira asked with a smile.

"Chevy was brilliant. With this last woman, I couldn't stop focusing on the leg. But she went to airway and vitals first. It was a good reminder for me."

"Yep. ER doctors always ask, 'What could kill the patient first?' They focus on that and only move to the next thing afterward. But, hey, it looks like you were both very calm and did great."

Nabila's eyes crinkled with a smile. "Ready?" she asked.

Adira stood up, gear in hand. "Ready. But first, two deep breaths."

Together they took a few seconds to make sure their heads were clear.

When they arrived at the open space by the chip shop, Adira sorted through the growing crowd. Four chairs sat close together, three of them with patients. Just past the empty chair sat the old man she'd seen by the truck. He watched her intently.

"Where's the patient that was sitting here?" she asked him.

"My son. He is inside getting water. He is okay," he replied, his voice strong and low.

"The doctors will want to check him anyway."

"*Inshallah.*"

It was a commonly used statement meaning *as God wills*, and Adira took it in this case to mean the man understood. She turned to see Nabila with Amir working on a woman's nose. Adira recognized her as the passenger from the SUV whose nose had borne the brunt of the rapid deployment of the airbag.

Chevy kneeled in front of the young man from the sedan, treating him with words and a smile. Adira remembered that in their first run-through, he was uninjured and suffered more from shock than anything.

"So who do we have here?" Adira asked, taking a knee next to Chevy.

"This is Juma," she said with a smile. "Thanks to a few minutes with his head down low, he's doing great."

Juma looked up at the two women. "It was very frightening, but I am better now, thank you."

Chevy reached out and took the man's hand. It looked to be a friendly gesture, but she was assessing pulse, temperature, and tension through touch. "So Juma," Chevy asked, tilting her head toward Adira. "What's more frightening: Truck falling on you? Or this girl's crazy eyes?"

Chevy wanted to see his response and reaction. Adira turned her eyes on Chevy and wrinkled her nose in mock displeasure.

Juma gave a short laugh. "More frightening for you than for me," he said.

Chevy patted the top of his hand. "You're going to be fine, Juma. Call the clinic if you wake up with a headache or feel nauseous, okay?"

"I will. Thank you."

They checked one more woman, who appeared to be fine, before seeing the last patient had returned. He sat next to the old man, and Chevy looked him over. Adira stayed by her side, conscious of the man staring once again.

When Chevy was done, the old man spoke to Adira. "Miss, may I ask where you are from?"

She turned. The man bore a friendly smile. Just a curious elder in the village, interested to see a foreigner. "America," she replied.

"I see," he replied. "I watched you at the accident. You were very calm and observant."

She guessed he was in his seventies but taller and heavier than most men his age. There was a gleam in his eye and confidence in his deep voice. He'd been strong in his earlier years. Yet still, there was an affable air about him. "Good teachers, I guess," she replied.

"We are fortunate that you were here."

"Glad we were in the neighborhood," Adira said, wondering if the phrase even applied in a small village on the edge of the desert.

"I would like to show our thanks. Please join us tomorrow. We will have a dinner in your honor."

"That's very nice of you. But I'm afraid—"

He raised his hand and gestured to his son, who had walked to Amir and was obviously extending the same invitation. The doctor looked back to Adira and gave her a smile and a shrug as if to say, "Why not?"

"Well, it looks like that's been settled," Adira said. "My name is Adira."

"I am Taimur," he replied.

"We'll see you tomorrow, then."

The old man smiled. "*Inshallah.*"

***

Taimur lived deep in the sands, his compound of tents a good forty minutes from the village across barely visible tracks. Standing in a small, fenced courtyard, Adira slipped off her sandals just outside the largest tent. Clamping a small box of chocolates she'd brought as a gift between her knees, she lifted a scarf from around her neck. Using one of the folding techniques Zahra had shared, Adira placed the scarf over her head and wrapped first one side and then the longer one loosely around her neck.

"Get some more makeup on those eyes, Witchy, and you'll look like a local," chimed Chevy.

Adira gave her a shove as they walked inside.

Nabila had explained earlier in the day what to expect. She'd grown up with the nation itself, experiencing its evolution from the front row seat of her own conservative upbringing to her more progressive children. In traditional Bedouin camps, she'd explained, many of the old ways were still followed, and Adira shouldn't be surprised if they were separated from the men. It was simply the way things were done, typically described as a way to make everyone comfortable. Perhaps that was true for Arab women, but it still felt awkward for Adira.

A little girl of about seven or eight suddenly arrived at a dead sprint. "*Shukulata! Shukulata!*"

Adira bent down as the girl skidded to a stop. Her eyes flashed up to Adira's briefly. "Wow!" the girl beamed, her accent stretching the middle.

Adira turned to Chevy and dramatically opened her eyes wide. "Not as scary for her as for you."

Chevy laughed. "Shut it and give her the chocolates!"

Adira handed the box to the little girl and received a broad smile in return. She was gone in a flash.

More children arrived, quickly relieving the rest of the medical crew of their gifts with varying squeals in thanks before Taimur himself appeared. He greeted each of them by name, showing he'd done his homework, which Adira found interesting. Behind him, a significant number of people, from old to very young, chattered loudly.

Taimur noticed Adira was slightly taken aback. "I have quite a large family. Seven children and seventeen grandchildren," he said.

"You must be very proud," Amir said.

"Or exhausted," Chevy added.

The large man laughed. "Both! Now, please, join us," he said. His size and deep voice commanded attention. Standing with a cream robe over his dishdasha along with a colorful, striped mussar, Taimur had a presence. It was his face, however, that won the team over. Even with dark, leathery skin from years in the desert, the vast wrinkles at the sides of his eyes showed he was quick to give a smile and did so often.

He deftly escorted them around the tent, introducing his wife, Mariya, and a few of the grandchildren. They'd met some of his children, like the young man from the accident, before. But even without that, it was easy to feel how friendly and approachable the family was.

Much of their conversations as they circulated started with the tragedy the day before but soon flowed on to America and Australia, which led to discussions of cultures and food. On that note, Taimur led them outside, showing where two goats had been roasting over coals buried in the sand since the night before. The woodsmoke and spices had Adira's mouth watering instantly.

"That smells amazing," she said to the two men tending to the pit.

The men stood, and Taimur introduced them. While they dressed as men in the desert do, in dusty sandals, long dishdashas, and tasseled mussars atop their heads, she was surprised to hear that one was a web developer and the other an accountant in Muscat. Taimur explained that while opportunities in the cities lured younger generations, the desert would always be home. For their part, the men nodded in agreement, saying weekends in the sands recharged their souls.

Taimur eventually brought them back inside, where three circular areas had been set up with colorful pillows. He divided the newcomers, spreading them among his family and ensuring everyone was introduced. Rather than being seated separately with women, Taimur brought Adira to sit in a mixed group next to him.

Again, he noticed her surprise, and as they sat, he said, "We are family here, men and women, all one and the same."

Before Adira could reply, a large platter arrived and was placed on the carpet in the center of their circle. Steam from the rice encircled the goat meat and carried the powerful fragrances of cumin, coriander, cinnamon, and cardamom. Adira soaked in the glorious scent before watching to see what everyone would do.

"Have you tried shuwa yet?" Taimur asked.

"A beef shuwa in Muscat, yes."

"At a restaurant? That is not shuwa!" said a young man across from her.

"Here," Taimur said. "Like this."

He moved to show Adira how to pull off a piece and add it to some rice with only a few fingers, but she surprised him by expertly mirroring his movements.

"Ah, someone has been practicing!" he said with joy.

They ate and chatted with ease, sharing stories with Adira as she shared her own. It was a happy atmosphere like little she'd experienced before, with laughter and harmless teasing flowing back and forth. As the groups moved their seats around to chat over dates and coffee, Adira found she didn't want the night to end, which was quite unusual for her.

Taimur explained to Adira that he wanted to show her something, and after she helped him get to his feet, they stepped out of the tent and into the darkness.

They walked barefoot through the sands, past a water tank raised on stilts, to the edge of a dune. Taimur gestured grandly to a nighttime sky filled with stars.

"It's beautiful," Adira said.

"The stars aren't like this in Muscat. Here, with nothing around, they shine brighter. Their colors come out."

And indeed they did, creating a soft glow cropped beneath by the flowing silhouette of dunes.

"My family has enjoyed getting to know you," he said.

"I've enjoyed them as well. They're all wonderful."

"If you don't mind me saying so, I noticed that you were very quiet when we talked about family."

How could she discuss something she'd never had? But she'd become adept at dancing around the subject over the years. "Yes, well, mine was nothing like this."

"What was your childhood like?" he asked.

A vague answer followed by a quick deflection back to the interrogator's own life had always proven to be the best approach. "Chaotic," she replied. "What's childhood like in the desert?"

"Fleeting."

Adira looked at the old man in the faint light of the stars. "That's a cryptic answer."

"As was yours," he said.

"Touché."

He smiled and turned his eyes back to the sky. "But we find peace in the sands. Perhaps someday you will let me teach you about the Bedu, about our history and heritage."

The old man made her feel comfortable, welcome, and at ease in an altogether strange way. She surprised herself with her own response. "I'd like that. I'd like that very much."

9

The day after dinner with Taimur and his family, the foursome packed up the Land Cruisers and made their way to Nizwa, where they stocked up at the hospital before climbing into the Al Hajar Mountains.

The landscape was more dramatic than Adira had ever experienced. Rocky cliffs towered over deep crevasses, the sides occasionally spotted with the remnants of old stone buildings or lush, green terraces of farmland. Serpentine roads, most with precarious drop-offs, eventually led them to a small village.

With Adira in the passenger seat and Chevy following with Nabila, Amir checked one of the two GPSs mounted to the dash. He took a look at his phone and pointed ahead. "Should be the white one," he said.

"Is it always like this, roaming from place to place?"

"Not always. Nabila and I are based in Muscat with a few other teams. We travel for a month, then work for two months in the hospital. Occasionally, once a tertiary hospital has been built, we'll return to help them hire local people we'd interviewed before."

"And the MOH finds homes for you at each stop?"

"Yes. Some are rentals, and some have been built by the government for people visiting from the various departments. This one," he said, pulling into a walled courtyard, "looks rather nice. I would guess it's an Airbnb."

It was in stark contrast to the old house in the desert. Instead of dusty paint crackled by the sand, this one was bright white and recently built.

"Nice!" Chevy said as she stepped out of the second Land Cruiser. "I love it when we get a holiday rental!"

Grabbing their personal bags, they entered the house. The interior was new and especially clean. Chevy and Nabila went one way, and Amir went the other. Adira, though, was drawn to the glass doors across the living space.

She opened one and stepped onto a deck cantilevered over the cliff's edge. Immediately below her were the steep walls of a valley, one side of which held terraced slivers of green farmland. Trees dotted the edges and marked passages where farmers could move level to level.

Nabila joined her, arriving from a door farther down the patio. "You can see why we call this Jebel Akhdar. The green mountains," she said.

"First, I swam with turtles in turquoise water, then the desert, and now this. All in less than a week," Adira said. "You have everything imaginable packed into this country, don't you?"

Nabila smiled. "We have been blessed this way."

"And we have been blessed with four bedrooms, each with an en suite!" Chevy said, joining them. "Wow! This view!"

"We have also been blessed with a fully stocked refrigerator," came Amir's voice from inside.

"Any alcohol?" Chevy asked as Amir came out, his hands behind his back.

"There was a box of beer, but I have sculled them all," he said, pretending to be dizzy. "But perhaps this will make you happy?" He held up a bottle of white wine.

"Praise be to—" she started, reaching for the bottle.

Amir pulled it back and wagged a finger at her. "No, no. You will not reference Allah with regards to drink."

"Praise be to you, then!" Chevy said with a laugh, snatching the bottle away. "Let's get this opened and get some dinner going."

The next day, they set up for vaccinations in a parking lot between a mosque and a small market in a small village. They used two pop-up tents, one for patients and one as the designated clean area. Adira showed Nabila how pop-up vaccine sites in California organized patient flow and supplies for maximum efficiency.

"How many patients should we expect today?"

Nabila checked a tablet and soon replied, "Sixty-four today. Tomorrow, you and I will come back for a dozen vaccine appointments in the morning while Amir and Chevy do a follow-up with two patients before we leave."

"This stop should be easy," Adira said. "Double appointments in ten-minute increments?"

"Yes, but there are usually some gaps."

Adira double-checked around the site. "Looks like we're all set to meet some farmers. Yee haw!"

Nabila waved her hand, pretending to be exasperated. "You are beginning to sound like Chevy!"

Adira laughed. "Now, that is how you get someone to be quiet!"

With that, an emphatic, Aussie-tinged "Yee haw!" echoed from the other side of the clean tent and likely carried through the entire valley.

Their day moved at a good pace. Not too fast nor too slow, with enough flexibility to accommodate locals and their families that ran early or late. Nabila handled check-in and records updating, Chevy and Amir inoculated and checked in with the patients, and Adira handled the vaccines and disposed of the sharps and other waste. During the lulls, some locals stayed to chat, interested to hear what Chevy and Adira thought of Oman. Some brought apricots, pomegranates, and vegetables from the farms, much of which they worked into dinner that night.

The next morning, the team woke to a strangely dark sky. As they left the rental, the skies opened up with a soaking rain.

"Rain? Really?" Adira asked Amir. "I thought this was the desert, the driest part of the world."

He smiled. "We have nine days or so of rain each year. It is always a surprise to visitors."

"At least it's beautiful," Adira said, seeing the scrub trees glisten as their headlights swept by.

"And helpful to the farmers. But it will make slow going back to Muscat this afternoon. We'll have to watch for floods."

"And wait for everyone to remember how to drive in the wet?"

"That too."

Thankfully, the leader of prayer in the mosque, the imam, offered the building for the morning appointments to keep everyone out of the rain. While women do not share the central prayer room with men, Nabila and Adira were welcome as long as they kept their heads covered and shoes off. Nabila always wore a hijab, but Adira was thankful she'd taken to keeping a scarf around her neck.

By early afternoon, the team had the Land Cruisers packed and set off for Muscat. The roads were soaked, with water streaming across the surface on valley bends and a few rockslides they needed to navigate. At one point, the road paralleled a swollen river downstream from a wadi that had exceeded capacity.

While Amir concentrated on the road and runoff from the cliff to one side, Adira watched the rushing brown waters below. What was a dry gully just a day before had swollen into a river at least thirty yards wide and moving at a speed faster than their own. Sludge drained in from cracks in the bank, merging with brush and debris rushing down the valley.

A bridge farther down the road curved over the water. Thankfully, it was a fair distance above the surface, though the white water crashed violently against the supports.

For a moment, Adira thought she saw the flash of a person in the river. She concentrated on the spot and the river just past it. Just as she decided it was her imagination, a head broke the surface.

"Amir, slow down. There's someone in the river."

He slowed and switched the hazard lights on to warn Chevy and Nabila behind them.

"See him?"

"Not yet," Amir replied. He scanned between the road and the river.

"There!" Adira shouted, pointing just ahead.

"I see him."

It was a young man—a teenager—holding onto something just below the surface of the raging current. He strained to keep his head above brown, swirling eddies of water.

Amir pulled over parallel to the boy. "I will call it in." Thinking quickly, he added, "There's a tow strap in the boot. Back left."

"Got it," Adira said. Chevy and Nabila were getting out of their truck as Adira retrieved the strap. She found it quickly and took stock. The bright yellow strap was folded tightly and felt small in her hands. "Grab your tow strap, Chevy," she said. "Plus anything you think will float."

Adira assessed the situation as she stepped over a guard rail. Amir came quickly to her side.

They stood at the top of the bank. Below them, the slope fell steeply, perhaps at a forty-five-degree angle. It was a mix of large rocks and gravelly dirt, slick with rain, and several yards above the river's surface.

"We have called for rescue," Amir shouted in Arabic when the boy came up for a breath. "Stay calm, and we will try to help."

Chevy arrived, uncoiling her strap.

"We'll tie them together," Adira said. "Did you find anything that will float?"

"This," Nabila said. "Empty and ready." She held up a hard plastic medical kit, much like a large tackle box.

While Adira knotted the straps together, Chevy tied one end to the box. "We'll throw this upstream and as far opposite him as we can get it."

"I'm not sure it's long enough," Adira said.

"Only one way to find out," replied Chevy. "I think you have the best arm, Amir."

Amir began forming a loose coil.

"He played cricket," Chevy explained to Adira. "Might be the only time that would ever come in handy other than curing insomnia."

Amir moved upstream, and Nabila shouted to the boy to get ready to grab the strap.

The rain increased, and Amir wiped his eyes with his arm before swinging the box like a pendulum. On the third swing, he heaved, sending the box over the river. It fell three or four yards short of the boy before being quickly pulled downstream by the current.

He pulled it back in and tried once more. This time, the strap went its full length. Still, it fell short.

"Not long enough," Amir said, scanning the bank for a safer spot closer to the water's surface.

"There!" Chevy said. She pointed to a spot below them where the water spun in a slight eddy. "Look at the water. I think it's shallower there."

"Untie the box and give me the end," Adira said. "Hold on to the strap, and I'll go check the depth."

Adira took one end of the rope, clipped it around her waist, and went down the bank. Her first steps found purchase, and she descended in a semi-controlled fashion to the river's edge.

This close, she could feel the roar of the water and its raw power. She probed the edge with her feet and took a few hesitant steps, acutely aware that she was in a high-risk position. The boy shouted something to her she couldn't make out. But she knew he would be getting weaker by the minute, and if he lost hold of whatever he had a grip of, it would only take seconds before he was swept into the bridge pilings.

Where the bank entered the river, it flattened out slightly. Conscious of the others having a good grip on the line, she waded in further, water at only shin level. The current wasn't as strong as it was in the center of the river, and she found she could stand without too much difficulty.

"If the three of you stand between here at the edge, you can anchor me," she shouted to the others. "I'll go out upstream, then swing down to him!"

She was asking a lot to have them come down the bank. They would know, even better than she would, that floodwaters can rise rapidly and carry dangerous debris.

Yet even before she'd finished calling up to them, they were making their way down, knowing the boy could be swept away in an instant.

Once they were down, Amir looped the opposite end of the rope around his waist while Nabila and Chevy took strong holds just in front of him. As they firmed up their positions, Adira stepped into the river.

She moved with purpose, keeping her stance strong and probing ahead with each step before transferring her weight. The water came above her knees, and she could feel its strength. If it reached her upper thigh, she'd lose grip and be swept into the current.

The boy was seven or eight yards out and just as far downstream. She willed herself two steps further. Then another. The next step was deeper and right onto a large, smooth rock. She lost traction. And swam like hell.

Adira drove her arms forward with purpose and kicked as fast as she could, propelling herself through the current. While she swam straight, her actual path formed an arc, bringing her closer and closer to the boy. She held her head up, judging her target. But the rain and murky water made it hard to see anything more than a blurry, dark form. Just as she was two strokes away, his head ducked below the surface again.

She closed the gap in a fraction of a second, reaching both hands out. Finding nothing.

The river had her now, and the branch the boy held on to tore into her side, trying its best to flip her over.

Adira swam hard, trying to extend as far as she could before the current and strap swung her back. A foot flashed in front of her. Her arms shot forward, catching one ankle and then the next. She pulled, scrambling for extra grip and wrapping his legs with both arms just as the strap went taught. She held firm to the boy as they were pulled downstream toward the bank. Inching her arms up as they floated, she reached first his knees. By the time she had a secure grip around his abdomen, her body had turned to shield the current and debris from him. But even as the water tossed and wrestled them, she could not feel him breathe.

Her back scraped across the bank, the boy protectively held on her stomach as the strap effectively beached her. She coughed and sputtered as Chevy ran to her side. "I've got him!" she shouted.

Free of the boy, Adira rolled onto her knees and coughed. Amir dropped the strap and joined Chevy while Nabila helped Adira move away from the edge of the river. Adira took quick stock of herself. Her head and limbs felt fine, but her side throbbed. She lifted her shirt to find a Y-shaped laceration on the left side.

"Are you okay?" Nabila said, studying her eyes and head before checking the wound.

"Nothing major," Adira replied. "The boy?"

Nabila looked up. "They have him breathing now."

Adira rolled back on the rocky bank and caught her breath. A roar from the sky overpowered the rush of the river as a helicopter flared to land on the bridge. Four medics leaped out carrying gear bags and a stretcher.

Adira stood and carefully made her way along the bank to the others with Nabila. The boy coughed up some residual water and shivered, but appeared lucid.

"How ya doing, buddy?" Adira asked.

He formed a weak smile before coughing up another spray of water.

"Save your breath. Everything's going to be okay."

"Thank you," he sputtered.

"You're welcome," Adira said, lowering down to her knees.

The boy rolled off his side in an attempt to sit but was quickly overcome by coughing once again.

Adira gently pushed him back down. "Stay on your side for a minute. We'll let the rest of the water come out."

The boy moved his elbow back to hold her hand in place.

Some small rocks rolled down the slope next to them as two EMTs descended on ropes. Amir conveyed the boy's condition. Adira squeezed her hand and said, "These nice men are going to take you to the hospital. But don't worry, you're looking great."

The coughing stopped, and he rolled over onto his back. His deep brown eyes still wide with shock, he thanked her once again.

A stretcher had been laid next to him. Two EMTs helped him into the basket and carried the boy up to the road.

A third EMT, burly with a beard and crooked smile, remained with the medical crew. He pointed to Adira and let out a joyful string of Arabic. Nabila and Amir laughed.

"What?" Adira asked.

"He says you should be on the National Swim Team!" Amir translated.

Detaching a few extra ropes from his harness, he began securing each of them, still laughing.

With the help of the safety lines, they were able to climb back to the road and over the guard rail. The large EMT exchanged a few words with a colleague, one of whom came over with a trauma bag.

They moved to the back of one of the Land Cruisers, and using the cargo door as a cover from the rain, Adira leaned against the back bumper.

"May I?" The burly man asked, using English after he'd heard Amir translate.

Adira lifted her shirt. "It's only a scratch," she said.

The wound was a few inches long with a deeper cut in the center. The EMT set about cleaning it. "You were in the water when we arrived," he said. "We had moved overhead when you slipped and had to swim."

"Not my finest moment," Adira said.

He stopped and looked up at her. "You don't understand. He lost his hold right before you grabbed him. The loadmaster had just started to send me down. I would not have reached him in time. Your timing was perfect. You saved his life."

"It was a team effort," Adira said.

"We saw you lowering down," Amir said to the EMT, "but then the helicopter moved closer to the bridge."

"Just in case," the man said quietly. None of them wanted to face the thought he'd moved to the bridge in the event they'd been swept away. Nor acknowledge the fact that he wouldn't have been able to save them all.

"Ya did good, River Girl!" Chevy drawled, breaking the spell. She cupped Adira's face and gave her a kiss on the forehead. "And you too, you big hunk!" she continued, giving the EMT's helmet a couple of pats. "Go take care of the kid. We'll finish patching her up."

The EMT said his goodbyes and walked back to the helicopter. Not long after, the whine of the engine increased and the helicopter rose into the sky.

From the opposite bank of the river came a baying sound. The team looked over to see a goat with a short length of rope around his neck.

Adira pointed to Chevy. "That one's all yours!"

***

As Adira and her friends set off for Muscat once again, inside the gates of Al Alam Palace, Zahra responded to a ping from her phone. It was one of her two emissaries, and the message sent a shock through her system. A few nervous hours later, the second messenger shared a similar report.

She had planned for this eventuality, or perhaps *dreamed of it* would have been a better description. But having confirmation in hand was entirely different. Until the wee hours of the morning, she prepared, making phone calls, reviewing documents, and revising them as she went along. Only when she felt she was finally ready did she send a last message.

The activity on the Palace network didn't go unnoticed, and a systems administrator deep within one of the administrative buildings soon made his own call.

"Your Excellency, we have an anomaly on one of the accounts you wanted us to watch. Zahra al Abdali," the sysadmin said once the line to Deputy Defense Minister Rashid had opened.

"An anomaly?" asked Rashid. "What sort of anomaly?"

"Well, it's a variation from observed patterns. We have a machine learning algorithm that monitors—"

"I don't care about this nonsense!" Rashid said sharply. "What was she doing?"

The sysadmin knew he'd been put in his place and became suitably demure. "Sorry, Your Excellency. There's been a lot of activity on a cloud server outside the network. And—"

"What sort of activity?"

"Accessing small files."

"Can you see what's in them?"

"No, Your Excellency. They are encrypted."

"Decrypting them is your job, isn't it?"

"Well, actually, my job is to ensure the network—"

"Yes, Yes. What else did you say you have?"

"Messages. She's been messaging frequently with two phones not on the Palace network. Again, they're encrypted, so we can't read the content. But I can tell you where those phones have been, which is the strange part."

"Where?"

"Well, right now, one is in Boston and the other near London."

"Why does this matter?"

"Because I've been able to trace the cell towers they have accessed. Both of them have spent full days at universities. Harvard and Oxford. In both locations, they seem to triangulate over medical facilities."

Rashid processed this for a moment.

"Your Excellency?"

"Decrypt the messages. And the files on the server."

"Sir, I don't think I can—"

"You will."

Rashid closed the line. *What is she up to?*

To be sure, there were plenty of people in the Palace Rashid kept an eye on. But this little woman had been spending time with the sultan of late, something that had piqued his interest given the sultan's condition.

As the sultan's stay at the hospital extended, Rashid knew the pancreatic cancer was spreading. But his Palace informants had explained that while His Majesty was receiving fewer guests by a significant amount, Zahra al Abdali's time with him had increased. The young woman with the limp held the meaningless title of Special Assistant to His Majesty the Sultan, yet she'd collected a small team of computer experts. At one point, he'd heard that her job was some sort of social media nonsense. He'd inquired about her with the Deputy Minister of Information, also a cousin, but he'd never heard of a social media position within the Palace Office itself. At the time, he and his cousin had written her off as yet another leech clinging to the sultan's robes, someone to be promptly removed once Rashid took the seat of power.

But now, she was sending staff to medical laboratories. Why? Was there some cure for the sultan's cancer? Surely, if that were true, he would have heard of it by now.

10

Given their next clinic was not far from Muscat, the team elected to go to their respective homes for the night. Amir dropped Adira at the Al Bustan Hotel, where she spent an hour in the tub warming up and washing off silt from the river.

The team met at the small fishing village on Al Sawadi Beach the next morning. Arrangements had been made for them to use a courtyard outside of a mosque very near the water. While they waited for Chevy and Nabila to arrive, Amir took Adira across the road to the beach, where a group of low-slung clay houses stood.

They were rough, small, and less refined than the newer homes just across the road. Small fishing boats rested between them, waiting on their sides for their next launch. The sun warmed their hulls, filling the air with the smell of fish and the sea. Outside of one house, a man sat on a stool, sipping coffee and watching ripples in the shallow water. They gave him a wave, and he raised his coffee in return.

"This is a hard job," Adira said.

"It is. But they are good people. You will find them animated and cheerful."

"Most everyone I've met is cheerful. But a few here and there have given off a bit of tension."

"What do you mean?"

"I don't really know. Just a feeling. I wrote it off as my being a foreigner, maybe a foreign woman with some of the men. But we passed a small group of people holding signs yesterday, and it reminded me that I'd seen a small protest like that my first day."

"You've come at an interesting time. Our oil reserves, which were modest to start, are shrinking. His Majesty has been directing investments in other areas to diversify our economy, but they will take time to develop. His Majesty is very ill—pancreatic cancer—and does not have much time."

Adira lowered her eyes. "I heard he was sick."

"Yes. And there is no heir, nor a successor named. So what you sense is uncertainty."

Adira understood uncertainty. "No one knows if the next sultan will follow through with those plans."

"Exactly. But it is deeper than that. His Majesty loves the people of Oman, and we love him for all he has done to develop this country. In other kingdoms, monarchs use oil money to build their own gold-plated towers, and if the people are lucky, a check for their small share of the remainder comes in the mail each month. Here, oil money goes to health, education, and infrastructure. It's been used to give each of us our own opportunities to succeed."

"He's given you pride."

"Even more than that, so perhaps I am rambling."

"No, I understand. Perhaps I should have said *independence*. The chance to make your own successes."

"Yes, I like that."

"So what will happen when this sultan passes away?"

He pointed a finger to the sky. "No one knows. We hope a man who shares His Majesty's values will be selected. But it will likely be our Deputy Defense Minister."

"Wait, the protests. Is he the one campaigning for some big purchase the people don't like?"

"Yes. It is idiotic. A country with no enemies buying jets and tanks? Enemies will find us now. We made the same mistake decades ago. Do not ask Nabila about him. She is livid, afraid that he will take all the oil money for himself and not use it to build our country like His Majesty. And she's terrified about how he may see women."

"What's the alternative?"

Amir's shoulders gave a shrug. "The foreign minister, Omar al Fallah, would be better. He is well-liked here and abroad."

"Well, write to your congressman, or the sultan himself, and tell him."

"It does not work that way." Hearing voices, he stopped and turned. "Looks like they're here."

Adira snuck one more glance at the sea. "Thanks for explaining it to me. Zahra didn't tell me about the problems you might face. She only talked about this sultan and was very positive."

"Well, she works for the Palace. But she is right. We have been fortunate to have him as our leader," he said. They took a few steps before he quietly asked, "What is she like?"

"Zahra?"

His head bobbed rapidly.

Interesting, Adira thought. She'd come to consider Amir as a complete professional, the perfect example of a well-educated doctor setting out to consistently deliver well-considered care. He was just so intelligent and perfect that seeing his cheeks turn a little rosy for the first time was quite amusing. "What do you mean?" she giggled.

"Ah…"

"Is she nice? Does she scowl at kittens?"

"No, no."

"Or did you *really* want to know if she is single?" she teased.

"Adira, I, well—"

"Relax, Amir, I'm just pulling your chain. She is very nice and unmarried. But during my few days with her, we did not encounter any kittens. So you have some risk there."

Chevy and Nabila had walked out to greet them. "What're you two talking about?"

"Amir has a thing for Zahra," Adira said, holding her hands beneath her chin and making an adoring face."

"Who's Zahra?" Chevy asked.

"The woman from His Majesty's office who sent Adira to us," Nabila explained.

"Oh, the fancy chick. I never met her. But I do remember Amir going on about her not long ago."

"Will you please stop!" he said. The color in his cheeks deepened. "She is most likely above my station anyway."

The three women stopped and gave him a stern look. Chevy spoke first. "You are a doctor, and one of the most gentlemanly gentlemen that's ever walked, okay? Posh girl's got nothing on ya."

"Do people even date here?" Adira asked.

"In my generation, no," Nabila said. "Our families would arrange marriage. But some young people do now, and it is allowed if they prefer."

"It's not like Oz or the states, though," Chevy said. "They actually talk stone sober!"

"Shocking!" Adira said. They all shared a laugh.

"Now, if we could turn to more serious subjects," Amir said, gesturing toward the trucks. "We do have a vaccine clinic to put on here."

Chevy went skipping ahead of them, singing, "Princey's got a girlfriend! Princey's got a girlfriend!"

They set up the two tents, and the hospital delivered the vaccines and some additional chairs to supplement their own small set. Before long, they were up and running, taking appointments booked on the Ministry of Health's app, along with a few walk-ins.

It wasn't long, however, before one of the young fishermen became quite excited. Adira had just come out of the clean tent with doses for Amir and Chevy when Amir's patient pulled out his phone. He tapped a few times, then looked more closely at Adira.

"*Fatat alnahr!*" he said to her.

Amir laughed, and a quick exchange in Arabic followed. The young man showed his phone to Amir.

Adira remembered that *fatat* meant *girl*, or was it *woman*? "What are you two saying?"

"YouTube!" the young man said. "You are on YouTube! Instagram! The ah—"

"River girl," Amir said, translating. "Remember the EMT yesterday? He must have had a body camera. Come, look."

Adira went to their side, and the man replayed a heavily edited video of her swimming through the river and being swung around by the others. It even showed Chevy calling her "River Girl," even though she looked like a wet rat.

The patient beckoned some of his friends from the waiting area over, and before long, they were asking for selfies with her. She let it go on for a couple of minutes before shushing them and sending the newcomers out of the tent.

"Somebody is famous! Somebody is famous!" The sound of Chevy's singing came from her side of the tent.

"I feel like I'm in a preschool today!" Adira exclaimed.

Chevy continued the tune as she went about her work, mixing her teasing of Adira and Amir up and then throwing in a few more silly taunts for good measure. Adira had to laugh. It did make the day easier to have a chuckle now and then.

As they packed up late that afternoon, a police car pulled up. The Royal Oman Police were not seen as an aggressive security force. Instead, they were there, like the saying goes, to protect and serve. As police stations went up in towns, they helped residents with automobile paperwork, licenses, and even passports, which could be had in less than twenty-four hours. These policemen, Mahmoud and Rafi, were no different. They'd also seen the video and wanted to say hello but were happy to jump in and help the team close-up for the day.

After everything had been loaded, they sat on a small wall looking out to the sea. Adira handed out the last of the waters and then took a spot near the older policeman, Mahmoud. He appeared to be around fifty, with a quiet but wise demeanor that Adira appreciated.

Adira let out a sigh, impressed by the view even more now as the sun lowered enough to cast a golden glow across the sea. Some fishermen unloaded their nets into a pickup truck parked in the glistening sand. The wind carried what sounded like cheerful banter as they loaded dozens of huge fish.

Nearby, two older men tended a fire. One monitored an old pot while the other cleaned a fish atop an overturned bucket. Two women soon joined them, one laying a carpet nearby, the other depositing several bowls before returning to a home not far from the fire.

"So peaceful to see families having dinner right on the beach," Adira said.

"I have not seen this very often," Mahmoud said. "More often, they go out to fish in the evening."

The fishermen finished emptying the net. While a few men began folding it, another hopped into the truck to drive the haul to market. He stopped as he passed by and waved. Adira and her crew waved back, and soon there was an exchange in Arabic.

"What did he say?" Adira asked.

Mahmoud hopped off the wall. "We have been invited to join them."

"What? Why?"

"They are celebrating. One of the children has been training to be a pilot. His first day is tomorrow."

Their generosity surprised Adira. She caught Chevy's eye and the two exchanged a smile. Chevy shrugged as if to say, "Why not?"

Slowly, the group hopped off the wall. Nabila begged off, wanting to spend the night with her husband. Amir and the policemen decided to drive to a nearby shop so as not to come empty-handed. Adira and Chevy joined the family and jumped right in to help.

The family group had swelled and seemed to include a few neighbors at this point. Another rough carpet was added, and before long, Adira and Chevy kneeled with some of the women and began slicing tomatoes and cucumbers. Along with limes and some small, hot peppers, they were a typical side dish with any meal. One of the women seasoned a fish and, after showing Adira how it was done, left her to it.

Amir and the policemen soon returned and passed out cups of water and orange soda. They had brought bread as well, which was wrapped in foil and set near the fire to warm. After Amir spoke with the parents, he knelt down next to Adira.

"Zahra has messaged us. She would like you to join her at the Palace tonight for dinner."

"Whoops. Haven't been checking my phone," Adira said. She then waved her hands at the dinner being prepared. "I can't now," she said.

"I told her we were eating on the beach, and she understood. But she will come by in an hour to pick you up if that is okay."

"I'll tell her," Adira said. "Thank you for letting me know."

Adira withdrew her phone and sent Zahra a quick message before joining everyone.

The conversations came in a mix of English and Arabic. Adira found herself at one point engaged in conversation with the new pilot, whose English was perfect. He told her about his parents and growing up in the village but also asked plenty of questions about America.

Plates were soon passed out, filled with fragrant rice, the vegetables, and fresh fish. Adira and Chevy were offered spoons, but impressed everyone by declining and using their hands.

Behind them, a few men in Royal Guard uniforms arrived at the wall where everyone had sat earlier. They quietly spread out and cast their eyes across the beach and the surrounding streets. Only Mahmoud noticed their arrival, which he found curious more than anything.

Eventually, Zahra arrived with another guard from the detail by her side. She was happy to see Adira and the two doctors sitting in the dwindling light with a family. She enjoyed the sight a moment before taking off her sandals and walking across the sand.

Zahra said hello as she approached and exchanged pleasantries with the family as introductions were made. She was asked to join but politely declined.

"Are you sure?" Amir asked her. "The fish is delicious."

Adira and Chevy exchanged a glance. Chevy silently mouthed the words to her song earlier today and wiggled behind Amir. Adira did her best to keep a straight face.

"Yes. You are very kind, but I need some time this evening with Adira."

Adira thanked the family, making sure to speak with each of them individually before walking back to the car with Zahra.

"That looked fun," Zahra said.

"It was an unexpected pleasure," Adira replied. "I am still impressed with how welcoming everyone has been."

"Well, you made an impression!" Zahra said, holding up her phone.

"Oh no. You saw the video?"

"I think everyone has!" Zahra said, laughing.

Adira buried her head in her hands before joining in with a laugh of her own.

Zahra asked about Adira's work over the past week as they drove, peppering her with questions along the way. After a time, they pulled into Al Alam Palace, where a large ornamental gate was quickly opened for them.

They were driven to an ornate door framed in gold leaf beneath tall pillars of gold and blue. Four guards snapped to attention as they approached, and the large main door opened to reveal a vast tiled gallery. Overhead lights glistened off every highly polished surface, giving the large space a mystical feel in the evening light. A back wall filled with windows overlooked a garden and the old harbor, both peacefully glowing in the moonlight.

"Amazing!" Adira exclaimed.

"Impressive, isn't it?"

"What is this place?"

"A reception area, mostly. His Majesty uses this particular part of the Palace to receive state visitors. Kings, queens, PMs, and a few American presidents have been met in this very hall," Zahra said, her excitement bubbling to the surface. "Can I give you a tour?" she asked.

"Sure. A little Palace glamour would be fun."

Zahra smiled and turned. Leaning only lightly on her cane, she led them across the room to a hallway divided into several rectangular galleries, each featuring a variety of large paintings.

Two uniformed Royal Guards followed them. Another pair of men in suits walked ahead. They seemed more alert than a visitor would be, and Adira concluded they were also guards. "Afraid we'll steal the silverware?" she asked, raising a chin in their direction.

Zahra looked up at the men in plain clothes. She made a waving gesture with her free hand and the men promptly vanished. "Just security," she said, turning back to Adira. "For the Palace."

Adira held up her hands. "I'm not a threat," she said with a smile. "Promise!"

Zahra gave a mock skeptical look before ushering Adira forward to a large painting. "Do you remember His Majesty's full name?" she asked.

Adira tipped her head forward. "Hamad Sabir"

"Close. It is Hamad bin Sabir al Sabir. That translates to Hamad, son of Sabir, of the family Sabir. The end of a name after 'al' can also reference where a family is from, and you don't often have that repetition at the end. But our names here are a long trail of ancestry."

"The 'bin' connects them?"

"Exactly. It means 'son of.' In Christian names, you do something similar."

"We do?"

Zahra nodded. "A name like 'Robertson' or 'Peterson' means that at some point, that person was the son of Robert or Peter. The same for a name like McNeil or O'Neil; the son of Neil. We would use 'bin Neil' here."

"But you don't have a 'bin' in your name."

"I do, actually. Only for women we use 'bint,' which means 'daughter of.' My name is Zahra bint Mohammed al Abdali. For Western purposes, it is simplified to just my given name and surname: Zahra al Abdali."

"And this guy?" Adira asked, pointing to the eight-foot-tall portrait of a bearded man with a jaunty turban.

" 'This guy' is Ahmad bin Sabir, the first of the Sabir family to become sultan. He was elected after the Persians had been expelled, at a time when the economy desperately needed repair. He leveraged our central location and the maritime skills of our people and brought us to the forefront of trade in this part of the world. That, in turn, allowed Oman to build a thriving agriculture industry."

"What's the difference between a sultan and a king?"

"That is an important question, especially since there are only two sultanate nations in the world, Brunei and Oman. The word itself means 'ruler' and is unique to Muslim countries. *King* is a secular title and can be used by any monarchy regardless of religion."

"So it's just a different word?"

"It is far more than that. Monarchies have a king or queen as the head of state and a prime minister or president as the head of government. The two govern side by side, although to varying degrees depending on the country. Think of the United Kingdom, where you have both a king and a prime minister."

"I never really thought about that arrangement," Adira admitted.

"A sultan is both the head of state *and* the head of government. He is what's known as an *absolute* monarch."

Adira leaned close to Zahra. Speaking quietly, she said, "I don't really know how to ask this, but how do you feel about living in a monarchy instead of a democracy?"

Zahra smiled. "You don't have to be secretive, Adira. Fair question though. We have a sultan who cares for this land and has used our resources for our benefit. He is fair and just, as well as wise. Today, our system of government works for our country."

"But you don't get a say in anything."

Zahra waggled her hand. "Maybe not to the extent of America. But to a certain degree we do. We have a council—much like a parliament—where one chamber is made up of elected officials. While they don't write law, they do assist His Majesty in policymaking decisions. Our voice is heard through them."

Adira nodded. "Sorry for the detour there."

Zahra touched Adira's shoulder. "It is fine. You can ask me anything, okay?"

"Thank you. So back to the title of sultan. I guess it's passed down from father to son?"

"Always. Beginning with Ahmad," Zahra replied, tilting her head toward the painting. "While he actually *was* elected, through the process, he realized that the system was fraught with bribery, conspiracies, and excessive self-promotion. He decided it was in the nation's best interest to establish a hereditary system of rule. The system that endures to this day."

"And the crown goes to the first son?"

"We don't use crowns here, but you're right for the most part," Zahra said, leading them farther down the hall before stopping at another of the paintings. "This sultan, for example, had a firstborn son who was disabled, so he handed the throne to his third child."

"Adding insult to injury."

Zahra continued on to the next gallery. Pointing to another image, she said, "It is not always perfect. Sultan Faisal had twenty-four children. He handed the royal seat to Taimur, his second son. Taimur himself had six wives and six children."

"His home life wasn't easy."

"It was harder than you think," Zahra said. "One wife was from Yemen, and another was a slave. Two others were cousins of his."

"Yikes."

"In addition to wives, he accumulated significant debt. For financial reasons, he had to abdicate the throne to his first son, Sabir."

"Thanks a lot, Dad."

"Not only did Taimur leave the debt to Sabir, but he also severely held back his exposure to the world, even preventing him from reading Western books. I think it was because of this upbringing that Sabir was skeptical of the emerging Gulf currency: oil. Oil would have allowed him to clear our debts if we'd worked as fast as the Saudis. But Sabir, a bit of a recluse himself, kept us very isolated."

"So what happened?"

"He had a son, just one, who he sent to England for schooling. To Sandhurst, the military academy, which led him to serve in the British army for a short time. When he returned to Oman, Sabir was deposed, and the son became sultan. That son is our leader today, His Majesty, Sultan Hamad bin Sabir."

"Amazing. So if his father was holding the country back, everything I've seen here—from prosperity to your amazing healthcare system—have only been developed in Sultan Hamad's lifetime?"

Zahra nodded. "His Majesty is the father of *al nahda*. The Omani renaissance." Moving into the last gallery, she led Adira to see a variety of paintings and photographs showing Sultan Hamad in different parts of Oman. While a few were formal portraits, most showed His Majesty with the people of Oman. On the shore with fishermen, talking with merchants in souqs, and walking the desert with Bedouin. The largest painting showed him with a beautiful woman, her eyes a brilliant light turquoise.

"Who is this?"

"That is Fatima Salmi, the sultan's wife for a time."

"She's beautiful."

"Indeed she was. Please, have a seat," Zahra said, gesturing to an antique love seat facing the royal couple's portrait in the center of the room.

"*Was* beautiful?" Adira asked once they'd sat down.

"Fatima was not married to His Majesty for very long. While it was a marriage with purpose, arranged to ensure continuity of our leadership, they truly adored one another. Alas, a child was never born in the Palace, and Fatima, being very honorable, knew it was her duty to leave, to allow the sultan to find another woman who could carry an heir for him."

"Did he marry again?" Adira asked.

"He did, and quite quickly."

"They had children, right?"

"No. They tried for several years without any luck before she eventually left him and moved to Saudi Arabia."

"So Sultan Hamad has no kids. How sad for him."

"Actually, Adira, that's not true. Let's go back to Fatima. As I told you, they really did love each other. On her last night in the Palace, they joined together once again. One final time. The next day, she left and moved into a magnificent home in San Francisco."

"San Francisco? Why there?"

"Two reasons, really. First, she didn't want to be a distraction to His Majesty. She wanted him to forget her and focus on his next wife. To focus on creating an heir for the sake of the sultanate. But also, she was ashamed. The establishment here, the traditionalist members of the family, were disappointed with her failure to bear a son. She was a pariah and understood she had to go to a part of the world where no one would find her."

"To San Francisco."

"Yes. London is usually the first choice of people from Arabia, probably since we all dream of the glamour and shopping in Mayfair. But His Majesty was against London and Monaco, and even Paris, knowing she would be subjected to the same criticism from ex-pat Arabs. He insisted instead that she have a fresh start in San Francisco, a city they always found beautiful. He bought her a home with sweeping views of the bay, and she was sent there with her maid and the maid's family."

"How sad."

"It became even sadder quite quickly. Two months after arriving in San Francisco, Fatima learned she was pregnant. Pregnant with the sultan's child from that final night."

"What did she do?"

"The day a physician confirmed she was with child was the same day His Majesty married his second wife. Fatima could not send word of her pregnancy on his wedding day. The scandal would be too great. She also knew that the new couple would immediately set to work on bearing a son. So she waited."

"This is getting more depressing by the minute."

"She wanted to tell him, and several times almost did. But eventually, Fatima learned that she was carrying a girl. Culturally, that was significant, and only compounded by the fact a sultanate—or any patriarchal monarchy—needs male children to continue. So she decided she would have their daughter in secret and allow the sultan to continue to focus on fathering a son."

"She had the baby without telling him? Alone?"

"She wasn't entirely alone. She was with her maid, Maha, and Maha's family, a husband, and daughter. They were very close, and she treated them as equals. As her own family. When the baby was a little more than a year old, Fatima still wanted to wait. She wanted to give the sultan more time and became quite obsessed with hoping he would have an heir with his new wife. It broke her heart, and I mean that quite literally, because Fatima died when the baby was only eighteen months old."

"How?"

"It has been hard to find this out as the records are thin. Fatima often used a false name when visiting the doctors to keep her secret. It is suspected that her lungs were weakened by illness at a young age and that she died of respiratory failure after complications with a virus."

"So the baby…did the maid bring her to Oman?"

"Maha and Mohammed, her husband, were bound by Fatima's wish to keep the girl a secret. It tortured them, as they were stuck between loyalty to a woman they loved and the royal baby of a country they loved. They decided they would keep the girl and raise her alongside their own daughter until the third anniversary of the sultan's new marriage. They had decided that if the Palace didn't have an heir by then, it wasn't likely to happen, and they would break their promise to Fatima and bring the girl to Oman."

"But wait. Earlier, you said the sultan didn't have a child. Why isn't she here?"

"When the girl was two, she was in the car with Maha, Mohammed, and their daughter when they were carjacked," Zahra said. Her voice cracked briefly, and her eyes began to swell. "Maha and Mohammed were killed. Their daughter was shot as well."

"Oh my goodness, Zahra. This is the most tragic story I have ever heard."

Zahra gave a clipped nod, trying to discreetly wipe the tears from her eyes.

Adira watched this closely, wondering why she'd suddenly become so upset. But then it hit her. Zahra bint Mohammed. Zahra, daughter of Mohammed. Carefully, Adira said, "When their daughter was shot, the bullet went into her hip, close to the spine."

Zahra bowed her head and put her hands over her eyes.

Adira moved closer and placed her hand gently on Zahra's back. "I am so, so sorry, Zahra."

Zahra took a few halting breaths and sat back up.

Adira let a moment pass before quietly asking, "What happened next?"

"There is only so much of the story I remember," Zahra said. "The bullets that hit me had passed through my mother first. She was shielding me with her body, and I lost consciousness when we fell to the ground. But from what I have been able to piece together from fragments of memory and the police report, I unbuckled the little girl, put her outside the car, and told her to run. After that, I went to my mother's door. She was panicking, struggling to unclip her seat belt."

"You went to help her, just like you helped the little girl."

"It seems I was able to help her out. Out of the car only to be shot."

"That's not your fault, Zahra. That was the carjackers. Not you. You were helping your parents, and both of them would have been proud of your courage."

Zahra reached over and squeezed Adira's hand.

"So what happened to the little girl?"

"She was lost. For years. When I awoke in the hospital two days later, a man and woman were waiting for me. They were emissaries sent by the sultan to bring me back to Oman. I asked if they had Amal, if they had found her."

"Her name was Amal?"

"Yes. It's a beautiful name that means 'hope.' I begged, asking where my sister was, as that is how I always knew her. They asked the hospital and the police and found nothing. They called a great-aunt of mine in Oman, who explained that I was an only child, and our family records proved it. Eventually, they decided that Amal was either a stuffed animal I had lost or some sort of post-trauma artifact. They brought me back to live with the aunt, my only relative, who died nine years later."

"Zahra, I am so sorry."

"The sultan had been keeping track of me, as he knew how fond Fatima was of my family. When he heard I was left on my own and not yet sixteen, he brought me here to be looked after by the Palace staff. When I came of age, something happened that helped the search for Amal. My parents' things, their belongings from San Francisco that had been moved back and placed in storage, were delivered to me for my apartment here. In one of the boxes was Fatima's journal, which told Amal's story."

Adira moved closer and urged her to continue.

"The staff that looked after me still didn't believe it was true, even with this proof. I was sent off to university. I was determined to spend the rest of my life finding Amal and wanted to be as prepared as possible. I studied digital forensics, how to hack databases, and everything I thought I would need to find Amal. When I was prepared, and had the credibility of a degree and some experience in one of our ministries, I was granted an audience with His Majesty. I shared the journal and my plan with him. He gave me the resources I needed, and for years I searched. You have no idea how hard it is to find a missing child, all of the cracks in life they fall through, all of the legal barriers, the privacy, the hopelessly poor records." Her eyes began to swell once more, and she struggled to speak.

"Oh, Zahra," Adira said softly.

"It was so hard every day, and as the days became years, I worried about that little girl more and more. She was growing up alone, without anyone to love her. I pushed so hard it nearly broke me. But how could I stop?"

"Zahra, you did so much for that girl. You gave your life to her, and I know she would understand if you allowed time for yourself, to heal yourself. You lost your parents too, and it's okay to grieve. She would understand."

"I can now, Adira," Zahra said, her brown eyes glistening. "Because I found her."

"How?"

"After the accident, some people must have come across her near the site. They took care of her that night and surrendered her to the authorities the next day. She was wrapped up and sleeping, dropped off in the early hours. A Child Protective Services officer entered her into the system, using a first name found in her clothing. That one stumped me for years, because the name they used was not her own. It was the name of the girl next door, a neighbor in San Francisco that had given my parents hand-me-downs for Amal and me."

"Has she come back to Oman? She must be old enough to have settled somewhere."

Zahra's eyes filled with tears, a few falling as her cheeks rose in a smile. "She came home ten days ago."

"That's about when…wait, you came to pick me up at the airport then. You should have met her instead!"

Locking eyes with Adira, Zahra said, "I did."

Slowly, Adira asked, "What was the name of the girl next door?"

"Her name was Adira."

Adira froze. This couldn't be true.

"I know it's sounds too incredible to be real. But it is, I promise."

For so long, Adira had moved home to home, each time hoping the next family would want to keep her. But with every new door, those hopes dimmed. Learning that someone had cared about her—actually *wanted* her—enough to search for years was, indeed, incredible.

"I will show you exactly how I know. First, though, I'd like to give you a hug."

The two women, separated for nearly twenty-five years, wrapped their arms around each other. Adira felt an entirely unfamiliar warmth grow from within.

When they pulled apart, Zahra grabbed Adira's hand. "Come," she said with excitement. "Let me show you."

She led Adira down another hall, through one of the Palace gardens, and past several buildings. She was close to running, her cane barely keeping up. "Slow down, Zahra. There's no rush now, right?"

But Zahra kept going, her limp not slowing her a bit.

They arrived at a white building with the old-fashioned jagged edges of castles at the top. Two uniformed guards stood at the sides of a door. Zahra spoke to them briefly in Arabic, and they politely bowed their heads as the door was opened and the women entered.

"My apartment," Zahra said. She kicked off her shoes in the foyer before entering a large living room with beautiful, tall ceilings. Only instead of couches and chairs and soft, welcoming furniture, the space was dedicated to three large computer workstations, each with multiple screens displaying a variety of images, all staged for her arrival.

"If you will indulge me, I'd like to tell a story."

"Please," Adira replied. Zahra's excitement was contagious, and Adira allowed herself to cautiously soak it in, if only a little bit. She hadn't been raised like most children. She'd led a rough life, a life where trust led to disappointment. Where letting down your guard got you hurt. So while she allowed herself to enjoy the moment, she remained alert for warning signs.

Zahra pointed to a government form with Adira's name in two of the boxes. "Child Protective Services filled this out. The name Eastmont, as you've probably guessed, came from the hospital where you were surrendered. I've learned that in America, the people filling out these forms can choose a name for you."

Adira had seen this take place at Highland Hospital herself.

Zahra moved to the next screen, showing a picture of the label on a small purple sweater. "The person who filled out the form is named Charles. We've spoken twice now, and I've thanked him for including this picture. It's the sweater you wore, the one from our neighbor, and the reason why he felt he had proof of your real name."

Adira moved close to the screen. Sure enough, her name appeared in clear handwriting on the label.

"These made a search by name impossible. And without a name, every record has to be reviewed one by one. It took us years to do this, and was made nearly impossible by the courts. We eventually had to hack the system, hoping to search surrendered children with amber eyes. But amber isn't a checkbox on the form, and the number of children with hazel or brown eyes is massive."

Adira nodded, amazed at the woman's perseverance.

"Fast forward to when you were about twenty," she said, moving to the next screen, again showing a form with Adira's name. "Do you remember signing up to be a bone marrow donor?"

"I do. A guy in my class at nursing school was diagnosed with leukemia. We all signed up."

"This was a long shot one of my colleagues wanted to take. He wanted to match DNA from the donor banks. It was a monumental task, and one we quickly learned would never work. They simply don't run DNA on the banks, at least a full study. So we went on blood type, narrowing the field down considerably."

"You had access to this?"

"No, and we couldn't hack it either. So we created a dummy corporation company to do a study, and received the bank's data that way, knowing we had made an assumption on blood type."

"Yeah, blood type isn't always dependent on the parents."

"Right. But both your parents had the same blood type: *B*. So the odds were good; in the US, that type is a significantly smaller population than *A* or *O* types."

Adira nodded.

"Then came the grind. We looked at every bone marrow donor with your blood type. We dug and dug, getting into databases that were so challenging. We even had the FBI on our trail for a while, which was terrifying."

"I can see the headline, 'A hack originating in the Middle East—' "

"Exactly. So we laid low for a while, and focused on females with birthdates around what CPS would have estimated yours to be. After a while, we narrowed the group from nearly a million down to eleven. Each one we visited or had brought here for some reason or another."

Adira took a step back. "This nursing program," she said. "It's not real, is it?"

Zahra paused, understanding Adira's concern. "The mobile clinics are real. And the nursing program—it is as well."

Adira's eyes narrowed slightly, sensing the slight hesitation. "But?"

"No, really. The program is real. Nurses from several countries apply for the position every year."

"I didn't apply."

Zahra looked down at her hands. "No, I am afraid I applied for you."

"And did you force them to accept me?"

"I encouraged it," Zahra said. Her voice quickened as she continued, "But the board said you would have been accepted on merit. You really do have strong credentials, Adira."

Adira felt a flash of betrayal. But just as quickly as she felt the rush of heat to her face, it dissipated. Much to her surprise, she understood Zahra's actions. "Go on," she said.

Zahra sat in a chair and rolled to another desk. "I can tell you are not happy with my ruse to get you here, and I am sorry. But if you did not like that, this may make you a little more upset." The monitors above the desk showed stains easily recognizable as a DNA test.

"You took a sample from me," Adira said, pointing to the screen. "The blood Amir drew, I guess. So he's in on it too?"

"Sort of. He doesn't know who you are, but he understood what we were doing. Please don't be upset with him. He actually likes you very much and said Nabila learned more about American nursing in a week than she had attending all of the seminars she'd ever been to."

"He's got the hots for you, you know," Adira said absently.

"Amir? Really?"

"Yes. Worried you're too fancy for him, though. That you're too high class."

"Men have never really paid me much attention. I'm well past the age people marry. And my limp doesn't help. Most men wonder if I have a birth defect that could be passed on to children."

"Doesn't bother him. But I might give him a limp myself for stealing my blood."

"Please," she said. But Adira waved the concern away, and Zahra continued, "Yes, he did take your blood, but only at my insistence that it was the wish of the Palace."

"Could've just asked me at the airport."

"What if you had said no and flown home?"

Adira held her hand out, palm up, unsure.

"I'm afraid we also took some hair from your brush at the hotel," Zahra confessed.

Adira's eyes narrowed. Her armor began to fall back in place. How could Zahra feel entitled to take hair samples? Blood? Did everyone on a sultan's staff feel so indomitable? A sharp reply hovered at the tip of Adira's tongue.

But she held back. Because it wasn't the Palace doing this. It was a woman. One woman who wanted to find the closest thing to a family member she had left. It could be excused, and her resolve could even be celebrated.

Adira let it go.

But Zahra had seen the flash in Adira's eyes. She said, "This search…you have to understand it's been my whole life."

Adira closed her eyes for a second. "I understand."

"The hair sample went to Stanford, and blood went to Harvard and Cambridge. We wanted the best genetic labs to do the tests. At each facility, the samples were divided, going to separate lead researchers who each performed multiple independent studies."

"How close was the match?"

"Ninety-nine point eight percent across the board," Zahra said. "You probably know that paternity index numbers never reach 100 percent, so that's as close to absolute as a scientist will go. And that was for *every* test, Adira, every test from six separate teams at three different labs."

Zahra turned to the monitors, seeing in the reports a finality to her search, closure to a lifetime of work.

But Adira hadn't had the same decades-long build up. This was a lot, and all very fast. "Impressive work, Zahra," Adira said, her voice quiet. Flat.

Zahra's shoulders fell.

"He here?" Adira asked, glancing back to the hallway behind them.

"I'm sorry, but his illness is quite far along. Most days he can't leave the hospital bed," Zahra said, her arms tensing as she pushed herself back in the chair.

Adira understood the illness. "He want to see me?" she mumbled.

"He does. But we have to wait for the doctors to tell us when he will be strong enough for you to visit."

Adira's reply was flat. "Hmm."

Zahra looked down to the floor, and in a near-whisper said, "I had hoped you would be more excited."

Adira looked up at the ceiling before replying. "Growing up, disappointment got to be a pretty strong muscle. When you're pushed in and out of those homes, you hope Mom or Dad will suddenly show up. After a while, you'd be happy with just a picture of them. Go through it long enough, you don't even hope any more. You're just a number, waiting to age out."

Zahra shifted uncomfortably.

"And the fancy hotel and fake job? My blood and hair going out to labs? I'm getting some flashbacks to being pushed around."

Zahra stood. "But—"

"I know you want it to be like a storybook, Zahra. But I've lost the ability to hope for that."

Zahra's hands clenched. "Do you think my life has been a storybook? I watched my parents die."

Adira closed her eyes.

"What we both went through was miserable," Zahra whispered. "But it doesn't mean we can't appreciate what's here and now."

"I grew up in those homes sad. Angry. It's hard to undo."

"I can only imagine."

The scar tissue deep within Adira that had protected her for so long finally began to let go. Her shoulders curled over her chest and her breath began to stutter.

Zahra stepped forward and carefully put her arms around Adira.

Adira leaned in and felt Zahra's warmth as the tears began to fall.

The two stood there, arms wrapped around each other, letting each sense the struggles the other had been through. Both growing up alone, parentless. Both fighting their own battles. Yet both finding each other today. The understanding went unsaid, communicated through physical touch.

After a time, they sat down in two of the office chairs, exhausted.

"If this was a storybook," Adira finally said, "you'd have more comfortable chairs in your living room and enough ice cream to drown ourselves in."

Zahra wiped the last of the tears from her red eyes. "Head down the hall," she said, reaching for the phone. "Maybe we can make our own happy ending."

Adira slowly left the living room, passing the entry on her way down a wide hall before entering a large bedroom. The space was divided in two, a long, marble console table separating the sleeping and sitting areas. The curtains weren't drawn as they'd been in the living room, and she could now see that the entire side of the apartment was at the water's edge. Small buildings with dim lights gave shape to mountains that framed a sparkling bay opening to the gulf. It was like a postcard. Adira stared out into the darkness, her tumultuous emotions of the past hour easing out to the sea beyond.

"I never draw the curtains in here," Zahra said as she returned. "I wake up to a sunrise over the sea every day."

"It's stunning."

"We can go out onto the balcony if you'd like," Zahra said, gesturing to one of the door handles.

Adira went out. It was, like every night she'd been here, a perfect temperature. A tiny hint of a breeze carried the scent of the sea.

A chime came from the front doorbell. "I'll be just a moment," Zahra said.

Adira closed her eyes. She let the fresh air of the sea settle her emotions. Eventually, the soft pings of china and silverware drew her back inside.

Zahra sat in front of a large silver serving tray complete with bowls, spoons, and three tubs of ice cream. "Will this help?"

Adira pulled a slow smile and let herself fall into a chair. "Absolutely," she said.

"We have chocolate, caramel, and cardamom-pistachio."

"Cardamom? I'll have to try that."

The two women made bowls and relaxed further into their chairs. Adira enjoyed the earthy taste and unusual flavor of such an aromatic spice in a sweet dessert. After a few bites, she pointed her spoon at some framed photos on the console table.

"Who are they?" Adira asked.

"Some friends from university," Zahra replied, setting down her bowl and getting up. "You might like this one." She walked to the table and picked the largest one up. She brought it to Adira.

"You and your dad?" Adira asked. The image showed a large man in a living room, sitting on the carpet next to a half-built playhouse. The remaining pieces, along with torn remnants of wrapping paper, were scattered about. His expression was one of mock annoyance, directed at a toddler standing in the middle of the playhouse with the little house's chimney on her head.

"Yes, that is my father. But I'm the one over here," Zahra said, pointing to a lump under a pile of wrapping paper.

Adira could just make out a nose and the bright white teeth of a young Zahra's smile.

"The chimney-head?" Zahra said. "That is you."

Adira inhaled abruptly. A rush of pressure went to her eyes and her lips went numb. "I—I mean we…we had a family," she managed to say.

"We did," Zahra said, returning to the table. She carefully selected two more photographs and handed them to Adira. "You will want to see these as well. All three of them came from my parents' storage years ago. I'm afraid that's all there was."

"You and me?" Adira asked while looking at a little girl holding a milk bottle for a baby in a stroller on a beach.

"In front of the Golden Gate Bridge," she said, pointing to dark forms veiled by a layer of fog.

Adira went to the next photograph. It showed a swaddled baby in the arms of a beautiful woman.

Zahra sat down on the arm of Adira's chair, and Adira felt a gentle touch on her back. "That is you with your mum, Fatima," Zahra said quietly.

Adira touched the glass, wishing she could remember the moment. Wishing she could feel it once more. Her mother was beautiful, her posture tender and loving. But in her eyes, Adira could see hesitance, a happiness being held back.

"Are you okay?" Zahra asked.

Adira set the photographs down and rested her head on Zahra's leg. "I'm happy, sad, confused, and exhausted. So, to be honest, I'm a total mess right now."

Zahra rubbed Adira's back. "Why don't you stay here tonight? I think we could both use the company."

"I'd like that, Zahra. But I have another day at the clinic tomorrow," Adira said. With a flash of reality, she raised her head and looked at Zahra. "Or *do* I have work tomorrow?"

"As I said, the job and the clinic are real. But you are the sayyida now, so work is really up to you."

"Sayyida?"

"Your title. It means 'daughter of the sultan.' In a traditional monarchy, one might say, 'princess.' "

"I just saw a picture of my mother for the first time, and learned that I was loved and cared for by a family who wasn't doing it for a couple hundred bucks every week," Adira said. "Let's enjoy that for the night and skip the title."

"But—"

"Please?"

"Very well, then," Zahra said, leaning down and kissing the top of Adira's head. "I have one last surprise. But let's get ready for bed first."

Zahra showed Adira the bathroom, pulling out an extra toothbrush along the way. She then led her into a large walk-in closet and helped her find something to sleep in.

When they eventually settled into bed, Zahra turned off the main lights. From a set of switches on her nightstand, she flipped a switch, and a lamp on Adira's side of the bed came on. She rolled back over to face Adira and handed her a small notebook. "This was among my parents' belongings as well. It is a journal your mother kept for a time."

Adira took the book, nervous as she pulled back the elastic band.

Her mother's cursive was precise and flowing, and thankfully, in English, with entries beginning soon after Adira's birth. While the passages were brief, they told a tale of love and loyalty.

She spoke of her daughter in angelic terms, every burp and babble as a joy. Her love for the sultan radiated through many entries, as did the torture her secret caused.

Many of the passages were dedicated to Zahra, with anecdotes of the older girl being absolutely in love with the newborn, spending every moment of the day helping Fatima raise her. Zahra had been there for Adira's first crawl, her first words, and her first steps, cheering her all the way.

And while the writings, like their life together, ended well before the journal was filled, they described a life Adira had never even allowed herself to dream of. A life in a home filled with care and love.

She rolled over to thank Zahra, only to find her sound asleep.

11

The next morning, Adira returned to the mobile clinic, having informed Zahra that she'd like to continue working while processing everything she'd learned. It was so much to take in, and while she knew it was much like burying her head in the sand, she needed to put herself to work.

The team had already arrived and set up the tents when Adira arrived in one of the Royal Guard's Land Cruisers.

"Did someone get lucky last night? You go, girl!" Chevy shouted across the parking lot.

By her side, Amir shrugged, and Nabila shook her head.

Adira went to work straightaway, grabbing cases out of a truck. "Didn't have the chance to," she said. "Got a ride here straight from the clubs."

Chevy spun in a ridiculous dance move and gave a loud hoot.

A hoot in return came from the beach. "That's right, boys! I'm back!" she shouted in the direction of the young fishermen.

Amir turned to Adira. "We can only hope to not be arrested when they deport her," he deadpanned.

They carried their gear to the tent while hospital workers set up chairs, tables, vaccine doses, and equipment. Nabila's tablet showed a full schedule of vaccinations, and they were quickly underway.

Adira had seen two Royal Guardsmen around the site that morning. Thankfully, her colleagues hadn't noticed. But midafternoon, several vehicles marked with the red crest had arrived, delivering at least two dozen guards.

This time, they didn't go unnoticed. Amir stopped a guard passing by the patient tent and had a brief discussion.

"What's up?" Chevy asked.

"He said they were just scouting the site to assess security. They probably are considering it for an event for the technical college here."

Chevy shrugged, deciding to ignore the soldiers.

Adira stole glances as she went about her work, hoping they would not pay too much attention to her. When she realized they were going about their own tasks and hadn't even so much as looked in her direction, she wasn't sure if she was relieved or disappointed.

After a time, they settled in to a few places around the mosque, and no one seemed bothered by their presence. The medical crew continued their work until late afternoon without interruption.

As they finished the last of their appointments and began to close down, a middle-aged woman came into the patient tent with a man who appeared to be her husband. She held a piece of fabric around her hand.

Adira had just returned from loading a case of gear and greeted them. After a brief exchange of pleasantries in Arabic, Adira switched to English to ask how she could help.

"I was coiling the net when it was pulled from the other end. I am afraid the line sliced my hand rather badly," the woman said.

Adira took her to a chair and kneeled opposite.

"It is my fault," the husband said. "I did not see she was holding it."

The woman said something gentle in Arabic and used her other hand to reassure the man.

"I am sure it was an accident," Adira said. "Let's take a look."

It was a good-sized gash across her palm and two of her fingers.

"I know this hurts quite a bit. But we can certainly take care of you. Let me grab some material and one of the doctors. I will be back in just a minute."

She found Chevy in the clean tent and explained the woman had a minor laceration as she collected a few items. Returning to the couple, she cleaned the wound.

"Tape is going to come off too easily," Adira said to Chevy. "Do you think sutures? Or maybe glue?"

"Glue will keep the site cleaner," Chevy said. "Nice idea."

Everything had been packed up except their wound kit and the tents. Adira retrieved the surgical glue. As she walked from the clean tent back to the patient, one of the Royal Guards stopped her.

"Miss Eastmont," he said. "Could you please join us in the mosque?"

"Can't right now. We are treating a patient," she said, walking around him.

"Miss, I am afraid I must insist."

"You can insist all you want. Just do it out of my way."

She arrived at Chevy's side, the guard following closely. Adira partially opened the pack containing the single-use glue dispenser and set it on the drape Chevy was using.

"Guy's got no mask and no gloves," Chevy said. "Get him out of here, please."

Adira turned and shooed the man back. "You heard her. Out. I will see you when we are done."

He reluctantly retreated.

"No stitches?" The husband asked as he watched Chevy hold the wound closed with one hand and run a line of glue down the seam.

"Not today. This is a type of super glue. She'll be able to use her hands, and it will protect the wound better."

Chevy held the wound closed for a full minute, then repeated the process on the two smaller slices on the woman's fingers.

"All set," Chevy said. "Why don't you stay here for a few minutes, and we'll let it finish drying? Keep it clean tonight and tomorrow—"

She was cut off when the husband suddenly stood. His quick movement startled the wife, and her hand pulled away from Chevy.

"Whoa there!" Chevy said, reaching out and trying to stop the woman from standing. Thankfully, she hadn't closed her hand over the glue. "Let's sit back down for a minute, please."

The woman sat but gestured with her other hand for Chevy to turn around.

"Bloody Nora!" Chevy exclaimed.

Adira turned. Behind them sat a man in a wheelchair. While he was paler, and certainly much thinner, he was instantly recognizable from the billboards, plaques, and even currency that bore his image.

"I daresay I hope I do not look that bad, Doctor," His Majesty the Sultan of Oman replied. While he appeared weak and frail, there was the hint of a smirk on the corners of his eyes.

"Ah, no, sir. I mean, ah, Your Majesty," Chevy babbled, clearly flustered. "It's just that, ah, well—"

While Chevy and the man and wife struggled to think of what to say and how to behave, Adira let out a little laugh. "You are the first person to have her at a loss for words," she said.

"Please, Doctor, continue," His Majesty said.

"Sorry, yes," Chevy said. Turning to the woman, she finished her instructions. "Keep it dry; no soaking in water. Be gentle with it. Nothing too strenuous like lifting and twisting things. The glue will gradually deteriorate as the wound heals. And, well, that's it!"

The woman thanked her. While she and her husband exchanged a few words with the sultan, Chevy leaned toward Adira. "This is insane!" she whispered.

"You have no idea," Adira said.

The reply puzzled Chevy. Even more so when the sultan asked Adira to join him inside the mosque.

A guard pushed the sultan up a gentle ramp to one of the mosque's doors and gestured for Adira to enter first. She pulled a scarf from around her neck and looped it over her head before removing her shoes and entering. Off to the side of the central area for praying sat a chair, and His Majesty was wheeled next to it.

"Please," he said.

Adira sat. Around her, guards stood by the doors, and a medical team in scrubs held station on the far side.

"Zahra was right," he said. "I have been blessed with the most precious treasure a man could hope for."

His Majesty was positively regal. He wore soft cream, perfectly pressed robes with gold piping. His mussar, a rich mixture of purples and golds, was tied perfectly. She also noticed—probably because it was unusual for hospital patients—that he wore two gold rings and a watch with two crossed swords beneath a *J*-shaped khanjar on the dial.

Adira had thought about this moment last night. About the time when she might meet the man who was her father and what she would say. She'd wanted him to feel guilty, to let him know she'd survived and succeeded in life without him. She'd wanted to be confident, even dismissive.

But the man next to her, while majestically turned out, was thin and pale. There were dark circles under his eyes and hollows beneath his cheekbones. An access lead was taped to a spotted hand, and another could be seen coming from the crook of an arm. It was clear that he would not be with the world much longer.

It was his eyes, though, that finally defeated her. She could feel in them both kindness and regret. He understood.

"I am sorry, my darling," he said. His hand reached out, and she turned her own to take it. The touch of her father, her very own father. Her eyes swelled with a lifetime of tears.

She let them come, if only for a moment, before forcing the nurse in her to return. "How bad?" she asked.

"Quite bad, I'm afraid. A week. Perhaps slightly longer."

"How have they been treating it?" she asked.

"The list could fill a book. Surgery, experimental therapies in Europe, and mountains of pills. But let us not worry about this, Adira. All of the doctors have been very attentive," he said. "Zahra has told me much about your childhood. I am very sorry it was not easy."

"You had no way of knowing, Your Majesty."

The sultan paused a moment before speaking. "I am your father, Adira. It does not feel right for you to call me Your Majesty."

"Glad to know we're both in unfamiliar territory."

"We have a few words for father here. *Abi* or *baba*. *Aboi* is also used."

"Which do you prefer?"

"I would be pleased for you to call me *Baba*. I've always found the term quite warm. Would you be comfortable with that?"

"Baba. I'll try that," she said, never imagining that she would have a discussion about what to call a father.

"I understand that you had many homes as a child and that they were largely unpleasant."

" 'Unpleasant' is an understatement."

He squeezed Adira's hand. "You have found your way back home, Adira. Your way back to me, back to the people of Oman. We are truly blessed with your return."

"It's a lot to digest, to be honest."

"I am sure it is, my dear. Take your time. Stay at Al Bustan as long as you like. And when you are ready, arrangements have been made for you to move into any palace you desire."

Adira shook her head from side to side. "That isn't necessary."

His eyes closed briefly. "As you wish. But the staff will always be ready for you."

How many times had she and her foster siblings dreamed of living in castles and palaces?

"There is much I should have been sharing with you over the years." He waved a hand to his abdomen and the vascular access line in his arm. "But with this illness, I am afraid that my movements are now rather restricted."

"I've learned plenty from Zahra, don't worry."

"There is always more to learn, Adira," he said. "I understand you met Taimur quite by chance."

"Wait, you know Taimur? The nice old man out in the desert?"

"I do, and very well."

Her eyebrows narrowed. "Was he part of Zahra's plan?"

The sultan gently shook his head. "Not at all. Many people know of our friendship, but even Zahra couldn't arrange a chance meeting at a traffic accident. You were brought together only by the will of Allah."

"So who is he?"

"As a child, I lived in the south, in Salalah, where I was largely kept within the Palace walls. I was sent at a young age to Sandhurst and later deployed with the British army. When I returned many years later, it was clear I did not know much about my own country. Taimur's father was my teacher and guide. He took me across our land, introducing me to the people in each region, sharing their strengths and struggles. Taimur and I were close in age and became the best of friends, as we are today." The memories brought a smile to the sultan's face.

"You miss those days."

"I do. We had our boys' own adventures together, some of which led to a smack from his father now and again."

"I saw a reference to a 'teacher' in Fatima's journal. That was Taimur's father?"

"Yes," he replied. "Her journal brought me great sadness. You are a secret she should not have kept."

"She did it for you."

"She did, and this both saddened and humbled me." He closed his eyes, clearly desolate. Behind them, afternoon light briefly snuck in through a doorway.

"What was she like?"

He returned his gaze. "On the surface, she was beautiful. You have the same eyes, you know. Hers were green, of course, but they glowed like yours. Beneath the surface, though, she was spectacular. She had a magical sense of humor and made friends with ease. She filled me with happiness every day."

He stopped to cough. Getting his emotions in check.

"On our last night, I begged her to stay. She told me that she loved me so much that she had to leave *for* me. It does not make sense, as I say it now. But it remains the most heartbreaking thing anyone has ever said."

"You still love her, don't you?"

"I do," he replied. "Even more so now that she has brought you to me."

Adira took her other hand and covered his.

A doctor approached to check on the sultan. "Your Majesty, it is time to go."

"Please leave us for a few more minutes," he said.

The man took his leave, and the sultan turned back to Adira.

He spoke quietly, "I know there is much a father should do for his child."

"Thank you, Baba," she said, surprised at how nice the word felt. "But you have your health to worry about. Not me."

"It is a blessing to be called *Baba* for the first time," he said with a smile. "But if I may finish. I cannot give you every experience a father should. But there is someone who can at least teach you as I would have done. Taimur."

"But I have a job here and—"

"My darling, please. I have an ulterior motive here. While I want you to experience your homeland, we are also approaching a time that history has shown may be slightly tense. It is a good time to move, as some say, 'under the radar.'"

"You'd like me out in the desert? With your condition, I'd rather stay close."

"Thank you," he replied, closing his eyes briefly. "But staying out of the reach of others would be prudent."

"This has to do with your cancer. And the successor afterward, doesn't it?"

The sultan nodded.

"I've heard the defense guy will take your place."

"You are quite informed."

"People talk at the clinics. But they don't like him. They're upset and want jobs they were promised."

"And they will have those jobs. Deputy Minister Rashid has been useful, but in this case, he has stepped beyond his authority. It is something I will have rectified."

"He's not going to like that."

"He has little choice."

"You might want to come up with a plan B for your next sultan if he's going to cause trouble. Everything is so peaceful here except where that guy is concerned."

"Until today, he has been my closest relative."

"Does it have to be a relative?"

"This role has been held by men in the family for fourteen generations."

"Why not change it up? What about the foreign minister that people like? Omar?"

"Fatima always liked him. But do not worry about Omar or Rashid. The Family Council will make their choice. I created the council to do just that: find the best successor."

"Who's the council?"

"Trusted friends. Those who have no designs on the throne themselves and have provided me with sage advice through challenging times."

"And they'll make the right choice?"

"They are the very few I have trusted all my life."

"And you want me out of the way? Up in the desert?"

"Not out of the way, but out of reach. Somewhere safe. When my time comes, I fear there will be some conflict. Old opponents will return and try to discredit me in their attempt to promote themselves for selection. I don't want them coming after you," he said before going quiet for a moment. "To be truthful, as much as I would love to take your arm and tell you everything about our family and our country, I cannot. I feel myself tiring even now. The medicine they gave me for just this excursion is wearing off already. Taimur can do this for me. It will give me great pleasure."

"But I can come see you at the hospital? Sneak up with the laundry?"

The sultan smiled. "I would like that very much."

The doctors approached once again, insisting that it was time for His Majesty to return to the hospital. Adira walked with them outside to an olive drab ambulance. After he was transferred to a gurney for his return to the hospital, she moved a medic aside and secured the straps herself.

After adjusting a pillow beneath his head, she placed her hands on his shoulders. "Thank you for coming to see me."

"Adira, you have made an old man very happy today," he said, placing his hands on her arms. "And very proud, as well."

"Thank you, Baba," she said. And much to her surprise, she found herself leaning down to kiss his cheek.

The ambulance and several Royal Guard vehicles departed. As the last of them pulled away, only the clinic's Land Cruisers remained. Chevy, Nabila, and Amir turned as one to look at her, with Zahra standing just behind.

Chevy, naturally, spoke first. "Your royal royalness," she said, exaggerating a curtsy. "I am but your humble servant and place myself at your mercy!"

"Zahra, call the Royal Guard and have this woman deported immediately!" Adira said.

They burst into laughter. "As you wish, Sayyida!" Zahra said with a mock salute.

Chevy came up and wrapped an arm around Adira. "Girl, you've got a lot to tell us. Fancy Chick here told us the good part, but I think there's more to the story!"

"Adira," Zahra said. "I've arranged dinner for us at Ubhar if you would like."

"We like!" Chevy said.

"I guess we're off, then," Adira said with a shrug.

"I'll take Nabila and Adira with me," Chevy said to Amir. "You take Fancy Chick, okay?"

Amir blushed and then looked at Zahra. "Would that be —" he started.

"Only if you promise not to call me 'Fancy Chick,' " Zahra said with a laugh.

Once the group had settled into a private room in the restaurant, and various juices had been ordered, Chevy set both hands on the table. "Whole story. From the beginning. Who's starting?" she demanded.

They all laughed before Adira gestured to Zahra. "You're on," she said with a smile.

Zahra told the story as she had the night before. Chevy, Nabila, and Amir interrupted frequently with questions. Adira listened silently, letting the details of this second telling soak in. The experiences she'd had in life had shaped her, but now, the ground had shifted. How was she supposed to make sense of everything now?

"Adira?" Amir said, bringing her back.

"Yes, sorry. Got lost there."

"We understand," he replied gently.

"So you were surrendered at the hospital, and then what?" Chevy asked.

"Child Protective Services," Adira replied. "Jumped around foster homes for a while."

"What about the family that adopted you?" Her question was natural.

"Never happened," Adira said with a shrug. "And as each year went by, the odds went down. I aged out, found a scholarship, and here I am."

Chevy knew she'd unknowingly hit a nerve. "And you turned into a success. Defied the odds," she offered.

After receiving a smile from Adira in thanks for happily ending that line of questioning, Chevy turned her attention to Zahra, asking how she had tracked Adira down.

Nabila had been even quieter than usual, so Adira slid her chair around the table to bring herself closer. "You look pensive," Adira said.

Nabila placed her hand on Adira's.

"I hope you're not upset I didn't tell you before, because I only just found out myself."

"I am not upset at all," Nabila replied. "It is the opposite. I am overjoyed."

"Phew. You kinda had me worried there."

"I am simply happy. Thankful, actually, for all of Oman."

"Whoa," Adira said. "I'm only a girl who found a birth parent."

"You know it is more than that."

"Actually, I don't. But I will say that as many times as I thought about what I would say to a birth parent, the sultan pretty much melted me like butter with his gentle nature."

"He is that way," Nabila replied with a smile. "I am happy for both of you to find each other. Allah brought Zahra to you both as a blessing."

Adira looked over at Zahra. She was floating on air, her eyes sparkling as she laughed with the others. "She is a blessing, isn't she?"

"As are you."

"You're going to have to stop saying that."

Nabila leaned forward. "But you have to know what this means. What it means for us."

Adira slowly let out a breath, a disappointed look on her face. She motioned with her hand for Nabila to explain.

"Are you sure you want to know?"

"Try me. Can't be as bad as shaking cigarette butts out of a bowl to heat up fake mac-n-cheese while hoping the house mother doesn't bring a stoned creep home again."

Nabila made a horrified face. "Perhaps not."

"So tell me. What's the big deal?"

"Right now, word is getting out. Oman is a small country; before long, everyone will know that His Majesty has a daughter. People will want to meet you everywhere we go."

"We've been working in some small places, so that won't be a big deal."

"I don't think you understand. This country prayed for His Majesty to have a child for years. You will be seen as a miracle. Work will be impossible."

"Okay, well, we'll deal with it."

"It also means that men with eyes on the throne will plot against you. Men like Rashid. I do not know what lengths they will go to take attention away from you."

Adira leaned back. "I don't want any attention. They can have it."

"It will come whether you like it or not."

Adira waved her hand dismissively.

"And women like me," Nabila said, pausing. "We will have some expectations."

"Expectations?"

"His Majesty had to fight for the equality of women here. He faced great resistance from traditionalists who only wanted women to take 'maternal' jobs, who wanted us to stay at home and not be seen in public."

Adira nodded. "And I think it's great what he did."

"You have to continue that, Adira."

"No, I don't. I don't have to either. A country doesn't just backtrack on those changes. They're here to stay."

Nabila shook her head. "These changes have only been around for one generation. Men like Rashid and the people he will appoint will push us back. That is how they define power."

"If that is the case, there's not going to be much I can do about it."

"But there is!" Nabila exclaimed, her voice firm. The others stopped their discussion and turned to watch. "You have a platform! You can make sure His Majesty's vision for Oman continues. It's something only you can do."

Adira shrunk back. This was not her.

Nabila leaned forward. "You are the sayyida. Just you, the only child. These next moments in our history are going to be about you."

"No, thank you," Adira said, pushing back her chair.

"But you must!" Nabila implored.

"Nope. That is not me," she said, her voice firm.

Suddenly, all eyes were on her. And all she wanted to do was be invisible.

"This is what you were trying to tell me last night, isn't it?" Adira said, her eyes on Zahra.

Zahra let out a heavy sigh.

"Nabila is right," Amir said. "We are at a crucial juncture in our history."

"I have a job with you and Chevy and the MOH that I was told was real. That's the job I want."

Amir stole a glance at Nabila. "That is going to be difficult now."

"So I'm fired?"

"Of course not. It is just that things will be…complicated," Amir said.

"Complicated is quitting a stable job for this one. Complicated is being told you have a 'platform' to take people here through a 'crucial juncture.' Complicated is having no skills to do that. Or desire! Oh, add to that the complication of learning that I did have parents, only one is dead and the other soon will be. That's complicated."

If Amir felt rebuffed, he didn't show it, and pressed on. "Yes, complicated for you. But this is also complicated for us. For Oman."

Adira stood. "I am choosing to uncomplicate my life by leaving this conversation," she said, edging her way around the table.

"Where are you—" Amir started.

"I'm just a normal person, a nurse. I'm not going to take that on. I can't," Adira said as she walked through the doorway of the small room and out to the street.

Zahra stood to give chase. But Chevy placed a hand on her arm to hold her back. "Don't. Let her go."

"But she needs help," Zahra pleaded.

"She does. You're right. But it has to come on her terms. When she's ready."

Zahra's hands clutched. Her eyes didn't leave the door.

"When you were searching for her, you ever do any research on girls that grew up in her circumstances?"

Zahra turned back to Chevy and lowered her eyes. "Not as much as I should have."

"Orphans that aren't adopted can feel defective, unworthy of love and affection. Not getting placed—moving home to home—like she did, she'd have faced rejection more than anyone. Statistics on abuse run high."

Zahra's eyes closed briefly.

"Kids from those circumstances? They can be reckless. Volatile. Distrustful." Raising a hand to the door, Chevy added, "And quick to run."

Zahra searched the windows. "I thought I could understand her since we both grew up without parents."

"You can. More than any of us. And because of that, you know those challenges actually make people stronger. Perceptive. Resourceful and disciplined. Interestingly, and I think very relevant here, is that once they let someone close, an intense loyalty forms. They nurture and protect those they trust more than the rest of us would. It's why she's such a good nurse."

Zahra turned back to Chevy.

"She's let you in. Us as well, but you most of all. I can see it in her body language."

"What should I do?"

"Don't push. She'll come when she's ready. And that's when you'll be there for her."

Outside the restaurant, Adira found two green Royal Guard Range Rovers waiting. After a bit of debate, and the threat of the newly found sayyida walking home alone, she was promptly returned to the hotel.

Once back in her suite, Adira went to the balcony and fell heavily onto a lounger. In the space of only twenty-four hours, her life had become a roller coaster.

She'd awakened happy that morning. Truly happy, much to her surprise. Learning of her mother and father, of Zahra and her parents, was like a miracle. And then, to meet her father, it was simply unimaginable. She wanted to talk to him more, to listen and understand. To see what similarities she could find.

But why did he have to be the single most prominent figure in the entire country? Why couldn't he be someone normal, like an electrician? Why did it have to be so political? So "complicated"? The daughter of a man pushing for greater equality in a male-dominant part of the world? Really? That was more than she wanted to take on.

It was some kind of torture. Give the girl a blessing, but follow it by dumping ten tons of baggage on her. She didn't have the energy to take on these dilemmas. She could never be the person Nabila or Amir wanted her to be. She'd only disappoint them.

Worrying about the pressures she felt was entirely selfish, given the poor man had only days to live. But unwanted feelings are often a tangled mess.

Lay low. Duck the storm altogether. That was how she survived in the system. Social worker comes by for a wellness check? Smile and say as little as you can get away with, lest a belt come out after they've left. House mom brings home a new boyfriend? Hide or get out. Avoid eye contact. Same applies here.

She'd go visit her father tomorrow and then go… somewhere else. California wasn't an option. She'd burned that bridge. The thought of applying for a job with Doctors Without Borders crossed her mind. Get a country nearby so she could sneak in a visit or two with her father without being part of the mess. Disappear. That would be best. The easiest, at least. Decision made, she rose from the lounger and made her way to bed.

***

Across the city of Muscat, phones were beginning to ring. The bits and pieces of information collected, both innocently and covertly, were being combined with vast amounts of speculation. Not all of the conclusions being drawn were pleasant, which was why Rashid bin Tamim was fuming.

"How is it that you can be so incompetent!" Rashid shouted.

On the other end of the line was the systems administrator Rashid had pressured to look into Zahra al Abdali's network traffic. "Your Excellency," he stammered, "The files you asked me to look into. I could not crack the encryption. My apologies, but—"

"Your apologies do no good now! Everyone has heard! That damn woman found Hamad had a bloody daughter."

"Yes, Your Excellency, and if you would like—"

"I would like you to do what I require, whenever I require it. Which is something you have so far shown yourself incapable of!"

The systems administrator was stuck between a rock and a hard place. While he didn't work for Rashid, when the Deputy Defense Minister approached him for Palace information, he'd accepted, thinking it would help him gain a better position once Rashid ascended to the throne. He'd regretted the decision ever since. "I will, Your Excellency," he said, defeat in his voice.

Just as Rashid was about to reply, his mobile phone rang, displaying a number he knew well. "I will be back in touch. You might do well to consider your career options for the future!" Rashid slammed the receiver down and took a deep breath before raising the mobile to his ear. "I suppose you've heard?" he said, dispensing with all pleasantries.

The voice on the mobile was a low rumble. "Of course I have. The question is, why did I not hear it from you first?"

"There was some incompetence on the part of an informant. It has been dealt with."

"So what, Rashid, will you do now?"

"Wait. This woman should not be a threat. She is a foreigner, and I suspect she will happily disappear once she collects some riches."

There was a pause before the voice replied. "You would do well to hope so."

The line closed, and Rashid was left looking at a black screen, his vision for the future beginning to crack.

***

Rashid's plan was one that had been set in motion by his father more than fifteen years ago when the young man had asked his father for help purchasing a platinum Rolex Daytona.

"We can try, Rashid," his father, Tamim, had said long ago. "But is it really these small expressions of wealth you want?"

At the time, Rashid found the question ridiculous. Of course he needed the watch! That one and more! He'd grown up following the young Saudis and Emirati on social media and wanted desperately to be part of the crowd.

"I thought, perhaps, you might be after more?"

More—more of anything—had always been of interest to Rashid.

And so Tamim brought his impulsive son into the study and laid a large, leather-bound book on the desk. "This," he explained, "is our family tree."

As far as family trees went, this particular one wasn't very deep. Nor wide. But it didn't need to be. What it needed to illustrate were three simple facts.

The first was to show that Rashid, as he well knew, was the only son of Tamim. The second was to illustrate the connection between Tamim and Sultan Hamad's grandfather, albeit within a mix of six wives and six children. The third, and most important, fact the family tree showed was the circuitous path between Rashid and the childless Sultan Hamad.

"So, my son, would you like a watch to attempt to illustrate wealth you know we do not have? Or would you like to swim the rest of your life in an entire sea of wealth?"

"You think that I could be made sultan? Me?"

"I think the opportunity is there if His Majesty remains childless. Let me tell you how." His father then outlined the plan for young Rashid, a plan that he had followed to the letter.

Upon completing school, Rashid joined the Royal Army of Oman as an officer. He made sure to maneuver himself into visible positions, take every opportunity presented, and make decisions that stood out. He took credit for all his underlings did well, and deftly avoided every criticism. He made sure his successes echoed in the halls of power and, as a result, propelled himself quickly through the ranks. Word of his desire to turn his "vast experience" into leadership was whispered into the right ears at the right time, and a successful leap from the army to the Ministry of Defense was made.

Once inside, his skill of using others for gain allowed him to maneuver up within the Ministry and even across to allied forces. On more than one occasion, his name bubbled up to His Majesty the Sultan himself. Eventually, he became the owner of backchannel connections to every one of the Gulf states. He was plugged in, and by the young age of forty-eight, graciously accepted the title of Deputy Defense Minister, a role that put him squarely in the spotlight.

It was the spotlight that Rashid wanted. Not for the same reasons he'd had as a young man. Back then, he'd wanted everyone to see him. Today, he wanted only a specific set of eyes on him—those of the Royal Family Council, the same body that would select the successor to the throne. Being visible—being successful and visible—would prove the boost his tenuous blood connection needed to propel him into the throne.

And it was on that throne that Rashid could swim in the sea of wealth he'd always wanted. Where Sultan Hamad directed oil money to the land and its people, Rashid felt no such obligation. The infrastructure was there for them, couldn't they figure out how to keep it running? He'd let the little people sort out themselves while he focused on the luxurious life of his dreams.

The problem was that no one knew exactly who was on the council. The secrecy of the members was intentional, an effort to make sure the group could not be pressured—or indeed threatened—while carrying out their mission.

Within the ministries and chambers of government, rumors had run wild for years. Some claimed the council consisted of dozens of members from the Majlis Oman, the state assembly of elected and appointed representatives. Others thought this ridiculous, knowing that in a monarchy, only the rich and powerful would be consulted. A few even thought the council was a myth, that His Majesty could only trust himself.

Rashid, though, knew the council had five members. And while there were four still to be uncovered, he knew one of them very, very well.

12

Adira woke to the smell of coffee. Not that it wasn't a good smell to wake up to, but it was unexpected enough that she thought she must be dreaming. She rubbed her eyes and took a few breaths. It must have been room service. They'd probably put a pot in the valet cupboard, the secret little closet that opened to a staff area on one side and into her suite on the other.

She walked into the bathroom and looked at herself in the mirror. "Last day, girl. Make the most of it," she said to her reflection. She worked a few tangles out of her hair, used the toilet, and washed her hands before walking into the living room.

"Good morning!" said a strong, low voice.

Adira let out a shriek and nearly fell over. "Taimur? What are you doing here? How did you get in?"

The strong old man held up his cup and grinned. "Coffee?" he asked.

"Yes. A lot. But what are you doing here?"

"Please, sit," he said. "Milk and sugar?"

Adira sat in the armchair next to his. "Both, please."

"Breakfast should be here shortly," he said while pouring her coffee. "The pastry chef here, who is the finest in the country, is a cousin of mine."

After he had added milk and a small spoon of sugar, he handed her the cup and saucer. "Passing through, were you?" she asked.

"Drink, Adira. You could use it."

Adira took a sip.

"Better?"

"A little. Still confused."

He smiled and leaned back. "You know, I knew you were their daughter when I saw you at the accident."

"How could that even be possible? No one knew then, not even Zahra."

"I spent much time with your father when we were young. And during their marriage, he and your mother would often join us in the sands. He was very insistent to always spend time outside the Palace."

"That was ages ago."

"It was, but the memories of good friends stay with you. I remember his face when he did something inadvisable. It was the same face you had in the video after you pulled the boy from the river."

"That was after the accident. Doesn't count."

"Very well," he acceded. "You hold yourself in a particular way. Like your walk, it's as unique as a fingerprint. At the accident, you stood as he used to. Relaxed but confident. Observant, but poised and ready to go."

"That's a lot to read into a stance," Adira replied.

"The two doctors that run the team. Did you notice they let you take the lead? It was interesting to watch," he said.

Adira waved it off. "That's just because I have trauma experience."

"Your eyes glow exactly like your mother's. And the way your brow furrows, that little wrinkle right here," he said, pointing between his eyes. "Your mother's face did just the same thing when she was concentrating."

"What was the face she made when she wondered what the hell was going on?"

He laughed. "We will have a wonderful time together, you and I! But to answer your question, it was just like the face you're making now!"

Adira couldn't help but laugh herself. The old man's smile —expansive, rough, and expressive—was simply contagious.

"My dear, what is going on here is that we are going to get to know one another, just as your father wishes he could."

"Taimur, I hate to tell you, but that's not going to happen."

His eyebrows rose in question.

"Don't worry, I am going to visit my father. Spend some time with him before I head out."

"And why would you be leaving us?"

"My friends here—Zahra and the people you met from the clinic—have told me that there's more going on here than a girl finding her dad."

His brows leveled in understanding. "This is true. But let us forget about that for a while, which will be easier in the desert."

"I can't. This idea that I need to stand up as, what's it called? Sayyida? That's not me. It's just too much."

He watched her, waiting.

But she could play that game too.

What he said was not what she expected. "Yes, well, I imagine running away would be the easy thing to do."

He was provoking her. She cursed herself for taking the bait. "I am not looking for the easy way."

"It sounds to me that you are."

"Arggh!" she said, setting down her coffee and standing. "I am not the type of person to raise my hand and say, 'Yo, peeps, how about having the poor girl from America tell you what to do?' "

The smile returned. "This is what you are worried about?"

"Well, yeah. That's what they were saying I needed to do last night. Stand for women's rights. Make sure an entire country doesn't regress! As if I know how to do that!"

"Adira," he said, his smile growing. "This is the easiest thing in the world to resolve. Is it why you are leaving?"

"Yeah," she replied quietly, caught off guard by his smug expression.

"Well then, let me explain something," he said. "There has not been a female telling male elders what to do in this part of the world since the Islamic era began. Leadership here, and in our neighboring countries, has always been male. This is progress that still needs to be made, I'm afraid. It is not something you need to worry about now."

Oh no. He thought she was being ridiculous. Adira quickly sat back down, embarrassed. "Really?"

"Really," he said, doing his best to appear earnest.

"I'm sorry, after dinner with everyone, I thought I was expected to give speeches all the time. "

"Please, do not apologize. You have faced a lot in the past two days," he said gently. After a pause, he asked, "Have we cleared this up to your satisfaction?"

She nodded slowly.

"So after breakfast, we may go?"

"No, no. It's still, well, I—"

"Tell me this, do you like it here?"

"Of course. The people are wonderful. And it's incredibly beautiful."

He nodded. "I could tell out in the sands. The tourists, what few we have, fidget a lot. You were uniquely settled. Calm. The desert was home for you."

"I did like it," she admitted. "Calming is a good word."

"Then I would be honored if you would spend a few days with me. Your father would like you to know our culture. Understand your heritage. If you still feel you must leave after that, I will drive you to the airport myself."

Adira thought for a moment. She tended to react too quickly sometimes. Or all the time. And now, with no expectations, it was easier. And it was only two or three days. "Okay," she said. "A few days. But that's it."

"Marvelous!"

"I am going to have a shower first," she said, standing once again. On her way back to the bedroom, she stopped and turned back to him. "Taimur, why are you doing this?"

He bent forward and looked down at his hands. "We are as close as brothers, your father and me. We see each other often, and this week, things have worsened. Going to see you yesterday, I fear, will have been his last outing. I saw him last night. He was awake for a short time and told me how proud he was to have a daughter. He was truly joyous. But he also said that his condition was deteriorating so quickly that he didn't want you to see him like that. This sickness is cruel."

His eyes moistened, and she could feel his sadness.

"He asked me to take his place. To share with you everything he would have as a father. It was something only I could do, he said. And it is a complete honor to have a man ask you for this. Even more so when the request comes from your dearest friend."

Taimur turned and looked out the window.

Adira could tell he wasn't looking at the view, but instead looking back. A man she hardly knew, who strangely was as familiar as someone she'd known forever, was willing to drop everything for the honor of helping his friend.

She walked back to his side and put her hand on his shoulder. "Let's make him happy, then," she said.

Taimur returned to the present. "We will," he said. "Now, off to the shower for you. Breakfast will be here any minute!"

When Adira returned, Taimur was seated at the dining table, speaking softly into his phone. He rang off as she sat down.

"That was one of my sons. The word is out."

Adira pulled the cloche off the plate that had been set for her to reveal an omelet and grilled vegetables. "What word is that?"

"You," he replied, picking up the television remote.

The screen came to life, and Taimur pressed a few buttons to find one of the local stations broadcasting in English. The screen showed a picture of her taken at immigration on her arrival.

"...*rumor that Miss Adira Eastmont bint Hamad is the daughter of His Majesty and Oman's former First Lady. While the Palace Office, due to His Majesty's current condition, has not responded to our inquiries at this point, we expect to learn more shortly. Efforts to locate Miss Eastmont for comment are currently underway. We have, however, been able to verify that this video, seen by much of the nation on social media earlier this week, was, in fact, Miss Eastmont rescuing a young boy…"*

Taimur gave Adira a cheeky smile. "I do love this video."

Adira rolled her eyes and continued eating. Once the EMT's body cam footage finished, the station cut to a clip of a middle-aged man with a neatly trimmed beard and wire-rimmed glasses walking into a government building. A voice-over identified the man as Deputy Defense Minister Rashid bin Tamim before switching to an interview recorded moments ago.

"I find it hard to believe that His Majesty has a daughter. If it is true, why has he kept it a secret for so long?" Rashid said to the off-camera reporter.

"So you do not think it to be true?" the reporter asked.

"His Majesty is ailing, and a girl suddenly appears with her hand out. Is she an opportunist? After riches?" Rashid said. He paused for effect and then continued, "Or is she perhaps a plant from the Americans? Do they have designs on our future?"

"So you think she is from the American government?"

Rashid shrugged and artfully brought the interview to an end with that question left in the air. "If you will excuse me, I have important matters to attend to," he said before turning away.

Taimur turned off the television.

"An American plant after riches! Now I know why everyone hates this guy!" Adira exclaimed.

"That was a British station, and I'm surprised the Ministry of Information did not stop them. It won't be on the replay. They will not be permitted to spread Palace rumors like that."

"Jerk probably called them himself."

Taimur nodded. "Omani stations will not play the interview, and the Ministry will find a way to end the speculation. Let's just hope they can kill any international curiosity."

"I just hope they leave me alone," Adira said.

"Arrangements have been made for us to depart through the service garage. Anyone inquiring with the hotel staff will be told that you have checked out and your itinerary is unknown."

"Oh, so now I sneak out like an 'American plant'?" she whispered.

"Did you bring a trench coat?" he asked.

Adira gave him a cockeyed smile.

"It was Zahra who did this. She is an impressive young woman."

"Determined, that's for sure. I'm a walking example."

"Indeed you are."

Adira finished her breakfast and then pulled together a small assortment of clothes. Soon after, Taimur led them down a service elevator to the staff parking area beneath the hotel. He led her to a decrepit four-door Toyota Land Cruiser that looked like a relic from the colonial era. The door opened without even a hint of a creak and revealed an interior as luxurious as a Palace Range Rover, if not more so.

"You are full of surprises," she said.

"You are not the first person who has been fooled. This truck, at least the outside, belonged to my father. Hamad and I spent a long time together in here. When my father died, Hamad asked if he could have it. I couldn't imagine why, as it barely ran by then.

"But a year later, it was returned. He knew my father loved this truck and wanted our memory of him to live on. The old body was put on an entirely new frame, with a modern engine and transmission, and the finest coachwork inside. 'The back seat was so bloody uncomfortable, someone had to put it out of its misery,' I remember Hamad saying."

Adira gave a laugh, and soon they pulled out of the garage, taking a service access drive out to the main road. A call came in, and Taimur explained that the sultan was sleeping after a difficult night and their visit would need to be delayed. Taimur took this in stride, his recent visits having shown that there were good times and bad. He made a quick call in response as they continued west, eventually pulling off the motorway and into a parking lot at the side of the Grand Mosque.

"Zahra's taken me here already," Adira explained.

"Has she? Good for her. But we are not here to see the mosque itself."

They parked and walked into the complex of white sandstone buildings. Adira lifted her scarf loosely over her head before leaving her sandals in an alcove of small cubbies. Knowing Adira had visited the prayer hall with its mammoth carpet and towering chandelier, he led her instead into the library.

"I didn't see this last time," Adira said. "Is this where the imams learn the Quran?"

"They can, as there is a considerable amount of literature here covering the history of Islam. But your father built this library for a greater purpose. He wanted it to be an epicenter for cultural, academic, and even scientific exchange between

Oman and the world. He also wanted to help Omanis excel here and abroad, and felt that understanding our history and culture was the starting point. Here, children and adults can find and experience everything from art and music to scientific journals on virtually any topic."

"But learning in Islamic countries is focused on men, right?" Adira said.

"Not at all, Miss Adira," came a new voice from behind.

Adira turned to find a short, middle-aged woman with a perfectly round face and prominent, rosy cheeks.

"Just look over there," she said, gesturing down a hall to a classroom window. Inside, a mixed group of boys and girls were painting. "His Majesty understands that knowledge forms a base of confidence for all Omanis."

"May I introduce Safa, our finest Islamic scholar," Taimur said. The woman beamed, her adorable cheeks practically bursting the snug white underlayer of her hijab.

"Nice to meet you, Safa," Adira said, extending her hand.

The woman surprised her by stepping forward and onto her toes to kiss Adira on the cheek. "And it is wonderful to meet you as well."

"I have to admit I'm a little surprised that there is a female scholar in a mosque."

"Most people are," she said. "Please, would you join me for coffee?"

Without waiting for an answer, she turned and led them through the library.

"I think you also might be surprised to learn that the mosque you visited yesterday is named after a woman," she said, leading them through a doorway and across one of the stone passageways.

"I'm surprised you even know I went to a mosque."

"It is a small country," she admitted with a shrug.

"But yes, I thought mosques were for men only," Adira said.

"Men pray separately. In many of the mosques His Majesty has built, there are also prayer halls for women. Of course, most women pray at home. But if they desire the community aspect of prayer, they now have that opportunity."

They arrived at a door and were led into a small sitting room outside an office. "So what woman was the mosque named after?" Adira asked.

Safa gestured Adira to a chair. Once seated herself, she replied, "It is named after your mother."

A warmth bloomed in Adira's chest. "Did you know her?"

"We met once, on the day I received my doctorate. Meeting her remains one of my most treasured memories."

An elderly man with a solid white mussar and matching long beard entered and set a tray of coffee and dates down on the table before them. Adira thanked him in Arabic and then watched him quietly sit next to Taimur on the opposite side of the room.

"How can Ibadi Muslims offer women educational opportunities and still be a part of Islam?"

"The Quran is a set of lessons set forth by the Prophet Muhammad. How people interpret those lessons is what defines their beliefs. In the case of education, the Prophet has told us that striving for knowledge is the responsibility of every Muslim. We interpret 'every' as meaning both men and women equally. Due to their interpretations of the Quran and local traditions, some countries do not see it this way."

"If men and women are so equal," she said, holding up a corner of her scarf. "Then why do we have to cover ourselves?"

"My, you do cut right to the chase, don't you!"

Adira worried she'd gone too far. "I am sorry to speak out of turn."

"Nonsense. You ask a fair question, and that is how we form our own opinions. So, I like to answer this question by saying it is *because* we are equal that we cover ourselves. The notion of covering ourselves is to prevent men from being distracted—or attracted—by our appearance."

"But it makes us invisible."

"We are never invisible. What we are when covered is seen and heard with the power of our bodies switched *off*. Without the influence of attraction, our voice becomes equal to that of a man."

"That's a perspective I haven't heard before."

"But you asked, and now you have another source of input. It makes me think of another verse from the Quran. Tell me what you think this means: 'In the sight of Allah, the worst of all creatures are those who do not use reason.' "

"I would say that means to form conclusions based on what you know, what you have experienced and value. To think for yourself."

"Exactly. And that is what you have been doing by asking me about women in Islam. You are taking my responses in, combining them with what you know, and creating your own fabric for reason. I am sure there are other ways you practice aspects of Islam in your daily life."

"Afraid not, Safa. Never been religious at all. Don't even know what I am."

Safa reached over and put a hand on the arm of Adira's chair. "What you are is Muslim, my dear, just as your parents."

Adira felt her chest swell. The only thing she'd ever belonged to was a wrinkled file folder in a Child Protective Services drawer. In the span of two days she learned she was part of a family, a country, and now, a religion. "Guess I have a lot to learn," she confessed.

Safa pursed her lips. "Yes, when you are ready. But I imagine you already practice some of the Prophet's lessons. You are a nurse, I understand?"

Adira nodded.

"Why did you choose this path?"

"There was a man, a doctor, who helped me through a difficult time. I think I wanted to do the same for someone else."

"And what do you like about this job?"

"You're healing. The smiles after you've helped someone through a difficult time, especially children, are a great reward."

"You might expand that to say that a person who does an atom's worth of good will see it, correct?"

"Let me guess, another lesson from the Quran?"

"Of course," she said. Leaning forward conspiratorially, she smiled. "I am a religious scholar, after all."

Both of the women laughed.

During the break in the dialogue, Taimur spoke. "If I may, we are going to visit His Majesty today. Thank you for your time, Safa."

"If you could give me a moment first?"

She went into the adjoining office and returned holding a wooden box.

"I have learned that you were an orphan as a child," Safa said to Adira.

Adira opened the palms of her hands. "Until just the other day."

Safa sat down with the box on her lap. She took a moment to run her hands across the carvings covering the dark wood. After a deep breath, she opened the box and withdrew a beautiful lilac scarf.

Unlike most of the scarves she'd seen, this one was not fine wool from Kashmir, but linen. The border was delicately embroidered with flowing patterns of Arabic script.

Taimur and the old man looked at each other. Their eyebrows rose in unison.

"The Prophet himself was an orphan, Adira. I think it is important for you to understand that." She folded the scarf in half on the diagonal and lifted it up. "May I?"

Adira removed her own scarf and bent down.

As Safa reached up, her voice soft and gentle. "I would like you to have this. To remind you that it was here that you found your family." The folded edge was laid just below Adira's hairline. One corner was wrapped around her neck and behind her shoulder, then the other.

Adira felt the luxuriously soft fabric beneath her chin. "It is so beautiful! Thank you, Safa."

"I am glad you like it," Safa said, her eyes glistening.

Taimur's low voice rolled gently across the room. "Safa, we know what you are doing here, and it is very special. Would you tell Adira why?"

Adira's head tilted to the side.

Safa reached out and smoothed a corner of the scarf. "I was the first person to receive a doctorate from the university your father established. Not the first woman, but the first candidate overall. At the graduation ceremony, there was one person who was even more proud than my parents."

Safa reached forward and clasped Adira's hand.

"That person was your mother. This scarf was Fatima's gift to me that day."

Adira's throat tightened. She ran her hands down the scarf at the sides of her head. "Safa, you can't give this away."

"I can indeed," she said, rising out of her chair. "The only better gift would be to see you wear it. We cannot bring your mother back, but we can share her love with you."

Adira stood and wrapped her arms around Safa. There was nothing more that could be said.

13

"What an amazing woman!" Adira said once they were back in the Toyota and on their way to the hospital. "Who was the man there?"

"The imam," Taimur replied.

"Oh, no!" Adira replied. "Did I say anything I shouldn't have?"

Taimur laughed. "Let's say you were straightforward. But because of that, you were brilliant!"

"Was this planned? The scarf and everything?"

"Not at all. I only let Safa know we were stopping by. The rest was all you and her."

"Really?"

"Really. The imam was even more stunned than I was when she brought out the scarf. It was given to her with a beautiful letter. Photographs of them were published in the newspapers. You touched her somehow."

Taimur smiled as they rode a private elevator up to the top floor of Muscat's main hospital. When the doors parted, soldiers from the Royal Guard greeted them. Taimur exchanged a few words with one before the soldier opened the door and gestured for Adira and Taimur to enter.

It was a large room, tastefully done and, while sparse, quite luxurious. In fact, the only resemblance it shared with any other hospital room was the mechanized bed and emergency equipment surrounding the headboard. The sultan, his bed elevated, spoke with a doctor and nurse.

"*As-salaam-alaikum*," Adira and Taimur said in unison.

The staff and His Majesty returned the greeting.

As the doctor stepped toward them, Adira stole a glance at the sultan. He was engaged with the nurse and looked alert.

"Hello, Doctor. I am Adira," she said, extending her hand. She recognized him from the day before. "I believe you were at the mosque."

He hesitated a fraction of a second before shaking her hand. "Yes. Daoud. David, in English."

"How is he doing, Doctor Dauod?"

"Tired. Weak. Losing his appetite."

"Pale, but his color has not changed," she observed from a distance. "How are his eyes?"

"Miss, I am not sure that—"

"She is a nurse and his daughter, Doctor. We may share," Taimur said.

"Yes. Well, then. There is no discoloration in his eyes. Some swelling of the abdomen and soreness in his back, however. We'd like to see him a little stronger. The trip yesterday was hard on him. I don't think he should have gone, and you may have—"

Taimur stepped closer to the doctor. "*La!*" he said. *No.* His voice was low but firm. "You will not put this on the sayyida. The decision to go was His Majesty's. And seeing his daughter for the first time has added to his life, not taken from it. No one is blaming you or the other doctors for the treatments failing, so do not try to do the same to others."

The doctor stood rebuffed. Adira, surprised by Taimur's reaction, attempted to help the doctor save face. She knew it wasn't personal, and only his duty of care. "It is a disease, and as much as all of us would like to control it, we cannot. I know you are doing everything you can, Doctor."

He nodded. "We hope to bring his strength back to try another round of treatment. But you know how things go at this stage."

Options at this point were indeed limited. "Thank you, Doctor. For doing your best and keeping him comfortable," she said.

The doctor was thankful for the excuse to retreat with some grace. He checked his watch and promptly left the room.

"This is what happens when you bring a lion from the desert," the sultan said.

"You have lions here?" asked Adira.

The sultan pointed a finger at Taimur. "Only one!"

The three of them laughed. The female nurse gave a smirk of her own.

"Hasn't lost his hearing, I guess," Adira said to the nurse.

"He has been known to pretend to," she replied. "I will give you some time with him now. We are trying to keep visits short, though. I know you understand."

"We do, thank you," Adira said as the nurse left.

After the door closed, Taimur said, "Quick, Adira. Tear the sheets into strips. We'll help him escape!"

The sultan smiled. Pointing to a chair, he gestured for Adira to bring it close by and sit down. "Not today, old friend," he said.

When she sat, the sultan leaned slightly toward her and extended his hand toward her neck. She moved closer, and he took hold of a corner of the scarf. "Safa?" he asked.

"You recognize it?" Adira asked in return.

"Her name is in the embroidery. And now I have put two and two together."

Taimur took a seat in another chair. "She wanted Adira to have it."

"Because Fatima gave it to her," the sultan concluded in a gentle voice.

"She was lovely, Baba." Using the nickname was somehow easier today. "But at the same time, strong."

"She would have seen those qualities in you," the sultan replied before looking down at the sheets for something.

Adira looked as well. "What do you need?"

"There is a buzzer," he said, finding one. "Not that one… ah, here."

"You have two call buttons?"

"My secretary," Sultan Hamad said.

"He has an office next door," Taimur explained. "While he is called the secretary, he is more like a chief of staff."

The door opened, and two men walked in.

Sultan Hamad gestured for Taimur to make the introductions.

"Adira, this is Samir, His Majesty's secretary," Taimur said, gesturing to a rotund man with dark skin and a thick beard.

Adira stood and shook his hand.

"And our surprise guest is His Excellency Qasim, the Chairman of the Supreme Court."

Adira extended her hand to the unusually tall man. He shook it, placing his free hand atop hers as well, and offered a genuine smile.

"It is very nice to meet you," the Chairman said. "I was next door with Samir, going over a few things, when you called, Your Majesty. I hope you don't mind, but I wanted the chance to say hello and meet your daughter."

"Not at all, Qasim. It is very good to see you, my friend." Turning to the secretary, Sultan Hamad asked, "Would you give the first folio to Adira, please?"

Adira took the folio and, after seeing Sultan Hamad wave his hand, returned to her chair. The folio was made of soft leather, embossed in gold with Arabic script and the crest of the sultanate. "Are we doing state business here?"

"Family business," the sultan replied. "I had an hour of state business earlier today. It is all I had strength for."

Adira didn't know how to reply. The idea of running a government when you were barely strong enough to move sounded impossible.

"Please open it," he said.

She did, and inside found two burgundy passports. She held them up. "We really are escaping!"

Taimur laughed as the sultan took a more serious tone. "Actually, Adira, they are for you. It is important to me that you understand you have a family and that Oman is your home."

Adira flipped open one of the passports. It contained the immigration photo that had been on television and her name in both Arabic and English transliterations. She checked the second passport, which was the same except for the name: *Adira bint Hamad al Sabir*. Adira, daughter of Hamad, of the family Sabir.

"Had we known each other since birth, my dear, your name would have included my own and that of our family. I did not want to be presumptuous and therefore had them prepare both. If you would select one, my staff have explained that it would be helpful for other matters as well."

"So I should choose my name?"

"Indeed. It is more choice than many of us have in the matter."

"You do know that Fatima gave me the name Amal?"

"Yes, Zahra told me. But she thought you would not be interested in changing from Adira."

"It would be pretty difficult."

"That is just as well because I find the name *Adira* beautiful."

"*Eastmont* sounds nice, but it was just made up, taken from the medical center where I was left."

The sultan nodded, not wanting to rush her.

Part of her thought of it as a significant decision, a question of her identity, not to mention the records that would need to be updated. But her father, the ruler of a country who could literally have anything done for him with the snap of a finger, was showing anticipation. This was important to him.

Adira set the Eastmont passport down and held up the other. "I would be happy to share your name."

"I am flattered," the sultan said, clearly relieved.

The secretary took the first folio from her and exchanged it with another. Inside was a Ministry of Health ID card on a lanyard similar to the one she had been given by Nabila, only this one showed her new family name. Beneath it was another card. "Driver's license?" she asked.

"National ID," Taimur said. "It is for identity verification and secure access to records. The driver's license is imprinted on the back."

"But you've never seen me drive," Adira said.

"Will you place your right hand over your heart and attest that you will not be a hazard to fellow Omanis on the road?" the Chairman of the Supreme Court said.

Adira held her hand to her chest and, with a laugh, said, "I do!"

"Congratulations, you just passed," the Chairman announced.

"If you two are done," said the secretary, holding out a card reading device. "We will need to secure your ID card."

Adira took the device from him and inserted the card. A small screen at the top of the machine came to life. She followed the instructions, and the tool stored her fingerprint and six-digit PIN code.

After removing the card, she handed the device back to the secretary. "Lot of security for an ID," she said.

The secretary exchanged a glance with the sultan before replying. "The card is also used for accessing records at the national bank. His Majesty has added you to a series of family accounts."

Adira had never been financially stable. While she'd had a full scholarship to nursing school, a small student loan had covered living expenses. Despite the high cost of living in Oakland, she'd been able to keep up with the payments. Mostly, anyway.

She shifted uncomfortably in her chair before holding the card back up for the secretary. "This is unnecessary. I'm not an opportunist. I came here for a job—one with very generous compensation."

"I know this," the sultan said. "I know you have used your intelligence and talents to build a career and an independent life. But as a father, I would like to offer stability. This is nothing more than what any father would do for his child if he was able."

Adira looked at him carefully.

"Your father is not doing this out of pity, Adira. Nor guilt. He feels it is right and in keeping with his personal values," Taimur said.

Adira turned the card over in her hand. "Can I ask a question about this?" she said.

"You may ask anything you would like," her father said.

"I, well, maybe this is something we should talk about alone."

His Majesty made a dismissive gesture with his hand. "You may speak freely."

She looked up at Taimur and the two men. Hesitatingly, she asked, "Your money—is it yours from the oil? Or is it the people's money?"

If the sultan was taken aback by being spoken to in this manner, he did not show it. "You are speaking of how kingdoms work in this region, I imagine," he said.

Adira nodded.

"You may be surprised to hear that I am very pleased you asked this question," the sultan said. "It is an important one. Much has been passed down through our family, and it has grown significantly over the years through investment. Did oil contribute? Yes, for a long time. But after a point, I understood oil revenues needed to be kept separately. Today they exist as an asset of the people, providing infrastructure, healthcare, and education, among other things."

Holding up the card, Adira said, "So this is yours, and using it does not hurt the citizens."

"You are correct, though I think of it as *ours*, not my own."

"I understand that the oil is running out."

The sultan nodded. "It is. Our reserves have one decade left, perhaps two."

"What happens to infrastructure and education then?"

"You have hit upon the most pressing issue we face. And while I have formulated several solutions, my illness means that much of this will fall to the next sultan to execute."

"From what I have seen, you advanced Oman two centuries in the span of almost fifty years, so you can be forgiven for not solving everything."

Adira had meant it to be a positive spin to keep her father focused on the positive. But it was clear the sultan took the matter very seriously. "It will not be easy. We should be thankful that the depression in oil prices during the pandemic showed us the world is headed away from petroleum. Naturally, we will still produce oil and gas, and even refine it for greater returns. But we must also focus the country on tourism and technology. There are also lessons for the future in the past, and I believe fishing and agriculture can return as valued segments of our socioeconomic fabric. Our family assets are now used to invest in various businesses and emerging industries here, giving them the boost they need to carry our economy in the future."

Adira could see the sultan becoming slightly distant as he worried about the future. "I am sorry to have asked. Didn't mean to upset you."

He came back to the moment and extended a hand for her own. "No. I am glad you asked. It makes me happy to help you understand our land."

"So Taimur tells me that you two rattled around the country in his old truck," she said. "I'd love to hear a story about those days."

"Did Taimur tell you about his father?" Sultan Hamad asked.

"No," Adira replied. "What was he like?"

"You recall that Taimur's father reintroduced me to Oman soon after I came to leadership?"

Adira nodded.

"He was, at the time, the most well-educated man in Arabia. An astonishing fact considering that he had been raised in the sands for much of his youth. Despite being Bedu and having the mind of an Oxford scholar, the man was, let us say, authoritarian."

Taimur chuckled. "Hamad, at that time, was an adult and had just become the sultan of a nation. Yet my father treated him like a petulant child! In some places, where the truck was not feasible due to the availability of fuel, we rode camels from camp to camp. I remember one night when we sat down to eat, he asked our travel companions if the camels had been fed and watered. They had not, and he promptly instructed His Majesty, the Sultan of Oman, to get off his derriere and see to the camels!"

The sultan assumed a low voice, " 'Go tend to them at once, Hamad!' he said. 'The camel has done more for this land than any bloody sultan!' "

All of them laughed, though the sultan's quickly deteriorated into a cough.

Adira handed him a cup from the nightstand. "Sounds like he was a character."

"He was a man that I detested, respected, and loved all at once," the sultan said after taking a small sip. Despite the water, his voice had weakened after the cough, and it was clear he was growing tired.

"I look forward to hearing more stories from Taimur," Adira said. "We should let you rest."

"I have very much enjoyed this visit, Adira."

"And I have as well. Thank you. I'm sure we will be back soon." She stood and held his hand before leaning down to kiss his cheek.

When she turned around, the others had already left. She gave her father one last smile and squeezed his hand before moving to the door. On the way, she looked back to find him watching her, his eyes held up by the hint of a smile.

Adira was enjoying this feel-good moment as she stepped into the private lobby where several uniformed soldiers of the Royal Guard were speaking in hushed, urgent tones. "What is it?" she asked.

One of the men looked to Taimur. Receiving a subtle nod, he replied, "We have found someone watching the hospital, sending messages on people entering and exiting this wing to an unknown number."

"He has been apprehended?" Taimur asked.

The man nodded. "Our investigation has already begun. We were just discussing how we will revise our protection plan."

The secretary had returned to his office. The Chairman took this as his cue to leave, giving Taimur's shoulder a squeeze and kindly lowering his head to Adira on his way out.

"Good," Taimur said to the officer. Judging by the marks on his uniform, he appeared to be in charge of the detail. "His phone. Did you look through the messages?"

Understanding why Taimur asked, he said, "We did. There was no mention of you and the sayyida or your specific vehicle. It only mentioned a 'Land Cruiser' entering and the time. Nothing describing it or who was inside."

"That is good to know, Major."

"We have not discussed security arrangements for the sayyida while she is with you."

Taimur thought for a moment before replying. "She will be my responsibility."

"Taimur—"

"It will be taken care of."

"She is a member of His Majesty's family now, which puts her at risk. She will need a protective detail."

Taimur leveled his eyes. "We have done this before."

The major nodded. "I have heard. But—"

"Right now, no one can find her. The fewer people who know where she is, the better, and you know that rotating detail will involve a lot of people."

"I will have to clear this with the colonel."

"Do as you need to. I will let your office know if conditions change."

"Please do."

"And make sure that no mention of our visits is recorded. Order your men to remain silent as well."

"We log every visitor," the major said.

"Not this one. She is a ghost."

The major nodded reluctantly. Taimur reached out and shook his hand before waving Adira to the elevator.

"Is this something we should be worried about?" Adira asked as they rode down to the car park.

"No. Threats appear for any leader. Usually, they are nothing in the end," he said.

They walked side by side to the truck. Oddly, he walked to the passenger side.

"Wait, you're not driving?"

"It is time for the practical part of your test," he said with a halfhearted chuckle. "I would like to make a few phone calls."

"But I have no idea how to get back out to the sands."

"We will do it the old-fashioned way."

"The moon? A trail of camel dung?"

Taimur leaned over the center console and pushed some buttons on the dash. "GPS."

14

Adira and Taimur took the highway through the Hajar mountains, winding up rocky passes where each sweeping turn opened to dramatic gorges below. Taimur told legends of the old villages as they passed through. Newer towns were used to describe the sultan's development plans, while older communities and ruins led to stories and myths of the past. Every now and again, Taimur's phone would ring. Adira enjoyed the cadence of his Arabic and found herself able to pick out a few phrases in the lengthy exchange of greetings.

After two hours on the road, the pair stopped at a café for lunch. Not long thereafter, they entered a small village with brilliant dunes towering in the background. Taimur guided her through the dusty streets to a small gas station where an attendant topped up their fuel and let a small amount of air out of the tires to facilitate driving in sand.

It was difficult to tell if the town was expanding into the sands or the sands were reaching into the town. Buildings thinned, and any semblance of a road vanished. Taimur simply gestured in the vague direction he wished her to follow.

Once they passed the last of the modest dwellings, Taimur pointed to a particularly large dune. "Up that one," he said.

The steep golden mountain was at least two hundred feet tall and towered over them. "We can't drive up that. It's huge!"

"We can. Circle around to the side. It is not as steep there."

Adira did. When she felt the wheel float, she slowed down.

"Don't slow," he said. "Keep your speed even with a little throttle. When your wheels are turned, they act like a plow and slow you down. You need to keep your momentum."

Adira tried a turn in the other direction to get the feel before turning back.

"Good. Now set it in four-wheel drive."

He pointed to a knob by her knee, and Adira made the adjustment.

"Now, when climbing a dune, always go straight. If you turn, it's easy to slide sideways and end up stuck or upside down."

Adira concentrated, but found it remarkably easy. Soon they were at the top. "That was fun!"

"It is not terribly difficult, is it? Ready to go down?"

"Ready."

"Over there," he said, pointing.

"That's the steep part!"

"It will be fine. Again, go straight. No turning."

Adira brought them to the edge. The hood appeared to hang straight off a cliff. All she could see was sky and scattered structures in the distance.

"Gentle and smooth," he encouraged.

She led them over the ledge. The sensation was not the fall she expected. It was more like tilting and compressing onto a large pillow.

"Very good. You want the feeling of moving just a touch faster than the sand sliding below us."

Their speed and Adira's confidence built as they descended. When they reached the bottom, Adira raised her fists and let out a triumphant squeal. "That was great!"

"You did very well!"

"Have I told you that I've never even owned a car?"

Taimur covered his eyes. "Now you tell me this?"

"Sure. I'm a pro now. What better time?"

Taimur shook his head and directed them south, deeper into the sands. He continued his instruction, teaching her how to navigate ruts and old tracks. They traversed the dunes for nearly a half hour before arriving at Taimur's camp.

They parked near a portable water tank resting precariously on a square of scaffolding about head height. A short length of hose was attached to a simple lever valve before splitting into smaller hoses in several directions.

"Desert shower?" Adira asked.

"It's also for drinking, cooking, and cleaning. Would you like a tour?"

Adira nodded. "It will be good to stretch my legs."

"The water is filled regularly by the wilayat and is the same as delivered to homes in the village via pipe."

"Wilayat?"

"Oman is divided into eleven governorates, which are like your states. Wilayat are the next division down."

"Like counties."

"If you say so. I have only visited Amrika once, and it was many years ago."

Adira pointed to a small wooden structure set away from and slightly lower than the main tents. "I imagine that is the bathroom?"

Taimur nodded. "More primitive than your hotel, and I am afraid it is on the floor and not a chair. But it has its own water for washing, and there is paper if you prefer."

Adira had learned to deal with the squatty potties, but not yet the little hose used for washing. She'd taken to carrying a pack of tissues with her and was thankful this one would have toilet paper.

Taimur circled them around the tents to another wooden structure farther away. It was a shed of a decent size that opened to a fenced pen. Inside were a half-dozen goats snoozing on some blankets and scraps of dried grasses.

"We use them mostly for milk," Taimur said.

"Mostly?"

Taimur waggled his hand back and forth, knowing she really didn't want a response.

They ambled up to the tents and around a small courtyard that had been made.

Adira looked back in the direction they came, eventually turning a full circle. Other than Taimur's camp, there was nothing but sand. "I didn't imagine there was a place on earth where you could see absolutely no one else."

"Head out that way," he said, pointing to the southwest, "and there truly is absolutely nothing. It's the Empty Quarter, the harshest environment in Arabia. This is lush in comparison."

Lush wasn't the word Adira would use. But it was beautiful. With rolling, golden dunes flowing to the horizon, the land here was somehow gentle. She slipped out of a sandal to feel the sand on her toes. "It's not hot! We're in the bright sunlight, and the sand isn't scorching. How is that?" she said, stepping out of her other sandal and burying both feet in the sand.

Taimur smiled. "Why would you think it would be hot?"

"I don't know. Maybe beaches? They get hot in the sun."

He shrugged. "It is just the way the sands are."

"I love how peaceful it is," Adira said, closing her eyes.

"It is why we come here. Please, I will show you around the tents."

Adira slipped her sandals back on, noticing the sand didn't stick to her feet like beach sand. It simply rolled off as if made of silk. She followed Taimur into a small courtyard used for greeting guests. A simple fence of sticks roughly defined the entry and offered protection from the wind.

At the center was the large tent where Adira had joined the family previously. Separate, smaller tents for sleeping were connected on either side, one for men and the other for women. Taimur walked them into the central living area, which was decidedly quiet compared to when she'd come for dinner.

"Where is everyone?" she asked.

"It is a weekday, so everyone is in Muscat. They will return this weekend. But Mariya and one of our daughters, Asma, are here. Some nephews will also join us. Come, I am sure they are in the kitchen."

He led them through a slit in the tarps into a tent dedicated to cooking. Battered, long tables served as work surfaces, one for prep, another with a few portable propane burners, and a third with buckets and a makeshift tap for cleaning. A stubby old fridge stood sentry in the corner, softly wheezing.

"*As-salaam-alaikum,*" Adira said as she entered. "It smells delicious in here."

"*Walaikum as-salaam,*" Taimur's wife, Mariya, and Asma replied in unison.

Mariya came forward and held out her hands to grasp Adira's. "It is our pleasure to have you visit again," she said. The elderly woman's hands were dry and wrinkled, but strong.

"Thank you for having me," Adira replied. Taimur's daughter sat in front of some books and a laptop at a round table off to the side. Adira turned to her and said, "Asma, it is good to see you again. I am sorry we didn't have the chance to talk much last time I was here."

"We will have time this week," she replied. "No classes for me."

"You're at university?" Adira asked.

"Teaching, actually. Research as well. Postdoctoral work." She raised her palms up. "I know; what is a forty-five-year-old woman doing back in school? But my children are all grown, and I needed a new challenge."

"Asma is focusing on land rights and the Bedu," Taimur said. "Somehow, she balances research for the Chairman of the Supreme Court with her own research."

"And teaching," Asma added.

"I am very impressed," Adira said.

"I am very close to needing to turn some research in today," Asma said.

"How do you submit any work out here? There's no cell service, and I didn't even see a light last time I was here."

"There's a small generator, and a sat phone if we need to hotspot. But it's so slow that I will dash down to the house before dinner."

"The house?" Adira asked, confused.

"He didn't tell you?" Asma said, the sides of her mouth turning up. "We just come here on weekends. You drove right by the house on the way up."

"So are you a fake Bedouin!" Adira said to Taimur with a laugh.

Taimur held his hands wide in innocence. "How would I be able to watch Formula One here?"

All four of them laughed.

"The days of the roaming pastoral Bedouin are passing us, I'm afraid. The towns have drawn everyone in with the lure of easy access to the horrors of fast food," Taimur said.

"And electricity," added Asma.

"Which we don't always need," replied Taimur, raising a finger.

"Except during Formula 1," Asma said.

"We honor our ancestry by spending our weekends here as a family." Taimur turned to Adira and pretended to whisper, "It is helpful that the races are on Sunday, which is not the weekend in this part of the world!"

"It is actually very nice," Asma said. "My husband and children have enjoyed coming to the sands on the weekends their whole lives."

"It's freeing to be out here," Adira said.

"Exactly," Asma said. "But I'm off now. See you for dinner."

"*Ma'a ssalama,*" Adira said.

Her parents bid their goodbyes as well.

"Can I help?" Adira asked Mariya.

"I would like that very much," Mariya replied.

Adira went to work chopping onions, chilies, garlic, and other vegetables. Mariya ground cumin, coriander, and cinnamon, and cracked cardamom pods to extract the small black seeds. Standing side by side with Mariya was comforting, but also new. In the homes she'd been shuffled through as a child, food came from boxes and drive-through windows.

They set about making a base for curry first, allowing yellow onions to sweat and slowly caramelize before adding garlic, ginger, and chilies. After a few minutes, Mariya instructed Adira to make a well in the middle, to which she added cumin, coriander, and cinnamon. As the spices toasted and their oils released, the tent filled with beautiful scents. Turmeric and some cloves were added, followed by toasted coconut powder and a broth before being set aside. Mariya explained that vegetables and chicken would be added later.

Another pot was pulled from beneath the table to make a coconut creamed spinach. Again, Adira began with onions before adding chili, tomatoes, and spinach. A small amount of water and coconut powder was added, and the pot was left to gently simmer.

Adira walked around the tent. The structure was held together mostly with wooden poles, with carpets covering the sand, and thin slivers of wood or rattan on the walls and beneath the tarps that made the roof. On one of the support poles hung a crooked picture of the sultan. Another showed a middle-age woman with a loving round face and a broad smile.

"Who is this?" Adira asked.

"This was my mother, Shamsaa."

"A beautiful name."

"Thank you. It means 'sunshine.' She brought light with her wherever she went."

"I can see it in that smile," Adira said. "Did she teach you to cook?"

"She did. Her ancestors were from Zanzibar, where the spinach recipe is from."

"And the curry?"

"That is from India. Our food is a history book for Oman. Every taste has its roots in a different part of the world."

"The smell," Adira said, inhaling deeply. "It's the smell of these dishes that is so beautiful."

"You are very kind, Adira. But I am sure you would like to rest before dinner."

Mariya took Adira through the main tent and out to the women's tent, where a small room had been created with fabric hanging from wood slats in the ceiling. A bowl and pitcher sat in the corner, and Adira washed before letting the silence of the desert lull her into a peaceful sleep.

The sun had just set when Adira returned to the kitchen. Two large platters rested on a table, each with a bed of rice covered by large portions of spinach and curry. Mariya slid one to the edge of the table and carried the other into the main tent. Adira followed right behind.

Asma and Taimur were in quiet conversation when the ladies joined them. Taimur's eyes lit up at the sight of the food. "I do love your spinach!" he said.

Mariya smiled appreciatively and set the platter on the carpet between them. They sat down, and Adira asked, "What were you two talking about?"

Asma stole a glance at Taimur before replying. "I was just hearing about your day," she said. "You met Doctor Safa? She's one of my heroes."

"She was spectacular," Adira said. "She made me feel so comfortable. Even confident in a strange way. It was great."

Asma showed a broad smile. "That's exactly her! I don't know how she does it."

"And I imagine your other hero is your father?"

Taimur rolled his eyes, and Asma chuckled. "Of course!"

The four of them took their time enjoying the meal, laughing and sharing stories. Afterward, Adira helped Mariya and Asma with the dishes, a little surprised at how easily she'd fallen into a traditional female role.

As she set a dried pot down on one of the tables, she remembered the second platter of food resting in the empty space earlier. At dinner, they'd only used one. Perhaps the second was simply left too cool and would be served tomorrow.

15

The following day, despite sleeping on a thin mattress in a tent in the middle of the desert, Adira was well-rested. The family gathered in the kitchen for a breakfast of breads and coffee before Asma left to return to the city. Mariya and Adira cleaned the kitchen, batted mats and carpets, and prepared for meals later in the day. Taimur joined them in the kitchen to help Adira with her feeble Arabic. When the kitchen chores were done, Taimur and Adira refilled the kitchen water supply and tended to the goats. As the day became hotter, Taimur declared it an ideal time to continue her language lessons in the shade of the tent.

While Adira had wanted to make the drive back down to the hospital the next morning, the doctors asked for another twenty-four hours. His Majesty had been uncomfortable the night before and had not slept well. Taimur continued to work with Adira on her Arabic before moving on to a history lesson.

He began not with Oman but East Africa, where climate change had sent early man across a then-shallow Red Sea to the Arabian Peninsula in search of more habitable land. As these tribes settled across the Middle East, Muscat became a central hub of trade.

Ideally situated for access to Africa, Arabia, Persia, and India, the eastern point of the Arabian Peninsula became well known for its merchants and well-protected harbor. Naturally, local copper and frankincense changed hands, but so did silks, spices, pearls, and gold. Everyone from the Babylonians to the Persians and Assyrians cast an envious eye on the Pearl of Arabia.

As Islam expanded in the seventh century, one group saw Oman as a place of refuge. After being forced out of Persia for not taking a side in the civil war following Mohammed's death, the Ibadi Muslims settled in central Oman and formed an imamate system of governance.

For centuries, Oman was divided by dynasties, imamates, and foreign empires desperate for control. Persians, Ottomans, and the Portuguese all made valiant efforts, and all had some success in conquering certain regions, but they were never able to control the entirety of Oman.

The first to do so was an imam in the seventeenth century who drove the Portuguese out and expanded Oman down the east coast of Africa. In 1749, amid the turmoil following the Persians trying once again, the first of Adira's relatives came to power. His reign was powerful and prosperous, and the empire expanded even farther into what is known today as Pakistan.

But as the reins transferred down the family line, clashes between the religious interior and the coastal seat of power saw vast swaths of territory lost and the economy collapse. By the early 1960s, tensions with the south escalated to full-scale civil war. Rebels from Dhofar fought the sultan's control with an eye to form their own nation.

British troops arrived to support the sultan, fighting a war not unlike the one Americans were fighting at the same time in Vietnam. As battles raged on, it became clear that the only solution would be a leadership change. Knowing eyes turned to a young Omani who'd recently graduated from Sandhurst.

"And who do you think that might have been?" Taimur asked.

"Hamad bin Sabir," Adira replied.

Taimur nodded. "Your father."

"So what happened? He just walked in and stopped a rebel movement? I don't think it's that easy."

"I will leave that to our dinner guest to explain," Taimur said.

"Who's the guest?"

"One of the rebels," Taimur said with a wink.

Mariya, who had clearly been listening to the Taimur's stories from the kitchen, arrived then with a late lunch. Afterward, Taimur left to pick up their guest, and Adira helped Mariya clean the kitchen and prepare for dinner.

Adira took a walk around the compound and decided to visit the goats. After letting herself into the pen, two of them hopped quickly out of the shed and began to circle her.

"They think you have food," came a voice from above.

Adira jumped back, nearly stepping on one of the goats. Her legs crossed over one another, and she fell. A laugh echoed down from atop the shed, followed by the creak of a wooden ladder.

A young man came around the corner wearing a tan dishdasha and tasseled olive mussar. "I am sorry to scare you," he said with a cheeky smile.

A rifle hung loosely from his shoulder. Adira stood, unsure.

"Who are you?" she asked.

"I am Sam," he replied. Recognizing she was taking a step back, he held his hands up slowly. "I am a friend, Sayyida. Taimur is my uncle. He has asked my family to watch over the camp. Here, this is my brother, Wasim." He pointed to the form of someone on a cot that had been set up in the back of the shed.

Adira took a deep breath and collected herself, understanding that these were the young men Taimur had called in to look after them. She held out her hand, which Sam reluctantly stepped forward and shook. "*Ahlan.* Nice to meet you, Sam."

"*As-salaam-alaikum*, Sayyida."

"*Walaikum as-salaam.* Please, call me Adira."

He smiled and bowed his head, placing his right hand over his heart.

"What, exactly, are you watching for?"

"Uninvited guests," he replied. "My uncle wishes your visit to be quiet."

"You don't need a rifle for uninvited guests."

His hands opened. "Perhaps not. But if the guest intends you harm, it is better to have it, don't you think?"

Adira looked him over more carefully. His smile seemed genuine. He was about her age. Strong, and given his English, well-educated.

"I have heard from my uncle that the Royal Guard wanted to protect you here. But we are better," he said, steering them to the pen's gate.

Adira stepped through, realizing he wanted to talk without waking his brother. "How's that?"

"We have lived in the sands all our lives. This is our backyard," he waved a hand toward the dunes. "And you have given my family a miracle."

"How's that?"

"Many years ago, our grandfather protected His Majesty in the sands when he learned from Taimur's father. So you see, us coming to protect you while you learn from Taimur? It has been our destiny all along," he held his hand to his heart again.

Adira was both touched and embarrassed. She'd never been one to draw attention to herself, as a child in the system or an adult at work. The fuss—from the news to how people had looked at her in the Palace—wasn't her. She'd felt studied like some form of object more than once over the past couple of days.

Sam, however, didn't look at her as a curiosity. He was genuinely appreciative.

Adira turned and faced him. "Well, Sam, thank you for looking out for us," she said. "Thank your brother too."

"Brothers. And cousins. There are more of us in the dunes and some in my uncle's house."

Adira's eyes widened briefly. "Wow. Sorry for the fuss."

Sam's smile widened even further. "It is our pleasure, Sayyida Adira."

She wrapped her own smile in mock disapproval. "I told you; it's just Adira."

He gave a wave and returned to his perch, leaving her to privately explore the dunes.

16

Their dinner guest was a slight old man. His rough, dark skin was heavy with wrinkles around his eyes and mouth, which gave the appearance of a permanent sneer. Taimur introduced him as Nadir.

"It is a pleasure to meet you," Adira said in Arabic. Knowing a male would never initiate physical contact with a woman, she reached out to shake his hand. Most of the men she'd encountered responded by extending their own hand in return.

Nadir did not.

Taimur interjected in an effort to move past the awkward moment. "I see you have been practicing your Arabic greetings. Please, go on."

Lowering her arm, she gave him a questioning look.

"Please, continue," he prompted.

"Yes, yes. Sorry." Turning back to Nadir, she continued in Arabic. "Welcome. How was your journey?"

"Long," he replied in English.

So the sneer came from inside, not decades in the desert sun. "Please, join us inside. Can I offer you water or coffee?" Adira continued, hoping her attempt at practicing Bedouin hospitality didn't sound as forced as it felt.

The little man made a clicking noise with his tongue and walked past her into the main tent.

Adira turned to Taimur, her eyebrows up in question.

"It was a long drive from the airport," Taimur said. "We will let him rest before dinner."

"I'll see if Mariya needs a hand in the kitchen," she said, leaving Taimur to deal with their guest by himself.

In the kitchen area, Mariya was rolling out flat rounds of bread and cooking them on a hot iron pan. "So you have met Nadir?" she asked.

"Tried to make a good impression," Adira said. "Didn't go so well."

Mariya stopped rolling and looked over to Adira. "Your Arabic has been coming along well. What was the problem?"

"Wasn't my Arabic. He just hated me."

Mariya gave a low chuckle. "He is old-fashioned, and gruff at times."

"A little different from that," Adira mumbled before asking, "What can I do?"

Mariya handed her a spatula and pointed to the pan. "That is ready," she said. Adira removed the thin round of bread and set it atop one cooling nearby. Mariya passed her the dough she'd been rolling, and before long, the two women had a nice stack wrapped in a towel to keep soft.

While Adira chopped Persian cucumbers, tomatoes, and red onions to make a salad, Mariya closely monitored the last few minutes of the beef she'd stewed all day. What had looked like a rather plain piece of meat in a simple pot of water that morning had become a soft, caramelized thing of beauty as the water evaporated and the spices intensified. When the last wisp of steam escaped to the tarp above them, Mariya shut off the burner and turned to find Adira standing beside her with two wide bowls.

"I see you have met the young men outside?" Mariya said with a smile.

"I have. Seems a bit silly."

Mariya shrugged. "It keeps Taimur happy," she said, spooning portions of the sticky beef. "And it is better than having His Majesty's guards here."

Adira nodded. "The boy I met was very nice, so I imagine it is."

Once Mariya had put half the beef into the first bowl, Adira placed a small stack of breads on top. With her other hand, she picked up another bowl already filled with half of the salad. Mariya stood to the side, allowing her to pass into the main tent. Instead, Adira went the opposite direction, nudging the layers of tarp aside to head out to the sands. "The boys have been out in the sun all day keeping us safe," she said with a wink. "I'll take this out and be back in a minute."

Mariya smiled to herself and began filling the second bowl.

Outside, the sun had fallen low on the horizon, hovering just above the goats' shelter. Adira could just see two forms on the roof. Sam and Wasim.

"Ready for dinner?" she shouted up as she approached.

"That is very kind, Sayyida Adira," came a reply. One of the young men stood up.

"I'll come around," Adira said. She circled the pen to find Sam standing at the foot of the ladder.

His face lit up in a smile as she approached. "*Shukran jazeelah!*" *Thank you very much!*

He took the two bowls from her and turned toward the ladder. Realizing he couldn't climb up with both hands full, he shouted up to the roof. "Wasim!"

"I'll take one," Adira said, reaching out for the salad. "Gives me a chance to see your view."

"Are you sure, Sayyida Adira?"

"It's just Adira, Sam," she said, grabbing the side of the ladder.

Atop the shelter, Adira introduced herself to Wasim before taking a seat near the edge facing the family tent and the valley below. "Nice up here," she said. "Bet the sunset is beautiful."

"It is," Sam said, though his tone contradicted the response.

Adira's brow rose in question.

Wasim explained, "When the sun touches the horizon, it glows brightly in one place. It blinds us from seeing that area."

"But it is only for one minute or two, Sayyida Adira. Do not worry."

"Not worried about that at all, Sam. I'm more worried that you have to stay out here away from your families. Are either of you married? Kids?"

Wasim looked at Sam and smiled.

"What?" Adira asked.

Sam replied. "Neither of us is married." His hand waved in the direction of Taimur's tent and the village. "And our family is here with us."

Adira looked at Wasim. "Then why are you smiling."

"There is a girl in our village that Sam would like to marry. He is hoping his parents and hers will come to an agreement while we are gone."

"Wasim! This is not the concern of Sayyida Adira!" Sam said, his tone beginning serious before a smile broke through. Wasim laughed, and soon the other two joined him.

"Well, Sam, I hope your dream comes true," Adira said, giving his shoulder a playful shake. "But I should get back. Taimur wants me to spend time with the old grump he brought in."

Wasim's lips tightened. "He is an important man, Sayyida Adira. You would do well to treat him with respect."

The sudden seriousness of his voice caught her off guard. "Why's that?"

The brothers looked at one another, not sure what they should say.

Finally, Sam broke the silence. "He is Mushir."

Adira gave him a questioning look.

"Mushir is the highest officer rank in the military. Like a general, perhaps more," Sam explained.

"Taimur said he was a rebel. From Dhofar."

"Yes, this is true. He was. But many years after the war, His Majesty bestowed this title upon him."

"So that crotchety man is in charge of all Oman's military?"

Sam waggled his head. "No. Mushir Nadir is an elder and is retired. His title is honorific, given to show His Majesty's trust in him as an adviser."

"Please, Sayyida Adira, be respectful to this man," Wasim said. "He is important to us."

"I'll give it a shot," she said, a resigned look on her face as she stood. On her way down the ladder, she pointed at the pair. "But only for you two."

They shouted down their thanks and watched her make her way back to the kitchen area.

Adira returned to find both Mariya and the serving bowls missing. Just as well, she thought. Remembering what she'd just promised outside, she pasted a halfhearted smile on and entered the main tent.

"Ah, there you are!" exclaimed Taimur.

"Wanted to get dinner out to the boys first," Adira replied. "Sorry I took too long."

Nadir regarded her with a stern look. Or perhaps it was his only look. Adira hadn't decided yet.

"When we were swamped in the hospital—after a large casualty event or anything awful like that—the staff gets worn out fast," she said. "I'd have food sent in and make sure the nurses, med students, and interns ate first. They're the ones working hardest, and we'd need to keep them on their feet," she said, carefully lowering herself onto one of the cushions encircling the dinner platters. "Even though the residents and attendings are higher ranking and act like princes, most of them get it."

Seated now, Adira turned her eyes to Nadir and smiled at her little dig. A silence hung between them.

Taimur's eyebrows popped up at the exchange. He let a second pass before reaching forward with a small piece of bread and using it to pinch some of the soft meat out of the bowl. "Smells delicious, Mariya," he said with a hint of a smile in the corner of his eye.

As they ate, Taimur explained the history he'd shared with Adira earlier in the day. Nadir would occasionally interject, directing questions or comments to Taimur, his disposition remaining surly. When they had finished, Adira went to stand and help Mariya. But Mariya placed a hand gently on her arm. "This time is for you, dear," she said.

Taimur lowered his head in thanks to Mariya and then turned to Adira. "I believe we left off with you asking how a new sultan might stop a rebellion?"

Adira nodded. "It sounds like the people of Dhofar didn't want to be a part of Oman."

"We didn't."

"So you rebelled. And fought."

"It was more complicated than that. Rebelling can be messy." Nadir paused, using the back of his hand to wipe the corners of his mouth. "Something I am sure you understand."

Adira conceded the point.

After a deep breath, Nadir continued, "The sultan at the time, Sabir, was disliked by the people of Dhofar. Our culture, and even our ethnicity, were different from his. As if this was not difficult enough, he pushed us back in time, banning our access to everything modern. We, the Dhofari, joined together in arms to escape his rule. Our forces were small initially, but our guerrilla tactics stung, and the British soon worried the sultan could fall. They sent troops to help Sabir hold his seat of power."

"But it wasn't your grandfather, Sabir, they were protecting," interjected Taimur. "It was the oil that was only then ready to flow. They weren't going to let it fall into the hands of rebels."

Nadir nodded. "While the British had been in the region for some time, the Chinese and Soviets—even Cuba and the North Koreans—became interested in our rebellion's opportunity. They brought arms and money and trained us in the arts of assassination and sabotage. At the same time, they planted the seeds of Marxism. Our simple rebellion soon became a war."

The story captivated Adira. "A proxy war. For communism," she mumbled. He'd been a part of a war that could have changed the balance of power in this part of the world.

"Exactly," Nadir replied.

"Why hasn't anyone heard about this? I mean, the Chinese and Soviets fighting the British? That's a pretty big deal," Adira said.

"Why do Americans not know about this, I think you mean? The answer is simple. You were involved with your own war at the time."

Adira gave him a questioning look.

"Vietnam," he replied.

Adira understood. "A conflict involving American troops would win in American history books."

"Indeed," Nadir said.

"So what happened?"

"The frequency and intensity of battles increased over several years. And even though Sultan Sabir was holding ground, he was stubborn and not proceeding as the British dictated. The risk if he lost terrified the British. A communist government had just formed in Yemen, our neighbor to the west. If Sabir fell and Oman became communist, it would impact the entirety of the Arabian Peninsula. The British needed to change the course of the war. They needed to play a trump card."

"They put my father into power," Adira said.

The two men nodded.

"But I thought he overthrew his father?" she asked.

"Changes of power are messy affairs," Taimur said. "The British turned one of Sabir's advisers and used him as an assassin. His attempt failed, but it was enough for the British to push your father into power."

"What happened to Sabir?" Adira asked.

"He was sent in exile to Great Britain, where he lived in The Dorchester for two years before passing away from wounds sustained during the coup," Taimur said.

Nadir continued the story. "His Majesty knew his entire life that he would need to carry the mantle of leadership at some point. The British pushed the first domino, and he knew his duty was to lead Oman out of this conflict."

"Duty to the people of Oman over family. Same as my mother."

Taimur looked down and slowly nodded.

"So this transfer of power ended the war?" Adira asked.

"No. Not for several years," Taimur replied.

Adira urged them to continue.

"Ending a guerrilla war is not easy," Taimur said. "To the rebels, at least at first, it was just another member of the same family in charge."

"And that was my mindset," Nadir continued, "when a communiqué came through requesting I meet with a delegate sent by His Majesty." His eyes closed, and his head tilted to the wooden poles at the top of the tent. He appeared lost for a moment, the scowl evaporating as he went back in time.

"It was the first 'peace talk' I had been a part of as the leader of a group of rebels. Our village had been one of the first to fight, and while many others fell for the lure of communism, we had not. Our goal remained focused on independence, which is likely why I was selected to attend this talk.

"The meeting was to occur on a flat expanse of rock at a wadi deep in the hills. I'd instructed most of my men to wait with me above the wadi. If it was a trap, I wanted to have the high ground. Below us, carpets had been laid where the meeting would take place. A few of my men were stationed there, presenting themselves as a receiving party, which I was sure the Palace delegation would expect.

"The day of the meeting came and went, so we stayed in position through the night. At dawn the next day, my men fired up a small stove to make tea and we circled around it for warmth.

"A voice came from behind some rocks. 'May I offer some bread in exchange for a cup of tea?' the voice said. We looked up to see a young man wearing a tattered dishdasha, carrying something wrapped in a purple mussar.

"One of my men asked who he was. The others leveled their carbines in his direction, worried the stranger was hiding a weapon.

"Slowly, the man lifted a corner of the mussar, and with a smile, he revealed what was, in fact, a large stack of fresh bread. In the calming voice we will always know him for, he said, 'Sorry to be late, Nadir. I am Hamad.'"

Adira laughed. "He snuck into your camp?"

"We never even heard a footstep," Nadir admitted.

"But that was your chance. Your chance to kill him and win the war," Adira concluded.

Nadir's mouth flattened and he nodded.

"But you didn't. Why?"

Nadir did not reply.

"The bread?" she asked. "No, wait. It's because he asked for tea. You can't decline to help someone in the desert, right?"

"Not even your enemy," Taimur said.

Nadir waved his hand. "It was those things, of course. But we were honorable men of war and had given our word to meet. Hamad came forward slowly and took a seat between my men. He spoke with them first, asking their names as he handed out bread to them. He inquired as to the status of our food and water supply, offering to have some brought up. They declined, of course.

"Eventually, he spoke to me. 'Thank you for meeting me here, Nadir. I have come to ask a simple question. What do you and your men want? What do you fight this war for?'

"I explained to him that we wanted our freedom from the sultanate.

" 'Yes, I understand this,' he replied. 'But what do you want independence for? Why do the Dhofari need your campaign to be successful?'

"I remember then becoming angry. I explained how as a people, we were seen as secondary to the sultanate, an afterthought. We needed hospitals, schools, and roads. Access to the outside to provide opportunity for our people. We needed to be seen, our culture respected.

"I remember standing up, ranting and insulting. But the whole time, your father remained calm. Listening. When I finally ran out of steam, he turned to my men. By name—he had remembered each of their names—he asked each of them the same question. They, too, were angry. Strong in their beliefs.

"When the last man had finally finished, your father opened his arms and looked directly at me. 'I want you to have these things. I want all of our people to have these things. And I will honor this request. Our people deserve no less.'

"This, of course, was ridiculous. I knew it was a trick. I recall spitting on the ground, asking him, 'So now you will want a cease-fire. For us to turn in our weapons and bow before you as our supreme leader?' I asked him.

"He was so calm then, just as he has always been. 'I do not expect you to bow, nor do I want your weapons,' he said. 'But I expect you—each of you—to think about my promise to you before you raise them in anger again.'

"I laughed in his face. 'So this is all you offer us? A promise?'

" 'It is,' he replied. 'My promise to you.'

" 'Young sultan,' I said to him. 'I will enjoy slitting your throat when your promise proves hollow.'

"Your father then reached down to his waist and unclipped the leather belt holding his khanjar. You know the khanjar? The knife we carry on our waists? He wrapped the belt around the silver scabbard and held it to me, saying, 'If this day comes, I deserve no less.' "

Adira blinked, processing how tense this exchange must have been on top of a mountain in the middle of a war. She regarded the little man more carefully and asked, "So that meeting stopped the war?"

Taimur laughed. "Not even close."

"The war continued with its ebbs and flows for quite some time," Nadir said. "One day, my men and I returned to our village to find a crew of men next to the mosque. They carried only tools and supplies and not a single weapon. They had just laid the foundation for a school. It was only then that I believed the young sultan."

"He was true to his word," Adira said.

Nadir nodded. "Word spread, and soon more rebels switched to his side. They, too, saw him live up to his promises, and eventually, our nation found peace."

"Sounds to me like you're the one responsible," Adira said to Nadir. "If you hadn't given him a chance, we might not be sitting here now."

Taimur let out a hearty laugh. "That's exactly what Hamad always says!"

Nadir's serene expression began to fade. He grunted and turned to look outside the tent to sands that had turned dark. After a moment, he slowly turned back to face Adira. "Your father surprised you as well," he said. "After what you've learned about your family, what do you plan to do?"

She'd not drawn the exact parallel. "My father and Taimur think it's a good idea for me to spend some time out here. My plans after that are open-ended."

"You've arrived to find your connection to royalty. I am sure you've considered this…considered what you may feel entitled to."

Heat filled Adira's cheeks and rose to her ears. Why this snide little man had come to visit was now clear. "You're interested in what I want. You think I'm here to take something."

"We've had centuries of invaders. None of them came out of the kindness of their heart," he quipped.

"Invader?" she replied to his affront. "I didn't come here looking for anything."

Nadir nodded, his eyebrows inching up.

Adira leaned forward. "That insinuation means so much, coming from a terrorist who declared war on my family."

Taimur raised a hand. "Adira, that is—"

"Let her finish," Nadir commanded.

"I was invited here to work. It was something I did precisely 'with kindness in my heart,' " Adira said, her cadence slow and deliberate, her gold eyes locked with Nadir's. "It is something, really the only thing, that I do well. I look after people who need a little help."

Nadir let out a grunt of displeasure and then went silent. Adira eventually stood.

She moved close to the old man without breaking eye contact until she stood above him. Slowly bending down, she brought her face inches from his own. "I came here to give. I don't want to take a goddamn thing."

She remained there a moment. Waiting. When he didn't snap back, she finally spoke. "Maybe it's you that wanted something all along. Maybe back up on that mountain, you wanted to throw my father off the edge and take the throne yourself?"

Taimur was clearly upset. "Adira, you've gone too f—"

Adira turned to him and quickly held up her hand. "Too far? Maybe so."

She stood up and looked down at Nadir. "But I've found that almost everyone here is far more hospitable than you. Chief among them is my father, and I'd rather be with him in his last days than sit here with someone still bitter over the past."

She turned and walked toward a flap at the back of the tent. Before pulling the canvas aside, she looked back. "I'm also getting my job back. You know, the one that helps people rather than puts them down with wild accusations? So it looks like I'll be here a while, Nadir. Maybe we'll meet on a mountain top someday, and *you* can apologize."

And with that, she strode purposefully into the night.

17

Adira woke the following day in Muscat, nestled in her soft bed at the Al Bustan Palace Hotel. After stretching her arms above her head, she rang down to the front desk, ordered breakfast for three, and then showered.

She'd just finished dressing in long pants and the one clean top she had left that covered her shoulders when the door chimed. The clatter of metal and plastic on tile followed. A torrent of Arabic came next.

"Relax, guys, it's just breakfast," she said, walking into the suite's living room. "Put the gun down, Wasim. Eggs aren't a threat."

The boys had been happy to see her turn up in the goat shed the night before. The feeling quickly disappeared when she'd asked to borrow their car. They explained that there was no way she could possibly leave Taimur's camp, and a brief argument ensued. It didn't take long for them to realize that she was leaving with or without them, and that the best course of action would be to stay with her.

Adira opened the door and greeted two of the restaurant staff. They set the table in the dining area and efficiently laid out an assortment of dishes. The boys' eyes went wide as the cloches were removed. They didn't have to be asked to take a seat.

As they dug in, Adira poured a cup of coffee for each of them and, last, herself. "Thank you for the ride down here last night. I know it wasn't what you were expecting."

Sam waved his hand across the table. With a mouthful of date bread, he said, "This does not make up for it."

Adira picked up a bowl of golden scrambled eggs and spooned some onto their plates. "Not even a little bit?" she asked with a cheeky smile.

Sam reached out for a croissant. "I will decide after I try everything."

Adira smiled. "You do that. When you're done, I'd like to go to the hospital. If you want to go back to the sands, I understand. The hotel can give me a ride."

Sam shook his head. "No, you are our responsibility, Sayyida Adira. We will take you."

Adira looked over to Wasim.

"We will take you," Wasim said. Looking down at his phone, he added, "Some of our brothers are here now too. They will help."

During their drive, Adira had seen Wasim on the phone and expected he'd been in touch with his family. It made no difference who knew where she was now. Her mind was set. She'd stay in Muscat for her father's final days, visiting him as his energy level permitted.

But after that—what to do after his passing—was a question she'd frequently asked herself over the past few days. The urge to run, to hop on a plane out of the country, was surprisingly absent. More than anything, she was determined to rejoin her friends at the clinic. Her time with them was exciting. Rewarding. She'd felt valued. Like she belonged. It was, she reflected, the happiest she'd ever been. No matter how many people told her it was impossible, she would get her clinic job back. As the boys finished breakfast, she messaged Zahra and Amir to see if they might join her for dinner.

It was at the hospital an hour later that the elevator doors on the sultan's private floor opened to chaos. The Royal Guard commander on duty was in a heated argument with a bearded young man with a carbine hanging loosely over his shoulder. While Adira hadn't met him, the family resemblance to Sam and Wasim—not to mention the dusty sandals and old rifle—made it clear her desert guardians had sent a brother or cousin in advance.

"Gentlemen," she said, striding up to the pair. "You will lower your voices right now. We would all like His Majesty to weather his illness in peace."

Her boldness and calm authority shocked them enough to immediately cease.

She knew better than to ask what the problem was, knowing full well she was it. "Officer," she said to the guard that appeared in charge, not really knowing his rank. "I know this is unusual, but these men are with me. They will only be here during my visit and will be respectful of your authority."

She looked both men in the eyes, then quickly continued before they had a chance to protest. "I will check with the doctor, then pay His Majesty a brief visit. No argument is going to be worthwhile. You're all here for the same goal. Align in that purpose."

And with that, she turned and strode swiftly past them to the large desk where a female nurse sat, Dr. Daoud right behind her.

"Nicely done," Daoud said to her. "It usually takes thunder, lightning, and floods to stop an Arabian argument."

The nurse smiled conspiringly. "Or one sayyida."

Adira gave her a wink before asking Daoud, "How is he doing today?"

The doctor took a deep breath. "He's taken a downward turn. Symptoms are worsening, and his energy today is very low. I am sorry, Sayyida."

"Is he awake? Can I go in?" she asked, pointing to the door.

"He has a visitor, I'm afraid."

Adira flicked both eyebrows up.

"They have long been friends, I understand. He said his visit would be brief."

Adira nodded. Without asking, she walked to the door and entered. A man seated close to His Majesty's bed turned at the sound.

"We have been blessed by Allah today," the man said, his voice low and powerful. "She looks just like you, Hamad!"

"*As-salaam-alaikum,*" she said. "I am Adira."

"I know, dear girl." He broke into a smile. "I am Omar."

"It is a pleasure to meet you," Adira replied, taking in the man she had heard good things about.

While the comparison in a Muslim country wasn't fair, Omar looked like an Arab version of Santa Claus. Round with a full white beard and a twinkle in his spectacled eyes. It would be difficult not to like him.

Adira moved to the bed to see her father. His skin color had changed, and his eyelids hung low. But she could see his eyes held a smile. "Hello, Baba," she said, grabbing his frail hand.

"It is good to see you, darling," he said. His hand turned to grip hers. The movement was slow, with less strength than she'd hoped.

"Feeling a little low today?" she asked, sliding a chair over and taking a seat next to Omar.

"I have finally resorted to this," His Majesty said, lifting a handle with a small button. Morphine.

"Use it as you need to. But no operating heavy machinery afterward, okay?"

Hamad turned to Omar. "Have the valet take the bulldozer back to the car park."

"Of course, my friend," Omar replied with a sad smile.

"Adira spoke of you recently," Hamad said to him. "I am glad you have this chance to meet."

Omar gave her a questioning look.

Adira shrugged. "I've been working at a mobile clinic. Your name came up, always in positive ways."

Omar opened his hands. "Your father granted me a position that affords some exposure. With his guidance, it has generally been successful."

"Foreign Minister, right?"

Omar nodded. "Like the Secretary of State in America."

"A friend told me my first day here that Oman is friends with everyone. That can't be easy. The world can be a messy place."

"Ah, the messy problems we leave in the desert for the sands and time to hide!" he joked.

Adira waited, letting him understand her question was serious.

"As a goal, it is quite simple," Omar said, his throaty voice softened by a gentle smile. "If we appreciate that each nation has taken its own path through history, it allows us to respect the differences in culture and governance."

"You make it sound much easier than it probably is," Adira said. "What if the other country is bad? Evil?"

Omar turned to Sultan Hamad. "My, she does get to the point, doesn't she?"

"If I've stepped too far—" Adira started.

"No, this is good. You ask, essentially, how to face someone with values that oppose your own."

Adira nodded.

"When we engage with other nations, it is very often as a mediator. We enter these negotiations knowing our path through history, and therefore values, will be different. But our role is always to remain neutral. This is the way we can bring peace."

Adira's head rose to break in. Omar gestured for her patience for a moment longer.

"Are some states labeled evil by other states, such as America? Of course. But if we maintain our neutrality—if they have our trust—then we've opened the door to talks that would otherwise be shut. If those talks can bring peace—save lives, even if only for a moment—don't we have the responsibility to do so?"

Sultan Hamad observed the expression on Adira's face. "I see that you can understand this, Adira. That you've drawn a parallel to your own experiences."

She turned to him and nodded softly, surprised he could tell exactly what had run through her mind. "It's not exactly the same, but yes. I understand. I understand your duty."

Sultan Hamad turned to Omar. "Our Adira is a nurse. She has undoubtedly used her gifted hands to heal those who have harmed."

Adira opened her hands. "At the hospital, we, as you say, remain neutral. Our job is to heal. We let judges judge, not us."

"So you understand. It is not always easy," Omar said. A moment passed before he sat upright and rubbed his hands down his thighs, signaling a change of subject. "What are your plans, Adira?"

"Hopefully, meeting up with some friends and getting my job back," she replied.

Sultan Hamad smiled. Omar regarded both of them curiously. "Your job?"

"I was invited here as a nurse."

"Why are you having her work, my friend?" Omar asked Sultan Hamad. "Surely this isn't necessary."

"He's not *having* me work. Working is *my* choice," Adira replied icily. "At least it was. Now I have to convince them I won't be trouble."

Sultan Hamad slowly raised a finger. "Perhaps before that, you might speak with Taimur? I understand you left rather unexpectedly?"

"You've been with Taimur?" Omar interjected.

Adira responded to both of them with a forward tip of her head.

"And will you go back to the sands?" Sultan Hamad asked.

Adira pitched her eyes to the ceiling. After a pause, she brought them down to meet her father's. "I will," she finally responded. "Today was to visit you and talk to the doctors about rejoining the clinic."

Sultan Hamad reached out a hand to touch Adira's. "They will be fortunate to have you."

Omar glanced to the door before standing. "I will let you have a moment."

Adira stood as well, though she wasn't sure why. It just seemed the right thing to do. "It was very nice to meet you, ah, sir."

He leaned forward and quietly said, "Your Excellency. At least, that is what people are instructed to say. Though I would be honored if you would call me Omar."

Adira saw him wink. "Of course. Omar, then," she said.

He turned to the sultan. "Goodbye, my friend. I will see you soon,"

Sultan Hamad nodded, and Omar left the room.

"Wow, he has a presence," Adira said, retaking her seat.

Sultan Hamad nodded before changing the subject. "You know, do you not, that I consider Nadir a friend."

"I do," she said, offering nothing further.

"It is worthwhile, with some people, to make an effort."

"I agree," she said, sitting up straight, preparing for the lecture that might very well come. "You might remind him of this."

To her surprise, His Majesty the Sultan closed his eyes and laughed. "Yes, he can be insufferable sometimes."

Adira was happy to laugh with him.

"I suspect," Sultan Hamad said, "that he was presenting a challenge. 'Pushing your buttons' as some say. It is his way of seeing how resolute one is in their beliefs."

"There are much nicer ways to do that."

"Certainly," Sultan Hamad said before reaching out and touching her arm. "Taimur's nephews…I understand they came with you?"

"They weren't too happy about it."

"They are Bedu, not city dwellers. Allow the Guard to take care of you while you're here. Let the boys return to the sands. They can take over the duty tomorrow when you return."

Adira readied a protest. But the look in the sultan's eyes made it clear. "Okay. I'll let them go. But I don't want the Guard to make a fuss over me."

"They will not," he replied. "Now, if you don't mind, my dear, I am going to rest."

"Of course, Baba," she said. At the door, she turned back to him. "I'll stop by on my way to Taimur's tomorrow."

"I look forward to it," he replied. Already, his eyelids were growing heavy.

Back in the lobby, she was happy to see her desert companions and the Royal Guard were no longer sparring. Once in the center of the large space, she waved for the leader of the Royal Guard contingent, Sam, and Wasim to join her.

"Boys, my father has asked you to head back to the sands —"

Sam interjected. "But—"

Adira reached out and gently touched his arm. "I know, Sam. And I feel the same way. But we're going to allow both of you—the Guard and your family—to take turns. The Guard will look after me in the city, and you will do the same in the sands."

Sam lowered his head and rubbed his eyes.

"It will give you the chance to rest." She gave his arm a squeeze. "Maybe see that girl of yours?"

A smile came in return.

Adira turned to the Guard leader. "Will that be okay with you, ah, sir?"

"Major," he replied. His shoulders pulled back, and his head bowed slightly. "And it has already been arranged. His Excellency, Minister Omar, has provided his vehicle, driver, and personal protection for you."

"What, did he take an Uber or something? That's not really necessary."

"He insisted, Sayyida. Said you would be far more comfortable in his car. He has left with another team."

"We're not going down the street with lights and sirens, okay? I don't want a fuss."

"Sayyida—"

Adira held up a finger. "His Majesty explained just now that you would be subtle."

The major's lips tightened. "I understand. But there will be a lead and trail car."

Her eyebrows twitched.

"They will be discreet," he said, moving his hands out, palms down, in a placating gesture.

Adira held his stare for a moment. "Okay, then. We're off."

"Where might you like to go, Sayyida?"

Adira checked her phone. While there was no response from Amir, Zahra had messaged, asking if Adira would join her for tea. "Know the Amwaj Lounge in the Kempinski Hotel?" she asked.

"Right away," the major said, raising a radio to his lips.

"As for you two," Adira said, turning back to Sam and Wasim. "Skedaddle. I'll see you tomorrow."

"Ska-dad-el?" Wasim said, a puzzled look on his face.

"It means go away," Sam said to him. Turning back to Adira, he smiled. "But in the nice way that a friend would use."

"I'm not going to say it a nice way the second time!" she said, shooing them off.

Once they had left, the major escorted her to a glossy black Rolls Royce SUV in the garage and introduced her to the guard Omar had offered to provide personal protection. He was tall with broad shoulders, and stood with the confidence of an athlete.

"Sayyida, my name is Moosa," the guard said. "It will be my pleasure to escort you today."

"Nice to meet you, Moosa," she replied.

He bowed his head ever so slightly and opened the rear door, which was strangely hinged in the back, resulting in its opening in the opposite direction. Adira took a seat on the sumptuous white leather. While it was luxurious, she felt out of place in such an extravagant vehicle. The lumpy back seat of Sam's dusty hatchback was a little more her speed. After the door had closed with not much more than a whisper, Moosa joined the driver in the front.

Before long, they arrived at the front door of the Kempinski. Adira wasn't accustomed to waiting for her door to be opened for her and was stepping out before Moosa could turn for the handle. He awkwardly stood by the open door and took the opportunity to scan the entry area.

"No one knows who I am, so don't get too worried," quipped Adira.

"Still, Sayyida, we must be prepared for unwanted attention," Moosa replied.

"I look like a tourist." She gestured toward him. "If we get any attention, it's because of this car and your uniform."

He instinctively looked down at the black tunic with its gold piping and perfectly polished buttons before returning her gaze. His face remained impassive. "Perhaps, Sayyida. Let us get you inside," he said before speaking briefly into his radio.

The expansive hotel lobby was framed with symmetrical rows of columns shaped like golf tees—a modern interpretation of the same shapes used at the sultan's Al Alam Palace. The marble floor echoed the crisp clicks of Moosa's polished boots and the dusty scrapes of Adira's sandals.

Zahra met them outside of the tea lounge. Handing her cane to Moosa, she fully embraced Adira. "I have missed you, Adira!" she exclaimed.

Adira returned the hug with equal enthusiasm. "You look wonderful, Zahra!" She looked down at the flowing rose-colored slacks, matching jacket, and hijab Zahra wore.

"Thank you!" Zahra replied. "Come sit! I want to hear about your time with Taimur!"

Adira followed Zahra into a space considerably more intimate than the lobby. The room was quiet and peaceful and decorated in neutral grays and calm butter tones. They moved to an *L*-shaped couch and took seats close to one another in the corner. A thin young man promptly appeared to take their order. Adira gestured to Zahra, who made her request quietly in Arabic.

"I've ordered tea and some small sandwiches. I hope that will be okay."

"Of course," Adira replied.

"So you have been at Taimur's camp, I hear. How was it? What have you been doing there?"

And so Adira told her about her time in the desert, the visits with her father, and the people she'd been able to meet. When Adira became vague about the experience with Nadir, Zahra gave her a knowing look.

"You're going to need to get used to it, I am afraid," Zahra admitted. "There will always be some people who feel your sudden appearance—especially the timing—is a little suspect."

"I shouldn't have to get used to it."

"No, you shouldn't. Especially since both were my doing and not your own."

"Don't even take that on, Zahra. I'm lucky you found me, that you connected me with my family. That we were able to get to know each other. A little time away helped me understand that even more."

Zahra smiled softly.

Adira leaned forward and briefly rubbed her hand on Zara's thigh. "Our conversations seem to always be about me. I have to say I am not used to that at all. I want to hear about you. What have you been up to this week? Your makeup, this awesome outfit, you look like a superstar!"

Zahra held a hand over her mouth while she smiled, a quirk of modesty that was endearing. "Well, let me tell you," she began. "I have an actual lounge now!"

"No more computer stations?"

Zahra spread her hands toward Adira. "We don't need them any longer!"

Adira gave a laugh.

"One of the Palace decorators took the desks away and replaced them with proper furniture."

"Have you actually lounged in your lounge yet?"

Zahra popped her eyebrows. "Not only have I relaxed; I've had a visitor."

"No!"

"Mm-hmm!"

"And did this handsome visitor happen to stay the night?"

"Of course not! But he's been twice now."

"Twice! It's love! Amir and Zahra!"

"He is very charming. The first time he wanted to see if I'd heard from you. He was distraught after our last dinner."

"It was a bit of a low point for me," Adira admitted quietly.

"I know. But then I heard from Taimur's daughter Asma— we have a mutual friend—that you were out at the camp."

"And the second time you saw him? Was it a date?"

Zahra could barely contain her smile. "It was. He took me to dinner. I invited him inside to see the apartment when he brought me home."

"So were there kisses? Fireworks?"

Zahra blushed again. "Adira, I can't…"

Adira gave an evil look and gestured for her to continue.

"No, he did not kiss me, okay? But I did have some butterflies in my tummy, and I think he may have too."

"I can't wait to see him tonight!"

"Chevy will join us as well. I hope that is okay."

"Of course! How about Nabila?"

"I'm afraid she cannot make it."

"That's a shame. But still, at least I can make my case to Amir and Chevy."

"Your case?"

Adira nodded. "I want my job back, Zahra. I know the program was a put-on, but the job was real."

"It was," Zahra said. "So that is what you want? You are the sayyida and would like your job as a nurse back?"

"I do," Adira replied.

"In a hospital?"

Adira shook her head. "A mobile clinic."

"Are you sure I cannot convince you to stay in Muscat?"

"And give speeches? Like Nabila suggested?" Adira leaned back and shook her head. "That's not me."

"I know it is not. I think we all know that now. No, what I meant was that you might slow down some, enjoy life."

"Still not me." Adira sighed. "I'm sure you think it's because I'm just being defiant. It's not that."

Zahra waggled her chin from side to side.

"Really. I'm not an opportunist, like Rashid or that asshole Nadir think."

Zahra placed two fingers over her lips. "Much of the older population has a great deal of respect for Nadir."

Adira's hand quickly made a slowing gesture. "I know. Sorry."

"So what you want is a dirty truck?"

"I was helping people. Real people. The ones that work hard every day and need a hand when they're sick. I loved being out there with them. I loved exploring the places they lived. It wasn't a grind like working long shifts in a hospital. It was…rewarding."

Zahra held her eyes for a moment. "You were happy out there, weren't you?"

"Not an ounce of weight was on my shoulders. Just being present in the moment."

"No Mayfair or Monaco?"

"I still don't know what or where Mayfair is. And from the pictures I've seen of Monaco, it's for people a lot fancier than I am."

"You know, no other woman, upon discovering she is the sayyida, would ever make this choice."

"I'll take that as a compliment. Now I have to convince Amir and Chevy."

"You don't need their permission."

"Maybe not. But I want their blessing. I want them to understand that this is how I can contribute. How I can be a part of Oman."

Zahra took a deep breath. As she leaned back, a smile grew.

"What?"

"More than once now, I thought you would leave, and I would never see you again. And now I hear the words 'be a part of Oman.' "

"I wanted to leave here more than once. This last time, when I left Taimur's? I felt bad afterward. Running—and more often than not setting off a bomb when I pull the rip cord—has been my way out. It's a reflex."

Zahra leaned forward.

"I don't want to be like that. I'm happy here and don't want to run anymore."

"And I don't want you to feel the need to run ever again."

Adira exhaled. "Thank you. I'm going back to the desert tomorrow to apologize to Taimur."

"He will appreciate that." Scooting closer, she held out her arms. "Now I would like a hug, please!"

They embraced, rubbing each other's backs and enjoying the peaceful moment.

When they finally released, Adira took a deep breath. "So tonight, where would you like to go?"

"Given that neither you nor Chevy are fans of anything 'fancy,' how about my apartment?"

"I don't want you to spend what's left of the afternoon in the kitchen."

Zahra chuckled. "And I don't think you would like that either. I am not much of a cook. But one of the Palace kitchens can prepare dinner for us."

"That sounds great, not just because I don't have anything nice to wear to a fancy restaurant."

"Give me your wallet," Zahra demanded, holding out a hand.

Adira reached into her pocket and withdrew her phone. She flipped it over, which hid the crack in her screen, but revealed the dirty and tattered card holder stuck to the back.

Zahra unsuccessfully tried to hold back her reaction.

"It works for me, okay? I work with my hands. I can't carry around a fancy bag."

"Well, at least it's not an elastic band," Zahra replied, pulling the contents out. Her eyes went wide when she saw the Omani ID card.

"His Majesty's idea. Maybe Taimur's too."

"Miss Adira bint Hamad al Sabir, is it?" Zahra said, smiling. Only this time, there was no modesty.

Adira shrugged. "Eastmont was a made up name anyway. Now that I have a real one, I should probably use it."

Zahra held the card to her chest and wiggled her shoulders. "I love it!"

"I think my father did as well."

"I'm sure he was delighted." Finding the credit card she'd given Adira on arrival, she held it up. "Have you used this yet?"

"I bought food for the team a couple of times. Is it the receipts you need? I'm sorry, but—"

"No, no," Zahra replied, holding back a smile. "I wanted to ensure you had it and tell you to use it. Go get yourself something nice to wear. You're celebrating a new job! That you will stay here with us!"

"I don't need—"

"You just said you don't always have the right clothes. Use the card to fix that. End of discussion."

Adira could only roll her eyes.

"So off you go to the shops," Zahra ordered, getting to her feet. "I am going back to my apartment to make a few phone calls and prepare for my very first dinner party!"

The two laughed their way to the lobby, where Adira found Moosa in a fresh dishdasha and embroidered kummah. "Nice disguise, Moosa!" Adira said, impressed that he had made an effort.

There was the hint of a smile on the otherwise stoic guard as he walked her to the Rolls Royce. After waving a last goodbye to Zahra, Adira asked Moosa and the driver to take her back to the Al Bustan. Browsing through designer stores wasn't her thing at all. She'd have the hotel do some laundry for her and make do with what she had.

They made their way east, hugging the coast past the airport and eventually merging into the main road where they wound gently through the patchwork of low-slung commercial buildings. After cresting the jagged ridge surrounding the old port, they began their descent into Mutrah. With the driver taking this more scenic route, Adira had an idea.

"Would it be possible for us to stop in the souq?" she asked. Negotiating an inexpensive dress—or a nice top and slacks—in the ancient market was more her speed than a modern mall's shiny floors and bright lights.

"Of course, Sayyida," the driver replied as they wound down the hill toward the harbor.

As they looped around the first of two roundabouts, Adira saw a group of protesters had gathered at the waterfront. While they hadn't blocked the road, traffic slowed to a stop at the second roundabout at the corniche. Forty or fifty people were gathered in a wide plaza at the water's edge.

"What are they chanting?" She asked Moosa.

"It is made to rhyme," he replied. "So it does not translate exactly. But it is like 'No planes, no Rashid; jobs, jobs, jobs.' "

"Rashid? The Defense Minister?"

He nodded. "Deputy Defense Minister."

"I'm not a fan. What do the signs say?"

"The same. Some call for reform."

"This is unusual, isn't it? The marching?"

"Very much. We are a peaceful nation. I have only seen a protest here once before, when I was a boy."

"Why protest now?"

"Some people can be difficult," he said, distaste in his mouth.

Adira could not tell if he disliked the protesters or the issue. She watched the people, almost all men, march in a circle. As they chanted, one man tripped and fell. The chanting quickly stopped, and a group gathered around to help him up. He was having difficulty standing, and they lowered him back down.

Adira took a bottle of water from the holder in her door and hopped out of the vehicle.

"Sayyida!" Moosa shouted. It was too late. He watched Adira dash across the street as he jumped out of the vehicle.

Once on the black-and-white marble tiles, Adira slowed and politely pressed her way through the crowd. Space was made for her to kneel next to the man.

"*Kaif halak,*" she said to him. "My name is Adira. It looks like you had a fall there."

The sun was high overhead, bearing straight down on his face.

"Can you hold one of the signs up? Make a shade for him?" she asked the onlookers.

They formed a cover above him, and she opened the bottle of water. "Feel like sitting and having some water?"

The young man nodded and slowly sat up. Adira looked him over carefully, seeing that apart from being a bit too thin, he didn't appear injured. But his face was flush, and he was sweating considerably. Heat exhaustion, most likely. Thankfully, his eyes correctly focused on her.

She let him take hold of the bottle and take a drink. "Take your time. We'll get you cooled down a little. When you're ready, we'll move you into the shade." She looked for a tree or something that offered shelter from the bright sun.

"Thank you, miss," he said, managing a feeble smile.

"I have some more water," said another man bending down next to Adira.

"Thank you," she replied, pulling the scarf from around her neck. She folded it over several times and then doused it with water. She said to the young man sitting down, "Let's put this on your head and bring your temperature down a bit."

The newcomer helped by removing the man's kummah. Adira set the damp scarf over the young man's forehead and thick hair. He reached up and held it in place, closing his eyes as some water dribbled down.

"I've seen all of you protesting before. A couple of weeks ago, not far from here," she said to her new helper.

"The Defense Ministry. They waste money on weapons. Weapons we do not need."

"What do you hope this will accomplish?" she asked, stalling while the water had a chance to work on her patient.

"His Majesty said we would have five thousand police jobs. But instead, we will waste money on jet planes and bombs. We have no need for more bombs."

"Employment here a problem?" she asked.

"Not always. You are from America?"

Adira nodded. "I am."

"Unemployment here is like America. Good most times. But the point here is that a promise has been broken."

"The jobs are needed in the villages," the young man added, showing he was cognizant of the conversation. "But this man is right; it is important the government not break its word."

Adira looked at the young man and asked, "Feel up for moving to the shade?"

He nodded, and with the helper on one side and her on the other, they gently lifted the young man.

"Sayyida, please, let me," said a Royal Guard soldier she'd not seen before. He must have been from a car following them.

"Thank you." Pointing to a thick concrete railing near the water that provided a generous band of shade, she said, "Let's sit him over there."

"Sayyida?" the helper asked, looking at Adira.

"Let's just get him in the shade," she replied.

They set the young man down, and he leaned against one of the stubby columns. "This is good. Thank you."

"You're welcome," Adira said, sitting beside him.

"Sayyida," the guard said, looking out at the crowd who had resumed their chant. "We should go. The crowd is growing—"

"We're out of the way," she said. "Let's just keep an eye on him for a minute."

The crowd was not growing but converging. A small group of policemen had arrived and shoved the protesters off the street. A man fell, and behind him, Adira saw a policeman's hands quickly pull back.

She was on her feet in an instant and marched directly to the policeman. "There is no need for that," she said politely but with authority. A second policeman extended his arm to prevent the confrontation from escalating.

Moosa appeared at the policeman's side. A few words were exchanged, and the policeman lowered his arm. Both policemen took a step back.

"Thank you," Adira said to Moosa and the policemen. "If you need to move them for their own safety, please be gentle. They are not harming anyone."

"This is not allowed in Oman," one of the policemen said, pointing to the crowd.

"Doesn't mean you need to knock them onto the ground," Adira countered. Not wanting to hear more, she quickly said, "There's a boy with heat exhaustion over there. Bring some water so that we can help him."

The policemen exchanged a glance. Moosa said something to one of them, who quickly ran off. Adira returned to the young man and sat back down.

The helper, who had watched with curiosity, asked, "Why does he call you sayyida? His Majesty does not have a daughter."

Adira shrugged.

His eyes went wide.

Adira shook her head. "No one's more surprised than me."

He looked confused. "Being sayyida surprised you?"

"It's a long story."

One of the policemen came over with two cold bottles of water. He handed them to her beneath the protective gaze of Moosa. Adira opened one and passed it to the young man.

"I would like to give my best wishes to you and His Majesty," the helper said. "He is a good man. The best man for Oman. If Rashid becomes sultan, it will be very bad for our country."

"From what I've heard, there aren't many options," Adira said.

"Minister Omar al Fallah. He has respect in the world, and we respect him."

Adira gestured to the crowd. "Use the protest to show your support for him. Send a positive message instead of a negative one."

"Maybe you should tell His Majesty," the man replied.

"Maybe," she said with a smile.

The helper turned to the people clustered around them. Surprisingly, a few women had also appeared. As the helper spoke, the crowd's eyes turned to her. "What's he saying?" she asked the young man.

"He is telling them what you said," he said. Listening for another minute, he continued, "He is saying that we should make signs for Minister Omar."

The helper continued to speak, and suddenly the crowd threw their hands up and began shouting, "Say-yi-da! Say-yi-da!"

"I don't need a translation for that. Please, ask him to stop," Adira said.

"It is too late," the young man said, smiling.

Moosa reached a hand down to her. "I must insist, Sayyida," he said.

"You going to be okay?" she asked the young man, wanting to be sure he was okay.

"Yes. Thank you for your help," he said, handing her the wet scarf.

"Keep it on your forehead for a little longer. And stay in the shade for a while, okay?" She received a nod in reply. She took Moosa's hand. "I think you're right. Time to go!"

They strode briskly through the crowd to the waiting vehicle. Adira leaped into the back seat and closed the door. After a few beeps of the horn, they were moving once again.

"I think we'll skip the market," she said to the men in the front seat. "That was enough excitement for me."

"That was very kind of you, Sayyida," Moosa said. "Reckless, but kind."

***

"Everyone! On your feet! Her Royal Protestness hath arriveth!"

Adira shook her head and closed the door to Zahra's apartment. "Thank you for announcing my arrival, Doctor Difficult. Is there a reason you haven't been banned from the Arabian Peninsula yet?"

"I tried, Adira," shouted Zahra from the kitchen. "But the Royal Police are all terrified of her!"

"Damn right they are!" Chevy said, wrapping her arms around Adira. Her face close, she said, "Missed you. You good?"

"I'm fine, Chevy. Thank you."

They disengaged, and Adira greeted Amir and Zahra before looking around the room. On her last visit, the space looked like a Silicon Valley startup with a patchwork of cluttered workstations. However, it now took the shape of a sumptuous residence befitting a palace. A low-slung modern taupe couch faced a pair of inviting bouclé chairs, all opening to expansive glass doors over the harbor. The setting sun cast a rosy glow on the twinkling water's surface, matching the linens on the round dining table set for four.

"Wow! What a transformation!"

"You like it?" Zahra asked.

"I love it!" Adira said, walking to the kitchen tucked off to the side. The counters held a half-dozen covered dishes, the earthy fragrance of rich spices escaping around the edges.

Drinks were poured—wine for Chevy and water for the others—and the four of them took seats in the living room.

"How was shopping today?" Zahra asked, not hiding the mirth in her voice.

"There was a slight detour," Adira said.

Amir held up his phone. "We saw."

"Uh-oh."

"Just had to be the social media diva, di'n'cha?" Chevy asked, rolling her eyes.

"There shouldn't have been such a fuss. Young guy had heat exhaustion, and I just happened to see him. That's all it was!"

"Mm-hmm!" Chevy mocked.

"Really!" Adira said, raising her arms in surrender. "If the Palace guys hadn't called me 'Sayyida' in front of the crowd, it wouldn't have been a big deal," she continued, her voice becoming softer.

"Sayyida, huh?" Chevy said.

"Means *princess*," Adira replied. "Still feels strange."

"How about the 'majesty' part, like when we're talking about her?" Chevy asked Zahra.

"I am right here, you know," Adira said. "My preferred pronouns are *she* and *her*."

"Not River Girl?" Chevy asked.

"You shall refer to Sayyida as 'Her Royal Highness,' " Zahra declared, pretending to sound official.

Chevy made a dramatic *pfft* noise and tilted her head back. "No chance of that!"

"Chevy, no one would expect anything different from you!" Amir said. "But Adira, you did the right thing. You had a responsibility to help the boy. Any of us would have done the same."

"Thanks. Doesn't really help my case, though."

"Your case?" Amir asked.

"I wanted to ask you for my job back."

"Adira, I—" Amir started.

"I know you said it would be too hard. Complicated. But I really want it, Amir. It's me. It's what I'm made to do."

Amir opened his mouth to speak, only to be cut off by Adira once more.

"And I think that working in remote areas, there'd be much less of a fuss. And after, well—after His Majesty's replacement is named, I won't need a guard anymore. It'll be just like it was before."

Amir nodded. Gently, Chevy asked, "How is your dad doing?"

Adira took a deep breath. "Weak. Only has the energy to talk for a little bit each day, so I've kept visits short. I hope the other visitors have too."

"They have, from what I hear," said Amir.

"Skin's pale; a little more discoloration today. And the pain is increasing," Adira explained.

"I'm sorry," Chevy said.

Adira nodded.

"Now, to get back to what I was trying to say," exclaimed Amir, distracting everyone from worrying, "Chevy and I looked in the Ministry of Health system today, and your job is still in the system."

"Even if it wasn't," Chevy added. "You know that you could, like, snap those Royal Highness fingers and give yourself any job you want, right?"

"I'm sure it doesn't work like that," Adira said. "But even if it did, I'd want you two—and Nabila—to actually want me back. Speaking of Nabila, why couldn't she come tonight?"

Chevy looked to Amir, who said, "At this question, we were instructed to respond that she's sorry but something came up."

"But?"

"She feels responsible for your leaving the other night. She is worried she pushed too hard."

"She came on a little strong. But I was the one who ran out; she didn't drive me out. Tell her I'm sorry, and I understand."

Amir nodded.

"Back to the clinic. Will you have me back?" Adira asked, opening her arms to them.

"Babe, we'll have you back in a heartbeat, okay?" Chevy said. "You know your stuff, work your butt off, and are a lot more exciting to have around than anyone else the MOH could possibly give us!"

Adira couldn't hide her happiness at hearing this. But she wanted to make sure Amir agreed and turned her eyes to his.

"Absolutely," he said with a smile. Zahra, seated next to him on the couch, reached over and grasped his hand.

"Thank you!" Adira said, relieved. "I need to go back to the hospital tomorrow, then out to the desert to patch things up with Taimur. I can be ready in two days. Will that work?"

Chevy looked at Amir. "New girl's asking for time off already. I don't know."

Amir nodded solemnly. "I had hoped she would not be this difficult."

"You two stop this right now!" Zahra said, slapping Amir on the leg. She stood up. Taking hold of her cane, she waggled it between Chevy and Amir and said, "It's time to eat, and you two are going to behave!"

"No chance of that, sister!" Chevy exclaimed.

They all erupted in laughter before getting up and uncovering the dishes in the kitchen. They were brought, along with the wine for Chevy, to the table.

Once they were seated, Adira leaned toward Chevy. Whispering in a not-so-quiet voice, she asked, "Did you happen to notice someone holding someone else's hand earlier?"

"Fancy Chick's got the moves, doesn't she!"

Zahra covered her face with her hands in an effort to hide. But there was no concealing her smile.

***

The mood less than a mile away, in one of the majestic homes mixed in with the embassies at the edge of the sea, was, on the surface, equally as playful. Lowering his bulk onto a hearty armchair, the heavy man held his hand out. His tall, athletic protégé placed a mobile phone in his hand, Rashid bin Tamim's contact card already showing, the phone number ready to be pressed.

When Rashid's phone rang, his emotions were on the opposite side of the spectrum, as evidenced by the sizable difference in the amount of scotch in the nearby bottle at the beginning of the evening compared to the present.

Rashid looked at the screen and reluctantly swiped to answer. "I hope you will be able to tell me what is happening right now," he scowled, not bothering with a single pleasantry.

A low chuckle came in return. "Ah, so this is troublesome?"

"Of course, it is 'troublesome.' It is, in fact, far worse than 'troublesome'!"

"That is good, my dear Rashid. It means you care."

"This woman is a nuisance! She was helping people protesting me! Who does she think she is?"

"She was quite good in those videos, wasn't she?"

"Good? You call that good? Why didn't the police stop them? It's what they're bloody there for!"

"I think she shared a word with them. Preyed on their sympathy for fellow citizens."

"How could this happen? How can a woman be creating this trouble? She should know her place!"

"I do think, Rashid, that you should be worried. She does seem to have the people on her side. They love her. One of my protégés," he began, looking across the room, "says the word in English is 'viral.' She has gone viral, and I would say for very good reason."

"What good reason could there possibly be for this insolence!" Rashid shouted.

"She cares, Rashid. As ridiculous as it is, she cares for the masses. She's also fearless. I think you saw the river video?"

"Of course I saw the video. The boy was an idiot to be near a culvert during a storm."

"Yes, but what the average person saw was a woman risking her life to save a boy. They will remember that. What will they remember you for?"

"I will not be spoken to this way! Not even by you!"

A gruff chuckle came in return. "Relax, Rashid. I simply want you to understand the enormity of the risk she presents to your plans."

Rashid exhaled. His free hand pinched the bridge of his nose. "I know. Especially hearing their idiotic chants."

"The chants are not the problem. The influence she has with people is where the problem lies."

"Are you calling to gloat at my expense? I have no time for this."

"Of course not. I am calling with a solution."

"I'd like to hear your solution, but I don't even know where the woman is!"

"The 'solution,' as one might call him, has been closely watching her for some time now. Presently, she is on the Palace grounds."

"Well, that's a bloody disaster. She's untouchable there. What are you proposing?"

"I am not proposing anything, Rashid. But if you would like to speak with this 'solution,' I am sure you could propose something that might solve your problem? Here," he began, pressing a few buttons and holding out the phone. "I have him on speaker."

"Who is this?" Rashid demanded.

The protégé stepped forward, closer to the phone. In a clear and calm voice, he said, "I don't think that is relevant at the moment, Your Excellency."

Rashid exhaled in resignation. "Fine, how close are you to this woman? Close enough to make her disappear?"

The man allowed a second to pass before responding. "Your Excellency, I need you to be a bit more specific."

"Specific!" Rashid shouted. "I want her gone! Gone between now and when her father finally dies. And twenty-four hours after that, since that's when the bloody council will meet. Kill her. Dump her in the desert. Sink her to the bottom of the sea. I don't care!"

"I understand, Your Excellency."

"Fine! Now get me off speaker!"

The heavy man pressed a few buttons on the phone and held it again to his ear. "My, Rashid, you could at least be polite."

"Can your man do this job or not?"

"Of course he can. He's in your chain of command, after a fashion, and has just received his orders."

"Good. Then I expect him not to make a mess of it!"

"Not in the least, Rashid. Take a deep breath now; your plans will soon resume."

The line, he realized, had already been closed. The large man set the phone down and looked up at his protégé. "That went wonderfully, I think."

"Your Excellency, are you sure this is absolutely necessary?"

The large man's face went cold. He was not used to being questioned, and the implication—the threat in his glare— showed as much.

His protégé had been under the thumb of his corpulent host since childhood, when the young man's father had used his position working in a government office to skim a small amount of money from the local treasury. The large man was the head of the province at the time, and pardoned the father. He knew perfectly well that in doing so, he owned his protégé's entire family, and could use them for whatever purposes he could dream up.

The protégé stood upright. "I understand."

"Good," the large man said. He glanced back to the blackness of the sea before continuing. "I tried long ago, you know. Back when you were just a boy. My intelligence was sound, and the men on the ground over there sounded competent. It worked well, or so I thought, for many years. Learning that she was alive came as an interesting surprise. I have to say that I've thought more than once this week about having her marry one of my sons. Getting that family into the bloodline could have been quite beneficial."

Raised eyebrows were his only reply.

"Yes, it's all true. But this is the safest option. For everyone, especially since the old man has only a day or two left in him. Take her deep into the desert and dispose of this girl. Let the sands bury this problem for good."

"It will be taken care of, Your Excellency."

18

Adira was welcomed the next morning with a glorious view of the sun glistening across the water. Zahra slept soundly on the other side of the bed. Slipping carefully out from under the covers, Adira padded silently to the kitchen. She filled the kettle and flipped the switch before searching the cabinets for the French press she knew Zahra had tucked away.

Finding it nestled deep in a drawer, she set it down on the counter and opened a bag of Tanzanian coffee she'd seen during the search. The boiled water followed four hearty scoops of coffee before she carefully set the lid.

While the coffee did its work, Adira took two cups, spoons, and a container of milk out to a small café table on the balcony. Returning to the kitchen, she lowered the plunger on the coffee halfway and brought it outside.

The sea below was calm, the surface reflecting the jagged hills framing the harbor. The early morning silence was broken only by the calls of a few seagulls in the distance.

She pushed the plunger down and poured herself a cup, adding a hearty splash of milk and giving it a stir. Holding the cup near her lips, she inhaled, taking in the mixture of fresh coffee and salt air. Embracing a peacefulness she'd only felt since arriving in the dry yet culture-rich nation.

After a time, the door opened behind her. "Good morning!" Zahra said, bending down and kissing Adira's cheek.

"Good morning to you. Thank you for letting me stay. Hope you slept all right."

"Please stop that. You know you are always welcome to stay here."

Adira poured a cup of coffee for Zahra. "It's strange for me. I've never really had a, well, a friend so inviting. So at ease with me."

"Adira, we were like sisters when you were a toddler. As far as I'm concerned, it's still the same. We just had a little time fall through the cracks."

"Not exactly a little."

Zahra wrapped both hands around her cup and took a sip. "No. I didn't much enjoy those years. But now I have you here. And I have to say I love it."

Adira reached over and squeezed Zahra's arm. "I love it too."

They fell into a comfortable silence, staring out to the sea. Adira poured more coffee for both of them.

"I set aside a few things for you last week. Clothes and a pair of shoes," Zahra said after a while. "We're about the same size."

"You knew I wasn't going shopping?"

"You're pretty obvious," Zahra replied with a smile.

"Thank you. I'm going to need to head over to the hospital soon. Then out to Taimur's."

Zahra stood, collecting her cup and the milk. "Then let's get you sorted out."

After a shower and changing into what she suspected were clothes bought specifically for her, Adira left the apartment. Moosa was waiting outside, standing next to a matte, desert tan Range Rover. While it appeared to be somewhat longer than the others she'd ridden in, it bore no crests or government markings.

"Good morning, Moosa," Adira said to him. "We going low-key today?"

The guard smiled. "As Her Royal Highness requested, I felt this car would be more discreet."

While Moosa had been stone-faced the day before, he betrayed a hint of emotion today. Disappointment, or perhaps resignation. "No driver?"

"No, Sayyida. I hope this will be okay."

"Better, as far as I'm concerned," she replied.

He clicked his heels and opened the passenger side rear door for her.

"If it's just the two of us, how about I ride up front?"

In his years of service to senior government officials, and to be sure during the half dozen with Minister Omar, not a single protectee had ever asked to ride in the front. "The back would be better, Sayyida. It will not be looked upon favorably if my superiors see me with you in the front."

"Okay, then. But only because I don't want you to get in trouble."

Moosa closed her door, then walked around and settled into the driver's seat. A glance in the mirror revealed Adira looking around the cabin.

"Wow, this is really fancy back here. Limos in the movies are like this."

"I am glad you like it. The seats recline, and there is a divider if you wish some privacy."

"I'm good. Could we please go to the hospital? And then Taimur's?"

"With pleasure, Sayyida," he replied.

Moosa was a skilled driver, handling the car expertly but in the gentle manner prescribed by those who drive senior officials. Adira hardly noticed the stops and starts, and turns were taken delicately.

They paralleled the sea, driving through the embassies, hotels, and luxury homes before sweeping around the airport and over to the hospital, where Adira was escorted up to His Majesty's wing.

Dr. Daoud wasn't behind the desk, but the nurse recognized Adira and picked up her phone. As she spoke, Adira used her hands to ask if she could enter the room. The nurse held up a single finger. Adira went to the desk and waited instead.

The nurse finished her call and hung up the phone. "Dr. Daoud will be here shortly."

"How is he doing?"

The nurse's expression wasn't positive. "This morning, he was in some pain. He is sleeping now. The doctor will be able to tell you more."

Adira nodded. "Could I see his chart?"

The nurse hesitated.

"I'm family, so it should be okay."

"Yes, but these things…you must understand. They are kept secret."

The doctor had approached from behind Adira. She turned at his voice. "The sayyida is a peer in our field and also His Majesty's only relative," he said, extending a hand over the desk. "To be honest, talking with staff and officials about his care isn't the same."

The nurse sighed in relief and handed the old-fashioned metal flip-top clipboard over.

"I can't think of a more stressful patient to have," Adira admitted. "I can only imagine the pressure you've been under."

The doctor's eyes lowered briefly. "It has been long enough that we're almost getting used to it."

"Thank you, Sayyida. I am glad you understand," the nurse replied, genuinely appreciative.

The doctor opened the clipboard, and Adira asked, "This is pretty old school. No tablet? Electronic records?"

"It is off-line," the doctor said. "We don't want specifics to get out."

"I'd guess with a patient like this, you'd consult with some specialists at other hospitals. How are you sharing images and bloodwork?"

"Electronically, like you said. Only manually entered under another name."

Adira understood and took a moment to look through her father's vitals, bloodwork, and treatments. Adira asked detailed questions, but even after a lengthy discussion, she realized they were where they were. The only direction for his care to take now was to maintain his comfort. She didn't want to ask the doctor how long her father had. No sense adding to the pressure he was under. From her experience, it was a matter of days, perhaps only three or four, five if she was lucky.

Adira closed the records and handed them to the doctor. "Thank you for sharing this. And for doing everything you can. I'll sit with him for a while if you don't mind."

Doctor Daoud bowed his head in thanks and walked her to the door.

Sultan Hamad lay asleep as she entered. The lights were dim, and the shades were pulled halfway closed. Out of habit, she scanned the monitors before taking a seat next to him.

"Good morning, Baba," she whispered.

Sultan Hamad's eyes were closed. He breathed gently, at a pace consistent with sleep in his condition. A nasal cannula provided supplemental oxygen.

"Got my job back last night, thank goodness. Being up at Taimur's, I missed it. The young professionals you have here, from Zahra and Amir, all the way to the doctors and nurses, are pretty amazing. The pride they have in their work, well, it's rarer than you think."

The words she knew were not heard and processed during sleep. But she'd always felt that some connection was made in those times, and it was always worth the effort.

"I'll work with the mobile clinic again. When you returned to Oman after being in England, you said you hardly knew the country. Taimur's dad took you around, introducing you to the people and places. That's really what the clinic team was doing with me. There's plenty more to see, though, and I'm really looking forward to it."

She scanned the numbers again, then looked carefully at the sultan's coloration, first his face and then his hands.

"When I was a kid, one of the homes they put me in had a Black foster mother and an Indian father. I've never seen that combination again, but they weren't the problem. It was this bitchy girl, the oldest of what might've been five of us. She was an expert at setting the others up, including me, for a fall. But anyway, I remember the girl grabbing my chin and saying something like, 'What are you, girl?' I told her I was a 'mix' because that's what someone in CPS said about me once. She laughed at me. Said, 'You the scariest mix I've seen. Ain't nobody got eyes creepy as yours!' "

Adira paused to see if he'd woken and quickly glanced at his white hair.

"Glad I left there. But it got me watching all the other kids. My skin was similar to some of the Black kids. But my hair's curls were more wavy than tight, and my nose was longer with a little bump. Got close on eye color with a few of the lighter hazel shades, though. The Latinas had hair maybe a little more like mine, but their faces were all cute and perfect. Mine was too angular. A couple of Indian kids lived on one of the streets they put me on—a girl and a boy. I kinda matched them but wasn't nearly as tall and thin. Once I started work at the hospital, I started seeing some women from the Middle East. Noses were closer to mine, and jaws were getting there. But their skin was usually lighter. Never did run into anyone with gold eyes, now that I think about it."

She stole a glance at him, checking his features once more.

"So I went through life never really knowing what I was. I mean, who can actually afford one of those ancestry DNA kits? Well, aside from Zahra. And you. But for me, that hundred bucks had a lot better uses. Fast forward to coming here. I look at you—maybe not now, but in the photos I've seen—and our color and overall shape perfectly match. And in that painting of Mom. Well, she's a lot lighter, but her nose and eyes are a pretty close match. Plus, there are plenty of other people in Oman's mix of African, Arab, and Persian that share some of our features here."

One of the monitors beeped. Adira did a quick scan and found it was nothing to cause alarm.

"Sorry for the long story. Haven't really talked this much in, well, my entire life. But I just wanted to tell you that I've wondered what I 'am' for my whole life. Then I come here, and I feel like I just fit in. It's been, well, comforting."

She planted her palms on her thighs and smoothed out the pants Zahra had given her earlier in the day.

"Speaking of fitting in, before someone tattles on me, I kinda jumped into a protest yesterday. Saw a young guy faint when we passed by. Heat, really, and maybe a little dehydrated. Got him cooled down. Water, shade, and a compress. Nice kid. They were protesting Rashid, in case your people don't tell you. I asked who they wanted to take your place, and they said Omar. I told them it might be better to protest for something instead of against it. It was almost all men, so I was pretty surprised when they listened to me."

"It is because you listened to them," came a soft, tired voice.

Adira startled. "You're awake!"

He turned his head toward her, and his eyes twinkled. "You showed empathy and conviction. The combination of both is your power, my dear."

There was a dryness to his voice. Adira checked his bedside and found a cup of water and a straw. "Can I raise you up a bit?" she asked, holding up the cup for him to see.

His eyebrows bobbed and she raised the bed enough that he could take a drink.

"How much of my rambling did you have to endure?"

"To be honest, I do not know. I just heard a voice. I wondered if it wasn't an angel."

"Nice try. Angels are a Christian thing."

"Actually," he said before taking another small sip. "We also have angels in Islam. God created them to bring messages to us."

"I didn't know that."

"Some take the role of guardian angels, and I wish for you to be blessed with many."

"Thanks," she replied. "Seems that's all I have here is people looking out for me. Actually feel a bit spoiled."

As he took a breath, the sultan felt a sharp pain in his abdomen. His eyes closed briefly as he collected himself when the pain subsided.

"Breathe," she said. "I can raise you up if going to a sitting position helps."

"The doctors have experimented with that. It is not terribly effective for me." He closed his eyes. "I might just rest for a little longer."

Adira stood and lowered the bed down. It was a reflex from her years with patients. But this wasn't just a patient.

It was someone she'd known for only a matter of days, yet they'd already shared a lifetime together. They were connected closer than any two people could be, and seeing him in the bed twisted her heart like nothing ever had before.

She watched him carefully for several minutes before leaning down and kissing his forehead. "I am going up to Taimur's now," she whispered. "But I'll be back soon. Tomorrow, or later tonight if I can."

He gave a gentle noise of consent, and after one last look, she turned and left the room.

Dr. Daoud was waiting at the desk.

"He woke up for a few minutes there," she reported. "Spoke coherently, but was a little hoarse, so I gave him some water. Maybe fifty milliliters. He experienced one shot of pain, abdomen or back."

The doctor gestured to a monitor that displayed live video from the room. "I am sorry I did not tell you."

Adira was not upset at being watched. "I understand. Hope I didn't bore you to death with my rambling on."

"Not at all. I asked the nurses to take a break and tried not to listen," he said.

Adira took a deep breath. "Not going to be long."

"It is not," he said. "But he will be well cared for. We keep many of the government people away and have help from the Guard," he said, raising his chin in toward the men in uniform by the elevator. "His assistants and friends keep their visits short. And it has been very good to have you here."

"I have to go now, but I will be back tomorrow. Tonight if I can."

He nodded.

"Let me give you my phone number."

He waggled his hand. "It's already been given to us."

"Please call if anything changes. I am sure you have a list of people to call, but fit me in if you can."

"If I'm here, you will be the first call. Family is important."

"I appreciate that. See you soon."

She turned and took one last look at the door before a guard escorted her to the elevator. Once in the garage, she joined Moosa in the tan Range Rover.

They left the hospital and were on the road to the desert just as the sun was at its peak. In the harsh heat, the mountains appeared dark and crystalline, almost brittle. They wound up and up, through and across the peaks and valleys. On one side of the road, Adira would see barren rocky cliffs. Yet, just opposite, a canyon could be green from the combination of enough shade and a spring in the right spot. Other turns revealed a cluster of buildings marking a village or a postage stamp patch of vegetation indicating a farm. It was a land of such varying terrain that it was a shame to classify the whole Arabian Peninsula as desert.

But after two hours, that's just where they were. At first, it was the rocky plains, with small villages marking their passing. She recognized certain ones now, thanks to the trips back and forth. A gas station here, a pleasant but rustic place to stop there. Even the edge of a camel racing track.

Every once in a while, she would catch a glimpse of the rolling sand dunes to her right. She remembered Taimur telling her how they shifted over time. The vast sands could envelop an entire region, hiding it forever, or just as quickly reveal the brutal hardscape below.

They passed what Adira came to think of as the last "big" town, mainly because it was the only town with a market that, while small, had some resemblance to a Western store. After this, she knew the following two villages were relatively sparse with supplies.

The first passed. And then the second. They would turn soon and stop in the gas station that Taimur used to deflate and inflate the tires. She'd be sure to show the place to Moosa if he didn't know.

She looked down at her phone and sent a quick message to Taimur so he'd know they were close. However, the message didn't go through when she tapped the button. A quick check showed she had no bars. Strange. This hadn't been a problem in the morning.

Looking up, she saw they'd missed the turnoff.

"Moosa, I think we passed it back there," she said. Few of the streets out here were marked, so it was an honest mistake.

He looked back at her through the rearview mirror. "There has been a change of plans, Sayyida. If you will be patient."

Adira shrugged it off, happy to be flexible. But just then, the divider between the front and back rows began to rise.

"No need to put that up, Moosa. I'm not a bigwig."

Moosa stared straight ahead. The divider had risen nearly halfway up. Adira looked around the center console. Finding a pair of buttons marked with arrows, she pressed the down button. Nothing happened.

She pressed harder, then pushed the up and down buttons again. Still, the divider rose, and was now eight inches from being fully closed. "Moosa, put the divider back down, please."

When he didn't respond—or even turn his head—Adira reached up and grabbed the top of the thick divider with both hands. Assuming there would be a safety mechanism to prevent fingers from being crushed, she applied pressure. First a little, then more. Then a fair amount of her body weight.

It didn't stop. It was being put up intentionally.

Adira didn't panic. The ER had taught her that fear and anxiety were never helpful. Instead, her muscles tightened with anger. Anger at Moosa. Anger at herself for trusting him.

And then she set about solving the problem. The divider was five inches from the top.

She needed something hard. Something to jam in the gap. Her sandals were too soft. The water bottle was flimsy plastic. Her phone was solid. She thrust it up. Too tall. Quickly turning it on its side, she held it firmly in place. The divider still pushed upward. A motor by her feet began to protest. Then the phone started to bend.

Moosa's hand flew up, violently twisted the phone, and tore it from the gap. The divider closed the last few inches and locked into place.

She turned her focus to the doors. They were locked, or at least the child locks had been set. Either way, they were inoperable from the inside.

Breaking a window was a possibility. But if this was one of the Royal Guard vehicles, it would be reinforced for bullet or impact protection. She rapped her knuckles against one. It made little, if any, noise. It had to be a half-inch thick, maybe more.

She looked behind her into the trunk.

A stiff shade covered the cargo area just behind the headrests. Latches held it in place in each of the four corners. She turned her body around and, kneeling on the seat, found two of the release levers.

Two corners of the cover popped up. She lifted one corner, pulled the other sideways, and eventually had the front half of the lid down. Hoisting one knee over and then the second, she landed with all of her weight on the cover, causing the aft catches to break.

Seated in the cargo area, she knocked on the rear window with her hands, again finding it was unusually thick.

Cars these days she knew had an emergency release tab for this exact scenario. She set about finding it and looked into one of the rear corners of the space. A seam defined a small hatch, tiny knobs in each corner.

One by one, she twisted them. On the fourth, there was a pop, and she pulled the cover away. Inside, several cable harnesses ran from front to back, ending where the taillights would be. She moved the wires up and down, looking for a handle or cable to release the cargo door.

Nothing. She briefly toyed with the idea of pulling some of the wires to flash the rear lights. But there were dozens and no way to tell which would have the desired effect.

She turned to the other side of the space and found another hatch. She repeated the process and efficiently removed the cover. The inside was the same. No emergency release.

She sat down on the cover and looked out the back window. They'd turned off and now traveled at pace on a gravel road. She caught a glimpse of a small village receding in the distance through dust clouds.

She looked at the rear hatch. It was split in the middle, allowing the upper half with the window to open separately from the lower portion. She ran her hand slowly across the seam.

Near the left side, there was a rectangular shape in the trim. Its purpose was imprinted in the plastic in small letters: EMERGENCY RELEASE.

She worked a fingernail under the edge without luck. Thinking it could be a lever, she pressed on one side. The opposite end popped out, and she took hold and pulled. It came off completely.

She looked at the back of the release. There was a catch where a cable would have been connected. It had been cut and removed. Inside the tiny recess was a hole where the line would have run. The loose end wasn't visible and had clearly retracted or been removed.

Adira's actions were methodical and efficient. Assess, prioritize, and act with conviction. Her priorities had been to stop the divider and gain exit. With both of those avenues shut down, she took a deep breath. She was being taken somewhere. Once there, Moosa, with or without accomplices, would have to get her out of the car. It would be another chance to escape.

Only five minutes had passed since the divider closed. It was time to see what other tools were at her disposal.

Something was under the cargo cover beneath her, but there wasn't enough room to maneuver. She found release knobs on the seat back and flipped one, then the other. Pushing the seat backs down gave her an ample, flat space to work.

She folded the cargo cover in half, realizing it could have some use as a clumsy bat if needed. Beneath it were two small coils of rope. The rope was thin and likely used for tying cargo.

She mentally filed the coils into the less-useful-right-now category.

Pushing the cover and rope aside, she looked at the thick carpet covering the cargo area. The spare would be in there. Perhaps some tools. She pulled the rug back, uncovering a false floor over what should be the spare. A firm tug on the nylon tab folded the floor back once, revealing half of the spare tire. She removed the rest of the floor and shoved it forward with the cargo cover and carpet.

"Now we're talking," she muttered to herself.

Nestled in a corner next to the spare was a jack. After fiddling with a pair of Velcro tabs, she was able to lift it out. A lug wrench and folded metal handle were clipped to the side. She detached both and laid them all on top of the spare. The other corners revealed nothing of use except small triangles of molded foam.

The road noise reduced as the vehicle transitioned from the rocky hard pack to sand. She looked out, and through the dust clouds, she could see they were now in the sands. Rolling dunes stretched in every direction. They appeared to be heading south, deep into the empty landscape.

The jack, which had to weigh ten pounds on its own, would be the most potent weapon. But lifting it from one end, she realized the weight would make it too slow to swing. The *L*-shaped lug wrench was heavy steel. A little more than a foot long, she determined it would be the most efficient weapon.

She held it, first by the short end and then by the long end. The long end would be better. She made a quick test swing and then moved to the rear window.

Spreading her knees into a broad base, she did another test swing. Feeling unstable, she lifted one knee up and wedged her foot next to the spare. Better.

She wound up and swung with as much of her weight as possible. The tire iron spun on impact, wringing the tool from her hand. It left only a tiny mark on the glass. She hefted the steel bar again, this time with the bent elbow facing the glass. The second impact came with a twang as the iron vibrated violently in her hand. The glass hadn't shattered or even cracked. The only result was a pea-sized white spot in the center of the glass.

She repeated the attempt with the heavier jack, her swings getting the same result. The reinforced glass was far more robust than she'd thought.

She looked forward at the black divider separating her from the front row. Lug wrench in hand, she crawled forward. Three swings at the partition proved that it, too, was reinforced. Flipping the tool over, she tried to pry back the gap from where the divider had risen. There wasn't enough room to gain purchase, and the fruit of her labor was nothing more than tears in the surface leather.

Keeping the lug wrench within easy reach, Adira sat on the back seat and caught her breath. Outside, the rounded pattern of the dunes extended endlessly in every direction.

Adira spent every moment attempting escape. She plied her tools on every window in the cargo area. She pried the edges, speared the glass with the pointy end of the lug wrench, and battered every surface with the jack. She used the jack to push the windows and doors. She even tried to use it to punch through the ceiling. But the windows never cracked, and the base she used for the jack inevitably broke before whatever she was pushing did. The result was loose seats, cracked plastic, and torn leather. With her still stuck inside, sweaty, scraped up, and exhausted.

The sun had edged closer to the horizon when the vehicle began to slow. This would be the challenging part. She grabbed the jack and the tire iron and moved back to the rear cargo door.

With the false floor back in place, there would be space to maneuver. She would have more room to attack when he opened the larger hatch than she would from a seated position by one of the back passenger doors.

Her plan was to come out on offense. Disable him and take the car if she could; otherwise, make a run for it. The second option, this deep in the desert, was her least favorite.

She held the tire iron with one hand and the jack with the other. Given the jack's weight, she needed to press the tire iron hand against it, helping her generate a little swing. Her plan was to throw the jack at Moosa's legs. When he looked down, she'd jump out swinging the lug wrench.

Her plan required speed and efficiency of movement. She'd run through each step in her mind and was prepared. All she waited for now was for him to get out of the driver's seat and come around to open the cargo door.

The Range Rover came to a stop. It was put in park and then switched off. Adira waited for the sound of his door.

To her surprise, the first noise was the cargo doors opening, first the glass top and then the bottom lift gate. Moosa hadn't moved; he'd simply opened the back with a switch.

Keeping the tools in her hand, she sat down on her bottom and carefully slid off the lift gate. She looked to her left, where a couple of posts stood with a rope between them. In the back of her mind, she processed this as a camel stop, as she'd seen one used as a place to tie camels and lay their saddle pads out to dry. What she didn't see as she scanned right were any accomplices. A small victory. She'd take it.

She took three steps away from the vehicle and considered her options. If she ran, he could quickly chase her in the Range Rover. She could bob and weave, but eventually, she'd tire and get run down. Her best bet was still to attack. She began to take a wide loop around to the front of the car.

The front door swung open. A hand, palm out, came first, followed by a foot. She rushed.

But in the time it took her to take three long strides, he was able to hop out of the vehicle. She turned her upper body and used the next step as leverage, hurling the jack straight at his knees.

He side-stepped quickly, and the jack dug into the sand. But Adira didn't stop. She moved in quickly, the lug wrench swinging straight for his head.

His left arm shot up with incredible speed, grabbing her arm and twisting violently. She was forced to drop the iron and bend down. On her way, she drove her other fist straight at his groin. Again, he proved to be astonishingly agile. His hips turned, her hand only making a glancing blow to his buttock.

Keeping hold of her right arm as she went down to her knees, he pivoted around her back. She moved with his twist, knowing he was very close to popping her shoulder right out of its socket. With a painful lift of her wrist, he commanded, "Stop!"

Understanding he had all of the leverage, she did. Not wanting to think about being raped and left for dead in the desert, she looked for something, anything she could use as a weapon. The lug wrench was on the ground behind her now. Beneath her knees was only sand. Her feral instinct was to grab a handful. Discreetly, she reached down.

"Please do not, Sayyida. A man does not grow up in a desert land afraid of sand."

"What do you want?" she growled.

"I do not want anything. This, sadly, is my duty."

"Sadly? I'm sure! You seem to be enjoying yourself!"

"This is not enjoyable, Sayyida. As I said, it is my unfortunate duty."

"To whom?"

He ignored the question. "What we are going to do now is get up and walk to the camel posts."

The hand on her back moved down to her arm, just below the shoulder, and began to lift. Adira leaned forward, and Moosa gave her arm a warning twist. The ligaments inside her shoulder were strained to the limit. "Stop! I'm getting up!"

The tension released the smallest amount. Adira shifted her weight back slightly and was able to awkwardly get to her feet.

Moosa kept a strong, twisting grip on her right arm and another hand on her back. There was no room to spin out of the hold, and she was slowly marched forward. She was steered toward a post. Once they were close, his grip loosened.

Before she had time to react, he'd kicked at the back of her knees, collapsing her down on her side. One arm was wrenched around the post, and the other quickly pinned by his knee.

She squirmed and swung her head, trying to make any contact she could. But in an instant, a loop of thin rope wrapped around one wrist and then the next. By the time she'd righted herself to a sitting position, her hands were firmly tied to the post behind her.

Moosa moved in front of her, his palms facing out. "That is all, Sayyida. You will not be harmed."

"Not harmed, Moosa? You just about tore my arm off, and now you've tied me to a post in the middle of the fucking desert!"

He closed his eyes briefly. "Please. I want you to understand that I do this out of goodwill. My—"

"Out of goodwill? Are you this nice to your kids? To your mother and father? Do you kidnap them and tie them up in the desert too?"

"Please—"

"What a noble man you are standing above a woman tied to the ground. Your family—when they aren't tied up getting the crap beat out of them—would be so proud!"

"Enough! I have no children!" he shouted.

Adira, against her instincts, went silent.

"My orders, Sayyida, were to kill you. This, I feel, is more kind."

"It's a hundred and ten degrees out here! The heat's going to kill me; it's just going to be a slow and painful death! You call that kind?"

He nodded solemnly.

Why was he showing what looked like regret? Adira changed the tone of her voice in the hope of sounding sympathetic. "Whose orders, Moosa? Someone in the Palace? Nadir? Rashid? Who?"

He turned away from her and looked up to the sky. "Of course, Rashid gave the order. The arrogant fool hates you! But his strings are pulled by someone far more dangerous. Did you know this—the sands hiding yet another of his problems —wasn't his first attempt?"

When had someone tried to kill her before? This was a surprise. "Who, Moosa? Who?"

"It was many years ago. He said it had happened when I was a boy. Strange, isn't it?"

"Who? I need to know who you're talking about, Moosa."

Moosa turned around, again looking at her. "I think he told me that story to remind me. Remind me about my father; that my family owes him. He could reach out and find us anywhere. So now I pay the price."

"Don't, Moosa. No man should have to pay the price for his father. Untie me. We can fix this. Together."

"It was an order, Sayyida."

"An American Naval officer I know would use the phrase 'lawful order.' Tying me up here doesn't seem so lawful."

"Americans always act so noble, don't they? But this is what I am trying to be now—noble—by not killing you, Sayyida. I want you to have a chance to survive."

He quickly walked to the Range Rover and returned with a small water bottle. He placed it near her legs.

"You are to be admired. I can tell that you are a kind person like your father. I do not want to hurt you. But I must do something. If I do not—if I cross these men—they will destroy me through my family. Through my mother and father. Through my sisters."

"Untie me, Moosa. Let me help. We can make your family safe," Adira pleaded.

He bent down onto one knee. "Please, Sayyida, do not return to Muscat. If you have the chance, run."

As he stood and walked back to the car, Adira shouted after him. "Moosa! Moosa!"

He ignored her and got back into the driver's seat. After making a large circle around the posts, he vanished in a cloud of dust.

19

A number of thoughts went through Adira's mind in the few seconds it took for the Range Rover to disappear. Who was after her and why were the first. But they weren't relevant at the moment.

Right now, she had one problem to solve: getting unhooked from the post. Sitting in the sand with her back to the post and her hands tied behind her back around it, she shimmied to the left and turned for a better look.

At the top of the post, a thick rope was secured with two steel bolts. The strong, nylon strand spanned a gap of eight feet, where the opposite end was bolted to a second post. If she stood, she could walk backward and end up with her hands only held by the rope. She'd still be stuck, but it would at least be more comfortable.

She tucked her feet beneath her and began to stand. But as her back pressed against the thick, old wood, it gave slightly. Once standing, she set her feet and pushed her butt hard into the upright. Again it moved. If she could get it loose enough, could she lift it out of the ground?

"Worth a shot," she mumbled.

The process was repeated, from one side of the post, then the other. Slamming backward again and again. Each time, it wobbled a little more. She shoveled as much sand as she could away from the base, giving more room for the post to shift and providing a ledge on which she could plant her feet for leverage.

Eventually, it became loose enough to try and lift. She squatted down low and squeezed her arms, getting as much grip as she could on the rough wood. Slowly, she rose, using the strength of her legs to force the post up.

It rose, just a little at first. But enough to encourage her. It was heavy, but she strained up, splinters driving deep into the soft part of her arms. She extended up to her full height, the post moving with her. She leaned to the side, hoping enough post was out of the ground to topple it.

But the post wouldn't fall. Her grip began to loosen, and before she could think about how to lower it carefully, it slid back down into the hole, taking a fair amount of skin with it.

She repositioned, lower this time, and tried again. Once she'd fully stretched, she scraped sand down into the base. She pushed as much as she could back into the hole before carefully lowering back down.

The process was repeated over and over, and the post had moved higher now. She decided toppling the post was worth another try. Again, she squatted down. Her arms screamed in pain, but still, she squeezed them as tightly as she could and stood. At the top, she went on to her toes.

Knowing it would hurt, she flung herself to the side. She landed hard, but the post had fallen with her, pinning her arm. She wiggled down its length, her arm dragging through the sand. The post ground across the abrasions on her arm as she moved, but she could feel the bottom of the post with her heels and knew she was close. Inch-by-inch, she worked her way toward the end until finally, her arms were free.

She pivoted to a sitting position and caught her breath. Getting off the post was a small victory, but her hands were still tied behind her back.

Toiling had stretched the rope around her wrists a small amount. She considered trying to work her hands under her bottom and then pass her feet through to get the bonds in front. She'd be able to see the knot, and it would at least be more comfortable. Doubting she had the flexibility, she stood, wanting to first try releasing the knot from behind her back blindly.

The sun had nearly reached the horizon now, but the heat remained. She prided herself at Taimur's for feeling quite strong in the sun, but wrestling the post in the relentless heat was a different story. She was already weakening. Sweat dripped down her nose as her fingers explored the rope behind her back. But the knot was just out of reach.

She stood up and bent backward, trying to ease her sore back. Stay calm, she reminded herself. Try another solution.

She bent down again and experimented with pulling her arms around her bottom. Were the ropes loose enough? There was only one way to find out.

She walked over to the second post, which was still securely planted. She bent over next to it, allowing her shoulder to rest against the wood and provide stability. She worked her hands down and got them past her hips and over her bottom. Reaching as low as she could, she raised one foot and tried to lift it through her arms.

The ropes stuck on her sandal, which she quickly kicked off before trying again. Pushing with the tips of her fingers, she was able to get it through. The second foot, with a little more room, came through quickly.

"Hell yes!" she shouted, standing with her bound hands in front of her stomach. The relief in her shoulders was instant.

Ignoring the bloody scrapes on the undersides of her forearms, she set about untying the rope. It was cotton and, much like the ropes she'd found in the trunk, was about a quarter of an inch thick. It was looped several times around each wrist and figure-eighted back and forth a few times. She could feel a knot just behind one wrist and set about gradually working it to a spot she could just reach with a couple of fingers.

It was slow going, tedious, and frustrating. After a while, she plopped down on the remaining post. The sun touched the horizon, and Adira smiled when it brightened and spread wide for a second before the bottom of it passed below the edge of the desert.

"We're going to do this," she decided. The knot had come around to the front, and using her teeth and tongue, she loosened it a little, then a lot. Finally, it came free.

"Yes!" she shouted. Uncoiling the last loop, she threw the rope down into the sand. "Take that, Moosa!"

Adira sat back on the post as the last sliver of sun disappeared. The desert was cast in a dim, orange glow which she knew would quickly fade. She'd dealt with her first problem; now on to the next. Getting out of here.

She'd noted earlier that there was not a single reference point. All she had at the moment was a couple of posts and the sun. Using her heel, she drew a line in the sand pointing to where the sun had set. She retrieved the water bottle and thought about her predicament. She could wait and hope whoever used this camel stop would come back. It could be locals, or it could be a safari tour group. There was no way to tell if they'd be back tomorrow, next week, or never again. Judging by the lack of footprints other than her own, she figured never was the safest bet, meaning she was in for a walk. A long one.

Still, banging inside the car for a couple of hours and then dealing with the post had taken its toll. She'd lost a lot of water and decided that a quarter of the bottle would be worth it. She unscrewed the top and tipped it to her lips. She was careful, measured, and slow and enjoyed every drop. Despite wanting to keep going, she forced herself to stop. A quarter was gone. If she was honest, maybe a touch more. She set the bottle on the post and stood at one end of her line. She rotated ninety degrees right. Given it was early fall, the sun would set a little to the north of west. How much, she didn't know, so she swung a few degrees left and settled on that as north. Again, she made a long line in the sand.

Looking at the mark, she tried to remember the maps she'd seen during her time with Taimur.

Moosa had turned south into the Wahiba Sands pretty close to where she usually turned off for Taimur's. Given that his place was only twenty minutes from the northern end of the sands and she'd ridden in the trunk for nearly three hours, something didn't add up.

She'd felt they were going south based on the afternoon sun coming from the car's right. They'd driven at a hearty clip, and in three hours, they would have reached, and maybe passed, the bottom end of the sands. The teardrop-shaped region was a hundred miles long and about fifty wide. Surely they would have passed through to the mountains if they'd gone due south.

She moved to the north tip of her line and imagined where the sun was as she'd scrambled around in the back. Maybe it had been coming in at ninety degrees from the side, and their actual direction had been southwest. That would explain why the desert here wasn't golden dunes but more like large patches of sand mixed with swaths of rock and gravel. It also meant that to the west was the Empty Quarter, the harshest desert environment in the world.

West was out. South was a possibility, but she knew that the population was thinner there, and she could find herself wandering for weeks before finding a town. East would bring her, eventually, to the sea. But the coast there was rocky with even fewer villages.

North, or north and a little east, seemed like the best bet. There were a half dozen tourist camps in the northern part of the sands she might hit, or at least an outfitter moving gear back and forth.

Despite having a plan, she knew the outlook was dismal. The thrill of freeing herself had worn off, and she realized she was utterly lost, in the middle of a deadly environment, with, at most, twelve ounces of water.

She told herself to stay calm. She'd gotten out of the car unscathed and freed herself. The next priority was finding people. People would have access to water, food, and transportation. Those things, in that order, are what she needed next.

The sky was just a glow to the west. To the east, it was turning black with pinpricks of stars beginning to show. Still, the temperature had dropped to a reasonable eighty-five degrees, and there was enough light to see features on the ground. Picking up the bottle of water, she oriented herself north, pivoted ten degrees east, and began to walk.

After thirty minutes, the sand she was on was stripped down to dry and stony land. It made the going a little faster, but she had to watch her step more closely. Thankfully, a little less than half moon provided just enough light to see. Another thirty minutes later, she was back in a large area of sand. The pattern continued through the early night.

Trying to make sure she maintained her course was the most difficult. The desert was absolutely void of prominent features. She soon found herself alternating between looking backward to see if her footprints were straight and trying to remember which set of tiny wrinkles in the distance was her target.

She wanted to get as many miles in as she could before morning. Hour after hour, she trudged on. In one rocky section, she lost her footing, stepping on a stone that slid out from under her. She recovered fine, but it was just the start. Undulations in the sand caught her off guard more than once. Fatigue was beginning to set in, something she knew would impact her decision-making.

She decided to stop and dropped down onto the sand. The water was tempting, but she'd need it in the sun's heat. She'd rest instead. Just a few hours, then get underway before the sun hits at full blast. She let herself roll to the side, lifting her scarf up just enough to rest her head. Sleep came in minutes.

***

Taimur had been concerned much of the evening. He'd expected Adira to arrive by sunset at the latest, and his calls to her had gone unanswered. He rang Zahra, who was just as surprised Adira hadn't made it to the camp.

Zahra, in turn, called Amir and Chevy, in the off chance Adira had joined them. She next checked with the Royal Guard contingent at the hospital. As they had been told not to record the sayyida's visits, there was nothing in the log relating to her arrival or departure. The ranking night shift officer phoned the major he'd relieved, who explained—after the urgency of the situation was emphatically communicated— that Her Royal Highness did visit His Majesty earlier in the day. He related that following her visit, she had been escorted into the garage by a pair of his young lieutenants.

The major, for his part, had both lieutenants roused from their billets at the Al Alam barracks. Both men reported that the sayyida had, at the elevator doors, pointed to a desert tan Range Rover and insisted that she was perfectly capable of walking to the car herself. While they did not enter the garage, they both observed a tall man in a dishdasha, which was also tan, exit the vehicle and open the rear door for her. Once she was inside, they pressed the elevator button and returned.

By the time these details circled back to the major, he realized that the buck, as Americans were prone to say, stopped with him. Expanding on that thought, he quickly realized that he would be in hot water, likely over his head, in a very short amount of time. As a result, he was swift to do three things.

First, he used his authority to mobilize a team to get on the highways between the hospital and Taimur's camp and scan every inch of the road and roadside. His thought, or hope, at this point, was that they'd suffered a breakdown or had an accident on one of the many sharp, cliffside turns on the road through the mountains. Second, he reached out to the signals intelligence duty officer to have them begin a search for Her Royal Highness's phone. Third, and most dangerously, he thought about how to cover his own ass. Only then did he call and have his commanding officer wakened and brought to the phone.

After colorfully explaining the direction the major's career path would now take, the commanding officer mobilized additional forces to scour the route. It was not until the early morning that details, now fourth- and even fifth-hand, made their way back to Zahra and Taimur.

***

Deep in the empty desert land west of Wahiba Sands, Adira woke to the rising sun. Surprised to have slept that long, or even slept at all, she rolled up to a sitting position and rubbed her eyes.

While her view might have been inspiring on a postcard, the reality was demoralizing. The land in every direction was totally barren. There was only sand and rocky outcroppings. Not a single shrub, animal, or man-made object could be seen.

Priorities, she reminded herself. Water, food, and people. The last would lead to the first two. She planned to walk north, hoping to find a camp in the sands or survive long enough to make it to one of the villages at the north edge of the sands.

She'd stick with her plan. Mainly because there was no alternative.

She checked her water, still only one-quarter empty. Convincing herself that a small amount would help replace a bit of the water she'd lost sleeping, she opened the bottle and took a sip. It was delightful enough that she quickly twisted the cap back on to remove the temptation to indulge in more.

She took the scarf from her neck and gently wiped her face. Feeling how the skin had tightened on her forearms, she inspected the abrasions. There were a few lacerations, places where the skin had broken, that had scabbed up overnight. She shook the sand out of her scarf and used the folds to remove sand that had stuck to the blood as it dried. While she tried her best not to reopen any wounds, tiny drops speckled the fabric.

She held it out and shook it once again. It was the scarf Safa had given her at the Grand Mosque. When Adira had dressed the morning before, she decided its splash of color went well with the white linen pants and top Zahra had provided. It still matched, though now, thanks to the dirty sweat stains that covered her head to toe.

"I might need your help today, Mom," Adira murmured as she stood. She took a bearing on the rising sun, oriented herself, and began walking.

The going was more manageable in the morning light. She could pick out undulations on the surface that had caught her out the night before, and her pace improved. As she marched through the morning hours, calculations ran through her mind. A hearty walking pace was four miles per hour. But with the sandy terrain, that would be knocked down, closer to two-and-a-half or three miles an hour. If she went nonstop for sixteen hours, she felt she could make maybe forty-five miles. Even if she'd been dropped all the way at the southern end of the sands, the villages at the northern edge were reachable within two days. And two days was within the amount of time a person could survive without water. It was doable, she told herself.

By late morning, she began to see what looked like mountains in the distance. It was only as she closed the distance and the shadows shortened that she understood the hills were actually towering dunes. At their base, folds of golden sand swept over the darker sand and pebbles she'd been crossing. She'd reached the edge of Wahiba Sands.

One foot in front of the other, she climbed the first dune. At the top, the pattern of flaxen folds stretched far beyond the horizon. It was a sight so vast that she began to seriously question the logic of her plan.

"No, this is right," she muttered. Pulling her scarf up to cover her head and provide a little shade for her eyes, she again set off.

20

By midday, a half dozen of the Royal Guard's senior officers had distributed a significant number of lectures, reprimands, and orders. People had been questioned, messages had been sent, and asses had been covered at a pace never seen before. The result, by midday, was a loose lead on what had occurred. An assistant to the general in command of the Royal Guard had communicated, at the general's direction, their progress to Taimur. Taimur, in turn, was quick to call Zahra.

"The news isn't encouraging," he confessed.

"What's the update?" she asked, her voice rushed. "My last call was overnight. They'd searched the road without luck and were going out again at first light. It's been light for hours now, and I haven't heard a thing!"

"While they were searching, the Palace guard roused everyone in and around the hospital. They're investigating what happened thoroughly."

"Investigating?" Zahra shouted into her phone. "Why aren't they searching? The skies should be buzzing with helicopters!"

Taimur was briefly silent before replying. "I know this is hard. Let me explain what I've heard. Please."

"Sorry, Taimur."

"It is okay. This is upsetting to all of us," Taimur said. "You know, I think, that her protection detail switched with

Minister Omar's? That it was a gift of sorts for him to give her his fancy car and detail?"

"Yes, she told me. And I saw the Rolls and the guard at the Kempinski."

"Good. The morning after your dinner, this guard, Moosa is his name, brought Adira to the hospital. At the end of her visit, she was brought down to Moosa, who was then to drive her up to the sands."

"So where's Moosa?"

Ignoring the question, Taimur continued. "Moosa explained that Adira became quite distraught in the car. He thought seeing her father's condition weakened her, and she could not stop crying. She—"

"Crying and distraught? That doesn't sound like her."

"I agree, but this is what they've learned. She asked Moosa to take her to the airport. A friend was flying in that she wanted to meet and bring up to our camp."

"No friend was coming in," Zahra muttered. "She would have said something."

"The guard was instructed to wait outside while she ran in to meet this friend. You know she has a way with these young men."

"Mm-hmm. Bossy."

"Exactly. Moosa has explained to his superiors that he waited almost ninety minutes. At that point, he went inside. After searching the arrivals area, he contacted airport security. They sent men to search the arrivals area and came up empty."

"Oh no."

"They checked the cameras. A woman in white pants and a shirt with a light purple scarf went to the Qatar Airlines desk and purchased a ticket to New York. The cameras tracked her through the airport and out to the gate. The flight left less than an hour after she walked in."

"No," Zahra whispered. Her stomach spun into a knot.

"I'm sorry, my dear."

"Why didn't the Royal Guard know? This Moosa, he should have reported it!"

"He reported it to Minister Omar."

"Omar is not his commander!"

"Only on paper," Taimur explained. "Omar brought him over from Internal State Security specifically to serve on his personal detail. For years, Omar has been his only manager."

"He should have gone to the Guard."

"Perhaps," Taimur admitted. "But he was with Adira on Omar's orders. She'd left the country, so he returned to Omar's office and explained what happened. Omar called me as well. He was very sorry to hear she'd left. He'd met her at the hospital and found her charming."

Zahra fought through her emotions and thought about how Adira had behaved the morning before. "It just doesn't fit."

"I understand how—"

"She had just confirmed her job with Amir. She wanted to stay, Taimur. She'd committed—really committed herself—to stay!"

"That may be. But she was taken to the airport. There is video of her going to the gate. I think we have to consider—"

"How good is this video? I need to see it. I need to see the ticket. The flight manifest," Zahra insisted.

"We are grasping at straws here."

"Straws smaller than this brought her here," she mumbled. "Any update on His Majesty?"

"It is not good, I'm afraid. I am heading down shortly. I want to be there for him when Allah decides it is time."

"I'm sorry, Taimur."

"Thank you, my dear."

"I appreciate the update. Let me know if you need anything at the hospital."

They said their goodbyes, and Zahra closed the line. She went to a cabinet and pulled her laptop out. After placing it carefully on the dining table, she opened it and got to work.

***

By late afternoon, Adira's pace had slowed considerably. Each dune she climbed stressed her tired, dehydrated body to the limit. Each step she took sank into the sand, making the next step that much more difficult. The sun stung like a hot iron, scorching everything it touched. While her tawny-brown skin had always been quite resistant to burning, exposure for almost the entire day had taken its toll. The backs of her legs were crispy, and her arms below her sleeves were tender to the touch. Her lips were chapped and swollen, and her eyes stung.

She'd laid the linen scarf over her head, allowing it to form a tent over her neck and shoulders. A fold had been made over her forehead in an effort to shade her eyes. But the motion of her steps and small bursts of wind kept flipping it down. A mile ago, she'd just let it hang. All she really needed was to see the next step. Then the one after that, and the one after that. Nothing else mattered.

She'd adopted a pattern of stopping every two hours. Or at least what she thought were two hours. She'd sit, put her head between her legs, and catch her breath. She'd allowed herself to take a sip of water during the last break. She planned to on the next one as well. It was almost all she could think of.

The size of the dunes made a number of things even more challenging than the sheer effort it took to climb them. Since walking up the face was incredibly difficult, she'd taken to scrabbling along the ridges, linking them as best she could while maintaining what she hoped was the right direction.

She could check if her bearing was straight where the dunes were smaller by scanning the trail behind her. But zig-zagging as she was, getting a sense of where she'd been had become challenging. The wind had also become a problem. Her footsteps along the ridges were often whisked away by the time she'd remembered to check.

With the sun lower, shadows began to stretch down the dunes. Looking down as she followed a curving ridge, the sunny side was a mixture of silver and gold. The shady side was in complete contrast, its tiny grains a warm mix of red umber with specs of pearl. After trying to name the colors beneath her feet for far too long, she realized it was time to stop. She'd been dizzy since her last stop, and a headache that started as a mild annoyance was building.

Before collapsing in the shade provided by the dune, she turned and looked back to track her progress. Already the wind had erased her presence. It didn't matter. The sun would have to be a good enough reference. She'd have a little rest and carry on at dusk.

She took three steps down the shady side of the dune. On the fourth, her weak legs gave out, and she fell. The landing was soft enough, though, and the relief of being out of the sun was immediate.

"The wind," she mumbled. Her voice was barely the hint of a whisper. "Moosa said the wind—no, the sand—would bury the problem."

Her mind, like her body, was depleted, making her thoughts a tangled mess. But she'd heard that phrase before.

"Omar. That's just what Omar said."

As her mind made the connection, she remembered he'd said that Omar had tried before when Moosa was a boy.

"How old is Moosa?" she wondered, the words barely escaping her lips.

He was strong. Young and tall. She'd seen no gray, but there were lines around his eyes. He would have to be a little older than she was, but not by much.

Exhaustion began to pull the shade down on her mind. She couldn't even understand why this mattered when her body decided sleep was more important than anything else.

She woke just over five hours later; the sun was long since gone. But a tiny part of her brain had been turning while she slept, and her first thought was Omar. He'd assigned Moosa to her, put him in a place where he could take her away at any time.

She had to get back if only to let people know that this man had a sinister side. She'd encouraged his appointment to the throne. To her father, as well as others. If the council passed on Rashid, the pressure from others might be strong enough for them to name Omar. She felt miserable for even suggesting his name.

She stood. A little wobbly and more than a little stiff. Setting the scarf down, she forced herself to stretch. As she bent side to side, she felt the urge to pee. Lowering her pants and squatting down, the experience was unpleasant. There was a slight sting and little result. What concerned her more was the strong smell. She decided that she would finish the water, make the most of it tonight when walking in the dark would cause less of it to sweat away.

Adira took her time, savoring every tepid swallow. When she finished, she crinkled the bottle enough to reduce its size and placed it in her pocket in case she came across some way to fill it. Then she climbed the ridge, made a best guess on direction, and marched on. It was time to make things right.

***

Moosa had finally made his way back to his tiny apartment after a long day of questioning. His ruse, everything from the second Range Rover that went to the hospital and the doubles for himself and Adira to the disposal of the first Range Rover, had, so far at least, worked.

A phone—not his main phone, but one from a set he kept for discreet conversations, rang. Only one person had the number.

"Your Excellency," he said by way of greeting.

"How did today go? What is our risk?" Omar demanded.

Moosa didn't expect a job-well-done again. He'd received that the evening before, once he'd ditched the Range Rover, its interior a tattered mess, at a disused mechanic's shop in

Nizwa. "We are fine. The Guard is quite sad the sayyida has decided to return to America."

"They'll trace her phone. I hadn't thought of this yesterday. Is there going to be a trail leading up to her resting place?" The voice asked.

"No. I used a jammer in the vehicle, and her phone was destroyed before the parts were disposed of. There's no trail there, Your Excellency."

"Good. Let us keep it that way. Come to the office tomorrow. We will keep you out of sight."

"As you wish, Your Excellency," Moosa replied.

"It will be 'Your Majesty' once the council hears that recording. And from what the hospital says, it will be very soon."

Moosa's clenched the phone. "You recorded the call?"

"Of course. What do you think the purpose of antagonizing this fool was?"

Moosa thought back. "*My* voice is on that call, Your Excellency. Is it really necessary?"

"Relax, young man. I will have the luxury of pardoning you once this business is finished."

"And if you don't receive that luxury?" Moosa's voice grew quiet with the realization that he would soon be a casualty in the quest for power. "Your Excellency, please…"

The line fell silent for a moment. "When the time comes, I will put you on security outside the building. If it appears my plan will fail, you will have the chance to run. I offer this as a token of my appreciation for your service. But I am certain it will not be needed."

Sweat prickled Moosa's forehead.

"We will succeed, I promise you. And the result will be far more than the money that fool Rashid wants to skim off our glorious resource. No, my friend. What will come is *true* power. The chance to bring our nation back on course. To end these silly notions of everyone being equal, of people having a voice. We won't let our country fall into the hands of fools! We will create a nation of strength!"

The line abruptly closed, and Moosa's shoulders fell.

"You had to do it," he reminded himself. But inside, he wasn't convinced.

21

Adira carried on through more than half the night. Her pace was slow, her body exhausted, starving, and dehydrated, and her feet swollen and blistered. Her stops were more frequent, but she forced herself to keep them short. She pushed on until, once again, her legs gave out. This time, she laid the scarf down in the sand and did her best to tell herself it was a bed. In her delirious state, her mind believed her, and she fell fast asleep.

At dawn, her outlook was bleak. She'd had no water for nine hours and very little before that. She hadn't eaten in nearly two full days, and at the rate she was burning through her energy and water stores, she had only a day before she'd be too weak to move.

But help wasn't going to find her here, so she rose again—slower this time—and did her best to stretch her legs. And more reluctantly then before, she put one foot in front of the other.

***

"Sheikh?" a nurse whispered to Taimur. "You have a visitor."

Taimur, tired from spending much of the night next to the hospital bed, stood and went to the door. "I will be just a moment, my friend."

Once in the lobby, he nodded to the doctor and scanned the room. Zahra waited expectantly for his gaze to reach her.

Once they caught eyes, she tilted her head toward a small conference room and preceded him inside. She leaned her cane against the table and set her bag down.

"Good morning," she said, pulling her laptop out of her bag. "How is he?"

"I think Allah would like to meet him," he replied. "It will soon be time."

Zahra went still at the sight of his pain. "I am so sorry. But I have something you must see."

Taimur took a seat. Zahra grabbed one as well and it around next to him.

Taking his silence for permission to continue, she sat and opened the laptop. On the screen was a video player. "These are from the airport. I pulled together what they had so we could follow her movement."

She pressed play, and an image of Adira walking from the curb to the airport doors appeared.

"The resolution at this distance is poor. I enhanced it, but this was the best I could do." They watched Adira take a few steps before leaving the frame as she passed through the door. Zahra pressed the space bar to stop the player. "What did you see?"

"A woman walking into the airport. Adira, I presume, if that matches what you saw her wearing in the morning. The blurriness and her hijab make it difficult to tell exactly who it is."

"Precisely." Zahra pointed to the screen. "That hijab. When have you known her to wear it?"

Taimur shrugged. "On and off. In the Grand Mosque. Perhaps when she met Nadir."

"Exactly. Sure, she always had one ready. But only for when it was required. Otherwise, it was around her neck."

"Zahra, this—"

"Wait." She held up her hand. "There's more."

Taimur made a gesture for her to continue.

Zahra pressed play once again. The camera was now in the ticketing area. Again, the angle was oblique, but a woman looking very much like Adira could be seen speaking with an agent and handing over a card. The agent typed, a passport was passed back and forth, and before long, a boarding pass was handed over. Zahra stopped the video again. "The rest of the footage is similar. This woman proceeds to a waiting area, sits for twenty minutes, and then goes to the gate."

Taimur nodded, not wanting to interrupt as Zahra flicked and clicked the trackpad.

The screen changed to a tabbed set of documents. She pointed to the first. "This is a record of the credit card I gave her." She clicked again. "This is from the bank card you and His Majesty provided. And this," she continued after clicking again, "is her original American credit card. None of these showed a ticket purchase."

"Aside from my amazement that you can dig these things up so quickly, they do not mean she didn't have another card."

"You are right. So I took a look at her phone. It has been completely out of service—completely cut off—since the day before yesterday, about two-and-a-half hours after she left the Palace. Of course, this would be the case if she was on a plane.

She would turn it off or put it in airplane mode. But she wasn't on a plane, and I know this for certain."

Taimur's gray eyebrows sprung up.

"I was able to, ah, gain access to the flight manifests. There was no Adira Eastmont nor Adira al Sabir on that flight. Nor on any flight the entire day."

Taimur leaned back. He looked up at the ceiling and took a deep inhale. Lowering his gaze back down, he asked, "Then where is she?"

Zahra's shoulders fell. "I have no idea. But the guard—Moosa—knows. He's who we have to find."

"You will need to do this, Zahra. If she is here—if she is alive—you need to find her," he said, his voice firm. Tilting his head toward the room where the sultan lay, he said, "I need to be here. For when it's time. To set the wheels in motion."

Zahra nodded. She'd seen the Royal Guard were now in their dress uniforms.

"Use your position in the Palace." Pointing again to the room next door, he continued, "He loves you, you know. And he values your abilities immensely for the job you did finding his daughter."

She humbly looked down.

"You're good at this. Find Moosa, then find Adira."

"*Inshallah*," she said, closing the laptop.

For almost all of the day, Zahra lit a fire under the Royal Guard and the Foreign Ministry. She chased every lead she could via phone, message, and in person in more than a half dozen government buildings. After tracking down Moosa's personal address, she even had the police break into his apartment. But finding him eluded her.

When she did eventually reach the assistant to the commander of the Royal Guard, it was explained that a cursory investigation had been done—via a phone call between Minister Omar and the assistant, making it highly suspect in Zahra's mind—and Moosa had been found to be conducting himself in accordance with his mission. It was simply a fact, the tiresome man explained, that the "American woman" wanted to leave, and so she had. He felt there was video proof; by contrast, there was no proof that she did not have another card or passport and leave under another name. As Zahra explained to him how preposterous this was, she was promptly hung up on.

***

In the middle of five thousand square miles of sand, Adira continued to plod along. She was nowhere near where she'd hoped to be, and her path had brought her in a broad arc that was now severely off course.

Her eyes, lips, and nose stung from the sun's intensity. Every muscle and tendon was depleted, screaming for her to stop. It was her body's effort to save the most important organs. Its instinct was to protect the brain and core functions for blood flow above all else. If that meant shutting down other parts, it would do what had to be done.

But Adira knew the body could take a more brutal beating than most people thought. What she felt now were just warning signs. A notification that she had some time, but she better hurry.

Deep inside, she also knew that she was tougher than most. She'd seen low points like few had, and she'd survived. This was just one more heaping spoonful of life's challenges.

Using determination more than anything else, she kept on. One step after the other. Again and again.

Thankfully, her mind hadn't fallen completely apart. She hadn't seen visions of palm trees and fountains. But nor had she seen vehicle tracks or anything man-made.

Until one tiny shape began to appear in the undulating waves of heat on the horizon. It was only a speck, yet had a hard edge, a distinctly vertical form poking up.

Worried it was her first mirage, she looked down at her feet for a while. When she brought her eyes back up, it was still there. She shifted her course to the direction of the shape and painfully carried on. After thirty minutes, she was sure it was a building. After an hour, she could tell it was a mosque. Standing there, all on its own, with nothing around. There were no other buildings, no cars. Nothing. But still, it was a mosque. There would be water and shade. And hopefully, people.

The last hour was extremely tough. She staggered with each slow step, her legs, feet, and even her mind at their limits.

A concrete wall surrounded the structure. Standing eight feet tall, it formed a large square around the mosque. Adira arrived at the side, close to the glorious minaret. It was painted a sandy gray, with vast detailing sparkling in gold. It was as if Allah had set it down in the middle of the barren land just for her.

But only if she could escape the blistering sun.

She followed the wall around, taking a turn to the right. This portion was more ornate, with wide arches painted in a contrasting color. She stabilized herself by putting a hand on the hot surface.

"Real," she croaked, her lips unable to even open.

She came to a double metal gate painted gold. If her body could form a tear, it would have come right then. But the gate wouldn't swing open. It was chained to its opposite.

She pushed on. A dozen steps later was a second pair of gates, also chained. She clutched the gold bars and leaned forward, trying to shout.

"Help!" she called. Her voice, however, had left entirely. All that came out was a fetid breath. Her head fell in defeat. But looking down, she saw that the chain on this gate was looser than the first. There was a gap.

She leaned in, pushing. Her fingers fumbled with the hot chain, ensuring each link was oriented the long way. A few had to be moved, and the gap opened further with each. There was room enough now. She moved one leg in, then a shoulder. Rocking her pelvis, she squeezed her torso through and then, with a hard scrape on her sunburned ears, her head.

She staggered across an expanse of checkerboard tile that filled half of the courtyard. Using her hands for support, she climbed a dozen stairs to a large, covered entryway. She allowed herself to collapse in the glorious shade, where she sobbed, her shoulders shaking with sheer relief.

The respite from the sun was glorious, but she still urgently needed water. She pushed herself up to find she was surrounded entirely by faucets. They ran along the sides of the covered space and turned in at the main walls on either side of the sets of doors leading to the mosque. A tiled collection basin ran between them, the ledge making a place for worshippers to sit and perform their ablutions before prayer.

She crawled to the closest faucet and turned the lever. A drop fell, and a second clung to the spigot. That was it. She licked the spout and used her finger to pick up the one that had fallen. Slowly she crawled to another faucet. It was empty as well. She went to each one with the same result. The water had been turned off.

She crawled to one of the large doors to the inside. Reaching up, she found it was locked. She banged a fist on the door twice, then moved to the next. Each of the four doors was locked. Again she banged, paused to listen, and banged again. There was no sound other than her short, raspy breaths.

The mosque was abandoned. It would be one for travelers, workers at tourist camps on the sands, or Bedouins who crossed the area during certain seasons. Her spirits fell.

She pushed herself to her feet and carefully shuffled down the stairs, intent on finding the water tank or a valve she could open. Slowly making her way around the building, she checked in every crevasse and behind every section of wall. She made one complete circuit, testing every door, yet finding nothing. The water must be controlled from the inside.

Her lap around the building was slow, and the sky had dimmed considerably. There was only so much light left, so she limped off for another loop, this time in the opposite direction.

She caught more on this lap, the most important of which was a set of young trees that had been recently planted. Running between them was an irrigation line. Even if the water was cut off, some residual water might have collected in the line's low points. If it had run recently, there was a chance evaporation hadn't dried them out completely.

She got down on her hands and knees. Weaving through the dirt were small feeder lines for each plant branching off the main hose. She got down on her hands and knees and freed one of the feeder lines. After wiping dust off the nozzle at the end, she wedged it between her dried lips and sucked. A little came out before turning to air. It was only about a teaspoon, but glorious, nonetheless. She crawled to the next one and was able to get only a few drops. She realized the plant she'd chosen was slightly higher than the first. Reversing course, she went down a few plants to the lowest point. From that one, she was able to get closer to a mouthful. Hearing bubbles somewhere in the line, she decides to detach the feeder and suck directly from the main line. Again she was able to get a mouthful.

She made her way around the courtyard, pulling the feeder line at the two other low points she found. Each provided nearly an ounce of water. She methodically made her way around, ensuring she'd tried each plant's feeder line. Some were dry, but several had anything from a few drops to half a teaspoon. But every sip, even the smallest, helped both mentally and physically.

By the time she finished, it was completely dark. The fatigue of walking for well over two days hit her hard, so she crawled back up to the covered entrance area and nestled herself against one of the large doors. She pulled the scarf around her neck and balled it into a tiny pillow. She laid back and closed her eyes.

22

A father, along with his almost-teenage son and eight-year-old daughter, rode together in a Toyota pickup truck. Much to the boy's dismay, he had been displaced from his usual spot in the front passenger seat by his younger sister, who had raced ahead when they'd left the shop, claiming an urgent need to control the radio.

The young girl had chosen a station that played an Arab pop song both she and her father knew. They sang along, the girl even going so far as to raise her hands in the air and wiggle-dance along with the beat as they crossed the eastern side of the sands. While the boy tried to maintain a pouty expression, behind the seat back, his hands tapped along with the beat.

The father made a slight course correction as the next song came on. To most, the sands could look uniform, nearly identical in every direction. But to this family, each set of dunes had its own character, and despite there not being a single marker, they knew exactly where they were headed.

By the time the next song ended, their destination was in sight. The father pulled the truck up to the gates. His son hopped out, keys in hand, and swung first one open, then the other. He was back in the cab a minute later, rubbing his eyes as they drove around to the side of the mosque. The early start to the day was hard on his fast-growing son, but they had plenty of work to do today. He turned the wheel and backed up as close as possible to a service door.

The son unlocked the door and propped it open with a rubber wedge. Afterward, he joined his father at the pickup's bed. There were a dozen cases of water to unload, along with some boxes of sweets, crisps, and other snacks the outfitters liked to have after prayers. The mosque wasn't used much this time of year. It was early autumn now, and visited just once a week. During the winter, when more people came out to the camps, it would be used daily and left open.

The boy took two boxes, and the young girl reluctantly took a third. The father grabbed a double-stack of waters and followed his children inside. They set their goods down on a long counter in what was called the kitchen but was really just a sizable back room space with a single slop sink.

Turning for another load with his son, the father spoke to the young girl. "Leila, go and turn on the water. Then press the button on the irrigation box. The new plants outside will need it. Do you remember which button?"

"Yes, Baba!" she called back, already skipping around the corner.

By the time the boys returned with their second loads, the pipes had given a *thunk*. Good, she'd remembered.

They'd just stepped out to take another load when the father heard air bubbling through the irrigation lines they'd run not long ago. The sound was normal. The fountains of water that erupted, spurting water every which way around the plants, weren't.

"Baba!" his daughter called.

"Leila!" he shouted. "Turn it off!"

"But Baba! There is a—"

"I need you to turn the water off now! Push the button again!"

"Baba, there is a woman here! In the front!"

The father froze. A woman? That was unlikely. But he went around the corner of the building anyway. He was sure there wasn't a woman there, but at least he could settle his daughter and turn off the irrigation. As he reached the bottom of the stairs at the front of the mosque, he could see what was, indeed, a woman. He was up and on his knees by her side in an instant.

Being raised on the edge of the desert, it took only a glance at her burned lips and red cheeks to know she'd been in the sun for too long and was severely dehydrated. He told his daughter to grab some water bottles before attempting to wake the woman.

"Hello," he said gently in Arabic. He tried again, this time rubbing her arm as he spoke. There was still no response. He grabbed her shoulders and gently rocked them, talking to her the entire time. He pressed a finger to her neck and felt a tiny pulse. It was rapid but very weak.

Leila arrived, and he took a bottle from her. Twisting off the cap, he poured water into it, then slowly tipped it to her lips. Almost all of it passed through to her mouth.

"Is she alive?" Leila asked.

"Yes," he replied. "But unwell."

He poured another capful into her mouth.

"Woman, it is time to wake up!" Leila crowed.

Her eyelids moved a fraction. The father reached and carefully pushed one eye open. It was rolled back. But then, with a flash, a golden eye centered. The other eye opened, and Adira began to focus.

"Good morning!" the girl said, delight in her voice.

Adira let out a weak cough.

"I am going to turn you on your side, okay?" The father explained, thinking some water may have been inhaled instead of swallowed.

He took hold of her shoulder and hip and gently rolled her toward him. Her top leg he bent to help her stay in place.

"Can you drink?" he asked.

A feeble nod came in reply. Holding the water low, he tipped it toward her lips. She was able to raise her head enough to take some of the water in. It stung as it made its way down her raw, swollen throat.

She coughed once more, but her eyes darted to the bottle for more. Once again, he tilted it, and she was able to get two sips down.

Slowly, things came into focus. She recognized that someone had come. Someone had come and saved her. Angels, they must be. Angels.

She tried to speak, but her voice was nothing more than a wheeze.

The girl had now laid down on her stomach, her face close enough to touch. Adira took another sip from the bottle and tried to curve her cracked lips into a smile.

"Your eyes are beautiful!" The girl exclaimed.

And with that, Adira's beautiful eyes were able to use the last of their reserves to create a single tear.

✳✳✳

Taimur had stayed at Sultan Hamad's side through the night, dozing off and on in a recliner next to the hospital bed. His Majesty lay still and silent, his body and spirit preparing for the inevitable.

At dawn, the hospital chief of staff, the head oncologist, and Dr. Daoud each reviewed the staff's overnight observations and conducted their own examinations. They worked in near silence around Taimur, sharing only sympathetic nods. After quietly leaving the room, they shared their conclusions in hushed tones. None were optimistic.

Taimur looked at his friend and saw not the man next to him now, but the lively young man who had made him laugh, cry, and cheer for so many years. A mosaic of memories flashed through his mind, from time in their youth, exploring, to official ceremonies in palaces, and even the intimate moments when the nation's leader conferred with him on decisions of state.

"I am going to miss you, old friend," he said, taking hold of Sultan Hamad's hand. "But stay close because I look forward to sitting by your side again in paradise."

The first rays of the morning sun crested the mountains and warmed the windows. In the glow, a hollow opened up deep in Taimur's heart. It was not pain or alarm but a shift, a change that let him know something had been peacefully released. A moment later, the monitor let out a slow, steady tone, and the colorful peaks and valleys on the screen fell to a flat line.

He placed a hand on his friend's cheek, then silently stepped back as doctors and nurses converged on the hospital bed. As required, they did their best to revive him. But His

Majesty, the Sultan of Oman, had decided it was time to step into the afterlife.

Taimur stayed with his friend as the doctors removed an array of leads and tubes. A nurse then crossed His Majesty's hands on his chest and tidied the bedding with precision and care. Once the carts of machinery had been removed and Taimur was left alone in the room, he went down to his knees. He touched his forehead to the floor and prayed.

When he finally stood, he called for the Royal Guard to station two men in the room. One would stand guard and make sure His Majesty was never alone, and the other would hold the flag of the nation he'd so proudly led.

Taimur went to the secretary's office next door. Together, they assembled and reviewed a series of documents. Once everything appeared to be in order, the two of them relocated to the small conference room where several people had gathered. Arrangements for this day had been made years ago, soon after His Majesty's diagnosis. As Sultan Hamad's closest friend and confidant, Taimur now had the duty to set those plans underway.

Seated at the conference table were His Majesty's lead spokesperson, the Chairman of the Supreme Court, the commander of the Royal Army of Oman, and the chairmen of the two houses of parliament, the Majlis al-Shura and the Majlis al-Dawla, within the Oman Council. The imam from the Grand Mosque was also in attendance, standing off to the side. The secretary and Taimur took their seats and explained the protocols framing what would soon become a hectic day.

The Islamic religion views death as a passage to the afterlife and has specific customs concerning the deceased and burial. After death, the body is to be washed by a family member of the same gender, wrapped in three white sheets, and buried within twenty-four hours or before the next sunset. Taimur had made the decision that His Majesty's funeral would be at four o'clock that afternoon. Leaders from other nations would want to attend, and the short notice would make that impossible for some. But he did not want his friend to wait.

He then confirmed that the next three days would be national days of mourning. With the funeral time set and the days of mourning determined, the spokesperson quickly reviewed the content that would carry the news around the world. He confirmed that prior to their broad distribution, the Foreign Ministry would contact all of the Omani embassies. Next, the leaders of the Gulf states would be notified, and then each nation with whom the sultanate maintained direct relations. After those messages were sent, the international press would receive word.

Even upon His Majesty's death, the sultanate was not without leadership. Provisions had been put in place long ago that assigned ultimate authority to the commander of the Royal Army of Oman until a new sultan could be appointed by the Royal Family Council. The Chairman of the Supreme Court confirmed this fact and asked the two Chairmen of the Oman Council to verbally assert their understanding and acceptance of the role the military would play during this time of transition.

Next, Taimur informed the group that the Royal Family Council would meet tonight at eight o'clock to appoint the next Sultan of Oman. The timing of this had been debated in the past, but everyone understood that it was in the best interest of the nation to provide stability for its people. He informed the group that he had in his possession the names of each council member and would personally notify each of them as well as those with material purpose for attendance. A few eyebrows rose in surprise that Taimur knew who was on the Family Council, and that one of the guests with "material purpose for attendance" would become the next Sultan of Oman.

When the meeting concluded, everyone filed out with the exception of Taimur and the imam. Taimur stood and put an arm around the old man, and together they went to wash their friend and prepare him for Allah's protection.

23

At the mosque in the center of the sands, Adira pushed herself to a seated position. Her back against the door, she thanked the father and daughter in a coarse whisper of Arabic.

They helped her drink from the bottle at first. As her strength returned, she was able to hold it herself. The son returned with more water, as well as a hastily assembled handful of snacks from the boxes they'd brought in.

"I don't think packaged goods like this will be good for her, Ravi," the father said.

"These?" Adira whispered, pointing to a bag of sweet gummy treats.

Ravi opened the pack and held it to her. She took two and ravenously chewed them before drinking from a second bottle and extending her hand for more.

"You will need something better to eat," the father said. Reaching forward, he asked, "May I?"

Adira nodded and held out her hands. The man helped her up and then put his neck beneath her shoulder. Together, they walked to the pickup truck. With Leila in the back with Adira, and Ravi back in his usual place, they set off for their home at the edge of the sands.

"My name is Adira," she said, her voice growing stronger.

"I am Khalil, and this is my daughter Leila. My son is named Ravi, and we are very happy to help you."

"Thank you, Khalil." She placed a hand on Leila's leg. "Your eyes are beautiful too."

The family brought her to their modest home in a small village of only eight or ten buildings. Ravi must have sent a message to his mother because a lovely woman in a cheerful yellow-patterned dress was waiting just outside.

The woman ran to the side of the pickup and helped Adira out. She said something about going inside that Adira didn't quite understand. "Forgive me, but would speaking English be okay?"

The woman froze for a second, surprised. "Of course. My name is Hana. Let us get you inside. I think you have had enough time in the sun."

She was brought into a small living room with very tall ceilings. The cushions upon which the family would usually sit were assembled against a wall in the shape of a bed and covered with a fresh white sheet. Adira sat down and then turned. Hana helped her adjust the pillows, and soon she was in a perfect raised position.

Khalil and Ravi followed Hana into the kitchen. But Leila couldn't take her eyes off Adira. She came and sat cross-legged right next to the makeshift bed. Glancing down and seeing there was still a gap, she scooted even closer.

Leila held a bottle up and asked in English, "Water?"

"Yes, please," Adira replied. She had been steadily drinking but trying not to take too much each time.

"Where are you from?"

Adira smiled. The girl was curious about her speaking English.

"America," she replied. "And Oman. Both."

"How can you be from two places?"

It was a good question. "If I have to choose, I'd say Oman. But I lived in America for a long time."

Leila nodded, content with this answer.

"Your English is excellent. How old are you?"

"Eight. Why did you sleep at the mosque?"

"I was lost. And very tired."

"Did Allah find you and bring you there?"

Adira closed her eyes and wondered precisely the same thing. "He did," she finally replied. "And He brought a friend."

"A friend? Who?"

Adira held out her hand for the girl to take. "You."

Hana walked in with a small tray holding a sliced apple and a bowl of khabeesa, a warm Omani porridge flavored with cardamom. The smell was heaven to Adira, and she tore right in. It was everything she needed: soothing, filling, and absolutely delicious. The bowl was finished in an instant.

"Well, I better make some more." Hana took the bowl back to the kitchen with a chuckle.

Adira was feeling better already. She finished the apple and a second bowl of khabeesa before yet another bottle of water.

After clearing away the tray, Hana turned her attention to Adira's rough appearance. They went together into the bathroom, where she was helped out of her soiled clothes. Adira cleaned herself thoroughly and, after seeing the dark swirls twist down the drain, did so once more. They applied a balm to Adira's lips and her cuts and scrapes. She was given fresh underwear, a pair of pants, and a comfortable dress. Despite feeling refreshed, Adira's eyelids were growing heavy.

Inside, her body was working hard to process the fluids and restart her digestive tract.

"I need to let someone know I'm okay. I—" Adira's stomach cramped, and she doubled over.

Hana guided her to the makeshift bed and helped her lay down. "Right now, you need rest while your body adjusts. When you wake up, we'll call everyone you need to."

Adira didn't even have the energy to reply.

***

"Hello! Time to get up!" Leila cooed, giving Adira's shoulder a shake.

Adira startled at the touch, her eyes popping open. The room quickly came into focus, and for a fraction of a second, she wondered where she was. But then she saw the smiling face of cute Leila. "Hello," she replied. "Wow, I was out."

Leila nodded. "Mama said I could wake you. She said you need food."

Adira rubbed her eyes. "Sounds good. Please tell her I'll be right there."

"Your clothes are dry now," Leila said, pointing to a tidy, folded stack. "Your scarf is okay, but the others, not so much."

Adira picked up the scarf and looped it around her neck. "That was very nice of you."

Leila dashed off to the kitchen. "Mama! Mama! She is awake!" she shouted on her way through the hall.

Adira rose slowly. She had a bit of a headache and still felt a little woozy but was eventually able to stand and make her way to the kitchen.

Hana got up from a small table where the family sat and helped Adira to a chair. A large platter of chicken kabuli sat before them, still steaming. More importantly, two bottles of an electric blue sports drink were at the ready by her seat.

"Oh, thank you!" she said, twisting the cap off one and taking a hearty swig.

"Khalil found them at the shop. They have some things in them that should help."

Adira's head bobbed as she drank greedily.

The family watched in amusement.

When she finished, she gave them all a smile. "What, have you never seen a girl revive from being half-dead in the desert?"

"Not in at least a day or two," Hana said with a chuckle. She handed her a spoon and pointed to the platter, "Now eat. You need to get your strength back."

Adira reached out with her spoon. The rice dish was fragrant and delicious, peppered with nuts, raisins, and moist pieces of chicken. Adira complimented Hana between bites as the children began to eat as well.

Hana explained where the dish came from and how it was made. Adira was sure the family was holding back a thousand questions and that Hana only gave the lecture to give Adira the chance to eat.

Once she was full, Adira set down her spoon. Hana and Khalil then began to eat themselves.

She took a sip from the second bottle and declared herself done, full, and extremely happy. She thanked each of them, one by one.

And then she answered the question they'd all been too polite to ask. "I'm sorry to have wrecked your sprinklers at the mosque."

Khalil smiled and made a dismissive gesture with this spoon.

"Three days ago, I was taken and dropped out in the desert. I'm not entirely sure where, but I think it was pretty far on the other side of the sands. I was trying to get up to the villages near Bidiyah. Am I close?"

Khalil and Hana looked at one another, their eyes wide. "Not really," Khalil said.

"Adira, we are on the eastern side of the sands." She pointed out a window. "The sea is about thirty kilometers that way."

"And Bidiyah," Khalil said, pointing another direction, "Is 100—and probably more—kilometers that way."

"Oh, shit!"

Hana gave her a stern eye.

"Sorry!" Adira said quickly. "Sorry!"

"What does 'oh, shit' mean in English?" Leila asked.

Ravi let out a chuckle.

"It's a bad word, Leila. I shouldn't have said it." Adira glanced between Hana and Khalil, silently mouthing another apology.

"Who put you in the desert?" Leila asked.

"A bad man. At least I think he was bad," Adira said. "Which reminds me, do you have a phone I could use?"

Khalil went to stand, but Hana waved him off and fetched her own phone. Flipping open its case, she handed it to Adira.

The screen showed it was two-thirty in the afternoon. She'd certainly caught up on her rest. But Adira had no idea what number to call. The curse of modern phones was that numbers never needed to be memorized.

"Do either of you know how to call Al Alam Palace? Like a central operator?"

Again, Khalil and Hana locked eyes.

Ravi, who had been mostly silent, asked, "The Palace in Muscat? His Majesty's Palace?"

Adira nodded. "Yeah, I need to call someone who lives there. It's pretty important."

"I don't think that will be possible today, Adira," Khalil said. "We were just watching the news on television. I think every official will be at the parade and ceremony."

"What parade?" Adira asked.

"His Majesty the Sultan died this morning. They are holding a funeral soon," Khalil said.

Adira's eyes swelled. Her hand went to her mouth.

"Yes, we are all very sad at this news. He has been a wonderful leader for all of us."

Her eyes, moist and out of focus, began to well. "Are you sure," she asked, her voice breaking.

Hana exchanged a glance with Khalil before turning to Adira. "Are you okay, dear? It is sad news, but you've gone a little pale."

Adira held her napkin to her eyes and slumped, hiding. The rush of emotion surprised her. After wiping tears away, she turned to Hana. "He was…he was my father."

"Oh, wow!" Leila said.

Hana put her hand on Adira, who leaned into her touch.

Khalil, mystified, asked, "Are you sure? Your father?"

Hana shot him a dirty look despite wanting to hear the answer to the question herself.

Adira nodded.

"She is. It is on social media. Look," Ravi said, holding out his phone.

Khalil leaned over and looked. Leila dashed around the table and pushed in between them.

Hana stayed where she was, her hand on Adira's back. She caught eyes with Khalil, who nodded.

"We best see about making that call to the Palace then," Hana said, removing her hand and beginning to tap on her phone.

Khalil and Ravi were each on their phones as well. Adira looked out the window, her mind numb.

"Adira?" Hana asked, bringing Adira back to the present. "Try this one."

Adira took the phone, and an operator promptly answered. "Could you please connect me to the mobile phone for Zahra al Abdali?"

Adira could hear a keyboard clicking as the woman asked, "Who, may I ask, is calling?"

"Adira Eastmont," she replied. "Your system might also show me as Adira bint Hamad al Sabir."

The clicking stopped. "Right away, Sayyida Adira. And please, I am very sorry for today's news. We are all very sad."

"Thank you," Adira replied.

"I'll connect you now."

The line rang three times before Zara's voice came on. "Hello?"

"Zahra, it's Adira."

There was the sound of a quick inhale. "Adira! Are you okay?"

"I'm fine. A little dehydrated and beat up, but fine," she replied. "Thanks to some angels who rescued me."

Hana stood behind Adira and rubbed her shoulders.

"Where are you?"

"On the east side of the sands. Between the sands and the coast, it sounds like."

"Adira, I am very sorry to say, but—"

"I just heard," Adira said. "I'm…I'm going to miss him."

"I know. I know you will. We all will."

"I'm going to see how I can get back. It sounds like there is a funeral planned. I'll see if I can get back for that."

"I don't know how far away you are, but I doubt you will make it. The procession is starting soon, and the service will be before sunset."

Adira held the phone to the side. "How far away is Muscat?" she asked Khalil.

He shrugged. "Five hours, I think."

"Is there an airport here?"

He shook his head, and she returned the phone to her ear.

"Ugh. I'm about five hours away. But I have—"

"What happened to you, Adira? We've been looking for days."

"Minister Omar's guy dumped me in the desert. But the important thing, Adira, is that Rashid and Omar are the ones that made him do it."

"You've been in the desert for three days?"

"Two, two-and-a-half. But Rashid and Omar…they're the ones responsible."

"Moosa told you this?"

"About Rashid, yes. But he was terrified of the guy he said was pulling the strings. And I am pretty sure—no, really sure —it's Omar."

"Those are big accusations, Adira."

"I know. Has the new sultan been named?"

"Not yet," Zahra said. "They meet tonight. Taimur told me eight o'clock."

"They have to know, Zahra! You've got to tell them before they name Rashid. Or Omar. I told those people to make signs for Omar. How could I be so stupid!"

"I'll do what I can. But you have to get back here. You're the only one who knows this!"

"Moosa said one other thing. That Omar—it must be him —tried to get rid of me a long time ago, when Moosa was a boy."

The line was silent.

"It's strange, I know. Probably nothing. But get ahold of the council. I know it's some secret group, but work your magic. Tell them not to rush a decision. Please!"

"I will make some calls. But hurry back! We need you here to prove any of this."

"I'll do my best. I love you, Zahra, in case I haven't said it before."

"I love you too. Now go! I'll call you back on this number later."

Adira hung up to find four pairs of eyes locked on to her.

"What's the fastest way for me to get to Muscat?" She asked.

Khalil stole a glance at Hana, who quickly nodded. "We can drive you," he said.

"What about the kids? Will they be okay?"

Leila stood and declared, "We are *not* going to miss this!"

"You sure, Khalil? I'd like to go fast. They're going to name Rashid—or Omar—the next sultan if we don't get there by eight."

"We'll hurry."

The four of them dashed off to their bedrooms to collect a few things. Adira had just enough time to clear the dishes before Leila grabbed her hand and dragged her out to the pickup truck.

***

At that same time, a vintage Land Rover, modified specifically for its purpose today, was put in gear and rolled out between the gates of Al Alam Palace. On the extended bed, in a casket draped with the flag of Oman, rested Sultan Hamad bin Sabir al Sabir.

The old Land Rover followed the lead of a perfectly precise double row of twenty-four motorcycles. Through each turn, their movement was perfectly synchronized. Following were a dozen Range Rovers carrying various government dignitaries. And to the sides and bringing up the rear were another dozen armored vehicles.

They drove slowly, without fanfare or marching bands. Over the drone of the Land Rover's engine, Taimur could hear little more than the whine of the gearbox.

Taimur had actually been assigned to ride in one of the new Range Rovers. A senior officer in the Royal Guard, who had been—like the Red Arrow motorcycle team—trained specifically for precision driving was supposed to drive the old Land Rover from the Palace to the Grand Mosque. But as this was to be Sultan Hamad's last drive, Taimur insisted that he be the one behind the wheel.

The streets were lined with the citizens of Oman. As they made their way through Mutrah, the crowd was, in some places, four or five deep. Some waved the national flag, some wept, and many prayed. The leader they treasured, and who treasured them back more than they would ever know, was on his final journey.

At the Grand Mosque, the crowds were even greater in and around the meticulous rows of Army and Royal Guard soldiers in their dress uniforms. Taimur rolled the Land Rover to a gentle stop at the exact center of their formation.

He switched off the vehicle and exited, walking around to the back and placing his hand on the casket. Four soldiers marched in silent precision, two to each side of the casket. As one, their arms extended, and the casket was raised and pulled back.

They held His Majesty near the center of the casket, leaving room at the ends. Taimur took his friend's weight at one corner. The imam, the Chairman of the Supreme Court, and Nadir, who had only just arrived, took the others.

Together, they carried the remains of their leader and friend up the stairs of the Grand Mosque and set him carefully down on a beautiful stand in the center of the prayer room. The crowd inside, made up of citizens, soldiers, dignitaries, and leaders from nearly thirty nations, kneeled and began to pray. Their prayers asked for forgiveness from Allah, and for his protection as he ascended.

After the ritual had concluded, esteemed leaders in the government went to a podium set up at the entrance, facing the vast crowd.

Taimur stepped forward and looked across the sea of people wishing farewell. "It is with great sorrow," he began, "that we mourn the death of my friend and our beloved leader, Sultan Hamad bin Sabir al Sabir, who Allah chose to be by his side as dawn broke today. Now, we stand here with our hearts filled with faith in Allah that he will protect him, now and forever."

He then stepped to the side and turned toward Mecca. He lowered down to his knees again, as did an entire nation, and prayed.

The sultan was then brought to a field adjacent to the mosque, where the imam led prayers for a smaller group, away from the crowds. After the casket was lowered, the men gathered gently threw handfuls of dirt, interring their beloved leader.

***

From the back seat of Khalil's pickup truck, seated next to Leila and Ravi, Adira slowly told her story. They were kind— or perhaps shocked—enough not to ask questions while she spoke. When she finally finished, the questions came in rapid fire. There was sympathy, anger, and even a little laughter as she told them about her experiences.

But there was an undercurrent to her tale, a tension and sense of urgency they all felt. Halfway, which by some stroke of fate was exactly where Adira had been hoping to end her trek, they stopped for fuel and a very quick snack. Once they were back on the road, Khalil put a little more pressure on the accelerator than he had before.

Zahra called twice, the first to say that there would be no postponement of the Royal Family Council meeting and that His Majesty's secretary would not be able to give her an audience until just before the council convened, and likely not even then.

The second call was to tell her to hurry.

24

Just outside the gates to Al Alam Palace, along the ceremonial road used for arriving dignitaries, was a set of stately buildings. Their design and placement were such that those inside the secure Palace grounds could enter from one side and the public could enter from the opposite side. While both entrances were closely guarded, it was created as a place specifically for dignitaries and the public to gather.

Tonight was an occasion that Sultan Hamad had always insisted be open to the public. He wanted his replacement not to be selected from a back room in secret, but before the people he would serve. And as a result, the grounds surrounding the Palace were filled with citizens that had come not just from Muscat, but all across the nation.

The Royal Guard had assembled in its entirety, with men in their dress uniforms lined around the Palace in perfectly spaced intervals. They were there not for crowd or riot suppression—the residents who had gathered were extremely respectful—but to honor the change of leadership that would occur in the Great Library.

Adira and the family fought through heavy traffic, making it to the National Museum before being directed into a car park. After making his own space on a small island of shrubs, Khalil turned off the truck and looked back at Adira.

"Where to now?" he asked.

"I have to do this myself, Khalil. Thank you all so much for saving me, but I have *no* idea what will happen inside. You should go. Do you know the Al Bustan hotel? The Ritz-Carlton? I have a room there. Just give them my name, and they'll let you up."

"Adira, that is very kind. But we didn't come all the way here to just leave," Hana said. "You have a story to tell, and we want to help."

"Look!" Ravi held up his phone, which played a video from inside the Great Library. "They've started!"

The doors opened, and all five of them leaped out. "Follow me," Adira said. "We'll have to hoof it the rest of the way."

***

The meeting hall of the Great Library was an ample, tall space filled with ornate carvings and arches. A tremendous carpet of intricate patterns in reds and golds gave gravity to the room almost to the extent of the gilded ceiling.

The room had been configured specifically for this meeting of the Royal Family Council. A table far smaller than those used for stately meetings with visiting delegates sat perfectly in the center, with two ornate gold-and-red velvet chairs on one side, three opposite, and one on each end. Gold and crystal chandeliers hung above, casting the table in bright light, yet keeping the perimeter dim. Three of the walls were lined with similar chairs set two deep, allowing those seated in the first row to have assistants at hand behind them.

Outside one dark end of the room was a large lobby filled with the heads of each ministry, house of parliament, and military branch. Only rarely had all twenty-eight leaders within the sultanate gathered together.

They mingled freely, voices respectfully low, outwardly sharing words about the great leader they had lost, while inwardly nervous about what was to come. All except one. Deputy Defense Minister Rashid bin Tamin, dressed in his most delicate and ornate robes, circulated through the room as if on air.

A cue was given to the Royal Guard, and in perfect synchronization, the doors from the lobby to the meeting hall were opened. The broad delegation filed into the room and took their assigned seats. The doors to one of the four antechambers at the sides of the hall were then opened, allowing assistants or those second in command to come in and take a seat behind their masters.

The silence in the room was broken when the doors to another antechamber were opened, and the Family Council entered. While the five council members had never been named publicly, many could have guessed a fair portion of them, as they were often seen with Sultan Hamad.

He had assembled the council first to be his advisers, counseling him during significant decisions and, as he was wont to say, "To keep me honest." He would work with them individually and occasionally in twos or threes. On rare occasions, he would call all five of them together.

During one of those meetings, when the group had gathered quietly together, the sultan informed them he had been diagnosed with pancreatic cancer. He had invited them to share this news and to discuss an amendment to the constitution he'd authored for his nation in 1996. His proposal was that as he had no son, the five of them would select his successor immediately upon his passing.

The first to enter the room was His Majesty's personal secretary. With the help of his rather large staff, he had been directing the day's events. While not a member of the Royal Family Council, he would serve as the director of the proceedings.

As he took a seat at the head of the table, the first member of the council walked in, the Chairman of the Oman Supreme Court. He was well respected and known to be of humble upbringing, brilliant, and quite possibly the most level-headed man in the entire Gulf region. The heads of government surrounding the room nodded as if confirming he was a fine choice for making such a significant decision.

Behind him strode the small figure of Mushir Nadir. His story of helping bring together the southern Dhofar region with Muscat and the North was well known. It was also well known that while a close friend of His Majesty, Nadir had a sharp tongue and fiery temper. While a few heads nodded at his appearance, plenty of eyebrows rose in question.

Next to walk to the table was Oman's leading Islamic scholar. While most knew His Majesty would have wanted spiritual guidance on the council, they expected it to be the Grand Mosque's imam, known to be a personal friend. What the gallery didn't know was that for many years, the imam was, in fact, on the council. But more often than not, the imam found himself turning to Safa for counsel on what advice to give His Majesty. Several years ago, the imam suggested that His Majesty "cut out the middle man, and put the smart one in place." This admission by the imam had only brought the sultan and him closer together.

Fourth through the door was the large frame of Taimur. As His Majesty's closest personal friend and a respected historian in his own right, the attendees all knew that Taimur would be part of this decision, and almost all were thankful for it.

Last in was Foreign Minister Omar. Again, many heads nodded. He was well experienced in government and well respected both here and abroad.

The one person who had no respect for him whatsoever was just now walking through an archway and into the Royal Square. Adira had seen the small British-style parade ground when leaving Zahra's recently. It was a football-field-size expanse of perfectly micromanaged gravel, surrounded on all sides by a covered hallway and perfectly spaced marble archways. It was a quiet and formal space that, at the time, she'd imagined was perfect for a procession of soldiers on horseback, resplendent with ornate uniforms and tall, feathered helmets.

Tonight, however, was a different story. The plaza had been designated as the place where the public could congregate to view the proceedings. It was packed with people all wanting to be close to the new sultan after he was named. Their attention was currently directed to an exterior wall of the Great Library where a vast sports-arena-size monitor had been mounted.

Displayed on the screen was a close-up of His Majesty's secretary at the head of the table where tonight's decision would be made. Adira and the family elbowed their way just inside the plaza and watched as he opened a leather folio and began to speak.

The secretary's voice boomed through giant speakers, "You have been brought together tonight at the request of His Majesty, Hamad bin Sabir al Sabir, Sultan of Oman. While he has ascended to join Allah's flock, I know he would feel blessed to have you here together. I will now read from a sealed note, as was his direction for this meeting."

The secretary took an envelope from his folio. Showing the seal to those seated at the table, he cracked the wax and withdrew a single sheet.

Adira realized that while they'd made it to the Palace in time, the meeting had started, and they still had a crowd to get through. "C'mon," she motioned to Hana.

They pushed their way through the throngs of people, most of whom were distracted by the screen and let them pass easily. As they neared the back wall of the Great Library, the layout became apparent.

For security purposes, there were only two sets of doors leading inside. A roped area separated a metal detector and at least a dozen Royal Guard officers at each entrance. Their faces were stern, showing they were there for security, not for ceremony like the others lining the walls.

Just before they reached the roped area, Leila stopped. Adira felt the tug and turned back. Standing next to the young girl, dressed in a set of MOH coveralls, stood a tall woman with spiky bleach-blond hair.

Adira gave Chevy a firm hug and then quickly introduced Leila and her parents.

Leila looked at Chevy and, in an earnest voice, said, "I'm the one who found her."

Chevy pursed her lips, impressed. "Betcha didn't think you were going to find a real-life princess today, didja?"

"She doesn't really act like one."

"Tell me about it, kiddo." Holding up a small medical kit to Adira, she asked, "Zahra was worried about you. Need anything? Your lips look terrible."

"Just to get in," Adira replied with a shake of her head. "Did she let the Guard know we were coming?"

Chevy shook her head. "She's worried about them. Said she still can't tell if this Moosa guy was just working for Omar or if someone higher in the Guard was also involved. She said you could charm your way in."

"I'm not very charming, Chevy. That's a terrible plan."

"She really isn't very charming, is she?" Chevy asked Leila.

"Not really," Leila said.

"But that's why I have a plan B." Chevy held up her kit again. "Got a set of coveralls for you along with a fresh copy of your MOH badge."

"Pose as medical?"

"Well, we *are* medical."

"Adira," Hana said, tilting her head. "One of the guards is staring at you."

Adira didn't turn quickly to look. Instead, she pivoted behind Chevy and pulled the scarf from around her neck up and over her head. She then stole a look over Chevy's other shoulder.

It was Moosa, and he was making his way toward them.

Adira's legs tensed to run. Instead, she steeled her resolve and stepped forward.

At two paces away, Moosa stopped and held up his hands in a placating gesture. "You're alive," he said.

"I am, Moosa. No thanks to you."

Above them, the monitor broadcasted the secretary concluding his remarks with instructions on how members of the council could now present candidate names and debate their prospect. Chevy and Khalil could not hear Adira over the booming audio, but could see the tension radiating from her. They stepped forward, each taking a side.

Moosa held his right hand to his chest. "I had to do it, Sayyida. Please, I hope you understand."

"You want forgiveness? No chance," Adira seethed.

"Please," he pleaded.

"Want to prove it?" Adira pointed to the screen. "Get us in there."

Moosa looked up. On the screen, Rashid bin Tamin was walking toward the empty seat at the end of the table, barely able to hide the grin on his face.

"If they win, they'll own you forever," Adira explained. "They'll make you do worse than tie women up and dump them in the desert."

Moosa squeezed his eyes shut, still trying to reconcile his actions.

"Now," she demanded.

His eyes opened, and his shoulders fell. "I will take you in."

Chevy stepped in. "Not a chance we're leaving you alone with her," she snarled. "*All* of us are going in."

He nodded and turned to the guards. They were quickly ushered around the metal detector and through the doors.

Through the loudspeakers, the secretary read a document describing Rashid's relationship to Sultan Hamad.

In the center of the lobby, Moosa stopped and pointed to doors that led into the great hall, each protected by a pair of uniformed officers. "I must go now. These men will—"

"Don't chicken out now, Moosa. You're getting *all* of us *all* the way in," Adira ordered.

Moosa took a quick breath and approached the guards. He adopted a command tone befitting his rank, and ordered the guards to admit Adira into the room. The men hesitated, explaining the meeting was not to be disturbed under any circumstances. Rashid beckoned Adira forward.

"Do you recognize the sayyida?" Moosa demanded of them.

One nodded his head quickly.

"And given that it is the *Family* Council meeting, were your orders to prevent *family* from entering?" Moosa asked.

While the two men looked at one another, they didn't budge from their stance in front of the doorway.

The audio feed from inside continued. Omar was requesting to play a recording that would shed insight into Rashid's capacity to rule.

Adira moved closer. "Gentlemen," she said. "Inside that room, at my father's request, a decision is being made on who will lead our country. They are about to make a grave mistake."

In a friendly but firm voice, she continued, "My friends and I are going to walk through that door now, and I am going to tell them what I know in hopes to avoid this mistake."

Adira turned and waved the others for her. Then she placed a hand on one of the guard's arms and gently moved him aside. She pressed the door lever and quietly stepped across the threshold.

The thick carpet and grand scale of the room muted the sound of their entry. But that wasn't all that distracted those in attendance from noticing the new arrivals. Every eye was on a phone Omar had set on the table, and every ear was tuned to the exchange being played over the tiny speaker:

"Who is this?"

"I don't think that is relevant at the moment, Your Excellency."

"Fine, how close are you to this woman? Close enough to make her disappear?"

"Your Excellency, I need you to be a bit more specific."

"Specific! I want her gone! Gone between now and when her father finally dies. And twenty-four hours after that, since that's when the bloody fool's council will meet. Kill her. Dump her in the desert. Sink her to the bottom of the sea. I don't care!"

"I understand, Your Excellency."

Adira turned back to Chevy and the family and waved for them to move with her into the shadow of a large square column. She was surprised to see Moosa had joined them, and Chevy was paying particular attention to him.

In the center of the room, Rashid was losing control. "How dare you!" he shouted. "Clearly, this recording is fake!"

Omar leaned back in his chair. "Then where, my friend, is His Majesty's daughter?"

"The bloody girl left! Video from the airport has been all over the news!"

"Your appropriateness for leadership is the subject of this meeting," Safa interjected. "And I have to say, that recording puts your character in question."

"It is fake! Omar is manipulating you! The bloody American left!" Rashid shouted. "This has no bearing on my character whatsoever. My leadership of this nation's military for the past three years shows my *character* to be perfectly suited!"

Taimur stiffened. "You will not refer to His Majesty's daughter as 'bloody girl' nor 'bloody American' in the chamber," his voice boomed.

Rashid made a dismissive gesture.

"I, too, find this recording disturbing, in light of the fact that Her Royal Highness did not appear on any flight manifest," Taimur said. "Perhaps you would care to explain that?"

A rumble of whispers could be heard from the chairs surrounding the table.

"I suggest we get back on track," Rashid said, adjusting his robes and trying to establish control.

Nadir looked each of his council members in the eye, then turned to the secretary and said, "I am afraid that I must conclude that Minister Rashid be removed from consideration."

"How dare you!" Rashid shouted, jumping out of his chair.

"In addition," Nadir continued, "I request the police look into this recording and its relationship to the abduction of Sayyida Adira."

"You cannot do this!" Rashid shouted.

"I am afraid that is just what this council is charged with doing, Deputy Minister," the Chairman of the Supreme Court said. "You may go."

"I will not! As the only man directly related to His Majesty, this is my duty! My right!"

The secretary turned around and gestured to the back of the room. A pair of uniformed guards came forward and walked around the table to stand beside Rashid.

"Do not make a scene, Deputy Minister," the secretary said in a low voice.

"You cannot do this! I will have you dismissed at once!"

The secretary waved his hand at the guards, who promptly took hold of Rashid's arms and steered him, not without difficulty, into one of the antechambers.

Once his protests faded, the secretary addressed the council. "Do you have someone else to propose?" he asked.

The council members were quiet for a moment before the secretary spoke again. "I understand the need for this meeting to occur so quickly was to maintain consistent, stable leadership for all of us. But these events tonight have come as a shock. One choice you have is to allow yourselves more time to carefully consider all of your options."

The council members silently exchanged looks.

"Our country," the secretary continued, "is in capable hands with the general, and allowing perhaps thirty days would prevent us from acting imprudently. Shall we use the rules of this council—that of a unanimous vote—to elect to proceed this way?"

"If I may?" Omar said, his voice booming across the hall. Once he had everyone's attention, he continued, "I worry about the perception of military rule beyond our borders. While the general is, indeed, a perfect choice, there may be questions about our stability."

He allowed his peers to consider this for a moment before continuing. "It pains me to offer this, given the fact that His Majesty has understood for years that none of us had aspirations of leadership. But in the interest of stability—of consistency for our land—I would, humbly, offer myself to fulfill this role."

The Chairman of the Supreme Court spoke first. "My, Omar, you do surprise us. But I think this would be worth discussing. Shall we present the foreign minister with a few questions?" he asked with a glance around the table.

Adira turned and looked up into Moosa's eyes. He responded to her unasked question with a curt nod.

With this cue, she stepped from behind the column and into the light. "I would like to ask a question," she said.

There were gasps of surprise as everyone in the room turned to face her.

25

"Adira! Thank goodness you are safe!" Omar declared, ungracefully coming to his feet.

Adira stepped forward to stand behind the empty chair at the end of the table. Looking at the secretary, she said, "Thank you for dismissing Rashid. Aside from being generally disliked by everyone, he was partly responsible for my being left in the desert for dead three days ago."

"We are blessed by your safe return, Your Royal Highness," the secretary replied. "While we would all like to hear about your ordeal, this may not be the time. Is your question for the foreign minister material to this meeting?" he asked.

"I regret saying this," Omar said. "But the council is a closed group. His Majesty's guidance was quite clear."

"I, for one, would like to hear what she has to say," the Chairman of the Supreme Court remarked. "And as a member of His Majesty's family, feel she is entitled to speak. Perhaps we should put this to a vote?"

"I will, sadly, have to vote no," Omar said, regret thick in his voice. "And as our votes must be unanimous…"

"But, Omar," the Chairman said, "You have offered yourself as a candidate and therefore have removed yourself from the council."

Omar, a smile plastered on his face, turned to Adira. "My dear, this is not a matter for your concern. We, this council, all have decades of experience, and understanding of our culture and complex issues you could never comprehend. There is no need for you here. I am sure you will be well taken care of." He waved her back dismissively.

Adira stood her ground.

"I will put forward a question for the council," the secretary said. "Will you allow Her Royal Highness, Sayyida Adira, to contribute?"

The four members of the council, their eyes locked on Omar, agreed in unison.

"I believe the hot seat here is for you," Adira said, pulling out the chair at the end of the table.

Omar waved his hand for her to take it. As she came around, he leaned over and whispered to her, "We'll see what this charade gets you."

Adira sat down and took a deep breath. Then, in what she suspected was a breach of protocol in such a setting, she reached up and pulled her mother's hijab back and allowed it to fall across her shoulders. Looking down the table to Safa, she said, "I would like to be both heard *and* seen tonight."

After receiving the hint of a smile from Safa, Adira returned her attention to Omar. "Thanks for worrying about me. But the sands can't hide all of your problems."

Omar rolled his eyes. "If all you will do is be disrespectful to this council, then—"

"Tell us," she interrupted, her voice firm. "Were you complicit in Rashid's plan to have me killed?"

"Of course not. If that is all you came to—"

"If you weren't complicit," Adira continued, "did you give the order yourself?"

"Don't be absurd. How could I wish harm on a girl as beautiful as you? You should be treated as a sparkling gem, with—"

"What if there was proof? Like a longer version of that recording that included your voice?" She didn't have any such recording, of course. But she wanted him off balance, to see how he might react.

A murmur spread around the room as Omar tried to collect himself. "Unfortunately, I think we heard tonight that fabricating a recording is quite possible."

Nadir let out a huffing noise at this hypocrisy.

"Maybe so," Adira admitted. Then, as if the idea had just occurred, she sat up. "How about we ask the man who both you *and* Rashid ordered to kill me?"

Adira watched a breath seize in his chest for a fraction of a second. But having been at the center of tense negotiations on the world stage, Omar knew that maintaining a calm exterior —and not exploding with rage like Rashid had done—left more options on the table. He regained his composure quickly.

Adira held his eyes a moment before turning to the shadows behind her. "Moosa? Could you please join us?"

Moosa walked to the table and stood by Adira. His posture was rigid, his shoulders held back in attention. Omar, by contrast, began to deflate.

"I know this is hard," Adira said gently to Moosa. "But can you please tell us your order and who gave this command?"

To Moosa, there was no turning back. There would be consequences, but in his tortured mind, he prayed they would be his alone. "My orders were to kill you. To dump you in the desert or send you to the bottom of the sea, Sayyida."

"And who gave this order?"

"As everyone heard on the recording, Deputy Minister Rashid. But following that, Minister Omar reiterated the order."

"There is a perfectly good reason that was necessary," Omar protested. "I needed to expose Rashid. He needed to think I was on his side!"

"Moosa," Adira said, her calm voice in contrast to the tension radiating now from Omar. "Was this just a clever trap set by an innocent Omar?"

"It was a trap, Sayyida. But he is not innocent. He knew that with the recording, he could eliminate Rashid and place himself as our sultan. After disposing of you, he promised I would be pardoned."

Gasps rippled around the room.

"He also told me that he had tried to kill you once before," Moosa said.

Omar sat up to protest but was distracted when Zahra approached the secretary with a piece of paper. They whispered to one another briefly as Adira watched with curiosity.

While this discussion was going on, the Chairman of the Supreme Court addressed Moosa. "Will you be willing to testify to this?"

Moosa nodded. "I have lived in fear of this man for too long, Your Excellency. It would be my honor to testify at a trial, and my duty to accept the consequences of my actions."

"Minister," the secretary said after Moosa had finished. "It appears that you directed fifty thousand US dollars from your wilayat treasury to a man in the American city of Oakland twenty-five years ago."

Omar rolled his eyes. "We have consultants working all over the—"

"I am sure. But this particular man has been arrested more than half a dozen times and is currently incarcerated for two murders. I understand that he has very recently been forthcoming with the Royal Police."

Omar's face turned red, and his eyes closed as his entire life fell to pieces.

As Adira reached out and squeezed Moosa's hand, the secretary once again waved his hand, and Omar and Moosa were escorted silently from the room.

The gallery of people seated in the meeting hall could barely contain their shock. The impact of the two most likely people to carry the mantle of leadership being summarily dismissed shook them deeply.

"Quiet, please," the secretary commanded.

After the noise had settled, Adira spoke to the Chairman. "He should be charged with murder. Twenty-five years ago, Zahra saved my life, but her parents were killed. Omar needs to be held accountable."

The Chairman looked across to Zahra. "Those responsible will be brought to justice," he said. "You have my word."

Zahra was doing her best to hold back the conflicting emotions bubbling to the surface. The secretary caught everyone's attention by waving to one of the guards to have a chair brought forward for her. When Zahra sat and looked across the table, Adira gave a smile that showed she understood how hard it was to face the memories of her childhood once again.

"How would you like to proceed?" The secretary asked the council members, bringing the table back to order.

The council exchanged glances, each silently conferring with the others.

While they were looking at one another, Adira felt a tug on her top. Leila had snuck up to the table and wanted to share a secret.

Adira leaned down, picked the young girl up, and set her on her lap. Leila cupped a hand over Adira's ear and whispered, "Nice job!"

Adira suppressed a laugh and touched Leila's nose.

"If we are ready?" the secretary asked, not hiding his impatience.

"Sorry," Adira interjected. "Can I make a suggestion?"

All eyes remained fixed on her.

"I think there's someone else to propose. My guess is you're looking for someone with a strong love for the culture and people of Oman. Someone with a deep understanding of our history."

She received curious nods in reply.

"He's sitting right here. From what I saw from videos today, he's the one who led you through the mourning of my father. He's the one I suspect many of you turned to when you needed advice or a steady hand. Shouldn't Taimur be the one to lead?"

Safa smiled endearingly at Adira, her eyes glistening with respect for the young woman.

Taimur sat back and pressed his palms forward. "No, no," he said.

"She is right, you know. You've been the steady hand. For His Majesty and for all of us," Nadir said. "Especially myself."

"His Majesty shared with us all the traits that were important to him," the Chairman said. "We deviated from that path in presenting Rashid—thinking that his bloodline would compensate for his weaknesses."

"Adira," Safa said. "Tell me what qualities *you* think he exemplifies."

Adira thought for a moment. "There is no better authority on history, on the roots of Omani culture. But importantly, a leader needs to have a big heart. You might call it empathy, but I think compassion is an even better word. It's something he has in spades."

"Is that all?" Safa asked.

Adira thought for a moment. "Integrity. The resolve that one must always do what is right. That's not always easy, but a leader needs courage to do what's right with the people of Oman and the countries you—we—have to deal with."

"Thank you, Adira," Safa said, addressing the group. Looking at the council, she continued, "I would make one addition to the assets a leader should exemplify: Approachability. Perhaps in your private conversations with His Majesty, he told you that was a trait he worked on his entire life but never mastered. While his love for our citizens was unconditional, he felt that growing up in a palace with a royal family created a buffer around him others were scared to reach through."

Taimur looked around the room. "It is a trait to which all of us in these gilded halls should aspire."

The table fell silent. Safa looked each council member in the eye and received subtle nods in return. "We are in agreement," she said to the secretary, "and ready to vote."

The secretary gestured to the cards and pen set before each of them. "Then please write your nominations and pass them to me."

"Who are they voting for?" Leila whispered to Adira.

Adira pointed to Taimur. "The big teddy bear over there. You'll love him," she whispered back.

Thick cards were soon returned to the secretary. Once he had all four, he brought them together and tapped the edges on the table, making sure they were aligned. One by one, he silently read them, showed them to Zahra, and set them on the table.

"The decision is unanimous," he announced.

All eyes around the table, Adira uncomfortably noticed, were on her.

Safa stood and walked from her seat to Adira's side. She leaned down to Leila and said, "Can I borrow her for a minute?"

Leila nodded and slid off Adira's leg. Instead of returning to her parents, she stayed under the lights, holding the arm of the chair in the center of all that was taking place.

Safa took hold of Adira's arm and guided her to stand. "There is only one person who shares the traits your father valued most. Only one person who has the ability to wrap their arms around the people of Oman and walk together with them into the future."

Nadir stood next. "And who will look after her people before she looks after herself. This is, I feel, the most important trait of all."

The Chairman stood now as well. "And we find only one person suitable, by right of birth as well as character."

Adira had thought they were standing to thank her for suggesting Taimur. But with that last comment, her legs weakened. "No. No," she said. "I have no idea how to—"

"The fact that you don't want to is exactly why you should," Safa said, taking Adira's hand and pulling her close.

Taimur stood as well. "Adira, we know this will be difficult at first. But I want you to know that the four of us, as well, I suspect, as everyone in this room, will help you. We will stand by your side every step of the way. What you have to bring is *your* heart."

"It's a lot more than that, and you know it." Adira started. She released Safa's hand and gestured around the room. "This is a man's world. What do you see here? Four out of, what, twenty-some ministers are women?"

"Twenty-four," Safa said, her voice soft. "But what I see are four *courageous* women."

"And what about our neighbors? Muslim countries run by men. My guess is we have to deal with them every day."

Safa held Adira's eyes before replying, "The other side of that is that they will have to deal with *you*."

"Last time I had to deal with an aggressive man, I didn't handle it so well."

"Humans were created by Allah specifically with the capacity to err. It is how we assemble wisdom."

Adira gave Safa a sideways glance. "The Quran?"

Safa nodded. "You've learned from every life experience and will continue to do so."

Adira's heart raced. Her arms and hands were cold, yet she could feel a rivulet of sweat running down her chest.

"Adira," Safa said. "What we are asking is for you to stand up for us. For all of us—the men, the woman, the old, and the young. You've been doing it since you arrived. All we ask is for you to continue."

"Please—" she stuttered.

Safa retook Adira's hand. "I would like you to try it for us, dear. We see the strength inside you. But if you find it is too much, you have the power to convene a meeting just like this to appoint your successor."

Adira responded quickly. "I can do that? Anytime?"

Safa nodded.

"And you'll tell me if I'm doing a bad job?"

"The *people* will tell you that."

"And you'll be there to help?" she asked, looking around the table. "All of you?"

Again, Safa gently rocked her head.

"Even Nadir?" Adira asked, turning her eyes to him in question. "Because I think he hates me."

"I dislike your forthrightness," Nadir said. "Which is far from hate."

"I dislike your forthrightness too, Nadir. But you deploy it well."

The secretary cleared his throat, which had the desired effect of returning attention to the matter at hand. He gestured for everyone to sit, which they all did, including Leila, who returned to Adira's leg.

"The protocols for this meeting," the secretary began, "specified the manner in which a new sultan would be named. Not considered was what would happen if the leader elected by the council declined. Knowing this group as I do, I suspect they will not force you to take this highest burden of leadership. So I will ask you directly. Will you accept the role of Her Majesty, Sultana of Oman?"

The room went silent. Adira looked around the table. She sensed Zahra's tension and felt the weight of what she was being asked to do press down upon her.

Her eyes went to Taimur, who smiled. The confidence he had in Adira—that all of them had in her—gave her a strength she'd never felt before. For them, she would try. She would try her hardest.

"I will," she said softly. "It would be my honor."

The room rose to their feet as one and applauded, and Adira sat astonished at their show of support. She felt both embarrassed and determined. Determined to return the faith they showed in her twice over.

The secretary allowed them a few moments before holding a hand up and asking everyone to return to their seats again. "We have one more matter of business," he said.

The room fell quiet, this time out of curiosity.

"His Majesty, Sultan Hamad, asked me to read another letter he prepared." He extracted another envelope from the folio and once again showed the unbroken seal to those at the table and around the room. Perhaps more theatrically than needed, he cracked the wax and withdrew the letter.

"This letter was dated five days ago," he said with gravity. Waving his hand to the now-empty portfolio, he said, "As you can see, there is no other letter that was left by him for this occasion."

Everyone in the meeting hall was puzzled by the secretary's theatrics, something the stoic man was not prone to employ.

"I will now read the message he wanted you to receive at this point in the proceedings."

To the honorable Royal Family Council,

I express my gratitude to you for undertaking this challenge. Your choice today was not easy. You were forced to ask questions with only the most elusive answers. Who embodies the soul of our land? Who has the compassion to empower our people to further strive for greatness? Who is steadfast in the face of adversity yet desires not to win, but shape a mutual success together?

The leader you have selected has all of these strengths buried deep inside. They are raw and unrefined, but with your guidance, they will shine brighter than we could dream possible. This leader will be a beacon of light for everyone.

To the people of Oman, whom I will miss dearly, I ask you to open your hearts to her. She grew up without a home yet has found hers here with you. She grew up without receiving love, yet gives it without reservation. Embrace her the way she has embraced us.

Most importantly, know that she has grown into the strong woman that you see before you without a family.

I ask you to join together and become that family for her, for she is a gift to us all.

Finally, to Adira. Know there is no one I would trust more to take our hands and walk together into the future.

May the Almighty Allah protect all of you in His care and grant you success in pursuing the path to success that you will realize together.

Yours with love, honor, and respect,
Sultan Hamad bin Sabir al Sabir

The great hall burst into applause once again. The members of the Family Council made no effort to hide their complete shock at His Majesty's last message.

Safa came once again around the table. Taking hold of a corner of the scarf, she said, "If she were here, your mother would have been the proudest person in the room, and I would be a very happy second."

Adira reached down and hugged her. "Safa, there is so much that I have to learn. I am absolutely terrified!"

"You have less to learn than you think. But we will be here," she said, gesturing to Taimur, Nadir, and the Chairman, "every step of the way."

Several of the attendees approached, introducing themselves and offering their congratulations. Adira received them all with grace before excusing herself and joining a small group that was feeling a little out of place.

Chevy stood holding Leila's hand, her family close by. Behind them, Amir bore a wide smile.

"This was, I…ah," Hana sputtered. "It was incredible!"

Adira held a hand over her mouth and laughed. "I think I would have fallen apart if Leila wasn't there with me!"

Leila rushed to Adira, who kneeled down and wrapped her arms around the little girl.

"Gotta say that your pop's letter was pretty spooky," Chevy said to Adira.

"How did he know?" Adira said. "I mean, if Leila hadn't found me, or Moosa hadn't been here to call out Rashid and Omar, or if we'd hit even one extra traffic light…"

"But none of those things happened," came a voice behind her. "Because His Majesty had faith. He had faith in Allah and each and every one of us."

Adira turned to find Zahra, who, while projecting a smile, had damp red eyes and smudges in her usually perfect makeup.

"He had faith in you most of all," Adira said, firmly embracing Zahra.

"What were you doing up with the secretary after giving him the background on Omar?" Chevy asked.

"The secretary thought Adira might want a friendly face on her staff. He's planning to train me to do his work in the future." She looked at Adira and hastily added, "But only if you want me."

"Of course I do!" Adira said. "I couldn't do this job without you!"

"Oh, thank you!" Zahra said, and the two embraced once more.

"Who's that?" Leila asked Chevy.

"Fancy Chick? She found Adira last time."

"She gets lost a lot," Leila said.

"Yeah," Chevy replied. "But it's workin' pretty good for her so far."

Zahra broke free from the embrace and locked eyes with Adira. "Are you okay? Because there's one more thing that would warm a few hearts."

"What?"

"Outside are some people that were sad to lose a man they loved today. I think meeting you would help."

"Going to have to get used to it at some point," Adira said, taking Zahra's hand.

Zahra led the way, with Adira close behind. Sensing the others hadn't followed, Adira stopped and looked behind her. "C'mon!" she called, tilting her head. They quickly ran to catch up.

As they exited, Adira froze. If the plaza had felt crowded before, it was absolutely packed now, and roaring. Zahra gestured to a small stage beneath the giant screen where Taimur, Nadir, the Chairman, and Safa stood waiting.

Adira climbed the stairs to the platform. Taimur was handed a microphone, and for the second time today, addressed the nation.

"It was the will of Allah," he began, his voice instantly silencing the crowd, "that we lost the protected one, Sultan Hamad bin Sabir al Sabir. He was the greatest of men, and we are forever in his debt for all he accomplished in our name. His renaissance crystallized our nation and culture, which has become known around the world as a model of strength, stability, and fairness. We were truly blessed to have had him as our own."

He stepped forward to the edge of the stage and continued, "We are even more blessed to have with us someone who was born with his same strength of character. With his same courage.

"For those of you who do not know, Adira has known many hardships in life. From these struggles she emerged strong, and fought for a career as a nurse.

"It was not until we found her, just weeks ago, that she learned she was the only child of His Majesty. And what was her first request when she learned of this royal heritage? She simply wanted to work as a humble nurse to help *us*.

"Some of the men you saw tonight tried to take her from us. She was abandoned in the desert for days, and it was only through Allah's grace that she was returned. And it is through His grace that she will lead us now.

"I would like you to meet her. She is Her Majesty, Sultana Adira bint Hamad al Sabir."

The crowd erupted in roaring cheers, the noise so powerful as to shake the very foundations of the Palace.

Taimur handed the microphone to Adira, who stood shocked, terrified, and at a complete loss for what to do or say. She looked around the plaza, focusing not on the pulsing crowd, but on the individual people within. A father with his tiny son sitting atop his shoulders, a cluster of three girls linked arm in arm with tears in their eyes, a worker in a dirty dishdasha waving a flag twice as large as he was. Her eyes swept closer to the stage. Just below her stood Chevy and the family, and Zahra holding Amir's hand.

Next to Amir stood Nabila, her hands held tightly together below her chin, her eyes wet with tears. Adira smiled at her and then held the microphone to her lips.

"Hello, everyone," she said, silencing the throngs of people as if a switch had been flipped. "My name is Adira."

She made her way to the edge of the stage and sat down. "You will have to forgive me. But this is all very new.

"I want to thank all of you for the love you shared with my father today. I only knew him for a handful of days, but he sure won me over. He also left some big shoes to fill.

"A few of you have seen me out with the mobile clinic. Those that I had the chance to meet, know that from you, I learned how strong you are in character, brilliance, and heart."

Sliding off the stage, she walked up to Nabila. In a gentle tone, she continued, "Meeting you has been both humbling and inspiring.

"I am going to need your help to fill those big shoes," she said. "I want to hear *your* stories. I want to hear about you and your families. What you're proud of, and what keeps you up at night."

She walked deeper into the crowd. "I hope that through you, I can get to know my father a little better. But more importantly, I want to know what we need to do together. Because it's only *with* you that I can fill this role.

"I don't know how to sit on a throne in a palace. All I know is how to get my hands dirty and help. How to give someone a big push up so they can go off and succeed on their own. I'm going to do the same now, because you are the most caring and impressive people I've met."

She paused and allowed a moment to take a deep breath.

"I'm not sure how royal protocols work when an impromptu speech is over," she said humbly. "So I'll just say this: I love you all."

Adira lowered the microphone. Before her were the three teenage girls she'd seen locked together. As the plaza roared again, one of the girls extended her arms, and Adira happily embraced her. The next one pushed her way in, and then the next. More people approached, some smiling, some with tears in their eyes. The men did not, as it was not customary for men to initiate physical contact. But when they approached and placed their hands on their hearts, she opened her arms, and with that offer, embraced them as well.

She soon felt the fatigue of the physical and emotional stress of the past few days and made her way back to the lobby of the Great Library, where Zahra patiently waited, Amir by her side.

"I have placed Hana and her family in one of the Palace apartments for the night, Your Majesty," Zahra said.

"You," Adira said with a look of incredulity, "will never ever call me that again, okay?"

Amir burst into laughter. "I told you she wouldn't have it from you!"

"It's protocol. I had to try!" Zahra said with a giggle. "Follow me, *Adira*. Your apartment has been prepared. Chevy's up there already and would like to check you out."

"Lead the way," Adira said.

They made their way through the Great Library and across to the principal Palace residence. After climbing a set of marble stairs, they arrived in a luxurious apartment on the second floor with expansive windows overlooking the harbor.

At a sideboard holding several dishes, Taimur stood filling a plate. Adira walked to his side and let out a sigh before giving him a smile. "I saw video of you today. Thank you for taking such good care of him today."

Taimur set his plate down, and the two embraced. "We will all miss him."

Adira gave the big man an extra squeeze before releasing him. "Only knew him for just a little bit, but he won me over."

"He was that way, wasn't he?"

"When did he tell you to put my name on those little cards tonight?"

Taimur shook his head. "He didn't tell us to do anything."

"So it was the letter. You looked beforehand," Adira concluded.

Taimur's head turned side to side once more. "We didn't even know he'd written that letter."

Adira gave him a skeptical look.

Taimur opened his hands. "This is the truth."

"Kinda curious that I happened to have met every member of the Family Council, huh?"

Taimur's cheeks pulled up into a little smile. "I felt it would be good for them to meet you."

"And?"

"And nothing, Adira. Neither your father nor I were instructing anyone. The council did what they each felt was right for Oman. And that is you."

"Guess we'll see if you're right."

"The secretary and his staff will teach you procedures and protocols. But everything Oman needs is already right inside here," Taimur said, gently tapping her forehead.

"Everything *I* need is right there," Adira said, nodding in the direction of Taimur's plate.

He gave a theatric sigh and passed his plate to her.

"Really?" she asked.

"Not so fast, Sultey," came an Australian twang behind her. Taimur stifled a chuckle.

" *'Sultey'*? Really?" Adira said.

"Yeah. Works, I think. But c'mon, you and I have a date," Chevy said, taking hold of Adira's hand and leading her into a quiet bedroom where she was promptly seated on a long chaise longue.

Adira let Chevy go to work. Her pulse was checked, a blood pressure cuff went around her arm, and the cold bell of a stethoscope went first to her chest, then to her back. Her eyes and throat were inspected before she was instructed to strip down to her underwear. Adira was too tired to protest the pokes and prods, or even give much more than one-word answers to Chevy's questions. But thankfully, the exam was over quickly.

"Don't think you need IV fluids, but have this," Chevy said, handing Adira a bottle of Pedialyte. "I've put another bottle in the bathroom for you. Two should do it, but keep it up on the regular water too."

Adira quickly dressed and sat next to Chevy on the chaise. "I don't know how I'm going to do this." She sighed.

"You survived walking across the desert for three days."

"Two-and-a-half," Adira corrected. "The first half day was spent trying to break out of the trunk of a Range Rover."

Chevy's head pulled back.

"Yeah. So that you know, bulletproof windows are crowbar-proof too."

"I'm sure that will come in handy someday," Chevy said. "But out in the desert…at some point, you thought, 'Uh-oh, this is pretty grim,' right? So how'd you handle it?"

"Usual stuff. Deep breath, look objectively and prioritize. Tackle one thing at a time."

Chevy shrugged. "It's going to be the same thing here. Solve one problem at a time. You look after the people the same way you do patients and they're going to be the luckiest folks on the planet."

"You know it's more complicated than that. It's an entire government,"

"One problem at a time. And you've got great people here. Fancy Chick's got your back on how things work. Taimur is the national grandpa that everyone adores, and that Safa, she's a pistol."

Adira looked down and took a deep breath.

"C'mon, let's get you something to eat."

They walked together into the living room. Zahra gestured to the seat next to her on a couch. Set before it on a coffee table was a plate already prepared for her, and Adira was quick to dig in.

Taimur watched Chevy fall into a chair, then asked, "How is she?"

"Still difficult," Chevy said. "But otherwise okay. Leila's family took good care of her."

Taimur smiled, then turned to Adira. "Strong men, some very familiar with the sands, have died out there," he said with admiration.

"I was lucky to have run across the mosque," Adira said.

"The hand of God," Taimur said. "Speaking of which, the proper way to end a speech is 'may the Almighty protect you in His divine care,' or something to that effect."

"I don't know, Taimur," Chevy said. "Looked like 'I love you' worked pretty good."

He slapped a hand on his knee and let out a roaring laugh. "Indeed! Safa just about burst with pride!"

Zahra turned to Adira. "I think we all did."

Adira leaned over and gave Zahra a hug before asking, "I'd like to make a quick call back to the US. Can I borrow your phone?"

"Sure," Zahra replied. "There's also a Palace phone on your desk in the bedroom."

"Perfect, I'll use that one. Be right back."

Adira closed the bedroom door behind her and sat at the desk. An operator came on, and she gave a string of numbers from memory.

"Hello?"

"Hi, Dr. Green. It's Adira."

"Adira! How're things going in Oman?"

"Interesting, that's for sure. Your last day at Highland is coming up soon, right?"

"Ten more days and we're free as a bird."

"How about you and Imani come here for a visit? I've got a pretty good story to tell you."

Epilogue

Six Months Later

The MATC dug its knobby tires in and climbed the rocky ridge leading to a cluster of small dwellings. The Mobile All-Terrain Clinic—essentially the marriage of a beefy 4x4 to a state-of-the-art ambulance—was the first to have been deployed by Oman's Ministry of Health. The singular vehicle was undergoing trials in the central desert to identify any design changes needed before a more significant order could be placed.

The vehicle came to a stop next to a Ministry Land Cruiser already parked on the sandy plain. Dr. Saree al Taz, a tall woman who had recently left hospital work in Muscat to dedicate her skills to people in remote locations, stepped out of the driver's seat. Her passenger, Graeme, was a nurse from New Zealand, three months into his year-long contract under the Nursing Care Leadership Program.

A wave came from the doorway of a Bedouin dwelling that could only be described as half-structure and half-tent. Dr. Saree and Graeme walked over and introduced themselves to the other MOH team, Dr. Mahmoud and his nurse, a young woman named Jazmin.

Inside the dim dwelling, Graeme was surprised to see that Dr. Mahmoud's team had a second nurse, presently sitting with a pregnant mother.

"Our visitors," the nurse said to the mother, "have brought a new mobile clinic here and are going to examine you. It's a truck with an entire doctor's office on the back, and you will love it."

The mother nodded.

"It's nice and private inside. They will do a simple physical just like we did and then take a urine sample. I've heard they can even show you a picture of the baby like you saw a couple of months ago, if you'd like one."

"I would!" the mother said, placing her hands on the edge of the bed to stand up. "Now?"

The nurse let out a little chuckle and said, "Of course!"

Graeme had noticed the nurse's calm demeanor and the trust the mother had in her. "She's good," he said to Dr. Saree.

The nurse and mother followed Dr. Saree and Graeme to the MATC.

"Would you mind?" the nurse asked, indicating she wanted to take Graeme's place in the "box," as he thought of it.

Graeme was caught off guard by the nurse's gold eyes. After regaining his composure, he replied, "By all means."

The nurse led the patient up and through the door, followed by Jazmin and Dr. Saree.

Dr. Mahmoud and Graeme chatted while the women were inside, the doctor explaining that the patient's pregnancy was going well, but she'd had some headaches. Since the MATC was nearby, they thought it would be worth using the onboard lab for a urinalysis instead of simple test strips.

"So really, you just wanted to see the new rig!" Graeme said to him.

Dr. Mahmoud laughed. "You caught us!" he replied. "Now show me up front!"

Graeme waved the doctor to the driver's side, and the two hopped into the cab. They chatted about the truck's capabilities for a while, and the conversation eventually moved to discussions about different parts of the desert they'd been working in recently. They lost track of time until Dr. Mahmoud noticed Dr. Saree and Jazmin walking the mother back to her home.

Graeme hopped out and opened the door to the box, Dr. Mahmoud right on his heels.

The nurse with the bright eyes was still inside, sitting on a rolling stool and looking through some of the cabinets.

"Wow!" said Mahmoud, seeing the articulating exam table and equipment mounted to the wall.

"You carry kits into people's homes," Graeme said. "We bring them in here instead. All the same gear you carry, but we have the exam table, plus plenty more."

"This mini lab is great," the nurse said. "Having the vitals and imaging gear mounted by the exam table is much better than packing and unpacking kits all the time."

"They've thought of everything," Graeme boasted. "If you swing that arm out," he said, pointing, "and flip it over, you'll see that we have satellite access to MOH records."

The nurse pointed to the tablet computer that could easily be swung out. "Dr. Saree used it. Had the mother's last ultrasound up on the screen, and in a snap, the new image was in her file."

"We have something similar up front. Maps all the calls for us," Graeme replied.

"How's it handling the terrain?" she asked. "Capable?"

Graeme nodded. "We had one of the Land Cruisers for a month before this came. It's just as good. Inflating and deflating the tires from the cab is a massive win. But she can be a little top-heavy, and you have to secure the gear carefully. If the X-ray arm went down to the floor instead of to the side, that would help."

"You give that feedback to MOH?" she asked.

"Yeah," Graeme said, a little curious as to why a peer was questioning him this way.

"What else would make it better?"

"Still could use a little more storage. Under the exam table, there's some space wasted. I'd use that, probably for heavy stuff," he said.

The nurse bobbed her head. "Another team is scheduled to take this off your hands next month. When you bring it in, write up your thoughts with Dr. Saree. Send some pictures in too. It would be good to see what you don't need as well as what you do need. The manufacturers like seeing our load-outs."

"Sure," Graeme replied, puzzled.

The woman stepped out of the truck, and Graeme curiously watched three green Range Rovers crest the hill and head their way.

"Who are you again?" he asked.

She extended her hand to him, "I'm Adira, Graeme. Appreciate your feedback."

He shook her hand, wondering how she knew his name.

"Thank you both. See you soon," she said before dashing back to the patient's house to say her goodbyes.

"Good nurse," Graeme admitted to Mahmoud. "But a little bossy."

Mahmoud snickered. "She joins clinic and hospital teams all across Oman. Chooses a different one each week and stays for a day or two. It is a way for her to stay in touch with all of us, to understand how we think and what we need."

They watched her hug the mother and a few more people at the entrance to the house. After a few last words, she turned and made her way to one of the Range Rovers, where a uniformed guard held open a passenger door.

"Who *is* she?" Graeme asked.

"That, my friend, is Her Majesty, our sultana."

Author's Note

On January 10th, 2020, the Sultan of Oman, His Majesty Qaboos bin Said al Said, died after nearly fifty years of leadership. He was held in extremely high regard at home and abroad, particularly for his incredible transformation of the sultanate and his mastery of statecraft on the international stage.

As His Majesty had no children, he named his successor in a secret letter, the seal of which was only to be broken by the Royal Family Council upon his death. The mystery of who would be named was the subject of great speculation in Oman and abroad.

During a visit to Oman just weeks prior to Sultan Qaboos's death, the story captivated me. I couldn't help but ask: What if an heir to the throne had been lost in the tangled passage of time? And what if that heir was female?

It is commonly believed that no woman has ruled a Muslim monarchy during the 1,400 years of Islam. But there have, in fact, been fifteen female monarchs. These sultanas, malikaat, and khatuns—the last seen nearly nine hundred years ago—each have their own stories of courage, savagery, and brilliance.

Could it happen once more?

***

Self-published authors genuinely appreciate Amazon reviews from readers like you! Without the marketing power of major publishers, we rely *entirely* on your social media sharing and reviews. So if you have a minute to spare, please leave a review on Amazon and share a link via Facebook. If you do, I'd like to thank you personally, so please send a note to connorblackbooks@gmail.com.

My sincerest thanks to Lynne, Amy, and Niki for being the absolute best early readers. Your advice and critiques were invaluable! Saad and Hajer, thank you for your succinct advice on Arabic and Omani names.

To Oman, thank you for sharing your beautiful country with me and for understanding that this is entirely a work of fiction based on the imagination of someone inspired by your wonderful culture, history, and people.

About the Author

Connor Black is a freelance product designer for companies in the United States and abroad. He lives with his wife in Manalapan, Florida. They have two sons, both in Southern California, and their own sayyida: a royally spoiled rescue dog named Gigi.

Also by Connor Black